P9-BYP-078

A Warm and Witty Look
at Life in America

Since 1970, Nancy Stahl has been helping Americans laugh at themselves with her hilarious "Once Over Lightly" syndicated column.

Now, for the first time, the best and funniest of her works are collected in a sparkling journal that exposes the madcap hilarity behind the bland routine of suburban life.

It is a warm and witty celebration of the joys of family living. For the truest form of love is, after all . . .

laughter!

IF IT'S RAINING THIS MUST BE THE WEEKEND

NANCY STAHL

if it's raining this must be the weekend

nancy stahl

A BERKLEY BOOK

published by

BERKLEY PUBLISHING CORPORATION

This Berkley book contains the complete
text of the original hardcover edition.
It has been completely reset in a type face
designed for easy reading, and was printed
from new film.

IF IT'S RAINING
THIS MUST BE
THE WEEKEND

A Berkley Book / published by arrangement with
Andrews and McMeel, Inc.

PRINTING HISTORY
Andrews and McMeel edition published 1979
Berkley edition / March 1980

All rights reserved
Copyright © 1979 by Universal Press Syndicate.
This book may not be reproduced in whole or in part,
by mimeograph or any other means, without permission.
For information address: Andrews and McMeel, Inc., A Universal
Press Syndicate Company, 6700 Squibb Road,
Mission, Kansas 66202.

ISBN: 0-425-04460-2

A BERKLEY BOOK® TM 757,375
Berkley Books are published by Berkley Publishing Corporation,
200 Madison Avenue, New York, New York 10016
PRINTED IN THE UNITED STATES OF AMERICA

January 2

Most people break New Year's resolutions by January 17, simply because they have greatly over-estimated their capabilities.

Let's face it, anyone unable to do fifteen push-ups, lose twenty-five pounds, or make a lasting contribution to world peace last year has precious little hope of being able to accomplish it this year, either.

No, New Year's resolutions must be confined to smaller, more easily controlled foibles, sprinkled liberally with reminders not to repeat actions which were so asinine at the time that there is no possibility of their happening again anyway.

For instance, this year I resolve to:

1. Practice preventive dentistry at two o'clock in the afternoon, rather than phoning Dr. Epstein in the middle of his son's Bar Mitzvah.

2. Tell the children the facts of life, at least those I remember.

3. Turn the mattress every three months.

4. Wash all the silverware after meals, even the spoons which nobody used.

5. Take down the outside Christmas lights before Easter.

By the same token, I resolve not to:

1. Appear in the supermarket in white anklets and hair rollers, no matter how badly we need curry powder.

1

2. Put coffee grounds down the sink.

3. Tell any jokes unless I am sure I remember the punch line.

4. Stay up till 2:30 A.M. to watch *Godzilla vs. The Thing*.

5. Stick a fork in the toaster.

6. Take any miracle drug unless given proof that all of its original users passed away quietly in their sleep at the age of seventy-three.

7. Ride in an elevator whose safety inspection sticker has expired.

8. Lick the blades of an electric mixer that is still plugged in.

January 4

I truly admire people who love to entertain, people who are eager to share the warmth and hospitality of their homes. People who know instinctively who to invite.

By the time we have compiled a semiappropriate guest list, I find myself regarding the whole idea of entertaining with the air of heady expectation I usually reserve for a dental appointment.

It is considered important to ensure that there will be a similarity of background among your guests. While providing a common bond is perhaps a safe course of action, there exists the dreadful possibility that our guests will spend the entire evening discussing their kidney dialysis.

The obvious alternative is to aim for a delicious mixture of introverts and extroverts, intellectuals and bohemians. While such rich catholicity of taste and philosophy may indeed elicit fascinating repartee, it may instead be rather disconcerting when our guests discover that they share absolutely no similar tastes or interests. In fact, after three painful hours, they may realize that the single thing which they have in common is a friendship with us, a fact which they each silently resolve to rectify the very next day.

I know that we should invite the twelve couples we have owed invitations since last July and, in one grand gesture, wipe our entire social slate clean. Unfortunately, the only reason that we haven't as yet returned these invitations is that we vividly remember what a dismal time we had at *their* parties. Which leaves me with the depressing prospect of stuffing mushroom caps for twenty-four people I can't stand.

Instead, should we perhaps invite twenty-four new people who would, in turn, feel obligated to issue a return invitation? Witty, charming people who will hopefully wipe *their* social slates clean with a poolside extravaganza next July.

After deciding who to invite, the next problem is what to do with the guests. My problem is that I do not like party games.

In fact, I resent investing three hours at the hairdresser and five dollars on a new pair of support stockings only to spend the entire evening scampering around with a thumbtack taped to my forehead, breaking balloons.

It is even more traumatic to have a navel orange thrust under my chins, especially since the game invariably requires me to pass it to a man who is six-foot-eight and has no more chin than a turtle.

January 6

The only graceful way to camouflage the embarrassing stigma of dining alone in a restaurant is to bring along a paperback, thus implying to my fellow patrons that I have sought my solitary state by choice, preferring to peruse a classic piece of literature than to indulge in insipid social discourse.

A friend of mine from Newark claims that she has solved the solitary-dining problem neatly by assuming the role of a princess recently exiled from a little-known Eastern European principality.

Wearing fifteen dollars worth of cheap rhinestone jewelry, a slinky black dress, and a mantilla, she sweeps in carrying a copy of an Estonian newspaper that she found in the ladies room of a Boston coffee house in 1956. When the waiter comes to take her order, she smiles wanly, points to filet mignon, and murmurs "Biftik—rare."

Between bites, she scans the newspaper, sighs tragically, and crosses herself repeatedly with her dessert fork.

Not only does she have a marvelous time, but her waiter invariably refuses to accept a tip.

January 8

I have never felt the same about plants since I read that they have nervous systems which enable them to experience anxiety, joy, and—quite possibly—lust.

I've always *liked* plants, mind you. But heretofore I've regarded them rather like potholders—useful and decorative, but hardly something I could train to fetch the paper or catch mice.

In view of the vast body of knowledge which has recently emerged, it is no longer possible to regard plants as simply decorating necessities. Giving them bonemeal and tap water is not enough. If they are to thrive, plants need soothing music, inspirational verse, and verbal encouragement. Like petulant children, they must be cajoled into blooming. "Believe me, Harry, you'll feel better once you bud."

Since plants have come into their own, emotionally-speaking, anyone owning a philodendron can never feel himself to be completely alone again.

While this situation may be all very well should the owner be skittish about burglars, it presents a distressing prospect to those individuals who view being completely alone as an erotic pleasure second only to having their kneecaps stroked with goose feathers.

Personally, I find it next to impossible to cavort about the house wearing nothing but a pair of red woolen ski socks and risk offending the sensibilities of an African Violet.

January 9

I'm actually all in favor of couples living together before they get married.

But only if you have to share your illicit prenuptial bliss with a semi-housetrained puppy, two children with the flu, and a water heater that goes kerchook, kerchonk, kerchonk all night.

Under those conditions you could *really* get to know each other.

That's what "compatible" is all about. After all, you know from your first date that it feels good when he rubs your neck. What really counts is how he reacts when the baby throws up on his Harris tweed sport coat. While marriage is made up of a good deal of neck rubbing, there's also a substantial amount of throwing up involved, and if he's going to stomp his feet and throw things when it happens, well, it's just as well to know about it beforehand.

And if the fact that you wear a chin strap and cut your toenails in bed is going to bother him, now is the time for it all to come out in the open.

It might be a good idea to arrange for a power failure, too. Eating by candlelight is one thing. Shaving by candlelight is quite another matter. Especially when you have shaved your legs with the razor first.

If you can manage it, it might be handy to have a drippy faucet for him to cope with. Lacking that, flush a diaper down the toilet. See whether he goes all pale and trembly when you hand him a wrench and a plunger.

Engage in funfilled activities like rearranging the living room furniture, putting up storm windows, and wallpapering the bathroom ceiling.

If you find that you can still stand the sight of each other after two weeks of this, then you probably have at least a fighting chance of muddling through till your golden wedding anniversary.

January 11

My friend Marjorie has had a difficult time adjusting to the implications of the Women's Liberation Movement.

"I'm just a *housewife*!" she would wail. "I could have been a *surgeon*!" It did little good to point out that few, if any, surgeons insist on picking up calves liver with tongs because it feels "ishy."

Marjorie eventually took to refusing to accept her role. She baked pies only at night, put them in hat boxes, and insisted that she bought them at the A&P.

Suddenly, however, an abrupt transformation occurred.

"I took a course called 'The Managerial Perspective as Applied to Housework.' It changed my life. I never realized the fact that I am chief policy formulator, head decision-maker, an expert in domestic analysis."

"You bake super pies, too," I observed.

"I'm talking about roles," Marjorie explained. "My ability to appraised logistical dilemmas."

"Like folding a contour sheet!" I exclaimed.

"More than that. Do you realize the importance of analytic appraisal?"

"Like whether to soak a mustard stain in hot water or cold water?" I asked.

"In the area of food preparation alone," she continued, "the aspects of financial management are critical. One must achieve creative artistry, which is a true challenge."

"Especiall when it comes to canned peas," I agreed. "Tell me, did they happen to teach you how to overcome negative attitudes toward leftover tuna casserole?"

January 15

When women's magazines aren't exhorting me to knit my own lamp shades or create memorable holiday centerpieces out of the cardboard cylinders from toilet paper rolls, they invariably resort to testing my marriage: Does he bring you gin and tonic in the bathtub? Do you tuck lovenotes into his lunch bucket?

In the interest of realism, I have devised the following marriage test:

To be answered by women:

1. Your husband bought you a black lace negligee, size seven. Would you exchange it for: (a) a blue flannel Mother Hubbard nightie, size sixteen, or (b) a new toaster?

2. Three separate fortunetellers have predicted that you will be married twice. Do you: (a) cancel your order for monogrammed sheets, or (b) begin introducing him as "my first husband"?

3. There is a very young, blonde voice on the telephone wanting to speak to your husband. Would you say: (a) "Could you call back? He's busy bathing our six adorable children," or (b) "You'll have to wait a minute. He's busy cutting his corns"?

To be answered by men:

1. Your wife asks "Am I as attractive as when we first met?" Do you answer (a) "Yeah, I guess so," or (b) "More so. All those lines give your face character"?

2. Your wife complains that there is a big, hungry spider on the ceiling. Would you (a) hand her a rolled-up newspaper, or (b) hand her a fly?

3. Your wife loans you her section of the newspaper, saying "You have to read this article by George Plopnik on topless restaurants." Do you: (a) Read the article, then return it, saying "What's so funny about that?" or (b) skim the Plopnik article, then become engrossed in a feature on the rehabilitation of juvenile delinquents, leaving her nothing to read but a sixteen-page flyer on sale-priced snow tires?

- In each case, (a) is the correct choice and is worth five points. Give yourself one point for choosing (b). Combine your scores.

18-30—You will probably be together another thirty years. Isn't that peachy?

6-14—You need an outside interest. Have you tried creating memorable holiday centerpieces out of the cardboard cylinders from toilet paper rolls?

January 16

I recently read a magazine article entitled "Play 'Consequences' With Your Child." The author went on to explain that "Consequences" involves asking your child "What would happen if . . . ," thus urging him to develop his reasoning powers.

Playing "Consequences" with our children is a bit like giving Michelangelo a paint-by-number set. They have dedicated their entire preadolescent lives to determining vital issues such as: What would happen if I dropped jelly beans down the hot air register? If I put caramels in the toaster? If I flushed my rubber duck down the toilet? If I cut off my eyelashes?

Of course, the whole trick to playing the game of "Consequences" lies in keeping everything at a purely theoretical level.

"What would happen if Mommy didn't use a potholder to take the biscuits out of the oven?" I asked.

"You'd burn your hand."

"That's right!" I beamed. "Then what would happen?"

"You'd say %$*!"

"How many times have I told you not to say that word?"

"I didn't say it. I said that you'd say it."

Determining to avoid personal issues, I tried the game again the next day. "What would happen if the electricity went off?"

"We wouldn't be able to watch TV or shave or wash dishes or open cans. And my worms would melt."

"What worms?"

"The worms I put in the freezer last summer. I wanted to see what would happen if . . ."

January 17

One of the joys of family life lies in coming together at the end of the day and exchanging experiences with those you love.

In our house, the exchange takes the form of a game of verbal one-upmanship known as "Your Day Was a Picnic Compared With Mine."

"You should have *seen* the traffic on Eisenhower Boulevard!" I began last night. "It took me an hour and fifteen minutes to get home!"

"You think that's bad," retorted my daughter. "My bike got a flat and I had to walk two miles home from school."

"That's nothing," replied her brother. "Some gangster hijacked our school bus and got it up to 137 miles an hour on the freeway. If he hadn't sideswiped a dairy truck, we'd all be in Albuquerque by now."

"I tried a new place for lunch," I announced. "The food was rotten, and the prices were exorbitant."

"You think that's bad," my daughter said. "In our cafeteria some girl found a cockroach in her chocolate milk."

"That's nothing," insisted my son. "Our cafeteria has been closed down by the Board of Health. The entire fifth grade died from eating catfood sandwiches."

"You know, it's no fun being a working woman," I sighed. "Nobody appreciates you."

"Being in junior high is worse," insisted my daughter. "Nobody understands you."

"That's nothing!" bellowed my son. "Nobody believes a word I say!"

January 18

"You'll go into the hospital on Monday and be out by late Tuesday morning," the doctor explained. "There's really nothing to it," he added, patting my hand.

"*You* say there's nothing to it," I snapped. "It's not *your* ovaries they're tinkering with!"

Like any sensible person, I have studiously avoided any prolonged contact with hospitals.

For one thing, I hate the way they smell. It isn't *just* the smell, mind you. Beauty shops don't smell all that great either, but no one ever died from getting a permanent wave.

When I arrived at the hospital, I was amazed to discover that the entire main floor was done in burgundy and olive carpeting with modern pictures, indirect lighting, and huge potted palms, giving the entire room the air of the lobby of a two-star resort hotel.

"I'd like a room," I whispered to the girl at the desk.

"Do you have a reservation?" she inquired.

"Stahl," I murmured. "Ovaries."

It was at this point that the resemblance to a resort hotel ended abruptly. They whisked me to a lab, banded my arm as they would a migratory bird, and forcibly induced me to part with several specimens of bodily fluids.

It wasn't only my room, a singularly sterile cubicle overlooking the hospital parking lot, that destroyed the illusion; I know of few hotels which demand that you sign a paper releasing them from any obligation whatsoever should you, during the next twenty-four hours, either have your car stolen or die.

An hour before the operation, the surgeon inquired: "How are you feeling?"

"More important, how are *you* feeling?" I asked nervously. "I mean, you *did* get a good night's sleep, didn't you? You look pretty fit," I observed, "except for that hicky on your neck."

"That's nothing," he assured me. "I just nicked myself shaving," he snickered, nudging me jovially in the ribs.

Admittedly, my recollection of this dialogue is rather garbled, as all morning a veritable parade of people had been poking needles into all exposed parts of my anatomy. By the time I arrived at the operating room, I was grinning idiotically and insisting that I was the Duchess of Windsor.

One hour after the operation, I had ceased grinning.

"How do you feel?" my roommate inquired solicitously.

"Sick," I replied. "How else?"

"Would you like a beer?" she asked. "I have a six-pack hidden in my bedpan. It makes a swell ice bucket. Help yourself to some pretzels. They're behind the TV set."

"I want to go home!" I wailed.

"Whatever for? It's raining ice balls out there. Personally, I *love* the hospital. The meals are no worse than your own and you get your back rubbed twice a day."

January 20

There are some intimate subjects which one simply does not discuss.

Oh, I don't mean sex. Even my mother talks about sex.

In fact, she taught me all about sex. What she didn't teach me was how to shave my legs. Nobody teaches a thirteen-year-old girl how to shave. They just hand her a razor.

For the past twenty-five years, I've searched women's magazines for instructions, but all I ever find is self-help-articles entitled "Make the Most of Your Nose" and meat loaf recipes.

I've tried hanging around bathrooms watching men shave. While the basic principle is the same, men don't have shin bones on their faces or, for that matter, any area of face where one ill-considered swipe of the razor will peel off a strip of skin one-eighth-inch wide and fourteen inches long.

I have yet to resolve the basic dilemma of where women should shave. Shaving during one's bath seems like a logical first choice, but it rather defeats the purpose of meticulous personal hygiene to emerge from the tub covered from the neck down with tiny brown hairs and globs of Rapid Shave.

While men shave in the bathroom sink, I know of very few mature women who are physically capable of putting one foot up in a washbowl. I know even fewer who, once in, could get out again. Not only is there a vast degree of physical trauma involved in having one foot stuck in a washbowl for six hours, but there is even greater emotional trauma in having her loved one chortle "Henry, you'll have to excuse the funny way old Mildred is walking, but you'll never guess . . ."

January 26

In our house, the garbage bag goes out when it is full.

Unfortunately, "full" is an arbitrary word, applying generally to a plastic bag so crammed with moldy bread heels, Kentucky Fried Chicken bones, and pizza crusts that it not only smells like a dirty turtle bowl, but there's no slack on which to place a twist-tie.

The bag is left in this unenviable state until the next person attempts to empty a handful of peanut shells into it, whereupon three grapefruit rinds full of cigarette butts immediately dislodge and skitter across the kitchen floor.

While it is fairly simple to pick the extra garbage off the floor and reapportion it into a second bag, leaving the original bag empty enough to accept a twist-tie, once you attempt to lift it you discover a severed soup can lid has sliced a three-inch gash in the bottom, and six cups of wet coffee grounds are dribbling onto your shoe.

Clasping your hand quickly over the bottom of the bag temporarily relieves the leakage problem, but the only permanent solution lies in depositing the bag into another bag, preferably before the soup can lid succeeds in severing your right index finger.

January 27

In these days of skyrocketing food costs, I have found that it is essential to make a list of the items I intend to buy.

A list not only prevents me from intemperate buying, but it adds an aura of efficiency, and, with luck, will draw my fellow-shoppers' attention away from the fact that I have forgotten to change out of my bedroom slippers.

A list has certain drawbacks, however.

1. You must remember to bring it. It does precious little good to spend the entire morning noting down the ingredients for "Rainy Day Shepherd's Pie" and rummaging through the cupboard shaking bottles of bleach to determine whether you have enough for another week, only to arrive at the grocery store and discover that you've left the list on top of the refrigerator.

2. The list must be decipherable. While many women employ an elaborate code to protect the list from being translated, should it be confiscated, it is most distressing to realize that you have absolutely no idea what "PRTD. MST.!" might be.

Making a list is only part of the battle, however.

It is equally vital to visit the grocery store only when you have just completed a twelve-course meal and are so completely weighted down with starch that you can barely waddle.

It is easy to spot someone who has made the mistake of arriving at the store hungry and "listless." She is the woman who is guiltily unloading a cart containing a half-gallon of fudge ripple ice cream, three dozen Snickers bars, and a half-eaten box of Hostess Cupcakes.

January 29

I enjoy having overnight guests.

Not only does the prospect of entertaining company provide the necessary impetus for long neglected household chores such as cleaning the gnats out of the overhead light fixture, but the contents of the refrigerator experience a notable improvement in quality when overnight guests arrive.

But the fact remains that, unlike dinner guests who are entertained by candlelight and carefully confined to the living room, dining room, and powder room, overnight guests have the run of the house. And although they may not remark on it, they will definitely notice a furry green ring in the bathtub.

It would never do to let a guest suspect how you really live, so when the next one announces an imminent visit, I must remember to do the following:

1. Check the medicine cabinet for potentially embarrassing medicines and items of personal hygiene.

2. Clean all the cigarette butts out of the rubber plant.

3. Buy new toothbrushes.

4. Remove *The Joy of Sex* from the night stand. Substitute *Wuthering Heights*.

5. Iron a set of sheets.

6. Check the grooves of the window in the guest room for dead flies.

7. Invest in two-ply bathroom tissue.

But I also must remember that while such elaborate preparations are designed to make a guest feel at home, it will never do to create such a degree of comfort that he loses all desire to return home. After five days, it is perfectly proper to temper hospitality with the insistence that guests take out the garbage, feed the dog, and clean the furry green ring out of the bathtub.

January 30

The challenge of creating a memorable gastronomic experience out of two cups of leftover roast port does not exactly set my libido a-twitter. Generally speaking, I would rather run around the block stark naked when it's fifteen degrees below zero than cook dinner. Of course, it's all academic anyway, as I've never been offered the choice.

Lately, however, our daughter has begun to regard the oven as something more than a place to dry her tennis shoes. I supervised her early efforts and offered helpful suggestions. It soon became apparent that I lacked a certain objectivity and was prone to gasping and wringing my hands when she sliced a tomato.

Now I just sit in the living room with a tourniquet and a fire extinguisher, resolving not to take a bite of anything until I've counted her fingers.

I must admit that she's very innovative. Cookbooks inhibit her; she creates as she goes along. Meatball and banana casserole with chocolate biscuits was one impromptu offering. And none of us will ever forget the pork chops with blueberry-clam sauce. She had wanted to flame them with twelve-year-old cognac, but she had used it all making the mashed potatoes.

"What's for supper?" my husband asked.

"I'm not sure. It smells like sauteed rubber bands."

"It couldn't be. She served that just last night."

While her Daddy and I wouldn't dream of complaining, our son is apt to call a spade a spade and announce that he'd rather eat nightcrawlers than pork chops with blueberry-clam sauce.

"Mom and Dad like it. Don't you?" she asked us. We nodded solemnly, palming our pork chops under the table and attempting to interest the dog in them. He shuddered and left the room.

"Mom and Dad love you. They have to say it's good. I don't even like you very much, so I don't have to be polite."

February 2

I just read an article which began with the startling statement, "Your furniture says a lot about you."

I have spent ten grueling years attempting to convince the children not to reveal our private physical peculiarities, petty disputes, or bank overdrafts. Now I find that I should have concentrated on the blabbermouths in the living room. In fact, all that our assorted furnishings have in common is the ability to badmouth us:

Danish modern end tables, circa 1965, badly scarred: Teeth marks on legs of these early artifacts indicate regrettable lack of parental discipline. White ring on square table, evidently vestige of long-ago holiday merrymaking, shows traces of being treated with every chemical known to science. Ring regularly reappears like the Ghost of Christmas Past. Spot of wax on step table indicates that owners do not own a candle snuffer. Since everyone receives at least six sterling silver candle snuffers as wedding gifts, they undoubtedly never bothered to get married at all.

Early American wing chair, circa 1970, grape Popsicle stain on underside of cushion: Slightly later period, the fact that said chair has springs indicates increasing affluence, but tendency to pander to offspring still apparent if you turn cushion over.

French Provincial stereo, circa 1973, seven cigarette burns on top, spray can of furniture polish and filthy dust cloth inside: Cigarette burns indicate that one conscience-ridden spouse attempted to evade responsibility for the other contracting emphysema by the ill-considered ploy of hiding all the ashtrays. Furniture polish can an impressive housekeeping gesture, but has been empty for three months.

Italian love seats, circa 1976, covered in immaculate gold velvet: Relatively new, therefore use restricted to those bearing notarized affidavit attesting to personal hygiene. No one has bothered to acquire sufficient documentation, as the love seats aren't particularly comfortable, anyway.

February 5

I am sure that the main reason so many first-born children become famous is the onus of having to live up to those early reviews in their own baby books.

The life and times of our first-born child are chronicled in an elaborate pink satin volume with twelve smirking cherubs and a spot of what looks like strained peas on the cover. Every word that she ever managed to lisp out is documented like the Congressional Record, while truly momentous occasions, like the compelling saga of her first sneeze, run to three pages.

Slightly heavier than *Webster's New International Dictionary*, her baby book bulges with envelopes full of teeth, wisps of hair, and fingernail parings. Our daughter is probably the only girl in town who could take her own umbilical cord to school for Show-and-Tell.

I suppose that I saved these souvenirs because she was constantly doing *wonderful, exciting things* which I was terrified of forgetting. All mothers are alike in that respect. I know that my own mother would sooner part with her nose than relinquish a certain glutinous mass which she insists was once my rubber ducky.

This tendency to collect infantile memorabilia gradually wore off by the time our daughter was three or four years old and began doing *things* that were not *wonderful* or *exciting*, like dropping 150 miniature marshmallows down the heating duct and swallowing my best earrings, which I truly hoped to be able to forget just as soon as was possible. Besides, no one can bronze a pair of shoes after they have been flushed down the toilet.

February 6

Regarding child discipline, I favor the "early warning system," otherwise known as the "1-2-3 and you're out" approach.

Since I consider that first offenders are motivated by curiosity rather than malice, I deliver patient lectures with catchy titles such as "Why One Does Not Keep

Dead Sparrows in Vegetable Crispers" and "Nice People Do Not Drink Their Bathwater."

Second offenders must be dealt with in a stern fashion, as they are generally testing your authority with a little game called "Let's See Whether She Really Means It," as in the following situation:

Child in muddy cowboy boots stands upright on the back of the sofa, grasps his nose between his thumb and forefinger, shrieks "Geronimo," and jumps into the seat cushion. The sofa bleats like a mortally wounded elk.

"Look, I've told you not to jump off the back of the sofa!"

"No you didn't. You just said not to jump off the back of the *chair*!"

"Well, I'm telling you now. If you do it one more time I'll send you right to bed." Notice that the child is thus being given freedom of choice. Of course, if it happens to be an hour past his bedtime already, he may realize that he not only has nothing to lose if he opts for a final jump, but in the ensuing crisis may very well avoid having to brush his teeth.

When confronting a child with a nasty alternative to continued obnoxious behavior, it is imperative to keep a bit of perspective and remember exactly who it is you are punishing. While "If you stick one more marble up the baby's nose, I'll make you stay in the house all weekend" may possibly restrain him, on the other hand, it very well may not. One more marble will leave you no alternative but to have him underfoot for the next forty-eight hours, whiling away his time by jumping off the piano while protesting, "No you didn't. You just said not to jump off of the sofa or the chair."

February 7

I enjoy receiving a bunch of cut flowers. Since they are technically *in extremis* when I receive them, no one expects roses to live. It is only a matter of postponing the inevitable. Even though I dutifully go through the motions of shaving their stems daily, and plying them with aspirin and Vitamin C, after a week I know that no one will fault me for throwing the whole sodden, brownish mass down the garbage disposal.

On the other hand, a potted African Violet is *alive*, a supposedly *lasting gift*. Even after it has become *my* African Violet, and as such could, in theory, be chopped up for salad greens, the giver retains a certain proprietary interest in "Our African Violet's" well-being and feels entitled to poke his finger into the potting soil and make snide remarks about my watering habits.

The situation is even more tense when people insist on giving me a cutting off the ancestral ivy. This is a semireligious ceremony which leaves me feeling a bit like Moses receiving the Ten Commandments. "Grandmother Nelson dug the parent plant from the Happy View Cemetery in Lincoln, Nebraska, in July, 1901," they will say. "We only give cuttings to our very dearest friends."

Resisting the urge to genuflect, I gaze despairingly at the sprig of ivy, which has begun to wilt in my sweaty palm. After a while, under the watchful eye of Grandma Nelson's shade, I dutifully plant the ivy in the exact type of soil recommended for heirloom ivy.

But even though I use nothing on it but seventy-eight-degree distilled water and spend all afternoon hauling it from one shaft of sunlight to another, it reacts just like a rose. Whenever we sit down to eat breakfast, decaying ivy leaves begin plummeting into our porridge. After a week I throw the whole sodden, brownish mass down the garbage disposal.

I have to admit that none of my best friends are potted plants. Anything that demands such care and feeding should have the decency to lick your hand or apologize when it dies.

Now my son—there's a talented green thumb.

Some children long for Santa to bring them shiny red wagons, hockey gloves, and toboggans. Others wistfully yearn for an electric train, a woodburning set, or the latest Judith Blume books. My son wanted a Venus Fly Trap this year.

Whatever the psychological significance of this request, it is definitely nothing upon which I care to speculate.

A Venus Fly Trap is an insectivorous plant which catches its prey like a steel trap. The two halves of the leaf, about the size of nickels, are hinged in the middle. When an insect walks on its surface, the leaf snaps shut, the toothed edges mesh, and the plant squeezes its victim against the digestive glands on the leaf surface until the insect's body is decomposed by enzymes. Yo ho ho.

A Venus Fly Trap cannot be purchased in this active state, however. It is native to North Carolina (and that's what I like about the South), from where it is exported in a dormant state. Encased in a plastic bag, the Venus Fly Trap exhibits all the intrinsic charm of a spider that has been run over by a skateboard.

With a modicum of luck, it will remain in this enviable state and can be simply thrown away in six weeks or so. Unfortunately, my son's Venus Fly Trap (which he named Fang) germinated into quivering life and soon began opening its revolting maw for food.

Fang, we soon discovered, can distinguish between living and dead objects (such as Cheerios), and exhibits utter disdain for the latter. While in mid-July we are plagued with veritable hordes of flying insects, it is a rare phenomenon to find a horsefly in February. Fortunately, our basement has become the Capistrano of the crawling insect world.

While Fang lacks a certain aesthetic appeal, I must admit he is doing an exemplary job on the silverfish problem. Besides, he is the only one of Santa's gifts that isn't either too small, broken, or out of "D" cell batteries.

February 10

"Fred and I are having a party two weeks from Saturday," the voice on the telephone said. "We were hoping that you folks could come."

"That sounds fine. Hold on just a minute while I check the calendar." (Checking the calendar is a cunning ploy to convince people that we are constantly in demand. Actually I don't have to check. I already know that our only social obligation for the next six weeks is to take the dog to the vet for a rabies booster.) "We're free that night," I said, trying to sound mildly surprised at the fact. "We'd love to come."

Unfortunately, being in the mood for a party is like being pregnant. At any given moment I can tell whether I am or I'm not. Two weeks from Saturday, who knows?

Two weeks from Saturday, as I gingerly applied lipstick over the cold sore on my upper lip, I felt definitely unpartyish.

"The Monster from the Black Lagoon," my husband announced glumly.

"Haven't you ever seen a cold sore?" I snarled.

"I mean on the eleven o'clock TV movie. Can't we stay home?"

"I hate to cancel out so late," I mused, "after I've shaved my legs and all. But I do have a little headache that I'll bet I could worry into a throbbing migraine by 10:45."

"Make it 10:30 to allow for traffic," he cautioned as we left.

But by 10:30 it became apparent that one of us was having a smashing time. Since I was being treated to a cost analysis of secondary sewage treatment systems in Los Angeles, it obviously wasn't me. My husband, however, was in deep conversation with a redhead who was wearing one of those push-me-up bras and looking at him as if he'd just discovered the wheel.

"I don't suppose that I still have a headache?" I asked him, temporarily disengaging myself from Los Angeles's sewage problems.

"Not on my account," he said hastily. "Besides, you did shave your legs and all."

February 11

Every year, I find the remaining bits and pieces of Christmas decidedly depressing.

February is a grim enough month anyway without impaling my foot on a pine needle still imbedded, pointy end up, in the carpet, whenever I walk barefoot in the living room.

Having been on the receiving end of seven Christmas fruitcakes, we have been reduced to eating fruitcake sandwiches, French-fried fruitcake, and creamed fruitcake on buttered fruitcake points. Not only do they show no inclination to get stale, but their strength is like the strength of ten because their hearts are pure brandy. I made the mistake of throwing two cups of fruitcake crumbs outside for the birds last week. Half an hour later, six sparrows were staggering along the telephone wire singing "When It's Springtime in the Rockies" in close harmony, while a cardinal was Indian wrestling with a Siamese cat. And winning.

Our son has developed a musical fixation on Christmas carols. Here it is mid-February and there is still a partridge in his pear tree.

Every day we receive sternly worded documents from the local department stores, requesting that we pay for our December magnanimity, all of which has either broken, shrunk, or is sitting immobilized for want of fresh batteries.

Our outside lights are still hanging glumly from the roof. Only ten weeks ago, a heady infusion of holiday spirit enabled my husband to leap smartly from my shoulders onto an icy rooftop, wrap his legs around the chimney, and clip red flashing lights onto the shingles to spell out *Peace on Earth*. Five weeks ago, natural attrition had reduced their message to *Peace o Ear*. Last week when they further abridged themselves to a rather ridiculous *Pea*, I finally turned them off.

"At least you could replace the red bulb in the porch light," I said to my husband.

"Why? It looks festive."

"A red light over the door was festive two months ago. In February there is only one excuse for that light, and our area isn't even zoned for apartments!"

Especially depressing is the five hundred-piece jigsaw puzzle I purchased for the family as a present. Rather than the standard "Venice at Sunset" or "Miss December" variety, this puzzle is a giant gum ball machine.

Two things became obvious as soon as we began the puzzle late in the afternoon of December 27. First, one gum ball looks depressingly like another. Second, two-thirds of the puzzle is solid black.

Unfortunately, before we could adopt the sensible approach of simply shoving all 500 pieces into the trash can, my son put three pieces together, thus morally committing us to assembling the remaining 497. For the past eight weeks, we have eaten in the kitchen, standing up at the counter, the dining room table being completely covered with gum balls.

Now a jigsaw puzzle may be approached from either of two directions. Some maintain the philosphy that one must sit and stare speculatively at the puzzle, looking for a particular piece with the appropriate configuration. The other approach, based on the theory that seven monkeys sitting at seven typewriters will eventually type all of the books in the Library of Congress, consists of trying every piece in every hole.

Unfortunately, these two approaches are often incompatible in practice.

My son, the sitter, objects violently to his sister's shotgun approach.

"Those pieces don't go together," he protested last night.

"They do now!" she replied, hammering two gum balls violently with her fist.

"Anything worth doing is worth doing *right*, you jerk!" he bellowed.

"Maybe," I replied, "but unless we try shaving little bits off some of these pieces, we'll end up eating Thanksgiving dinner standing up in the kitchen."

February 13

Every night at dinner my children play a game entitled "Top News Story of the Day". It's a variation of the "If You Think Your Day Was Bad . . . " game, and the rules are simple. Whatever bit of folksy information my daughter reports, her younger brother must counterattack immediately by injecting a more bizarre incident, beginning with the words "That's nothing. Some kid in my class . . ."

A typical exchange runs much along the following lines:

Laurie: "A guy in my class named Michael Harris got cross-country skis for Christmas."

Eric: "That's nothing. Some kid in my class got a three-hundred-speed bike for Christmas. It goes seven-thousand miles an hour. His mother is a black belt in karate, and his father is a Russian spy."

Laurie (desperately): "Carlene Shultz can burp at will."

Eric: "That's nothing. Some kid in my class can pull his eyes right out of their sockets, get a whole grapefruit in his mouth, and make his nose bleed by pulling on his earlobes."

Laurie, understandably miffed at being continually

upstaged, will occasionally exhibit a bit of skepticism as to the authenticity of these events. For example:

Laurie: "Ritchie McGrath ate a fly today."

Eric: "That's nothing. Some kid in my class swallows rats."

Laurie: "Don't be dumb. Rats are too big to swallow."

Eric: "I didn't say big rats, smarty. He swallows little rats. Babies."

Laurie: "Sara Jenkins brought her basset hound to school today."

Eric: "That's nothing. Some kid in my class brought in his pet gorilla. I petted him and he let me feel his muscles."

Laurie: "Oh, brother!"

Eric: "What do *you* know? You don't even go to my school!"

February 18

Over the years I have learned that motherhood is much like an austere religious order, the joining of which obligates one to relinquish all claims to personal possessions.

Not only is my badminton racquet referred to as "*The* badminton racquet" and as such regularly loaned to friends, left in hedges, and used to strain the water out of the pan full of Kraft dinner, but the children fight over which one of them gets to chew up my last sheet of personalized stationery to make spitballs.

Just last week I bought a pair of black leather gloves to go with my good black coat. As I was dressing for a luncheon date yesterday, I saw my daughter through the bedroom window wearing my black gloves to school. There was nothing to do but wear her brown knit gloves. Just then I spied my son walking down the street in her brown knit gloves. I was the only woman to arrive at the luncheon wearing green and yellow snowflake mittens with one thumb unravelled.

Occasionally, however, there are opportunities to get a little of my own back.

Last night the children appeared clutching a pair of blue jeans which each adamantly insisted was his.

"All right," I declared. "I'll cut them in half. Each of you gets one leg." I reasoned that the rightful owner would love his jeans enough to relinquish his claim to save them. (This worked admirably for King Solomon in a dispute involving ownership of a baby.)

Unfortunately, as both children agreed to the division, King Solomon was forced to reverse his decision. It's one thing to chop a baby in two, but no wise king cuts up a pair of perfectly good jeans. He wears them himself, even if he can't quite zip them up.

February 25

I am completely accustomed to feeling inferior. I learned twenty years ago that not only was my prowess at simple stain removal woefully nonexistent, but that I lacked the ability to boil water without scorching it.

I have learned to live with my inadequacies.

But thanks to the candid approach recently adopted by even the most staid journalistic sentinels of womanhood, I find that I am equally ill-equipped emotionally.

It is frightening to envision the editorial upheavals that must have occurred at even the most hallowed publications. China-painting experts, origami geniuses, dried-flower impresarios—all must have been abruptly terminated in this new wave of women's journalism.

It is all very well to accept my inability to embroider my own pillow cases. I don't even *like* hand-embroidered pillow cases; the French knots always leave dents in my cheek. But it's quite another matter to discover that I am shamefully unassertive, psychologically repressed, and sexually naive.

It is most disconcerting to find that the very same people who tried—unsuccessfully, I might add—to instruct me in the intricacies of preventing the interfacing in my collar from curling, now are confiding that if I stop smoking, my sexual appetite will increase.

Don't get me wrong. An increased sexual appetite is without a doubt a Good Thing. But I can't help remembering what trouble I found myself in trying to interface my collar.

February 27

Somehow I had expected the Women's Liberation Movement to relieve me from the drudgery of housework.

But what Germaine Greer fails to point out is that just as the rain falls on both the just and unjust, so dust is no respecter of a raised consciousness.

As one must, of necessity, deal with housework, the following courses could raise apparent drudgery to a truly creative level, commensurate with an emerging woman's new-found capabilities:

1. *The Managerial Perspective as Applied to the Linen Closet 101:* This course stresses appraisal of the existing situation, as well as covering policy formation regarding the use of shelf paper. Advanced students with a strong mathematical background will benefit from Course 102: *Solving the Logistical Dilemma of Folding a Contour Sheet.*

2. *Interfacing with Milkmen 310:* Interpersonal transaction is emphasized in this course. Stroke theory is offered as a medium for obtaining specials on cottage cheese two weeks after the offer has expired.

3. *Stain Appraisal 440:* The decision-making aspects involved in the use of hot or cold water are emphasized. Attention is given to the pragmatic approach to mustard and blood, as well as the Freudian implications of "Ring Around the Collar."

4. *Workshop in Leftover Cookery 560:* Truly invaluable for the aspiring financial manager, this results-oriented approach to peas, mashed potatoes, and bacon fat begins with a comprehensive overview of existing materials, examines restructuring techniques to achieve creative expression, and finally addresses itself to

methods of overcoming negativity, rigidity, and natural aggressiveness to Shepherd's Pie.

Instead of advanced education, one can always opt for a maid.

While it isn't easy to get hired help, it is even more difficult to get rid of hired help.

If a maid proves herself to be lazy, surly, and unbearably slovenly, I simply assume that it was my own fault for having hired such an incompetent in the first place. Her presence becomes a cross that I must bear, rather like a weird relative who collects peach pits and, unless watched carefully, runs down the street stark naked, barking and chasing cars.

My first experiment with household help was named, as best as I could ever discover, Nijishruljhi. Whatever her linguistic abilities were, they stopped well short of English.

Ignoring the unmade beds and greasy oven, Nijishruljhi spent her entire first day removing the mineral deposits from the holes of the shower head with a straight pin.

Using a series of expansive gestures, I tried to convey the fact that I desired a more macrocosmic approach to housecleaning.

The next Wednesday I arrived home to find that she had ripped out eighty square yards of wall-to-wall carpeting and was waxing the plywood subflooring.

Fortunately, at that point, Nijishruljhi declared through a series of eloquent gestures that she intended to find a family who appreciated clean shower heads. It cost me $107.50 to have the carpet relaid.

Finally, I engaged a woman named Griselda, a strapping lass with arms the size of Smithfield hams, who assessed my inadequacies with uncanny accuracy during her first day. The next week she arrived with a stack of *True Confessions* and a bottle of gin, both of which she consumed while I worked, looking up only long enough to raise her feet (which, incidentally, were encased in my bedroom slippers) so that I could vacuum under them.

Six weeks later, after foiling a would-be exhibitionist two blocks from our home (and in the process breaking both his legs and badly mutilating him), Griselda declared our neighborhood to be too risky, and quit.

March 1

I don't know why people bother to name cats. One might as well stand outside at midnight in the rain calling out his street address or phone number as "Here, Muffet." Muffet will only come when she's ready. And she won't be ready until you are in bed with a mustard plaster on your chest.

Of course, when someone yells, "Who ate my alpaca sweater?" you are able to answer, "Muffet," which is not only considerably shorter than "The %*&! cat did," but adds a nice, personal touch.

After six months of observing her apparent satisfaction with Captain Nemo cat food, we bought a sixty-can case of the stuff. We filled every corner of the kitchen with Captain Nemo and had to use the last sixteen cans in the den as bookends and paperweights. That night she took one look at a dish full of Captain Nemo, shuddered, and looked at us as if to say, "Not *this* slop again!"

March 2

Yesterday we were visited by the tax assessor, who was skulking around from door to door looking for undeclared half bathrooms.

He seemed a bit loath to believe that the only home improvement we had made in the past year was to hang three coat hooks last September, two of which fell off the next day. "I think that I'd better have a look around," he declared skeptically. "What's in there?" he asked, pointing to a closed door with a sign reading KEEP OUT—THIS MEANS YOU.

"That's our daughter's room."

"It looks mighty like a half bathroom to me."

"Well, I don't mind proving it, but maybe you'd better let me go first," I suggested. Entering our daughter's room can be something of risky venture. One can never be completely certain that either something small and furry or something long and slimy has not just gnawed its way out of its cage and isn't at this very moment crouched behind the door preparing to scurry or slither up the leg of the first person to come in.

Obviously, one does not enter such a room without exercising reasonable precautions. As I opened the door, I began flapping my arms and shrieking "Shoo!" at the top of my voice. The caged beasties replied by leaping, panic-stricken, into the air and scattering sawdust onto the already-littered floor.

The tax assessor, who was by now a bit gray around the lips, gave a strangled gasp and pointed to a black object lurking on the desk. I whipped off my shoe and whacked it three times. "It's all right," I said, realizing my error. "It's only a banana peel." It was a foolish mistake; actually our daughter is quite methodical and has a place for everything. Socks go on the study lamp, shoes on her pillow, dirty clothes under the bed, pajamas on the bed post, and banana peels on the desk.

Suppressing a shudder, the tax assessor grabbed his hat and left. He didn't even check to see whether we had converted the broom closet into a half bathroom.

March 5

I suspect that Supermothers wouldn't dream of sleeping late on Saturday mornings.

Supermothers probably consider 6:00 A.M. on Saturday an ideal time for creative activities such as baking gingerbread men and teaching their children how to make cunning papiermache hand puppets out of back issues of *The New Republic*.

I long ago disabused our children of the notion that I would engage in any maternal camaraderie on Saturday mornings before 9:30. I informed them that Daddy and I were to be awakened only in cases of fire, flood, or arterial bleeding. ("Yes, dear, the spurty kind") and that we were *not* to be roused from a sound slumber to be asked what language they speak in Zanzibar, how chickens reproduce, whether they can go to camp next August, or why the elephant painted his toenails red.

I wouldn't want anyone to think that I simply give the children laissez-faire to chop each other's ears off with rusty bread knives or set fire to the piano. Knowing that they wouldn't do anything expressly forbidden, I attempt to anticipate potential trouble by issuing an early morning ultimatum into the darkness. "Don't hit each other with blunt instruments, drink bleach, light matches, or go outside to make a snowman in your pajamas. And if you telephone Grandma long distance, be sure that you reverse the charges."

Unfortunately I am handicapped in that I don't think like a child.

If I had thought like a child last Saturday morning I might have added, "Don't put blue food coloring in your bathwater, Hershey Bars in the toaster, or wash Daddy's sweaters in the dishwasher."

Since I am woefully short on imagination, the children are doomed to spend the rest of their lives light blue from the waist down, the toast tastes like scorched rubber bands, and we now have four men's sweaters, size 6x.

March 8

I consider myself to be an honest person—except at parties.

The following is a list of remarks (actual meanings are in parentheses), which, when uttered at parties, have caused me to rush to the bathroom mirror and stare at my tongue to be sure it was the same one I had brought in with me.

"I know just what you mean. I was terribly glad to see the Christmas holidays end, too. It's such an exhausting time of year." (We didn't get asked out much, either.)

"Actually, we've had a pretty busy winter. In January we were involved in a sort of archeological dig. You know, unearthing and cataloging ancient artifacts." (We cleaned the basement.)

"Then in February we got terribly caught up in an exciting artistic project. Experimenting with new techniques is so exhilarating." (We painted the kitchen ceiling. Rather, I painted; my husband held the ladder.)

"Your son is really 'all boy!' " (Isn't it time he was in bed?)

"Yes, my husband is growing a beard. I'm getting to quite like it." (Actually it's exactly like kissing a Brillo Pad, but it does a great job of hiding a double chin.)

"What an attractive dress. Brown is certainly your color." (It makes you look like a walking bratwurst.)

"I know that your daughter would simply love ballet lessons. I do hope that you enroll her in our girl's class." (We desperately need someone else in the car pool.)

"Your dog certainly is playful!" (He just swallowed my watch.)

"You bet I agree that our elementary school is positively medieval in their teaching methods." (Your son must have failed Health Habits, too.)

"We're awfully sorry that we have to leave so early. This migraine hit my husband so suddenly." (Within thirty seconds from the time you brought out the slide projector.)

March 14

Recently we received a check with the instructions "Buy something that you all will enjoy."

Let's face it, there are precious few things that will appeal to both a forty-year-old and an eleven-year-old, except a steak dinner. Which isn't something that you can dust off and display prominently whenever the giver pops in for a visit.

Games are nice. But the children are hopeless at stud poker. The type of game they enjoy involves negotiating red plastic beans into a pot faster than anyone else. After playing it six times the first evening, we tossed it into the cupboard for six months or so, during which time the dog unearthed it and ate all the beans.

Having been informed by the children that they wouldn't particularly enjoy having a new mailbox, we settled for an outdoor birdfeeder.

We proceeded to fill the feeder with a mixture of suet, hemp, millet, canary seed, oat groats, and egg flake fortified with cod liver oil. The feeder contained everything, in fact, except birds.

During the first two weeks only one bird visited the feeder. He pecked around a bit, made a little gagging noise, and took off again.

Luring the birds became a personal challenge. We tried smorgasbord combination plates of popcorn, rice, Cheerios, and gingersnaps. Finally we hit upon a combination of fruit cocktail and sweet pickle relish.

Birds which normally feed exclusively on crabgrass and caterpillars, as well as others once thought to be extinct, began lining up at dawn and drawing numbers. Some feign broken wings in order to be first in line. If I am late in filling the feeder, they turn surly and begin hammering on the window with their beaks.

Actually we are enjoying the birdfeeder, but a new mailbox wouldn't cost us $3.58 a week for fruit cocktail and sweet pickle relish.

Thanks to our recent acquisition of a birdfeeder, I have taken up bird-watching.

In order to become a serious bird-watcher, it is necessary to obtain a copy of a bird identification book, which features full-color drawings of birds, all doing birdlike things such as building nests, digging worms, and picking lice out of their tails.

Unfortunately for your purposes, these birds are all standing still. Since any birds you will come in contact with will be flashing past at a dizzying rate of speed toward a rendezvous with a picture window, it is necessary to simulate this action by placing the bird book on the floor, covering it with leaves, and running past it as fast as you can.

Birds may be identified by inspecting their eggs, which are colored or speckled, and their beaks, which are small and pointy and ideal for pecking the eyes out of anyone who tries to inspect their eggs.

It is claimed that birds may also be identified by their call. Anything going "tweet-tweet" is most likely a bird. Conversely, birds which go "woof-woof" or "meow" probably aren't.

Many species cannot be distinguished from each other except by obscure markings under their wing-tips or on the bottom of their feet. To add to the confusion, the females of all species are brown.

Since birds take great pains to avoid showing you the bottoms of their feet, one must resort to the technique of bluffing.

If you do succeed in spotting a smallish brown something darting into the eaves, you must declare with conviction "Ah-hah! A Swamp Sparrow." It is possible that someone will have the temerity to say "Are you sure that it wasn't a Vesper Sparrow, Song Sparrow,

Fox Sparrow, White-Throated Sparrow, White-Crowned Sparrow or possibly a Robin?''

Simply reply scornfully ''Nonsense! Didn't you see the buff-colored patches under his warbles?''

I still can't help but feel that bird-watching is terribly presumptuous, though.

I mean, it's no wonder one has to get up at 5:00 A.M. and trip over all matter of nasty goo while traipsing three miles through the woods in order to try to spot a bird through a pair of high-powered field glasses that are never quite in focus.

The birds are hiding. And I can hardly blame them. What if positions were reversed?

What if a band of feathered people-watchers descended in great hordes, began pointing their wing-tips at *me* and exclaiming, ''Look! There's one now!''

''Where?'' the other would retort. ''You mean the flat-breasted one with the big tail?''

''That's the one! Notice how drab she is. Obviously the female of the species.''

''You're amazing. I can never seem to tell them apart.''

''She certainly keeps an untidy nest. Look at all the bits of string, bows from packages, dog-food coupons, and pork chop recipes.''

''Disgusting. I understand that she only feeds her young once a day at sundown. It's pitiful watching the fledglings foraging about on their own in the morning, bashing their beaks on the kitchen cabinet doors she's left open.''

''Disgusting, yes. But they're awfully interesting to study, actually, especially now that they're on the endangered list. Maybe that's why they're the only species that writes books on their own mating habits.''

March 15

One Friday morning, six weeks ago, I was taking a shower and singing a medley of Gershwin hits when my daughter began hammering on the bathroom door.

"Mom!" she bellowed. "The dining room ceiling is leaking like *anything*!"

"Nonsense," I replied, resuming a rudely interrupted chorus of "It Ain't Necessarily So."

Twenty minutes later I sauntered downstairs to find my son sitting under the dining room table, sailing a toy boat.

I called the plumber immediately. "Would someone be home all day?" they asked. Evidently they wanted to make sure that someone was going to be in. Someone *was* in all day, but not the plumber. He arrived promptly at 7:00 A.M. the next morning.

By then Lake Placid was completely dried up.

"Believe me," I said. "It pours like a faucet. Watch." I raced upstairs and turned on both taps. We watched for half an hour. Nothing. I took another shower, sang the same songs. Still nothing.

I wrote the plumber a check for fifteen dollars.

After he left, I turned the shower on again. Water cascaded through the ceiling in sheets. I rushed to phone the plumber.

"It's doing it again!" This time he arrived in half an hour. By then the leak had stopped.

"But you can *see* the water on the floor."

"Maybe you spilled something," he suggested skeptically. "Maybe the kids did it. What about the dog? Lady, I fix leaks, not puddles."

I wrote out another check for fifteen dollars.

This poignant drama has been going on for six weeks.

The plumber has torn up the bathroom floor, only to find it dry and dusty underneath. Yesterday, however, he finally came up with a solution.

"Lady," he said. "If I were you, I'd move."

March 18

I knew that my son was really ill when he passed up supper.

"But it's fried chicken!" I pointed out, waving a drumstick tantalizingly under his nose.

"My stomach hurts," Eric replied.

"He just wants to get out of walking the dog," was his sister's unsympathetic reaction.

For the past ten years I have viewed every pain occurring below the Adam's apple and above the knees as possible appendicitis. Seventeen appendicitis attacks have turned out to be stomach flu. Twenty-four have been constipation. One was a fractured pelvis.

I began gently prodding Eric's stomach.

"Cut that out!" he snarled.

"I'm looking for McBurney's Point."

"Who is McBurney, and what is his point doing in my stomach?"

"McBurney's point is a place between your hip bone and your bellybutton." As an aside to my daughter, I added, "If he screams when I poke it, he has appendicitis. If he laughs, he's just trying to get out of walking the dog."

"Yahgah!" bleated Eric as I located McBurney's point.

"By George, I think he's got it!" I gasped. Within twenty minutes we were sitting in the emergency ward of the hospital, where Eric reluctantly parted with several specimens of various bodily fluids and had his McBurney's Point ruthlessly prodded by two surgeons, three residents, and an inquisitive orderly. They disappeared for three hours, leaving us to watch the admissions of three automobile accidents, two drug overdoses, and a drunk with a broken nose. Meanwhile, Eric's appendix whiled away the time by flopping around like a dying mackerel.

By 2:00 A.M. the doctors announced that Eric and his appendix should part company immediately. I kissed Eric on the cheek as he was being wheeled into surgery.

"You shouldn't do that," he warned. "You'll catch appendicitis."

"Are you sure that he's all right?" I asked the surgeon after the operation.

"All right!" he laughed. "He isn't even out of the recovery room yet and he's asking whether we have any fried chicken."

Eric was keenly disappointed when the surgeon refused to give him his appendix, as he had planned to put it under his pillow for the appendix fairy, reasoning that if baby teeth were worth twenty-five cents each, an appendix could bring at least $7.50.

The appendix was next to have been featured in a Show-and-Tell presentation at school, then bronzed for his grandmother to use as a paperweight.

Eric shares a hospital room in the children's ward with another appendectomy, a case of colitis, and a rash of undetermined origin whose owner assured me isn't the least bit contagious—probably.

The boys spend their days checking the drip flow on each other's intravenous feeding bottles, swapping "why-did-the-elephant" jokes, and shooting rubber bands at the nurse's aides.

The day following his operation, Eric received four jigsaw puzzles, twelve comic books, twenty-seven greeting cards, and three hamburgers for lunch. Whereupon he announced that he was in no particular hurry to return home.

"They let me stay up till 10:00," he announced. "And we don't have to take baths," he added significantly, turning on the TV to watch a "Gilligan's Island" rerun.

By the next day, Eric had completed the four jigsaw puzzles, read all twelve comic books twice, and lunched on creamed spinach and carrot sticks.

"I kind of miss being home and going to school," he conceded, handing me a soggy napkin full of creamed spinach. "Especially since I have something for Show-and-Tell."

"Swell. What is it?"

"Billy's rash."

Since hospitals are inhabited solely by the Afflicted and the Healers, a visitor is clearly a misfit, looking neither sick enough to be a patient nor clean enough to be a nurse.

Feeling as welcome as a blizzard in May, I visited a friend Myra while checking on Eric. I found her sharing a room with a thin, blonde woman with a faint, black moustache who was scrutinizing her tongue in a hand mirror. Myra seemed a bit uncertain whether hospital protocol demanded that she introduce me.

"I'd like you to meet Mrs. Berger," she finally said.

"Colitis," announced Mrs. Berger, wrenching her attention away from her tongue.

"I beg your pardon?"

"Colitis," she repeated. "You wouldn't believe the misery I'm in." The three of us observed thirty seconds

of silence in wordless homage to Mrs. Berger's unbelievable colitis.

"Don't she look terrible?" demanded Mrs. Berger,
pointing accusingly at Myra. I had to admit that I had
seen Myra look better, but lying in bed for four days
watching your toenails grow isn't exactly calculated to
put roses in your cheeks.

I groped for an opening gambit. It seemed somewhat
pointless to say "How are you?" to anyone with
twenty-seven stitches in her stomach. "How do you
feel?" while a bit more appropriate, was likely to elicit a
lengthy and somewhat nauseatingly graphic reply.

"How are the meals?" I asked at last.

"Terrible. But everyone has to eat them eventually.
On Monday they give you a broiled chicken back. If you
don't eat it, the next day they chop it up with canned
peas and make chicken salad. If you still won't eat it,
Mrs. Berger says that they puree it and inject it into your
hip.

"Thanks for the flowers," she said, vaguely indicating a table full of vases. Since I had ordered them
by phone I had no idea which ones were mine. I tried to
determine which bunch looked most like $2.75. It cer-
tainly couldn't be the three dozen longstemmed roses. I
fervently hoped that mine wasn't the single lily in the
water glass.

Just then the nurse announced that since it was time
for dinner, I would have to leave. "Unless you'd like to
stay," she said, waving a hypodermic needle. "We're
having a lovely puree of chicken."

March 19

Last week my daughter approached me indignantly.

"Do you realize that I am the only girl in my entire class who still wears those crummy Fruit of the Loom undershirts? I want a bra. A training bra."

"Training for *what*!" I demanded.

"Don't be crude. Here in the mail-order catalog it says that training bras 'provide gentle support for the blossoming girl as she prepares to flower into womanhood.' I'm blossoming, in case you haven't noticed."

"My little girl!" I sobbed, clasping her tightly to me. "Are you *sure* you're blossoming? I mean, you seem pretty much like you always were to me."

She favored me with a huffy stare and stalked off to her room.

The next afternoon we visited the lingerie department of the local department store.

"Now, *that's* what I want," she announced, pointing to a display of purple lace bras with matching bikini panties.

"That's what is known as sending a man on a boy's errand," I informed her.

"May I help you ladies?" a salesgirl inquired. My daughter flung me a "So There!" glance.

"I need a new bra," she declared. "I don't exactly have a favorite brand," she added, gathering up fifteen assorted makes and sizes and heading for the fitting room.

The next morning my daughter appeared decidedly depressed at breakfast.

"It's tight," she complained.

"It's supposed to be tight."

"The straps cut into my shoulders."

"The straps are supposed to cut into your shoulders."

"Does it show through the back of my blouse?"

"Don't worry. You can't see a thing."

"Darn it. I'll have to change to a thinner blouse. What's the good of wearing a bra unless people can see it? You might as well wear an undershirt."

Who's to blame for this early interest in wearing a bra? Not me, that's for sure. It must be the constant barrage of advertisements.

Now I am sure that there is a valid need for such advertisements. (Actually, I'm not all *that* sure, but it seems appropriate to try to be positive.)

What I can't seem to understand is why underwear models, without exception, appear to be gripped in the throes of some unexplained passion. Evidently it is considered bad form to simply stand around in a Playtex bra, casually inspecting your fingernails; convention obviously insists that you must assume sultry expressions, thrust both arms upward in lascivious abandon, and fling locks of hair wantonly over both eyes, presumably leaving no doubt in the mind of the prospective purchaser that being encased in a Playtex bra is an erotic event.

The most intriguing advertisement of all is the "before and after" approach, featuring a hapless matron, her midriff bulging alarmingly and her posterior shaped like a brace of enormous butternut squash. The second view features the same matron wearing a girdle which has not only rendered her midriff and posterior svelte and smooth, but has inexplicably removed the circles from under her eyes, obliterated the gray from her hair, and capped her front teeth.

Ironically, no such miraculous transformation of libido and shape is hinted at by those who model men's underwear.

Invariably they are pictured either sitting sheepishly

around a locker room, shaking foot powder into their executive-length socks, or with one foot propped on a bench, staring grimly at the camera, obviously tormented by the crucial decision of whether to finish getting dressed or simply go back to bed.

March 20

Not only do many couples consider a double bed to be an ideal arena in which to resolve major conflicts, such as whether or not permanent-press handkerchiefs want ironing, but they bring to the arena two combatants with wildly divergent body temperatures—it being a proven fact that by 2:00 A.M. the female body temperature plummets to 89 degrees while that of the male shoots up to 112.5.

Consequently, a typical wife insists upon covering up her husband all night, reasoning that if she is cold, he must be too.

Her husband, in turn, spends the greater part of every night with beads of sweat coating his upper lip, dreaming that he has been staked out on the Sahara Desert at high noon as a penalty for not taking out the garbage.

In the throes of his discomfort, he occasionally succeeds in flinging his half of the covers over his sleeping wife, while whimpering "But the bag wasn't *full*!" Finally comfortable, he drifts off into a deep sleep, dreaming that he is swinging lazily on a hammock, deep in a cool forest glen, while six maidens hover nearby, ironing his handkerchiefs.

March 22

I must admit to being decidedly underimpressed with artsy-craftsy projects.

I have found that no matter how many red sequins you glue on them, bleach bottles still look inordinately like bleach bottles.

Pipe cleaners don't exactly set my artistic libido atwitter, nor do used S.O.S. Pads, empty orange juice cans, or the cardboard tubes from toilet paper rolls.

To my way of thinking, there is nothing remotely festive about a Christmas wreath made out of green garbage bags and a bent coat hanger.

Once, stricken with an acute attack of conscience over the ecological problems of our society, I went so far as to buy a bottle-cutter set which promised to enable me to make glasses out of those ten cases of empty beer bottles in the basement. I discovered that one case of beer makes more glasses than I'll ever need; instead of a bsement full of ten cases of empty beer bottles, I ended up with a basement full of 240 ugly brown glasses.

Unfortunately, I happen to live in an area of compulsive driftwood collectors.

"You're *not* going to throw away grapefruit

rinds!?!'' shrieked one of my neighbors, carrying on as if she'd just caught me rinsing my hair with Holy Water.

"What's wrong with throwing away a grapefruit rind?"

"You *save* it," she insisted, rinsing off the coffee grounds and carefully patting it dry. "Orange peels, apple parings—it all makes heavenly sachet."

Thanks to diligent hoarding, I now have seventeen little bags of garbage hanging in my closet.

Not only does everything I own smell like a fruit salad that sat out in the sun too long, but I draw flies.

March 24

There is something regenerative about the approach of spring. As the doldrums of winter begin to lift, I find myself seeking to rejuvenate my life, to cleanse my soul and greet the awakening of nature with a spirit of unadulterated purity and innocence.

I accomplish this by having a garage sale.

This year I resolve to be absolutely ruthless, there being no room for sentiment in an eight-by-ten storage room. While I intend to keep the four ping-pong paddles I found beside the washing machine in hopes that we get a table some day, I see no justification for keeping a repair kit for an air mattress that I left in Yosemite National Park in 1972.

And while I have no intention of having another

baby, if one came to visit I should probably be quite glad to have a wooden gate or two to keep between us.

While there is no possible way I could be induced to part with a crepe paper daisy costume from the second-grade production of "Bluebird Hill," a beer bottle covered with gold-sprayed macaroni shells, or a jewelry box full of the dog's baby teeth, the following items are definitely for sale:

Fourteen gallon cider jugs with strands of green mold inside.

One 1970 Denver, Colorado, phone book.

A sleeping bag that smells funny and has a jammed zipper.

One potty chair bearing the original price tag. Never used.

A jigsaw puzzle entitled "Aristotle Contemplating the Bust of Raquel Welch," with six pieces missing.

One bird cage, one hamster cage, one aquarium, one turtle bowl, a cat's scratching post, a rabbit hutch, three bags of cedar shavings, and a shoe box with holes punched in the lid.

Of course, along with the garage sale, spring also brings with it another primordial urge. And, overcome with the same inexplicable urge that sends salmon upstream to spawn, I know that I will come dangerously close to cleaning the house.

I don't mean simple "wipe-the-jelly-off-the-commode" type cleaning.

I mean real cleaning. Putting Spic and Span on a tooth-brush and scrubbing all the little knobs on the stove. Taking the TV set apart and dusting the tubes. Waxing the garage floor.

For anyone who comes close to pandering to this primordial urge, I recommend asking the following questions:

1. In these critical days of world crisis and economic

upheaval, can you in all conscience devote an entire day to rearranging your spice rack?

2. In the final analysis, will anyone really care whether the grout around your bathtub is gray?

3. Can you really leave this world knowing that your only contribution to global harmony is having a spotless broiler pan?

4. The last time you indulged in such an orgy of cleanliness, you gave birth two hours later. Granted, there may not be a causal relationship, but do you really want to take that chance?

March 25

Any mother with children at home who attempts to enjoy a short telephone conversation finds her attention constantly diverted by horrendous thumping noises, rather like someone throwing a cat down a laundry chute, followed by the less-than-reassuring exclamation "Boy! Are *you* gonna get it!"

If at this point she does not get up, the thumping will stop, unfortunately being replaced by a repetitious sound, vaguely reminiscent of the cry of an indignant moose, which indicates that someone is using his bed as a trampoline.

This temporary diversion soon gives way to the authoritative sound of nailing, pounding and/or sawing, as the children peremptorily decide to add or subtract a spare bedroom.

Actually, the most frightening sound of all is total silence, indicating that someone is either painting his shoes, cutting out all the pictures in the *Encyclopedia Britannica* to send to Grandma, or drinking an entire bottle of Mr. Clean.

March 26

At one time, I thought that it was a perfectly splendid idea for my son to have a paper route.

Wanting a paper route, I believed, exhibited an admirable desire to assume responsibility and would lead to a much needed appreciation for the value of money.

It also meant that I wouldn't have to raise his allowance this year.

I must admit that a paper route has, in fact, increased his sense of responsibility. As he feels an obligation to attend to his regular customers first, we now receive the last paper, the one that fell in the puddle and has the sports section missing.

A paper route has improved his regard for the value of money, too. Where once he was so unconcerned about money that I regularly would retrieve on the average of eighty-eight cents in change from the lint filter whenever I washed his jeans, now he refuses to deliver a paper to me unless he is paid in advance. And unless I tip him, he throws it on the roof. When anyone asks what he wants to be when he grows up, he replies "a tycoon."

In return for this semireliable service, I occasionally help him out when he is ill, has a detention, is practicing his trumpet, or has a blister on his heel. While he can lob a newspaper twenty-five feet directly onto the center of a welcome mat, the only direction I can throw is straight up. So far, I have heaved seventeen papers into trees, thirty-two onto roofs, and have witnessed four disappear completely.

This I don't mind. What I do not enjoy is collecting for him.

"You're not Eric!" one man said accusingly. Before I could explain coyly that he should notice a family resemblance, he marched off to the kitchen and said, "There's a new paperboy out there come to collect, Emma. Big gawky kind of kid. I just don't know what this younger generation's coming to; I could swear he was wearing curlers!"

March 29

I am not certain at just what age a birthday ceases to be a Joyous Occasion.

I do know that the period between "now I am old enough to" and "now I am too old to" is frighteningly short.

I find that these days, birthdays are less a question of doing something special than of remembering how to do everyday things. And wondering whether they're worth the bother.

"Why didn't you tell us that today was your birthday?" the children demanded recently.

"I forgot that it *was* my birthday," I admitted.

"But we could have had a party," they protested.

"I would sooner celebrate the Saint Valentine's Day Massacre. At my age, parties are in bad taste—kind of like setting off Roman Candles to celebrate the invasion of Pearl Harbor."

"Just think of all the neat presents you missed getting."

"Who needs six more flannel nightgowns?" I scoffed.

"Somehow I never thought you would be the type to be sensitive about getting older," mused my daughter. "Next you'll be telling us that you lie about your age."

"Of course I lie about my age," I retorted. "I tell everyone that I'm sixty-two."

"Whatever for? You could pass for thirty!"

"Think about it," I replied. "Which would you rather be known as, a dissipated thirty, or a remarkably well-preserved sixty-two?"

March 30

"I just can't understand you, Millie," I protested to my friend last week as we slid into her car. "You just don't seem like the type for a CB radio."

"Nonsense," countered Millie. "A CB radio enables me to add my voice to those of my fellow men, Sweet

Baby, Dirty Dan, and Big Foot. Together we sing the song of the open road. Or we will as soon as I learn the jargon."

"Super Stud calling those pretty little beavers in the pregnant roller skate," bawled the radio. "If you're making for Sugar Town on a big 10-17, I'd be more than happy to cover your rear."

"Just what does he mean by that?" hissed Millie, clutching the steering wheel grimly and peering nervously into the rear view mirror.

"I think Super Stud is either that orange van with the baby shoes hanging over the dashboard or the purple pick-up truck we passed that had the 'Honk If You Love Jesus' bumper sticker. He wants you to join him in singing the song of the open road. Or something."

"I don't care what you say," Millie insisted. "If my car breaks down now, I can use my CB instead of that 38-D bra I used to tie to the antenna as a distress flag."

"But you don't wear a 38-D bra."

"How much help do you think I would have gotten waving a Fruit of the Loom undershirt?"

April 2

Reading in bed is an art.

One must first choose the proper bed. A single bed is rarely wide enough to accommodate a sufficient number of pillows, not to mention a box of Kleenex, an ashtray, a plate of Things to Nibble On, and a second book to read in case you decide you don't like the first one.

A double bed is better, unless you must share it with someone who flops around and makes exasperated noises while you're trying to read.

Choosing appropriate food to eat in bed is a problem. One should avoid anything with seeds, as they invariably mix themselves up with the bedding and leave you with nasty looking marks on your cheeks the next morning. Although crumbs can be annoying, it is relatively simple to mop them up by dabbing at the sheets with a piece of bread covered with peanut butter.

Pajamas are a nice touch when one is reading in bed. They not only speak of elegance and refinement, but keep the crumbs off one's chest. Bottoms should be roomy enough so that one can slide down in bed without hurting oneself.

The book should be something light and entertaining, as it is patently ridiculous to make such elaborate preparations, only to fall asleep on page two of *Agriculture in the Middle Ages*.

April 3

Since we had children, I've discovered that housework is never really finished. At some point it becomes necessary simply to declare, "There now, that's entirely enough of *that*!" or you'll find yourself at 4:30 in the afternoon waxing the underside of the coffee table and sobbing.

As it is, after spending eighteen hours washing windows, sweeping floors, and scrubbing peanut butter off the TV screen, I fall into bed with a sense of accomplishment. Whereupon a still, small voice begins to whine, "Yeah, smarty, but what about all the toast crumbs in the silverware drawer?"

A friend of mine insists that all I need is a system, like her Room-a-Day method. On Monday, she cleans the living room; on Tuesday, the family room—and so on. Unfortunately, when I tried her system, the living room that I cleaned on Monday was not only full of old boots and Oh Henry! wrappers again on Wednesday, but I found that someone had traced a decidedly vulgar word in the dust on the stereo.

I'm not certain where kitchens fit in this one-a-day scheme. It's all very well to declare Thursday as "clean-the-kitchen" day, but what happens when the Sunday dinner ham shoots off the platter, slides the length of the kitchen, and bounces down the back stairs? I suppose that in theory one could refuse to deal with the twenty-foot smear of ham fat on the floor, it not being Thursday and all.

But unless one is willing to risk having a husband, two children, and the TV repairman bouncing down the back stairs as well, it becomes necessary to maintain a three-day vigil in the kitchen, cautioning, "Hop over the ham fat, dear" to everyone.

I prefer my "If-I-don't-see-it-nobody-else-will-either" attitude. But every system has its drawback. Yesterday I saw our son Eric and his friend down on their hands and knees, peering under Eric's bed. "Wow! You win!" declared the friend, and handed Eric fifteen cents.

"What was that all about?" I asked Eric later.

"Oh, I just bet Murray fifteen cents that I had more dust under my bed than he had under his."

April 10

I recently ran across a magazine article entitled "Ten House Plants Which ANYONE Can Grow."

If one is addicted to absurd hyperbole, this article ranks a close second behind the lead story, "How to Look Adorable When You're Eight Months Pregnant."

In the first place, the writer was adamant in insisting that plants need to be placed in an area of the house where they will receive sufficient light. Unfortunately, I have only one such area, and it is presently occupied by the refrigerator. Where I desperately need a plant is in the darkest corner of the living room beside the heat vent.

"Overwatering," contended the writer, "is probably the most common problem affecting would-be-gardeners. Over-watering causes the plant's leaves to drop off." As the leaves are likewise prone to drop off when the plant is underwatered, overfertilized, or afflicted with mealy worms, one can never be completely certain where one went wrong should the plant suddenly fall into the kitchen sink and lie there looking up balefully through the egg shells and coffee grounds.

"Try talking to your plants," urged the author in conclusion. "They'll love you for it."

Regrettably, he neglected to suggest suitable topics of conversation. Let's face it, an African Violet is verging on being inanimate; how can one discuss the problem of urban decay with something doomed to spend its entire life in a six-inch plastic pot?

I find that reading material on raising houseplants is much like reading the final chapters of *The Joy of Sex*; I know that thousands of people can follow the fairly involved directions and experience unqualified success and enjoyment, but can I? And even if I could, do I really want to?

It's not that I haven't tried.

I have a philodendron located on a window sill, carefully out of direct sunlight, which I regularly ply with the very best fertilizer and seventy-eight-degree distilled water. I protect it from drafts, loud noises, and rude language. We not only sit down for daily chats, but I play classical music to it and read it inspirational verse every Tuesday. Its only response is to sit there clasping its terminal bud dramatically, wheezing, and dropping leaves into the kitchen sink.

I called on my next-door neighbor yesterday only to find her practically lashed to the piano with tendrils of English ivy. While I watched, not only did three leaves unfold and six buds appear, but I could swear the entire plant was humming "Happy Days Are Here Again" in close harmony.

"Stop that, you little devil," she chortled, absently unwrapping a tendril that had entwined itself around her neck and was nibbling her earlobe amorously.

"Isn't it the oddest thing?" she exclaimed. "I simply

never remember to feed or water it. I can't understand how it stays alive."

"You must do *something*," I argued. "Your plant is so healthy it's almost embarrassing to watch!"

"Well, I do read to it," she admitted.

"Inspirational verse?"

"No," she blushed. "*The Joy of Sex*."

Something larger than houseplants looms before me now, however, and that is the outdoor garden. The two momentous decisions facing me (and every homeowner) this month are: (1) What to plant, (2) What to plant it with.

The first problem is more easily solved if you either lean heavily toward the practicality of cucumbers or vibrate whenever you spy a petunia. Unfortunately I tend to vacillate. I mean, petunias taste revolting, yet cucumbers won't fit in a bud vase.

One must also consider things like soil acidity, drainage, and exposure to the sun, a thorough study of which can stretch well into July, nicely solving the problem, as by then it is too late to plant anything but radishes.

Once you have determined what to plant, the next pressing problem lies in locating the proper tools. In my case, intense questioning administered under an extremely hot light elicited the information that the trowel had been used to fix a bicycle.

"How can you fix a bicycle with a trowel?" I wailed.

"You can't."

Muttering obscenities, I strode into the garden with sixteen packages of seeds and a tablespoon.

The package directions specified that the seeds be planted as early in the spring as the soil can be worked. It is extremely difficult to work soil with a nine-inch tablespoon. It involved getting down on my hands and knees and stabbing away at a clump of clay only to discover that, since the clump was in reality a beef knuckle bone that the dog buried last fall, the attendant vibrations loosened all the fillings in my molars.

Now seed packet illustrations should undoubtedly be given "The Most Blatant Example of False Advertising Award."

If only seed companies would feature color illustrations of green beans covered with slugs, cucumbers riddled with worm holes, and cabbages being engulfed by a slimy, reddish-brown fungus, one would at least be partially prepared for the inevitable.

Instead, seed companies insist upon presenting breathtakingly gorgeous, full-color views of a virgin tomato, unblemished save for a drop of morning dew clinging to its flawless stem, a pea pod bursting open spontaneously to reveal twelve perfectly matched peas, and a head of lacy lettuce coyly uncurling in the summer sun.

Those of us even remotely susceptible to the "Mary Mary Quite Contrary" syndrome inevitably go all to pieces in the face of such bounty.

I mean, if it all hadn't looked so gorgeous, I never would have forgotten that our entire garden plot consists of a six-by-six feet area beside the garbage cans when I snatched up twenty-seven packets of assorted vegetables that no one in the family likes anyway.

Eventually I reached the stage where I arbitrarily declared the soil to be ready.

But it was something of a shock to open the seed packages and discovered that the next step involved planting what appeared to be several thousand grains of pepper individually.

At that point it seemed infinitely more logical to simply rebury the bone.

"What did you plant in the garden?" my son asked.

"A cow," I replied. "And if it ever comes up, I sure have a lot of pepper to put on the steaks."

April 14

I am a firm believer in getting away from the children periodically.

Not only is a brief hiatus from sharing a common bathroom beneficial to all concerned, but a short separation from mother causes the children to appreciate her exceptional care and tenderness which heretofore they have taken for granted.

On the other hand, there is always the possibility that they will realize that they are not only perfectly capable of managing without you, but prefer it that way, and will answer your long-distance phone calls with "Mother who?"

Of course, one cannot simply pack a bag and slip away silently into the night, no matter how attractive the prospect may appear after an entire evening of watching them spit in each other's milk.

No, you must, in all conscience, recruit a caretaker to sleep in your bed till 10:00 every morning, watch "The Edge of Night," thaw the TV dinners, and otherwise function as you would.

One cannot turn such heady responsibility over to a stranger without first briefing her on family routine, personal idiosyncrasies, and the fact that there is a garter snake named Arthur loose in the house.

Consequently, I am leaving the following note for the sitter:

Dear Mildred:

It is Eric's turn to stomp on the Fruit Loops box so that it will fit in the garbage bag, and Laurie's turn to use the plunger on the kitchen sink.

The stuff in the green refrigerator jar is Hamburger Surprise; the dog food is in the pink refrigerator jar. Don't get them mixed up. The dog hates Hamburger Surprise.

The sugar is in the canister marked flour; the flour is in "Sugar." The one labeled "Coffee" has a bottle of cooking sherry inside; it's a little salty, but not too bad if you drink it fast.

As there is always the possibility that a parent who goes away from the children for a weekend of adult-type revelry may meet with some sort of fatal disaster, whenever I go away I take great pains to leave my dresser drawers in immaculate condition, ensuring that any concerned neighbors who begin rummaging through my personal effects searching for insurance policies and stock certificates will be impressed with my housekeeping skills.

I have likewise taken the precaution of tucking the following letter to the children under a pile of panty hose:

Dear Children:

I'm sorry that I'm not able to leave you much money. There would have been a lot more if your teeth had come in straight.

There is, however, a college fund set aside for you to use at any college you choose that doesn't have coeducational dormitories.

I want you to know that I loved you when you flushed your new shoes down the toilet, shaved your eyebrows off, and wrapped the dead sparrow in waxed paper, labeled him "Pork Chops," and put him in the freezer. It was probably hard for you to realize that I loved you, what with me going all white around the mouth and screaming "If you *ever* do that again, I'm going to *belt* you!"

But if I *didn't* love you, I wouldn't have cared.

I mean, you may not grow up to become presidents of the United States or nuclear physicists, but at least you won't grow up to be the kind of adults who go around pouring their Ovaltine down heat vents.

Love,
Mom

P.S. Better buy more dental floss; I used the last of it to tie up my suitcase.

April 16

While dinner should be an occasion of family harmony, all too often the evening meal is fraught with dissent.

What is clearly needed is the following "Code of Behavior at Mealtime," a copy of which should be conspicuously posted in the dining room.

Cleanliness: Children are required to wash all visible moving parts, i.e., hands, faces, ears. There is nothing quite so revolting as eating opposite someone with a Chiquita Banana label on his forehead or "I Love Rod Stewart" written on her hand in green ballpoint ink.

Food: Any comments on the quantity or quality of the food are restricted to those of an affirmative nature. Rhetorical questions such as "Why do we always have to have crummy old beets?" are detrimental to morale. Food is to be consumed as quickly as is politely possible, using only the utensils provided, i.e., there will be no manual arrangement of peas to spell "I Love Rod Stewart."

Physical Restrictions: Tipping chairs is positively disallowed, as are intricate balancing acts involving glasses of milk. Elbows and knees are to be kept off the table.

Conversation: Each member of the family may choose one topic and browbeat it for three minutes. Son may use his three minutes to describe how to make an amplifier. Daughter may explain how she is going to take a paper route to earn enough money to send for a Mark Eden Bust Developer. Mother may muse aloud on the difficulty of removing carbonized chicken pie from the inside of an oven. Father will use his three minutes for silence. Any topic is allowed, with the exception of those discussions beginning "Guess what I saw on the sidewalk on the way to school!"

April 19

Don't get me wrong. I think that pantyhose are possibly the greatest invention since sliced bread.

In theory pantyhose are the answer. But why can I never find a pair that fits?

I am either forced to spend the entire day encased in a pair of pantyhose so large thst even though I pull them up to my armpits, my ankles and knees are festooned with wrinkles, or I must attempt to wedge into a smaller size which never goes quite all the way on.

And it is most distressing to walk down the street with the elastic top clinging precariously to my hip bones, the crotch in the general vicinity of my knees, and the uneasy realization that any ill-considered physical activity will undoubtedly cause the entire effort to snap down around my ankles.

April 21

"You really should jog," a friend of mine declared recently.

"Whatever for?" I shuddered.

"It's such good exercise!" she crowed. Actually, as reasons go, good exercise does not exactly set me all a-flutter. I mean, it's not as if she said that jogging tasted good or paid $28.50 an hour.

Besides, I tried jogging two years ago.

The first morning I ventured out in a pair of emerald green stretch pants and a snappy red hockey shirt that my son had bought at the Salvation Army for fifty-five cents. Evidently this garb did not immediately identify me as a jogger. Not only did four buses stop to pick me up, but it took me fifteen minutes to convince a cruising member of the vice squad that I wasn't being pursued by a sex maniac.

I tried again a week later, this time wearing not only a

blue track suit but a sweatband around my forehead and a shirt cardboard bearing the number "27" taped to my back.

I was doing quite well until I was joined by a German Shepherd who seemed good-naturedly determined to hamstring me. He gamboled along beside me, slathering coyly, alternately licking my hand and making slashing motions at my ankles.

"Good boy!" I bleated. Obviously offended at this blatant bit of hypocrisy, Good Boy lunged for my throat. A burst of speed fortunately rendered this area out of reach, although he managed to snatch and eat my shirt cardboard.

This permanently retired both me and my number from jogging. At least until it starts paying $28.50 an hour.

April 22

While I was never particularly enchanted with the prospect of hauling an orange-and-white striped teddy bear, two dozen baby bottles, and a rubber sheet half way across the country, I've discovered that traveling with small children is a lead-pipe cinch compared with taking two children on a three thousand-mile trip to California.

In the first place, my son Eric insisted on packing his own clothes in a fourteenth-hand duffel bag that he bought for twenty-five cents at a Navy surplus store and arrived in California with six pairs of shoes, an electric blow comb, and twelve copies of *Mad* magazine.

"What do you mean, you 'forgot' underwear?" I demanded.

"I remembered to bring socks," he countered.

"Yeah. One green and one blue," I sighed.

"Where's my room?" his sister, Laurie inquired.

"You're standing in it."

"We're not all sharing one room!?! You mean I have to sleep in the same room with 'It?' " she wailed, gesturing toward her brother.

"Yuck!" Eric grimaced, indicating that he too was somewhat less than overjoyed at the prospect.

"Think of this room as our home away from home," I insisted. Within ten minutes they had draped their jeans over the chairs, slung underwear over the lamps, and taped three posters up on the walls.

"This place is as much a mess as your rooms at home," I complained. "I hope you're comfortable now."

"As comfortable as a growing boy can be without a refrigerator," Eric grumbled.

"And the phone," Laurie added. "I've been here for twenty minutes, and it hasn't rung *once*."

While on such a trip, one is happily freed from the onerous chore of meal preparation. The resulting euphoria is more than a little offset by having to take children to break bread, not to mention an odd dish or two, in restaurants.

As I discovered in California, a 7:00 A.M. breakfast is a hands-down favorite as the worst possible meal to eat outside the home.

While within the confines of familiar surroundings, a mother can shuffle aimlessly about the kitchen wearing a chin strap and clutching a cup of coffee, ricochet gently from the refrigerator to the stove, wondering idly where the toaster has got to. In the face of such amiable helplessness, the children may very well realize that she definitely is in no shape to be trusted with a bread knife and decide to fix their own breakfasts.

"You have blue eye shadow all over your ear," my daughter Laurie hissed as we entered a coffee shop in California.

"I *thought* my eyelids seemed bumpier than usual," I sighed.

"Am I ever *starved*!" my son Eric confided to our waitress, a motherly-looking woman wearing black fishnet stockings and a pink micro-miniskirt.

"Isn't he *cute*!" gushed the waitress, mentally computing fifteen percent of a $12.50 breakfast order.

"I'll have the Lumberjack's Special, with a double order of sausage, four English muffins, a bowl of Fruit Loops, and two large glasses of orange juice," Eric announced. "For starters."

"And I'll have a cheese and bacon omelette, hash-browned potatoes, cream of wheat, a Danish pastry, and tomato juice," Laurie said. "What are you having, Mom?"

"Black coffee and a glass of prune juice."

"It sure is embarrassing to eat breakfast in a restaurant with you," Laurie whispered.

"Lots of people drink prune juice," I replied huffily.

"Yeah. But not while they're wearing a chin strap."

April 23

The fantasy of Disneyland comes as no real shock to anyone who has already spent several days in southern California.

During those first necessary days, one loses the initial mistrust of California foliage, which is of the same bizarre, exotic quality which Northerners only encounter as decorations in third-class restaurants, as well as the uncomfortable certainty that on the underside of every leaf are the words "Made in Japan."

It is also necessary, as a prelude to Disneyland, to have made frequent stops at drive-in restaurants and experienced the ridiculous self-consciousness of having to recite your order to a large plastic clown.

Disneyland is composed of forty-two attractions, the lines for many of which were long, doubling back on themselves snake-fashion five and six times. The barriers which are erected to prevent interlopers from breaking into line are equally effective in keeping anyone already queued up from changing his mind and heading for a free exhibit instead.

Through sheer strength of numbers, the children forced me into a Matterhorn bobsled, which wound its way through a man-made mountain at a dizzying rate.

"I wish you wouldn't scream that way," my son observed.

"It's the only way I know!" I howled before lapsing into a moan-sob combination which lasted until we careened back down the Matterhorn.

While, with the exception of the Matterhorn disaster, I enjoyed Disneyland, I was evidently not the only one struck by Disneyland's pervading unreality, which extends even to its restrooms. I watched a six-year-old boy, obviously distraught, rush back to where his mother stood waiting.

"Quick! Quick!" he bellowed. "Am I a 'Prince' or a 'Princess'?"

April 25

It has often been said that the best part of traveling is coming home again.

This is not necessarily true.

This is especially not necessarily true when one is returning home in the company of two children who have spent an entire week combing southern California beaches for "souvenirs," which, more often than not, turn out to be recently-deceased marine life.

"You smell funny!" I whispered to my daughter as we waited to go through the airport security check.

"It's not me," she declared. "It's my starfish. I bet I'll be the only one on the entire plane with a starfish."

"You'll probably be the only one on the entire plane—period!" I gasped, struggling to move upwind of the pungent bulge in her jean jacket.

"Where are your socks?" I asked, noticing that she wore none.

"They're in my suitcase. I have clams in one, dead hermit crabs in another, some weird sort of black, slimy thing with six legs in . . ."

"What in heaven's name are you going to do with that stuff?"

"Give it all to Jane," she replied. "To show her I was thinking about her."

"I can see it all now," I said sarcastically. "Here's a black, slimy thing with six legs, Jane. When I saw it, I immediately thought of you."

"Jane will think it's cool," she maintained stubbornly.

"You don't have any souvenirs in *your* socks, do you?" I asked my son.

"I didn't bring any socks, remember?"

As it turned out, he did bring home a souvenir. A perfectly spectacular, absolutely authentic case of athlete's foot.

May 6

I am not particularly fond of animal acts. Rather than watching a bear in red velvet knickers ride a motorcycle, I would much prefer to see him out in the wild, doing something that nature intended him to do. Like raiding garbage dumps.

Over the protests of the children, I have vetoed their attempts to teach our dogs to do any of the following tricks:

Shake Hands: While I've never been accused of being a fanatic on hygiene, I'm not particularly enchanted with the prospect of shaking hands with anyone who spends the entire day tromping through freshly fertilized tulip beds and spilled orange juice.

Beg: I'm not sure what other people feed their dogs, but I'd be embarrassed to suggest to our dog that he beg for the revolting muck that we put into his dish. It's terribly good for him and all, but he greets every meal with a resigned sigh and holds his nose with one paw while he eats.

Speak: I've never heard of a dog saying anything constructive, or even remotely entertaining. When you teach a dog to speak, you teach him to bark, which is precisely the same thing that you bashed him with a rolled-up newspaper for doing just yesterday.

Besides, with one child launching into a lengthy diatribe on the impossibility of functioning in an inflationary consumer-oriented society on an allowance of $1.50 a month, the other child complaining that he's the only boy in the whole school who has to carry a pink lunchbox with a picture of Cinderella on it, and a husband wistfully asking where all his clean handkerchiefs have gone—the last person I need to hear from is the dog.

Play Dead: I'm admittedly squeamish about this accomplishment. I mean, suppose he became really *good* at it. You could go around for weeks remarking on how clever he is, only to take him in to get his rabies shot and have the vet tell you that it really isn't necessary, as he isn't playing after all.

May 10

A whole new phenomenon is sweeping the nation. Mothers are going out to get a shampoo and set or buy a loaf of pumpernickel and simply disappearing for good.

I cannot imagine that every woman simply deserts the ship without leaving a note telling those left in command where the life jackets are stowed. A note, perhaps, like the following:

Dear Jim:
I promised to fix the children blueberry pancakes for breakfast. I'm not sure just where the spatula is; you might try looking in the toy box.

Tommy has volunteered to bring cupcakes to Cubs tomorrow night. Bake forty-six chocolate and two white; chocolate gives Howie Sherman the hives.

If the baby says "Wah-Wah" it means either "I want a drink of water" or "The dog is being sick again."

Shirley owes us two onions. We owe Myra two extra-large disposable diapers, a vacuum cleaner bag, and a can of cream of mushroom soup.

It is Billy's turn to fill the ice cube trays and say grace. It is Karen's turn to drink out of the Fred Flintstone mug and plug in the vacuum cleaner.

The produce man will give you old lettuce for the guinea pig. Save any that isn't too brown for salads. The bird seed is in the liquor cabinet next to the fish food.

Thursday afternoon bridge is here next week. Barb bids a short club, and when Fran says "two no trump" it means she wishes she'd never opened in the first place. The sherry is in the liquor cabinet next to the bird seed.

Lots of luck,
Carol

May 16

In addition to a poor sense of rhythm, abysn coordination, and the inability to participate in "Ro

Row, Row Your Boat" without putting my fingers in my ears, I lack a sense of timing.

I rush to get to the PTA meeting at 7:30 P.M. only to find that there is no one there but the janitor. I spend fifteen minutes helping him set up folding chairs.

The plumber promises to come early Monday morning. For the first time in recorded history, he arrives on time. Just after I have shampooed my hair and applied a Moondust Blonde rinse that must be washed out in ten minutes.

After thirty years of waiting in dentists' offices, thumbing through two-month-old news magazines and torn copies of *The Little Red Hen*, I arrive fifteen minutes late. Due to a last-minute cancellation, the dentist is right on schedule and charges me ten dollars for the time he has wasted.

For me, the distressing aspect of being invited to attend a dinner party is that one never is certain when to arrive.

What time, exactly, is "sixish"?

There is a distinct possibility of arriving at a "sixish" dinner party at 6:05, only to be greeted at the door by a four-year-old holding a TV dinner and a glass of Welch's Grape Juice, who tells you that Mommy is still fixing her face.

There is no need to ask where Daddy is. Daddy is the one in the tub yelling "Who the hell is that at the door?"

For the next forty-five minutes the three of you sit cross-legged on the living room floor, watching the last half of "The Bugs Bunny Roadrunner Hour," during which time you develop a nasty stiffness in your knees and an indelible spot of Welch's Grape Juice on your dress.

The next time you are invited to dinner at sixish, you resolve to play it safe and check first to see whether anyone else has arrived.

Seeing no parked cars in front of your host's house, you decide to drive around the block for a while. Unfortunately, the other guests do the same; by 10:00 P.M. there is a cavalcade of twelve cars glumly circling the block, each determined not to be the first to arrive.

The distraught hostess, meanwhile, has locked herself in the upstairs bathroom, where she is having a spectacular crying jag and making plans to move to another city, while her husband, having polished off two pitchers of before-dinner martinis, is finishing his eighth helping of lasagna.

Ideally one arrives at a party only after it is in full swing, when three people are sitting on the mantelpiece doing an imitation of a stop light, five others are pelting each other with smoked oysters, and a scholarly gentleman is trying to convince a young woman to let him pierce her ears. One can easily slip in virtually unnoticed and observe silently until one feels either stimulated enough to join in, or sufficiently bored to go home and watch *Godzilla vs. the Thing* on the late show.

Unfortunately, there are pitfalls in this situation as well, especially if your husband is wearing a sport coat and everyone else is in a suit.

"You didn't tell me to dress up!" he will hiss accusingly.

Now, I have precious little sympathy for a man who gets upset when his coat doesn't match his pants.

Especially when the other women are floating about in long gowns, while I am wearing stretch jeans, a turtleneck sweater, and Girl Scout socks.

But perhaps worst of all is our son's birthday party. Six children invariably arrive an hour early and are treated to a view of me blowing up balloons in my slip. They squat at my feet and exchange remarks on how neat the little red veins in my cheeks look.

May 19

I decided, after beginning the garden last winter, that the first step toward a successful garden lies in conscientious soil preparation.

Every spring you will find that the typical garden yields the following crop of effluvia which evidently grew during the winter: one rusty skate key, six beef bones, a soggy Halloween mask, a Christmas card from Mimsy and Pudge, and half a jack-o'lantern.

Once you have harvested this bounty and put it into garbage bags, poke about in the dirt with a slotted spoon. Many purists will claim that one should use a rake or a spade instead. Disregard this nonsense. There are faddists in every discipline.

There is probably nothing more satisfying to the soul than turning over moist crumbles of black earth with a slotted spoon. Unfortunately, you do not have moist crumbles. You have solid clay, with a surface so impervious to manual disturbance that the slotted spoon rebounds from it with a force that loosens the fillings in your back teeth. Of course that occurs only when it is dry. After a rain, solid clay assumes the general consistency of Playdoh.

There is a remedy. One must add sufficient quantities of peat to loosen the soil. Peat is formed in bogs during a process that takes approximately two-million years. If you feel that you can't wait that long, however, you may buy it from a garden supply store.

While working in the peat, remind yourself that there is a lot to be said for growing your own vegetables. There is even more to be said against it, actually, but the human memory tends in a year to forget these disagreeable aspects. If it weren't for this fortunate mental lapse, not only would there be no tomatoes, but your brother would be an only child.

One of the more pleasant aspects of having a backyard garden is that it provides an acceptable topic of conversation should one encounter a neighbor out there.

"Certainly having a big problem with mealies on the conifers," my neighbor mused ruefully last week.

"Terrible! Worst I've ever seen!" I agreed, not having the vaguest idea whether a mealy is the weird red thing with six legs that I had just stepped on, or simply a dread fungus disease. It would have helped enormously if I could likewise identify a conifer, and possibly help them before the mealies got them all.

"Malathion," he declared, nodding his head solemnly. "Malathion's the answer."

"Perhaps," I countered guardedly, wondering what the question was and unwilling to give complete corroboration to something that might very well turn out to involve compulsory sterilization.

"It's got a great deal to do with acidity, you know," he confided. "Makes gardening a real chore."

"You can say that again," I agreed, musing that I can't even go to work without a glass of Alka-Seltzer, let alone garden.

"I've had a lot of luck putting compost on my privets," he announced, suddenly excited. "How about I come over and handle yours?"

"If my privets need handling, I'll do it myself," I stammered, backing away in terror.

"You don't use 2,4-D, do you?" he demanded.

"Certainly not!" I retorted haughtily as I stormed into the house. "I've never even tried marijuana!"

May 26

Over the years, my daughter has formed an almost pathological attachment to the telephone.

While other toddlers romped through the playground clutching frayed security blankets, my daughter lumbered after them with a toy telephone wrapped around her neck.

When she was three, she slept with her left thumb in her mouth and her right forefinger in the telephone dial.

When she was in grade school, I allowed her to use the real telephone. Since not one of her friends was considered old enough to make or receive calls, she filled the gap by holding thirty-five-minute conversations with Dial-a-Prayer and a recorded time and weather message.

Now she had developed into a lovely young woman with sparkling blue eyes, golden blonde hair, and one ear which is noticeably flatter than the other.

More often than not, she and her friends don't even talk on the telephone. They play records. Or one holds the line while the other washes her hair. When they communicate verbally, the result is a series of cryptic one-liners:

"No!!!"

"He didn't!!!"

"My mother is even worse!!!"

Recently I had a telephone installed with an exceptionally long cord, which, like a trail of bread crumbs in the forest, I follow whenever I want her. It invariably leads to a closet.

"Now hear this!" I bellow at the closed door. "I want my coat."

"I can't talk," a muffled voice replies. "*She's* listening."

May 28

Everyone knows that mothers are indomitable characters who never get sick. After all, she is woman; she is invincible—except during the flu season.

There is something vaguely pathetic about an entire family expressing complete incredulity at her obvious vincibleness.

"Have you seen Mom?" one child said to the other. "She's been sitting there on the bathroom floor for a couple of hours."

"Doesn't she know it's time to peel the potatoes for dinner?"

"You don't imagine she's sick, do you?"

"Not her!" the other child hooted. I haughtily refuted his ill-considered diagnosis by passing out cold on the bathmat.

To my surprise, my loved ones assured me that I would be given every consideration while I was unwell.

Household chores were performed gratuitously. The family hockey player did the laundry between periods of a street hockey game. That's the day I discovered what a hockey puck sounds like at one hundred revolutions per minute.

To keep Mom warm and toasty, the hot water bottle was deposited on her chest, neatly removing whatever unsightly hair remained after the mustard plaster had done its job.

Medicine was dispensed promptly and ceremoniously. The doctor (the hockey player/laundress) entered the sick-room every day with "Time for your medicine, Madam. And how are we feeling today?"

Actually we had been feelingg fine, until we discovered that the doctor, capable as she was, had been regularly giving the dog my penicillin. I, on the other hand, had been fighting the flu with a daily ration of heart worm pills.

May 31

One of the lessons a man learns very early in a relationship with a woman is how to avoid obnoxious household chores.

He can, of course, simply refuse to do anything the entire weekend except lie on the living room sofa with a bowl of pistachios on his chest and watch "Wide World of Sports" all day. He soon learns, however, that this attitude is likely to result in his spending all night on the sofa as well, and having to go to work on Monday morning with pistachio shell marks indelibly etched on his cheek.

The astute male, on the other hand, readily perceives the instrinsic value of "Botching." Botchers volunteer to fix absolutely everything, then proceed to break, wrap, wrench, or step through several key parts before throwing their backs out. It is somehow unthinkable to fault anyone with a positive attitude and a slipped disc.

The more sophisticated male will even manage to avoid grocery shopping. Asked to bring home a loaf of white bread, a bottle of catsup, and one pint of cottage cheese, he will arrive home with tuttie-frutti yogurt, frozen daiquiri mix, instant expresso coffee, and a gadget to cut melon balls. Not that he will forget what he went to buy. But instead of white bread and catsup, he will bring home Jewish rye and taco sauce. And instead of plain cottage cheese, he will buy cottage cheese with pineapple chunks. Which you won't notice until you've already used it in the lasagna.

June 1

I've been victimized by a vacuum cleaner. It entered my life as a $29.95 reconditioned Christmas present, which explains a good deal of my resentment. When one is expecting a pastel mink luxury and receives instead a used metal utility, it is something of a disappointment. In a mood of poisonous venom, I christened it Beaver, after a coat that I had hoped to give to the Salvation Army.

The first victim of Beaver's ministrations was a lightweight doormat which he attacked with vigor, inhaling not only string, thread, and dirt, but the entire rug itself. Beaver belched to a halt, the half-digested pink mat hanging out his hose. I finally induced him to give it up, resolving to confine his diet to meatier, less easily swallowed items like carpeting.

Beaver glided over the broadloom with ease, but it soon became apparent that he was picking and choosing. He flatly ignored Fuzzies like thread and dust balls, devoting himself to Hard Little Balls like crumbs and diamonds from engagement rings. I urged him on, murmuring encouraging noises when he balked at a Fuzzy. Still he refused, unless I first bent down and rolled the Fuzzy into a Hard Little Ball between my fingers. This method, while successful, was so time consuming and exhausting (rolling up dust balls manually is hard work) that I temporarily abandoned the carpet in favor of the hardwood.

After carefully hiding my bedroom throw rugs, remembering Beaver's penchant for the doormat, I changed his attachment to the one to be used for floors. Oh, yes, Beaver came with all manner of goodies. He has, besides the floor and rug attachments, a drapery brush, paint sprayer, and a tiny brush for removing belly-button lint.

Beaver was noisy doing the carpets; on hardwood floors he wailed like a banshee. After answering a call from the SPCA and assuring them that I wasn't declawing my cat with pliers, I resumed the task. He did reasonably well, to a point. Or more exactly, to a corner. His attachment, while doing a great job on the straight-away, wouldn't touch into the corners. Consequently over the years, all manner of corruption has accumulated there. After all, I'm pretty well tied up rolling dust balls for Beaver, and I can't do everything by hand.

June 4

I don't believe that when I was little any adult ever worried about communicating with me. Present-day child psychologists warn against this and plead with parents to become pals with their children while still retaining parental authority. This is about as easy as whistling "Bye-Bye Blackbird" with a mouth full of Tokay grapes.

I tried communicating with our daughter, Laurie, but I couldn't get past threesies at jacks, and when I stood on my head I got a nosebleed. Not only was I a pretty hopeless pal, but I found that it's hard to retain parental authority while you're hemorrhaging on your last clean blouse. When I nearly strangled myself trying to skip Double Dutch, Laurie got a pained expression on her face and asked whether she could be excused to go and do her homework.

I decided that my husband would have more success with our son Eric.

"What do you mean, I don't communicate with him?" my husband exclaimed. "I said 'hello' to him just yesterday."

"I mean really communicate. Sit down and talk to him. Find out what he thinks."

"I know what he thinks. He thinks his sister is a creep. He said so at supper. He also thinks that Brussels sprouts taste like paint remover."

"Don't you ever share your opinions with him?" I asked.

"I shared my opinion that he'd better eat his Brussels sprouts even if they do taste like paint remover."

"That's not what I mean. You should share your views on life and establish a meaningful relationship."

"All right," he sighed, "I'll try." Half an hour later he returned, holding a bloody handkerchief to his nose.

"It was going pretty well. He showed me his bubblegum wrappers, and I let him look at my *Playboy* centerfold collection. Then he asked me whether I could stand on my head. I think we could have established a meaningful relationship if my nose just hadn't started bleeding."

June 12

As one of the joys of summer lies in acquiring a golden-brown complexion, the following is a layman's guide to suntanning:

Where to Tan: The question of where to do your tanning depends largely on how you look partially clothed. Consult a full-length mirror, inquiring "Mirror, mirror, made of glass, am I too fat across the shoulders?"

If the mirror replies "Speaking objectively, you look exactly like a giant, albino elephant," it may be wise to conduct your sun-worshipping from a strictly private area, perhaps the inside of the packing case from a grand piano.

What to Wear: Most people choose a small bathing suit. While it is permissible to lie on your stomach and undo the bra hooks to avoid the offending white stripe, bear in mind that you cannot jump up quickly when an enormous, hairy spider crawls across the back of your thigh.

What to Do while Tanning: Since you invariably feel silly lying there simmering in the sun like a gigantic rump roast, it is necessary to find something to take your mind off how ridiculous you feel and how unbearably hot you are.

You may try reading a book. If it is sunny enough to tan, however, it is too sunny to read, as the letters tend to cavort about the page like hyperactive fireflies and form idiotic sentences like "Srum, whep heliop das freezen."

You could invite someone to tan with you, preferably someone whiter, ideally someone inclined toward blotches or freckles. Never invite anyone with an olive complexion who will turn golden brown in thirty-five minutes while you lie there encased in skin that is the same attractive hue as the underbelly of a mackerel.

You could always drink. But since one drink in the sun is equivalent to two in the shade, there is a distinct possibility that after one Planter's Punch you will not be able to get out of the chaise longue, and will have to lie there all afternoon, helplessly chortling over the sentence, "Srum, whep helip das freezen."

June 13

I am becoming more and more convinced that the entire new wave of women's journalism is dedicated to making me feel inferior.

A few years ago, women's magazines only left me feeling slightly uneasy over my unimaginative meals, my inability to knit drapes, and my ignorance of how to remove the ten most common household stains. I realized my shortcomings, but I could cope. "Wood nymphs," I used to declare loftily, "don't embroider pillowcases."

But recently even the most staid women's magazines have begun to insist upon zeroing in on my love life.

One recent article spent several thousand libido-provoking words informing me that stopping smoking would vastly whet my sexual appetite. While I was almost ready to quit before reading the article, now I'm positively embarrassed to give up smoking. I mean, suppose someone offered me a cigarette. As soon as I said that I'd given them up, everyone would say "Ah hah!" and start snickering and nudging each other.

Worst of all, these magazines are showing me new, vital areas in which I am woefully unimaginative and ignorant.

It's all very well to declare oneself completely disinterested in the problems of interfacing a knit suit, but can anyone safely ignore an article entitled "Twelve Common Sexual Hang-Ups and How to Cure Them"?

Then again, suppose I *do* read the article.

While I can live with the knowledge that I am incapable of growing African Violets, can I likewise handle the realization that, out of twelve common sexual hang-ups, I have ten? All incurable?

June 14

Recently I ran across an article giving complete instructions on how to apply natural makeup.

Armed with twenty-eight dollars worth of non-makeup, I resolved to try.

The article stated that I must first contour my face. "A judicious application of blusher," the article maintained, "can effectively create the illusion of slimness." Reasoning that a judicious application of blusher certainly sounded far simpler than losing ten pounds, I began contouring. Unfortunately, the resulting illusion did not make me look slimmer, only in desperate need of a shave.

I likewise tried to raise my cheekbones by "artfully applying a darker foundation in the hollows below them." After fifteen minutes of intense searching, during which I discovered that I *have* no hollows, I chose random spots where I reasoned hollows should be. I only succeeded in looking dirty.

"Gleamer," the article asserted, "will impart the aura of dewy youth when carefully applied to the upper corners of the cheeks." Not only did gleamer look suspiciously like a grease stick, but it struck me as being nothing but a tube full of the very thing that I had just applied powder to cover up. The resulting impression was not so much that I possessed dewy youth, more that I had just played five straight sets of tennis.

"Eyes," the article warned, "need special attention. The darkest shade is brushed on next to the upper lashes, the lighter above it, the lightest stretching to the brow to raise and accentuate it." I soon discovered that while it is impossible to apply eye shadow to an open eye, it is likewise impossible to apply eye shadow with both eyes closed. One must apply it to a closed eye, while the other one watches to make sure you are doing it right.

While I rather like the overall effect, I have found that it takes me a good forty-five minutes of frantic activity to achieve the appearance that I am wearing nothing but radiant good health.

June 15

Many women these days tend to belittle the positive side of homemaking, overlooking the very real benefits of a homemaker's complete autonomy.

Aside from being the supreme arbiter of whether the toilet paper should unroll from underneath or over the top, a woman is free to determine when the vacuum cleaner bag is full and which socks do, indeed, match.

But perhaps the most heady aspect of being home alone all day is that you are able to engage in all manner of whimsies, up to and including petty vices, without the risk that someone will come roaring around the corner and warn you that what you are doing is tasteless, stupid, and will more than likely give you acne, or worse.

For instance, if I go back to bed every morning at nine o'clock, no one will know, unless I don't get up in time for the chenille marks to vanish before the children come home for lunch.

I can watch soap operas. I mean, there is no possibility of appreciating the tragic nuances of "As the World Turns" when a ten-year-old is sitting on the sofa going "yuk!!"

I can do exercises. One simply cannot do a successful bend and stretch when a preschooler is chortling "Make your tummy jiggle again, Mommy!"

I can go into the bathroom without closing the door.

And I can wear anything I choose. Or nothing at all, which my next-door neighbor swears not only cuts down beautifully on her weekly laundry, but adds a certain titillation to even such mundane chores as matching up socks.

June 17

People constantly express admiration for a small child who appears to be socially at ease in the presence of a large number of adults.

Nonsense.

A child in the company of adults is faced with a group of well-wishers who are genuinely concerned with making him feel that his presence is a welcome addition. Any child exhibiting the most rudimentary social graces is treated to a degree of praise which an adult achieves only by climbing the north side of a mountain or inscribing the entire New Testament on a ping-pong ball in Chinese.

"Imagine that!" they will exclaim. "I asked him his age, and he said 'six.' What a kid!"

Personally, I reserve my admiration for any adult who can stay in a room full of six-year-olds for ten minutes without bursting into tears, breaking out in a rash, or retreating to the bathroom and locking the door for the next two hours.

An adult in the company of small children is faced with a group of potential terrorists who vacillate between ignoring his presence completely and regarding him as an enemy spy.

Any questions directed toward the adult will be on the order of "Where did you get those funny wrinkles in your neck?"

June 19

I hate to see my children watch too much TV.

It's not the sex and violence I mind. For a child who has been raised on blind mice having their tails lopped off with butcher knives, "Kojak" is pretty tame stuff.

No, what I find to be thoroughly objectionable and potentially disillusioning are commercials.

Parents in commercials are unfailingly loyal. Who but someone in a commercial would refuse to take twice as much of another laundry soap rather than switch from Tide? I mean, twice as much is twice as much; so what if the white socks are gray for the next two months?

Parents in commercials are unfailingly cheerful. When you climb into a tar pit ten minutes before you are to leave for Grandma's house, a TV mother will merely chuck you under the chin and call you a "Bold One," rather than going all white around the mouth and locking herself in the bathroom.

Parents in commercials are always patient. When you, sixteen of your friends, and an enormous English sheep dog barge into the kitchen and drip muddy water onto a freshly waxed floor, a TV mother fixes everyone a huge pitcher of Kool-Aid instead of sobbing "Get out of the kitchen this minute, and take that lousy mutt with you!"

Finally, mothers in commercials are pretty. Since I am secretly sure that all TV children are really thirty-five-year-old midgets anyway, it is probably logical that their mothers all look twenty-two. But no mother that I know ever greeted her children at breakfast wearing blue eyeshadow. Not unless she had been to a party the night before and had been too tired to wash her face.

June 20

Personally, I am opposed to using grass.

Now I know perfectly well that thousands of respectable, taxpaying citizens not only delight in grass, but experience no physical or mental problems connected with it.

But for myself, I favor doing the entire backyard over in green cement.

I resent grass. I resent administering constant protection, dedicated feeding, and conscientious watering to anything that neither calls me "Mommy" nor licks my hand in gratitude.

Every spring, the backyard emerges from the snow, thickly matted with a lichenlike underbelly of winter's casualties, which must be meticulously combed from the lawn while it is still cold enough outside to make your nose run.

Any greenish bits that haven't become wedged in the rake and uprooted must be slavishly pandered to immediately, plied with organic fertilizer, and encouraged to spread sufficiently to fill in the inevitable bald spots.

Actually, after sufficient ministrations, the bald spots fill in remarkably rapidly—with chickweed. One is sorely tempted to simply give over to the chickweed, it being obviously fitter, as well as a great deal prettier, than grass. This will never do. Darwin aside, one can't go around liking chickweed, even pretty chickweed.

Once an exquisite green carpet is established, it must be watched like an eccentric uncle, lest it suddenly exhibit dangerous aberrations, and must never be left unattended for extended period of time.

And for what? All six patio chairs have to be put on an eight-by-ten slab of cement, because every time you sit on the exquisite green carpet, ants crawl up your legs.

One of the saddest misconceptions about gardening is that, while shrubs and trees are constantly demanding mulch and clamoring to have their terminal buds scratched, grass is simply laid down like wall-to-wall broadloom and forgotten.

It would help, of course, if once a lawn was laid out flat, it would remain flat instead of sinking in some places, heaving in others, and generally carrying on like a harpooned whale. Concealed hollows invariably contain potential hazards; more than one mower has been summarily abandoned with the dog's beef bone or leash jammed irrevocably between its blades. To make matters worse, someone in the family always insists on installing lily ponds at the bottoms of inclines, ponds just deep enough to engulf a fast-running mower up to the handles.

One of the first problems of lawn care is whether to leave the clippings on the lawn or remove them. Half your neighbors will maintain that the clippings provide the lawn with nutrients; the other half will insist that accumulated clippings deprive the lawn of necessary sunshine. Whatever your inclinations, do not argue with anyone wielding pruning shears.

If you do choose to remove the clippings, you will need a grass catcher, which is a piece of striped awning material hooked onto the mower. When it is not falling off, the catcher collapses periodically and must be kicked along with your free foot. This flattens the grass nicely so that the mower rolls harmlessly over, accomplishing nothing but raising a blister on your thumb.

Actually the disposition of clippings is rarely a problem as, more often than not, the green grass doesn't grow all around. Instead of forming a verdant carpet under the elm tree, it concentrates exclusively on poking itself up through the cracks in the front walk, and your entire lawn maintenance program will consist of digging it out with a fish fork.

June 22

When my parents noticed my marked tendency to bump into our door frames and wave to people's backs, they thought that I was simply stupid and clumsy.

Later, when I started school, they discovered that, in addition to being stupid and clumsy, I needed glasses.

After ten years of wearing glasses with lenses approximately as thick as the bottoms of coke bottles, I was fitted with a pair of contact lenses. I don't have to wear my contact lenses all the time. Only when I want to see.

Last Saturday afternoon, I was in the supermarket, leaning over the meat counter and wondering what tripe was and whether we were desperate enough to eat it, when my left contact lens fell into a pile of frozen pork chops.

"Hold on there!" I exclaimed grabbing a package of chops from an elderly lady. "My eye is on these."

"Not bloody likely, Toots!" she snapped, snatching them back, "I saw 'em first!"

While my attention was diverted during this caustic exchange, there must have been a veritable run on pork chops.

"Oh, no!" I shrieked, patting the now-empty compartment.

"Don't take it so hard, lady," the butcher said, patting my hand consolingly. "Why don't you try some nice spare ribs instead?"

"You don't understand! My left contact lens fell in there," I bawled, pointing to the meat counter.

"No fooling!" he replied, peering into the counter. "That's tough. Tell you what, though," he added brightly, "I'll give you a rain check on the pork chops."

Shortly after that, I arrived for my long-awaited appointment with an optometrist.

"Doctor will see you right away," his nurse announced.

Resisting the urge to genuflect, I fumbled my way into the examination room, banging my shoulder painfully on the door frame.

After first noting the vital information—whether I preferred to pay cash or charge it, Doctor instructed me to look at his right ear while he peered into my eye from a distance of three inches with a tiny flashlight.

"Your eye seems perfectly normal," he announced.

"So does your ear," I replied politely. He placed my chin in an enormous black machine.

"I want you to read the chart for me. What line can you read?"

"The one that says 'Made in Germany.' "

"Where do you see that?"

"Here," I pointed to a sign on the machine one inch above my nose.

"Look at the chart," he said, pointing to a fuzzy square of light at the far end of the room. "Tell me which is better, this," he said, changing lenses, "or this?"

One half-hour and twenty-seven agonizing decisions later, he announced that while I couldn't pick up the lens for a week, he would loan me something to use in the meantime.

While I'm quite eager to get my new lens, I don't expect to get a seat on the bus nearly so often once I give back the white cane he lent me.

June 25

I am desperately searching for the perfect summer camp—for myself.

I have come to the realization that I would much rather learn three dozen secret Indian hand signals than ten ways to remove tar spots from T-shirts.

I would like to spend my summer identifying birds, not skin rashes.

And I would much rather be lulled to sleep by a chorus of crickets than by the intemperate revelry at a pool party to which I wasn't invited.

I have never understood why summer camps are restricted to children, while their mothers are the ones who have been confined for the preceding ten months and suffer from tired blood and hot flashes. Like youth itself, summer camp is wasted on the young. The last time my son went to summer camp, it cost me $250 to have someone teach him to short-sheet a bed.

Ideally, campers should all be mothers, with first priority given to women who are over thirty-five and at least three inches too short for their weight. We seasoned mothers would make excellent campers. The challenge of making a campfire out of two sticks would be simple for anyone who, whenever the tweezers are missing, can pick gravel out of somebody's knee with a pair of ice tongs.

Not only would we not have to bring rubber sheets, but no mother in her right mind would ever complain about any food that someone else had cooked, even if it does have saltpeter in it.

June 26

"We don't need lunches today, Mom," my son informed me gently at seven o'clock this morning.

"Of course you need lunches. You can't expect to learn how to take the square root of pi on an empty stomach," I retorted, deftly turning the heels of the bread to the inside and hoping he wouldn't notice.

"But school's out," he protested.

"Out!?!?" I gasped.

"For the summer."

"For the entire summer!?!?" I bleated, clutching a kosher dill pickle to my breast.

"Yeah. Isn't that super? Do you know what I'm going to do?"

"Judging by past experience, you'll step on a rusty nail, sit on your glasses, and pitch a baseball through the window of the Presbyterian rectory. And tomorrow will be even more eventful."

"You don't sound glad that we're out," he sniffed.

"Glad? Why shouldn't I be glad? After all, when you're in school I never get to visit with the staff at the emergency ward or the optometrist's office, let alone have a heart-to-heart talk with the Presbyterian minister about the Decaying Moral Values of Today's Youth."

"This summer is going to be different," he promised loftily. "You forget how I've matured during this past year."

While his statement would have been a great deal more effective had he not jumped off the garage roof two hours later, he was right about one thing. With two broken arms, this summer is certainly going to be different.

June 27

A is for aphids, the greenish things floating in the pitcher of lemonade.

B is for bulbs, those nasty, onionish globs you found in the basement when you moved into the house. At the first sign of spring, unearth them, and throw them in the garbage.

C is for cuttings, those lovely green sprigs of other people's plants which you snip off carefully, wrap neatly in wet newspaper, and proceed to leave on the car dashboard in the sun for two weeks.

D is for dandelions. Dandelions must be recognized for the noxious weeds they are. Right-thinking people do not like dandelions, even though they are obviously hardier, and a great deal prettier, than zinnias.

E is for evergreen. Evergreen trees do not have leaves that turn majestic shades of gold and red every autumn, then fall to earth and form a gentle carpet of color. Hooray for evergreen trees.

F is for fences, the longish lengths of splintery wood and/or rusty wire over which one throws largish stones and the soggy tennis balls the dog has sucked on.

G is for geraniums, which are either the blackish sticks poking out of the ground beside the weeping birch or the moldy pot of "stuff" in the basement, depending on whether anyone remembered to lift and pot them last fall. Throw them into the garbage beside the bulbs.

H is for hoses, the long ropes of hollow plastic caught in the lawn mower.

I is for ivy, luxuriant, glossy vines which adhere to brick walls, create an aura of verdant beauty, and pull the mortar out.

J is for July, the month in which it is too hot to do all those things that it was too cold to do in January.

K is for kompost, a word which, as this is my book, I can spell any way I choose. Kompost is what non-gardeners refer to as garbage.

L is for lawn mower, which, although it wouldn't cut hot butter, has somehow managed during the winter to nibble through the plastic hose in thirty-six places. The term may also be applied to a male child under eighteen, should you be fortunate enough to have one.

M is for manure, which is called organic fertilizer because is sounds nicer.

N is for nemophila, which, although it sounds uncomfortably like something Nice People don't do, is actually a flower. Trust me.

O is for organic fertilizer (*see manure*).

P is for parties which gardeners can now have outside. Outdoor parties are nice in that you don't have to vacuum afterwards.

R is for run over, which is what you probably have done to the threaded metal end of the hose, irrevocably preventing it from screwing into the water outlet.

S is for sprinklers, capriciously shaped metal and/or plastic objects which either refuse to sweep from side to side or refuse to spin. Either is equally effective at delivering water in such an erratic manner that the flowering crab will become shriveled and desiccated while the petunias will wash away into the gutter. Or they would if you hadn't run over the metal end of the hose.

T is for toolshed, an unassembled metal contraption which, when erected, will be only half the size of the shed in the illustration. Toolsheds come with instruction sheets. Three pages of instructions, all labeled "Page 2" and beginning "Now that you have the walls erected . . ."

U is for urea formaldehyde, a type of plant food, the generous application of which is guaranteed to keep Avon from calling.

V is for verbena, which sounds a lot prettier than it looks.

W is for weed killer, an appallingly expensive chemical which must never be applied unless it is pouring rain and perfectly still, so that it can't blow onto the roses or a loved one.

X is for the bare spot in the lawn where the builders buried their beer cans.

Y is for yellow. Carrots should be; broccoli shouldn't.

Z is for your zone, which you soon discover that everything you just planted isn't hardy for.

June 30

I have given up smoking.

Actually, I was fairly certain that I had given up smoking six weeks ago. Being fairly certain you've given up smoking is like being fairly certain you're pregnant; it doesn't do to go around broadcasting the fact until you're absolutely certain.

There is nothing so unnerving to someone who suspects she may be either pregnant or giving up smoking than to have half a dozen concerned friends and relatives bleating, "Yeah, but are you *sure*?" every fifteen minutes.

I realized, too, that should I discover that the decision was a Dreadful Mistake, I could simply change my mind a week or so down the line without having to listen to anyone sigh and shake his head.

Besides, anyone who has given up cigarettes is twitchy enough for the first few days without having several people watching him covertly from behind copies of *Time* magazine, hoping to catch him in the throes of some sort of disgusting withdrawal symptom.

These same people peremptorily decide, in your best interests, either to hide your last pack of cigarettes, or to flush them dramatically down the toilet.

It does very little good to explain to these people that you *need* a last pack of cigarettes lying around waiting not to be smoked, that will power is not born of deprivation, and that as soon as they leave, you intend to tear the lining out of the pockets of every coat in the house to glean enough tobacco to make one final cigarette not to smoke.

July 2

I only say "no" to our children when I'm absolutely forced to, when my back is against the wall, and
they're clamoring to dye their eyebrows black, or have
"Make Love Not War" tattooed on their forearms.

But I'm far from being an overpermissive pushover. I
don't say "yes," either.

Instead, I've become a master at using the parental
equivocation of "we'll see," which has the convenient
ambiguity of meaning anything from "probably" to
"fat chance."

I have found that only immediate problems demand
an immediate response, and if necessary I can be quite
forceful. As proof, I offer the following actual conversation:

"Can I have a chocolate chip cookie?"

"How do you ask?"

"*May* I have a chocolate chip cookie?"

"What do you say?"

"May I *please* have a chocolate chip cookie?"

"No. It's too close to supper."

The situations which are bona fide "we'll sees" are
requests involving future events. I find it virtually impossible to project beyond what I'm going to fix for
supper; anything after that is clearly in the lap of the
gods.

Last week the children approached me as I was delumping horseradish sauce by forcing it through the tea strainer. (Note to children: Never ask Mommy *anything* while she is straining horseradish sauce. Mommy is always nervous and out of sorts at moments like this.)

"Let's go see *King Kong Meets the Creature from the Black Lagoon* and a *Daffy Duck* cartoon carnival at the drive-in on Saturday." Now at that moment I would rather have been hung by my heels over a live volcano than sit through *King Kong Meets the Creature from the Black Lagoon*, to say nothing about the *Daffy Duck* cartoon carnival. But after all, it was only Tuesday. Long before Saturday they might forget about it or the drive-in might be razed for a shopping mall.

"We'll see," I said. I wasn't really too worried. If they asked again on Saturday I could always employ the best answer of all: "Ask your Daddy."

July 7

Judging by the sales fliers we receive daily, everyone worth knowing is assembling his own metal toolshed.

Before ordering a box of shed, remember that when erected it will be only half the size of the shed in the illustration, as those two adults standing beside the shed in the picture are actually twenty-five inch high midgets named Sam and Zelda. Sam and Zelda earn $37,000 a year being photographed while sitting in above-ground swimming pools and illustrating adequate head room in camper-trailers.

This discrepancy is not immediately obvious, however, as the contents seem adequate to construct a medium-sized elementary school, there being at least three roofs, ten windows, and 637 assorted wing nuts, bolts, and screws, half of which spill out of the box and roll under the front porch.

You will notice right off that since the screw holes don't match, you must drill 243 new holes, thus giving the shed the same jaunty air as if it had been strafed by a machine gun.

Anyone with the normal complement of arms will need help erecting the walls, as all four have to be joined at once, a feat roughly equivalent to making a house of playing cards in a windstorm. While it is possible to use a friend's arms, remember that after you snarl "I said to hold it straight, you incompetent nincompoop!" three or four times, he won't be your friend anymore. Good friends are hard to find. Better use your wife's arms.

As you go along, you can even imply that it is her fault that all the original glass has shrunk down to a window the size of a shaving mirror and that the door meets only at the top. Actually you will find that it is such a serviceable shed that you may even sleep in it for the next three nights. It's ever so much nicer than the doghouse.

July 13

The unfortunate fact of the matter is that an actual camping trip rarely resembles those photographs of rustic togetherness which features Dad, Mom, and a brace of children sitting around a camp fire toasting wienies as the setting sun turns the sky into a symphony of color.

Of course, no one would ever go camping if they showed someone beside a fire taking a sitz bath in a two-quart saucepan. Or a candid shot of a garter snake crawling up Mom's pant leg while she is busy picking gnats out of the butter.

Anyway, you can't light a fire when it's pouring rain. On the one day it doesn't rain, the children, having announced that they have already seen a sunset once, insist on eating in the tent and reading comic books.

Now a tent is just like a bedroom. A tiny little bedroom. One that leaks. You share this tiny little leaky bedroom with three other people, one who twitches, one who snores, and a five-year-old who had six cans of pop before retiring. Not to mention four pairs of wet tennis shoes and a dog who has spent the better part of the day rolling in dead fish.

Next to a giant economy-size can of Raid, a camper's most valuable asset is a short memory. By the time he has silently folded up his tent and eased his scratched, mosquito-bitten body gingerly into the car to go home, he will have completely forgotten the agony of stubbing his big toe on a tent stake at 3:00 A.M., while taking a five-year-old to the comfort station, and will begin babbling rapturously about how lovely the pine trees looked in the moonlight.

July 14

To my way of thinking, swimming is less of a sport than something I do when I fall out of a boat.

It is most uncomfortable to find myself standing in water that is ten-feet deep, when I am only five-and-a-half-feet deep. In such a situation, swimming is infinitely more practical than walking, as walking requires the rather tedious process of continuously sinking to the bottom and hopping up high enough for my nose to clear the surface.

Floating—a process which involves lying back and filling my lungs with air—I have found to be a most unsatisfactory alternative, for while my lungs float beautifully, from the neck up and the hips down I am completely submerged. And not having mastered the art of breathing through my navel, I panic.

Actually, I restrict my aquatic activities to a rudimentary crawl and an admittedly abortive backstroke.

In order to do the crawl, you must scoop handfuls of water backward and duck your head periodically under your armpit to breathe, all the while executing a leg-motion rather like you would use to shake free of a gigantic man-eating squid.

Personally, I prefer the backstroke.

The major drawback to the backstroke is that lying on your back cuts down drastically on your field of vision, it being restricted to viewing cloud formations and a stray bird or two. The one time I was foolish enough to immerse my body in a swimming pool, I found myself suddenly in the deep end. Worse yet, I was in the middle of an impromptu game of water polo. I believe that I lost my taste for swimming immediately after the ball landed on my chest and fifteen people yelled "Mine!"

July 24

It is fatal to confess to anyone that you are thinking of going on a diet.

"You're nuts," one of my equally overweight friends declared as she handed me a second helping of devil's food cake. "It's taken you years of haggling to acquire a decent wardrobe tailored to your build. What are you going to do with a closet full of pantsuits with size eight jackets and size sixteen pants?"

"You don't look *that* bad," declared one of my very slim friends. (Narrow people are prone to sadism.) "What's your waist?"

"You mean *where's* my waist?" I replied morosely. "I haven't got one."

"Don't be silly. Everyone has a waist. It's about six inches below your bust."

"I don't have one of those, either," I wailed.

Only my children offered anything remotely approaching moral support.

"That's a terrific idea," my son agreed, spearing my second pork chop neatly off my plate.

"Great news!" echoed my daughter. "Can I have your dessert?"

While gluttony, like lust, is one of the Seven Deadly Sins, it is not nearly so easily assuaged by three dozen push-ups and a cold shower.

Initially, I attempted to sublimate my unnatural cravings by turning to television, only to have my favorite programs interrupted every ten minutes by Kraft food commercials featuring someone folding three cups of mayonnaise into a bowl full of melted caramels and miniature marshmallows.

The success of any diet is utterly dependent on the degree of your ability to convince your stomach that it is, in fact, full, so that it does not take umbrage and seize up on you.

Stomachs, fortunately, are the most stupid organ of the entire human body, forced to rely very heavily on messages received from your nose and mouth.

The following are three extremely simple mealtime strategies designed to confuse the stomach:

1. Chew each bite 3,427 times. Eaten this way, one-half a cup of cottage cheese will so exhaust your jaw that it will immediately jump to the conclusion that it has consumed a seven-course dinner.

2. If you feel you must use the good china for dinner, do not serve yourself on a standard-size dinner plate, as the sight of all those hand-painted flowers peeking through the peas will only emphasize the spartan size of your portions. Much more visual deception results from eating your entire dinner from the lid of a jar of Cheese Whiz.

3. Ten minutes before your evening meal, lick the glue off a whole box of airmail envelopes.

July 26

It seems that an inordinate amount of media coverage has been devoted to the problems of gays.

Personally, I have nothing against gays.

I mean, I certainly wouldn't want someone waking me up every morning by whistling "Happy Days Are

Here Again'' in my left ear, but a little gaiety in moderation is hardly cause for such violent emotions as are being displayed these days.

Gays, fortunately, are attracted to each other. Anyone who can tumble down a flight of steps, break his ankle in three places, and knock out four teeth, yet express delight that his Timex is still running, would find himself to be completely incompatible with a person who goes all white around the mouth if there's dew on his morning paper.

I think, while everyone agrees that two consenting adults should be free to be as gay as they please, no one should be forced to spend time with a person who tapdances while he brushes his teeth.

Anita Bryant contends that should we allow gays to educate our children, they, too, could become gay. I must admit that the thought does give one pause. The average mother has enough to do without having to contend with a brace of ten-year-olds calling her "Marmee" and being gay all over the back of her neck while she is down on her hands and knees, wiping grape jelly off the kitchen floor.

Which reminds me, while I've known several gay men, I have met very few women who were anything more than affable. Maybe it has something to do with having to spend a whole lifetime matching socks.

July 27

One of the major concerns facing our society is the growing rate of marriage breakdowns.

While lack of communication is frequently cited as the underlying cause in many cases, I am certain that there is a more basic problem.

Too many Night People marry Morning People.

Such marriages are effectively doomed from the start.

Your basic morning person arrives home at 5:30 P.M. Tripping over the bags under his eyes, he stumbles through the front door in a somnambulistic trance, only to be greeted by a Night Person humming "Come to the Cabaret" while clenching a flower between her teeth.

While Morning People retire at 9:30 P.M., Night People stay up until 2:30 A.M. to watch *The Man in the Iron Mask* for the fifth time.

When the alarm clock rings at 6:30 A.M., the Morning Person will vault gaily from bed just in time to witness the Night Person fling the clock to the floor and stomp on it until his feet bleed.

Morning People eat things like omelettes and waffles for breakfast. Night People begin the day with two Excedrin tablets dissolved in a glass of Carnation Instant.

While their friends respect Morning People, they rarely call them long distance at 3:00 A.M. to wish them a Happy Saint Swithin's Day.

It is just as difficult for a Night Person to establish rapport with a person who views his body as a temple as it is for a Morning Person to communicate meaningfully with someone who has no discernible stomach muscles.

July 28

For many women, holding down a full-time job has become an economic necessity.

Aside from the many mothers these days who have chosen careers outside their homes as a means of personal fulfillment, at least an equal number enter the work force simply to make ends meet.

But no matter what motivation causes a woman to combine motherhood with a full-time career, one common, inherent difficulty is the gnawing guilt one feels at mealtime.

"This is a TV dinner!" my son announced last night, pointing accusingly at his plate.

"What makes you think that?" I demanded, doggedly maintaining an air of righteous indignation, even though I knew full well that there were three still-warm divided foil trays hidden in the bottom of the garbage can. "How can you tell?"

"I don't have to chew the gravy."

"I feel so bad about this," I remarked later, slicing off three pieces of Sara Lee chocolate cake. "With me working full time, you never get homemade biscuits any more. You never sit down to spaghetti sauce that's simmered all afternoon, or help me roll out the dough for a homemade apple pie."

"I wouldn't feel so bad about it, Mom," my daughter retorted, patting my hand consolingly. "You never fixed any of those things before you started working full time, either."

July 30

Perhaps it's my own lack of savoir faire, but I always seem to have an inordinate amount of trouble in restaurants.

The maitre d' invariably leads me to a table behind a pillar, in a draft, or right next to the men's room, a table at which no one else will sit. If he were to ask whether this table suited madame, possibly madame might timidly venture the opinion that, although she doesn't want to be a bother, she'd prefer another one. One with four legs, perhaps, rather than three.

Of course, he doesn't ask. Rather he fixes me with a gaze so steely that it is obvious that, should I dare to complain, he will report me directly to the manager.

Once I am seated, my problems are not over. After twenty minutes, the waiter casually saunters over, picking his teeth with his forefinger, to take my order.

"I'll have the lamb chops," I venture. The waiter shakes his head.

"The chops are bad today. I suggest the stuffed tripe." Without waiting for a reply, he leaves. Now if there's anything I loathe, it's tripe, even stuffed tripe. Somehow I lack the panache to fling a bread stick at his retreating form and demand lamb chops.

One hour later my stuffed tripe appears. It has evidently tumbled off en route and been scraped up off the floor, as it is covered with light green carpet fluff. The waiter glares at me as if I am somehow personally responsible for staining his carpet. He slips the bill under my plate obviously hinting that the sooner a troublemaker like me leaves, the better.

August 1

Many of you undoubtedly just suffered through the harrowing experience of moving.

Before you begin congratulating yourself on having survived it all, make certain that you have ordered telephone installation. If not, you are facing probably the greatest trauma of the entire move.

"We have just moved to 3131 Hartwell Crescent, and I would like to order a telephone," you say, inwardly praising yourself on your forthright approach.

Unfortunately the disembodied voice of the business office shatters your aplomb by crooning, "How many rooms do you have in your new home?"

She might as well have asked how many second cousins your great-grandmother had. "Seven?" you quaver, it sounding like a likely number. "Nine or ten if you count bathrooms and kitchens."

"How many bedrooms do you have?" she purrs.

What ever is she driving at, you wonder, your cheeks reddening as you blurt out "four."

"My, that sounds lovely," she coos.

"It is rather nice," you admit modestly. "There's a wet bar in the basement, which is an authentic replica of an Old English . . ."

"You'll need at least six telephones," she announces.

"Hmmmm?" Your reverie shatters abruptly.

"That's one for each bedroom, one for the kitchen, and one for the Old Eng . . ."

"One phone," you insist.

"*One* phone!?" she gasps incredulously. "But you can't possibly . . ."

"One phone!" you insist.

"Would you like a touch-tone, Contempra, or our enchanting Princess-style with a lighted dial? Each comes in your choice of seven decorator colors —Seamist Green, Beautiful Beige, Sunrise Yellow, Pristine White, Achingly Aqua, Bucolic Blue, or Scarlett O'Hara."

"I'd like a plain black one. It should ring."

"Black?" she shudders audibly.

"Black is my favorite color."

"I'm sorry, but it will take six weeks to special order a plain black phone. We just delivered the only one in stock to a mortuary."

August 3

Every family must of necessity adopt some sort of position regarding weekend meals. One popular attitude is the laissez faire approach, whereby everyone over six years of age eats whatever he likes whenever he finds himself passing the refrigerator.

Unfortunately, left to their own dietary whimsies, people tend to ignore refrigerator jars full of leftover chicken a la king in favor of wolfing down huge slabs of the roast beef that you had hoped to stretch out through next Wednesday.

And there is always one member of every family who will shun anything vaguely nutritional and exist the entire weekend on a diet of marshmallows.

But those families who insist upon having three formal, sit-down type meals a day find themselves lacking a quorum more often than not.

People tend to rise on weekends as the spirit calls them. Our son's spirit calls at 7:00 A.M., while our daughter's spirit is completely mum until 11:00 A.M. An unwary mother may find herself faced with a steady rivulet of people trickling in asking for waffles with blueberry syrup all morning. By 11:30 the waffle iron is overheated, and mother isn't far behind.

Lunchtime is even worse. Everyone takes to whizzing through the kitchen on their way to trombone lessons, barber shops, and batting practices. Lunchtime becomes about as gracious as a pit stop in the Indianapolis 500.

The only meal for which I can count on full attendance is Sunday night supper. Sunday night we break bread in front of the television set with little plastic trays in our laps and improve our minds. Our children would prefer to improve their minds with a "Beverly Hillbillies" rerun, but we always insist upon viewing something educational. Last week while we ate, we were treated to a spectacular documentary presentation of a bull snake swallowing a field mouse.

"Keen! Look at that ol' snake—he isn't even chewing! Isn't that cool, Mom?"

"Cool," I murmured, resolving henceforth to cast my vote with the "Beverly Hillbillies" contingent. Sunday night togetherness may improve our minds, but it doesn't do much for the digestion.

August 4

Today we arrived at Shuswap Lake for three funfilled weeks of "romping across safe, sandy beaches or relaxing in our charming, rustic beach cabin while reveling in the enchanting vista of acres of pine trees mirrored in crystal-clear waters."

Or something like that. I can't remember the exact wording because our dog ate the brochure last month, but I do recall the picture of the girl in the wee red bikini. She is not romping today. No one romps when it is fifty-eight degrees. In spite of that, my husband is sitting on the porch eagerly peering down the beach, ready to suck in his tummy in case it warms up to romping temperature.

Considering the fact that the windows are glued securely shut with last year's flies, our cabin seems to lean a bit more heavily toward "rustic" than it does to "charming."

I've found that the first four hours in any cabin should be approached with extreme caution and a handful of bandages. During our first four hours, all the doorknobs fell off, the silverware drawer plummeted out and gave me a smart crack on the shin, and the toilet flushed itself continuously with hot water.

The walls of our cabin are done in what the children call "naughty pine" and are adorned with a 1969 calendar, several stern warnings from the management regarding misuse of the plumbing, and a few blobs which look vaguely like A-1 sauce.

But we are delighted to find that there is a complete absence of mosquitoes. In fact, we have it on good authority that there isn't a single mosquito within a five mile radius. It seems that the spiders have eaten them all.

August 8

Today is the fourth day of our vacation. The weather is still somewhat of a drawback, there being a lot more of it than we had been bargaining on.

Our biggest problem has been in amusing the children. So far, I have read them three *National Geographics* and one issue of *Business Week* cover to cover, and as of last night I owe our son $2,643 from the Slap Jack tournament.

Today the sun appeared briefly, the shock of which sent five toddlers into hysterics and caused three elderly women to drop to their knees in their Mackintoshes and begin crossing themselves. The rest of us shucked off our foul weather gear, grabbed our suntan oil, and hit the beach at a fast lope, oiling each other's back as we ran. Within ten minutes, however, the sun was swallowed up by clouds and the wind rose to forty miles per hour, immediately swamping two canoes, a water-skiier, and a Donald Duck air mattress.

Since the pilot lights on all the gas space heaters blew out during the gale yesterday afternoon, the inhabitants of all ten cabins met last night for a bonfire on the beach. Unfortunately we mistook a pile of "naughty pine" paneling for the pile of firewood. Our host made a terrible fuss and has flatly refused to light a single pilot light or give out any fresh sheets or towels for the next two weeks. Except for the fact that I dropped a whole bag of marshmallows into the fire and discovered that I was the only one who was old enough to know all the words to "Bye-Bye Blackbird," it was a huge success.

I'm afraid that we are having a bit of difficulty with our bed. Even though it is made out of top quality cornhusks, our mattress sags drastically in the middle, forming a trough which we have dubbed "Death Valley." Unless we lie on our sides and cling tenaciously to the edges, we roll into Death Valley and spend the night eyeball to eyeball, inhaling each other's exhale.

I suppose that I shouldn't complain. The couple in cabin seven have Bunker Hill instead of Death Valley and are forced to lash themselves together with the cord from his bathrobe or risk tumbling out altogether.

August 10

Every newspaper these days features a daily column devoted to horoscopes.

I have often noticed that not only are these daily horoscopes unfailingly optimistic, their character analyses of various birthsigns are invariably flattering.

Based on my experience as a mother—and as an Aries—I've figured basic characteristics which coincide with Zodiac signs.

Aries (March 20—April 19): Individuals born under the sign of Aries tend to be at least eighty-three pounds overweight and prefer the dark meat on a turkey. Basically sedentary, a pair of them make ideal bookends.

Taurus (April 20—May 20): Plagued throughout life by excessive earwax, those born under the sign of Taurus tend to be moody, irritable, and should never eat radishes. Taurus women love having their backs stroked with goose feathers.

Gemini (May 21—June 20): Thanks to the dual nature inherent in Gemini, individuals born under this sign can be counted on always to choose the correct fork at dinner, and to use it to pick their teeth.

Cancer (June 21—July 20): Cancer men are compulsive toenail-biters and invariably wear monogrammed undershirts, as do Cancer women. In fact, the former can be distinguished from the latter only by examining their palms for an outcropping of reddish-brown hair, especially obvious during the full moon.

Leo (July 21—August 22): Never loan your library card to a Leo. These individuals are basically parasites and spend their lives waiting for others to push them through revolving doors.

Virgo (August 23—September 22): Virgo women are known for wearing the same socks for a week and the inability to pronounce the letter "R." Virgo men are given to placing long distance obscene phone calls and reversing the charges.

Libra (September 23—October 22): Libra men are noticeable for their extreme overbite, enabling them to eat a ham sandwich through venetian blinds. Libra women are exceptionally frugal, devoting their entire lives to making evening gowns out of surplus parachutes and knitting their own drapes.

Scorpio (October 23—November 21): Those born under the sign of Scorpio are compulsive thumbsuckers who often suffer from acute dandruff, nervous tension, and yaws. Scorpio women have limpid, intensely beautiful eyes and bad breath.

Sagittarius (November 22—December 21): Sagittarius men are notorious in early life for practical jokes, liking nothing better than to serve twelve-year-old Chivas Regal scotch in a dribble glass. In later life they become convinced that they can walk on water. Sagittarius women suffer from ingrown toenails.

Capricorn (December 22—January 19): Although

frequently obsessed by the conviction that wasps have nested in their ears, those born under the sign of Capricorn enjoy simple pleasures and can often be found sitting in a linen closet smelling the clean sheets.

Aquarius (January 20—February 18): Unreliable, pessimistic, and subject to sties, those individuals born under the sign of Aquarius religiously eschew rough language, although a certain Aquarian was overheard to say "Darn it, anyhow" shortly after having been disemboweled by an enraged grizzly.

Pisces (February 19—March 20): Men born under the sign of Pisces are easily recognizable by their low foreheads, pendulous earlobes, and their inability to pronounce "aluminum." Pisces women are inordinately proud of their hair. No one knows why.

August 11

I know a couple named Bert and Brenda who spend the entire summer exploring side roads, the little tree-lined byways that most of us pass at fifty miles per hour while murmuring "We simply *must* take that road one of these days and see where it goes."

Actually I rarely pass these charming byways unless my gas gauge needle has just stopped quivering at a point roughly a quarter of an inch below empty. And it seems that every time I have gasoline, I am either escorting fifteen Cub Scouts on an educational tour of the local filtration plant or speeding toward the emergency ward with a child who has just lopped off an ear.

Bert and Brenda have no children, which leaves them relatively free to amble about the countryside discovering waterfalls, staying in quaint country inns which charge two dollars a night and include a three-course breakfast, and picking up ten-piece antique maple dining-room suites for $3.37.

The only likely-looking country side road I've ever explored turned out to be a farmer's driveway where I was met by three half-starved German Shepherds, one of whom ate my license plate. And no matter what the farmer said, he didn't even *own* a prize laying hen. Especially not the one I ran over.

It is, of course, entirely possible that Bert and Brenda have had similar unpleasant experiences while exploring side roads. In fact, I shouldn't be at all surprised if every third trip or so was a kidney-jolting journey to a dump. But, being childless, they can keep mum about the whole messy affair, which is a bit difficult to do when your son insists on taking a dead chicken to school for Show-and-Tell.

August 14

Since we have spent ten days here at the lake so far, we are enjoying a bit of seniority over the newcomers. They allow us to use the best ping-pong paddles and to chop all the firewood for the bonfires.

Our feud with the management broadened in scope last week as a certain *esprit de corps* developed among cabins one through ten. The main contention, you may remember, arose over management's refusal to light the pilot lights on the gas heaters or to supply clean linen and towels.

Our delegate from cabin two informed management that unless heat was forthcoming, concerted retaliatory action would be taken in the form of flushing great wads of paper towels and potato parings into his septic tank.

Management capitulated immediately; between the combined aromas of fresh linen and gas fumes, everyone is walking around in a state of euphoria.

Yesterday I discovered that our son has been wearing his "favorite" socks all week. Though admittedly unhygienic, it has helped cut down on visits to the laundromat.

Finally the weather improved sufficiently to allow a bit of waterskiing. Waterskiing is a lot like patting your head while rubbing your stomach; it looks easy when someone else does it. I could never finish murmuring the litany "skis up, knees bent, feet together, rope held to chest" before someone yelled "Hit it!" and I found myself face down, blearily gazing at the beer bottles on the bottom of the lake while the skis beat great welts in the region of my shoulderblades.

Took the children to a drive-in movie last night at a nearby small town. During the day, a local farmer grazes fifty head of Black Angus at the Starlight Drive-in. A trip to the concession stand in the dark was like walking over a mine field. It was quite an entertaining show starring a little girl named Jane Withers who bears a striking resemblance to Josephine the Plumber. Unfortunately they had lost the last reel, but they showed the first reel twice to make up for it.

Eric fell asleep on the way home, and I sneaked his "favorite" socks off. I had planned to wash them and drape them over the gas space heater, but the pilot light just blew out again.

August 17

In spite of it being a supposedly uplifting TV show, I find that whenever I watch "The Waltons," I invariably become depressed.

The sad fact of the matter is that our family is nowhere near as well adjusted as the Waltons. "Rats," I mutter every time I view the show. "There they are, poverty-stricken, victims of the Great Depression, struggling to wrench a meager existence out of the unyielding soil. Some people have all the luck."

I was determined to simulate the Waltons' spirit of family cooperation, their sense of participation, and by so doing to acquire their unfailing cheerfulness. First I concentrated on my son, Eric-boy, who was lying on the floor reading an issue of *Pop Music Today*.

"How're them chores comin', Son?"

"What chores?" he asked, looking at me as if I had suddenly begun speaking in tongues.

"Um, well, there's the butter," I mumbled.

"The butter?" he repeated, obviously mystified. Actually, I don't churn butter. And taking one pound of butter out of its paper and putting it on the butter dish isn't much of a chore.

"Have you fed the livestock?" I asked.

"You mean him?" he replied, pointing to Rover-boy who was absently munching a couple of bearer bonds. Just then his sister came home.

"Did you git them potatoes for me at Ike's on your way home?" I asked.

"No, I got them at the A&P. They give stamps."

"Well, let's git to it and russle up some grub," I chortled, sweeping her off into the kitchen. "You peel the spuds."

I think that there is a possibility of acquiring the Waltons' spirit of family cooperation and sense of participation. All we have to do is discover how to peel a box of instant mashed potatoes.

August 19

I am convinced that everyone is born with either a Number Mind or a Word Mind.

Number Minds go through life nonchalantly splitting infinitives and inferring when they should be implying. Those of us with Word Minds have to take off our shoes to add nine and eight.

Now I would never read mathematical puzzles were they not written in Words; I read "Fun with Figures" for the same reason I read the financial page, which, though completely unintelligible, is full of glorious Words like "optimum capital allocation" and "unprecedented maximization."

Yesterday's mathematical puzzle featured the following folksy dialogue:

"What's that label on our garage, Dad?" Alan asked. "It's a funny number anyway."

Dad smiled. "The building permit number," he replied. "What's funny about it?"

The boy grinned. "It's just four less than a seventh of what you get if you square its last three digits."

You figure it out.

Number Minds will undoubtedly convert that gay repartee into an equation and completely ignore the obvious pathos of the situation. There is Dad, just off the 6:20 train, wanting nothing more than five minutes alone in his vibrator chair.

Before he can get into the house, Alan, whom I envisage as an adenoidal twelve-year-old, and probably a bedwetter to boot, leaps out from behind the privet hedge and starts whining, "What's that label on our garage? It's a funny number anyway."

Dad, admirably restraining his immediate impulse to tell Alan to button his lip, smiles and explains. But instead of leaving well enough alone, he asks Alan what's so darn funny.

Alan chuckles (adenoidally) and begins to spout his nonsense about four less a seventh to poor Dad (plainly a Word Mind like me who gave up trying to balance his checkbook sixteen years ago).

The whole situation is almost as depressing as the financial page.

August 20

One of the fallacies of summer holidays is that you are going to get some serious reading done while you are lying on the beach.

Our house is full of volumes of Thackeray and Dickens in genuine, gold-leaf binding—really solid stuff that I've always meant to read but never have.

There is always the temptation to tuck one of these literary classics into the beach bag between the earplugs and the swim fins. What better time for communing with Tolstoy, you reason, than while you're basking idly beside the sea for seven whole days?

In the first place, Russian novels are out. Russian names are difficult enough to keep track of when you're sitting by yourself on a snowy Thursday afternoon. They become completely hopeless to sort out while your toes are being nibbled by sand fleas and a small girl is busily swatting the mosquitoes on your back with her Eskimo Pie.

If you will notice, used bookstores in resort areas invariably stock at least twenty-eight volumes of *War and Peace* with sand in the bindings that vacationers are determined not to lug all the way back to Des Moines again. I am not sure what the local residents do with that much Tolstoy, but by September they undoubtedly have enough to build themselves a dandy seawall.

No, for the beach you want something light and airy. The instruction manual for an electric coffeemaker is ideal. For variety you might include the washing directions for your husband's swim trunks or the label on the bottle of insect repellent.

Let's fact it, rather than reading anything, you will undoubtedly spend most of your summer holiday peering myopically in the direction of the water and wondering whether your son is the blond head bobbing fifty yards off shore or the boy who is scuttling along the beach waving the top half of someone's bikini.

August 21

Today, on the seventeenth day of our vacation on Shuswap Lake, we were informed that for almost three weeks we have been drinking unpurified lake water.

I had suspected as much when I found snails in the bottom of a pitcher of lemonade, but the rest of the family carried on as if Shuswap Lake was fed by the Hudson River. They immediately blamed the water supply for every complaint they've had since we arrived, from intestinal afflictions to heel blisters.

This morning I took the children horsebackriding. We were greeted at the corral by a man who I'm sure was Chill Wills. His upper plate was clacking so alarmingly that I couldn't understand much of what he said except "Howdy, Ma'am" and "Two dollars an hour each in advance." While the children were assisted onto two gentle mares, I found myself being heaved aboard a vicious looking sorrel who was chewing the bit and obviously wishing that it was a human ankle bone.

"You'll like 'Perdition.' He's got spunk," Chill Wills clacked at me.

"Spunk, my foot! He has rabies!" I replied as we left for what I truly believed to be the Last Roundup.

Soon we reached a gentleman's agreement; Perdition

would stumble along gnashing his huge yellow teeth and frothing at the mouth while I would content myself with clinging to the pommel with both sweaty hands and sobbing.

Alas, disaster struck in the form of a killer butterfly. When it fluttered past Perdition's bloodshot eyes, he gave a strangled scream and bolted across a marsh gibbering pitifully. First I yelled "Whoa!" When that seemed to drive him to even greater frenzy, I switched to "Help! Help!" I finally settled for a steady moan-sob combination, which my children tell me I kept up for an hour after Perdition halted abruptly to eat a patch of poison sumac.

I have the beginnings of an acute discomfort in the lower back, which by tomorrow gives every promise of developing into excruciating agony, should I be so foolish as to attempt to sit down.

But according to my family, Perdition had nothing to do with it; it's all that lake water I drank.

August 29

I recently extended a dinner invitation to friends of mine from New York City, a couple who have an eighteen-month-old son.

I checked with his mother beforehand to find out Bobby's favorite foods.

"Oh, any finger foods will do," she assured me. "Mashed potatoes, creamed carrots, Jell-O . . ."

"I'm afraid that I don't have a high chair," I said.

"That's no problem. We always carry the Manhattan yellow pages around with us. It makes a terrific booster seat. Of course, that's about all it's good for these days. Last Tuesday I went to call an electrician and found out that all the pages have been glued shut with blobs of gravy."

"I haven't had anyone Bobby's age around for a long time," I admitted.

"He's at a super stage," his mother insisted. "He's still too little to pick all the mushrooms out of his spaghetti sauce and roll them up in one corner of the tablecloth. He doesn't have any loose baby teeth dangling over his lower lip and threatening to fall out any minute. And he doesn't report all the revolting things he saw on the sidewalk on the way to school. In fact, he's only got one fault."

"What's that?"

"He's not sure where his mouth is yet. And there's nothing that dampens my enjoyment of coq au vin more than watching him stabbing away at his cheek with a fistful of creamed carrots."

August 30

I truly believe that one of the finest aspects of our modern culture is the growing lack of social pressures on a couple to have children.

There are, however, noticeable differences between

childless couples and those who have chosen to raise a family.

You know that you are in the home of a couple with children when you find yourselves playing bridge with an Animal Rummy deck;

—When the man of the house refers to his middle toe as "the little piggy that had roast beef";

—When you find yourself drinking a martini out of a Fred Flintstone mug;

—When you ask your hostess whether you can borrow her nail scissors and she simply looks at you and bursts into hysterical laughter.

On the other hand, you know that you must be in the home of a couple who have chosen to remain childless when you can use their bathroom without first removing a toidy seat;

—When the living room contains a white brocade sofa, a glass-topped coffee table, and sixteen current affairs magazines with the covers on;

—When your host informs you that he has *volunteered* to act as leader for a Cub Scout pack;

—When you notice that there is no lock on their bedroom door;

—When you discover that they don't know the location of the emergency ward at the local hospital.

September 8

I have to admit that I'm overjoyed that my children are back in school.

Don't misunderstand me; I like my children. But I like them in their place. Unfortunately, their place closes down for two months every summer.

While the first day of summer vacation is taken up with whooping "No more pencils, no more books, no more teacher's dirty looks" and feeding their geography notes to the dog, by mid-afternoon of the second day both children are reduced to lying under the dining room table and whining "There's nothing to *do*!"

"What do you mean, 'there's nothing to do'? Just look at your room!" is met with stony silence. (Mothers, it must be admitted, are not overly sympathetic toward people who have nothing to do. It is a callous attitude acquired in the process of folding diapers with one hand while stirring chocolate pudding with the other.)

I confess to being a bit out of sorts as well. Not only has my consciousness-raising session been canceled for the summer, but I must remember to close the bathroom door again.

As the summer progresses, my children seek out others with whom to mope. They follow me around the house like a Greek chorus, watching me dust.

While I am grateful to acknowledge the end of

summer, I pride myself on the fact that I did adapt. I learned not only to live with a refrigerator full of Kool-Aid and a kitchen floor liberally sprinkled with granulated sugar, but I even occasionally yielded to the temptation to surreptitiously hoof my way through a chorus or two of "Me and My Shadow" while peeling potatoes.

Fortunately, last month the children were too caught up in the heady decision of whether to buy two-hole or three-hole filler paper to notice that the flush of excitement that had begun rising to my cheeks in late August was something more than simply hot flashes.

The children's annual return to school signifies a further step in their educational experience, a continuation of the emotional and intellectual awakening process so vital to maturity.

It also means that I can again go to the bathroom without closing the door and watch "As the World Turns" instead of "The Three Stooges."

Since their return to school, the children have displayed a great deal of solicitous concern as to my psychological welfare, suddenly bereft of their company as I am.

Of course it would never do to let the children know that I am simply ecstatic that they have returned to school.

"I'll bet you miss those great Monopoly games we had in July. I'll bet nobody ever played Monopoly for forty-seven hours before," my son sighed.

"And remember the time we went to the beach and that fat little kid dropped his Eskimo Pie on your stomach?" his sister added.

"Mom's lucky, though. We have to go to school every day, but she can still watch 'The Three Stooges' every afternoon."

"Somehow it isn't the same program without you," I assured him.

"Sure must be dull around home these days."

"Yeah," I sighed blissfully. "Sure is dull."

September 9

While a cat or a dog is usually considered a family pet, a child may beg for something in a cage or a bowl to keep on his bureau as his very own.

As a public service for mothers (who invariably will be obliged to feed these pets, clean their cages, and pick cedar shavings out of the child's underwear drawer), I present the following Child's Garden of Pets:

The Turtle: Isn't he tiny? See him swim? See him sun himself? He does everything but eat. Have you tried dried flies? Have you tried lettuce? Have you tried hot pastrami?

The Hamster: Isn't he cunning? Watch him store food in his cheek pouches. My he smells odd! See him run around in his exercise wheel? He does that all day long. He does it all *night* long, too. I've *tried* oiling the wheel. Let's put his cage in the basement behind the woodpile.

Tropical Fish: Aren't they lovely colors? No, you can't kiss them. They are very delicate. They live in a special $12.98 tank with a $17.50 heating element, a $14.95 pump which uses granulated charcoal and a fiberglass filter, and we put algae retardant in their water and feed them brine shrimp eggs. No, I don't know *why* they are all floating upside down.

The Parakeet: Aren't his feathers a pretty shade of blue? They match the rug so well. Isn't that handy? Let's teach him how to sit on our finger. Where are all those bandages I bought last Tuesday?

The Mice: Mommy mouse is pregnant. Isn't that nice? She has six darling little babies. No, I don't know why Daddy mouse ate them. Maybe they made too much noise and jumped on their beds.

The Snake: Yes, he's very pretty. Yellow and black are *my* favorite colors, too. I'm sure that he's not a bit slimy. No, I don't want to hold him!

The Chameleon: Did you know that he changes the color of his body to match his background? Isn't he clever? That is called protective coloration. It makes it very hard for his enemies to see . . . Well, don't just sit there, look for him!

September 11

As much as it might seem that way, mothers are not with their children every minute of the day.

Consequently, all manner of things go on that mother never knows about. Which is undoubtedly all for the best.

You must impress on the children that you'd just as soon not know that Susie is blowing bubbles in her Ovaltine again, but if she is sitting on the living room floor drinking Mr. Clean, you'd like to be told.

When the children misbehave, threatening them with

"Wait until your father comes home" is not a particularly good idea, as this tends to make Daddy about as popular as Atilla the Hun, and the children will await his homecoming with the same degree of enthusiasm as they do a flu shot.

Besides, Daddy is apt to be unreliable. After a particularly irksome day of watching the Dow Jones averages go down and feeling his collar trying to strangle him, Daddy may regard the fact that Marvin ate $6.98 worth of artificial fruit as being vaguely amusing. Marvin, sensing a potential ally, makes Daddy a nice, strong drink, leaps onto his lap and begins stroking his cheek, leaving you brandishing half of a wax banana and demanding, "Well, what are you going to *do* about it?"

Since you are destined to be both judge and jury, you must remember the cardinal rule: *Never punish a child when you are angry.*

If you have gone all white around the mouth and are seeing red flashes, it's probably just as well to lock yourself in the bathroom, where you can howl, stomp your feet, and hold your breath until you turn blue. When the child knocks on the door and asks if you are ready to punish him, put your mouth to the keyhole and yell, "Not yet, dear. If I touch you, I might kill you."

In an hour or so you will find that you're calm, and the child is out in the sandbox making a castle. Go to him. Smile and say, "I'm not angry any more, Bobby. Now I'm going to whale the tar out of you!"

September 16

I never was a hypochondriac. Unless I was faced with evidence to the contrary, I always assumed that my spleen and pancreas were in there somewhere, plugging away at whatever they were supposed to be doing.

But last week we bought a life insurance policy. And instead of giving us another desk calendar or an ice pack, which we really could have used, our insurance agent presented us with a copy of the *Family Medical Encyclopedia*, a frank discussion of 2,400 medical subjects from *Abasia* to *Zymurgy*.

Now I'm not in favor of censorship in principle. But I do believe that certain types of literature are best kept out of the hands of impressionable people. Like me.

When my husband arrived home from work tonight, I was lying in the dark on the living room sofa. Across my forehead was a homemade ice pack (twenty-seven ice cubes tied in a hockey sock).

"What's the matter?" he asked.

"Agranulocytosis," I whispered.

"What's that again?"

"Agranulocytosis," I repeated. "Also called malignant leukopenia. A rare but often fatal disease in which the bone marrow is affected and the manufacture of essential white blood cells is severely diminished."

"You've been reading that darned *Medical Encyclopedia* again," he said accusingly, pointing to the well-thumbed book which lay, disease-down, across my knees. "Three days ago you were positive that you had scurvy just because your gums were bleeding."

"So I forgot that I had bought a new toothbrush. But this time I'm sure. In the first place I have a high fever and ulcerations in my mouth. Look," I said, pointing to my upper lip.

"That's a cold sore. What's for dinner?"

It's impossible to get any sympathy around here. I don't know how he can expect me to make dinner when I can't even make white blood cells.

September 18

I have always been amazed that for one woman "cleaning house" is a task to which she devotes forty-five minutes a week, while for another woman the job is literally full time, demanding at least eight hours a day.

Oddly enough, both houses look equally presentable.

I have recently devised a theory to explain this phenomenon: household dirt is composed of three layers. The first woman cleans only layer one; the second cleans all three layers.

Layer One: This layer is composed of highly visible effluvia, usually sticky. In this category is the blob of grape jelly on the stereo, the orange juice on the kitchen floor, the dab of French's mustard on the telephone, and the two cigarette butts stuck in the rubber plant. Also included in this category are items temporarily misplaced, such as the tube of denture adhesive on the piano, the empty ice-cube tray on the coffee table, and the living bra draped over the toaster.

Layer Two: Also known as the Twilight Zone, it consists of things you don't see unless you are down on your hands and knees looking for a cufflink. In this category is the tumbleweed of dust under the bed, the wad of chewing gum stuck to the back leg of the end table, and the beef bone buried behind the dresser. Many items considered hopelessly lost, such as library cards, tweezers, and the meat thermometer, are often lurking in Layer Two.

Layer Three: Layer Three is composed solely of things no one ever sees except mothers-in-law. It includes the four dog biscuits under the refrigerator, the dust on the tops of the drapes, the dried carrot stick stuffed behind the books in the bookcase, the price tags on the tops of the paintings, and the three obscene books tucked behind the spare blanket on the top shelf of the linen closet.

September 21

A popular women's magazine recently ran a test whereby the reader could determine her degree of assertiveness.

Each question presented a situation, your response to it showing whether you normally react in an aggressive, assertive, or passive manner.

Being masochistically addicted to personality quizzes, I endeavored to answer the following:

A friend asks you to accept a gift you do not want. You . . .

1. Accept the gift but indicate you don't really want it;

   2. Thank your friend but explain that you cannot accept this gift;

   3. Do not accept the gift.

Now, the major problem with this situation is that absolutely no hint is given of the type of gift that she offered. I mean, is it something small and intimate that I could simply tuck away on the top shelf of the linen closet, and later assure my friend that I was indeed using and/or wearing it? Or is it something three feet high at the shoulders with drooping jowls that will leak all over the new broadloom?

   Your husband has been throwing his clothes all over the bedroom during the past week. You . . .

   1. Put up with the mess as best as you can;

   2. Tell him you would appreciate it if he would try to keep his clothes hung up;

   3. Pick up the clothes because you want to help him.

Again, no hint is given as to *why* he threw his clothes all over the bedroom. No mention was made of what, if anything, I was doing with my own clothes. From everything I've been reading lately, a moderate amount of marital clothes-throwing is a good thing.

And it is a lot more fun than sitting around taking personality quizzes.

September 28

The person who said "Neither a borrower nor a

lender be" didn't live five miles from the nearest super-market.

Suburbanites shop but once a week. As I know of no one who is able to accurately predict his family's dietary whimsies over a seven-day period, between Tuesday and Friday of each week we are invariably found running between each other's houses carrying measuring cups.

Not only is the communal sharing of nature's bounty an expression of true humanitarian spirit, but it enables one to avoid the dilemma of making baking powder biscuits without baking powder.

Most of the neighborhood borrowing is confined to such temporary culinary short-falls as an egg, a small onion, or a cup of Vermouth. One woman, however, is notorious for stretching the bonds of Christian charity.

"How can anybody 'borrow' a standing rib roast?" I grumbled to one of my friends.

"You lent Joyce a roast?!?" my friend Alice ex-claimed, aghast.

"Don't be ridiculous. What would I be doing with a standing rib roast? Fortunately she settled for three pounds of hamburger."

"You have to understand about Joyce," Alice ex-plained. "I love the woman like I do my own sister, but she has never caught on to our system. No matter what she borrows, she always returns sugar."

"Sugar?"

"She figures everyone uses sugar, and it's simpler than remembering what she originally borrowed. Besides, she enjoys watching the expression on the bag boy's face every week when she buys 137 pounds of sugar."

October 1

To me, an autumn afternoon has always been a magic time, a time for a romantic stroll through a carpet of crisp, golden leaves, while the sun turns my hair to a burnished halo, and a cool breeze whispers a sad farewell to a waning summer.

To my husband, an autumn afternoon means lying on the sofa with a bowl of pistachios on his chest and watching six straight hours of football.

I suppose that there's nothing to prevent me from taking a romantic walk through carpets of crisp, golden leaves by myself. But bashing around in a pile of leaves alone is hardly romantic. Besides, I can hear the neighbors now: "Look at the Stahl dame, Fred, out there jumping around in a pile of leaves. Get the kids inside while I call the police."

The only alternative seems to be to put a bowl of pistachios on my chest and watch the football game, too. But I regard football games like I do taffy apples and kittens: one is plenty. By 3:30 last Saturday afternoon I had finished my pistachios and darned every sock in the house, including the ones my husband was wearing.

"Let's go play tennis," I suggested brightly, turning off the television set. My husband screamed as if I had driven a stake through his heart.

"The Jets have fourth-and-two on the three-yard

line!'' he shrieked as he leaped from the sofa. He wrenched the set on, only to hear the announcer say, ''Well, folks, you just saw probably the most electrifying play in the entire history of professional football.''

''No, I didn't!'' my husband bawled, pointing at me accusingly. ''She turned the set off!''

''I'm tired of watching football,'' I complained.

''I'll tell you what. Have you noticed that carpet of crisp, golden leaves outside?''

''I sure have!'' I said, expectantly.

''Why don't you go out and rake them? I'll bet they'd make a swell compost heap!''

October 2

Owning a grandfather clock is one of those mixed blessings like suddenly finding yourself in possession of a harem. No matter how proud of it you are, from then on getting a good night's sleep becomes a bit difficult.

The first night that we had the clock, I noticed that my husband was lying rigidly in bed with one hand on his chest and appeared not to be breathing. ''What's the matter?'' I asked anxiously. ''Are you sick?''

''It's my heart. I can *hear* it beating,'' he whispered in a stricken voice.

''Relax. It's just Big Ben downstairs.''

''How long does this go on?'' he demanded. I was

tempted to say "Till the old man dies," but I restrained the impulse.

During the next several hours, Grandfather's Westminster chimes effectively wrenched us rudely from the verge of sleep every fifteen minutes, melodiously informing us that it was quarter-past, half-past, or quarter-till. Grandfather left it up to us to figure out quarter-past, half-past, or quarter-till *what*. I suppose that it would have been simple enough for one of us to get out of bed and look. But getting up involved not only locating slippers but running the risk of finding ourselves wide awake and hungry. Instead, we decided to lie there and wait for the hour to strike.

But invariably, the striking of the hour—which is a veritable pops concert—was the one we dozed through, only to awaken fifteen minutes later to learn that is was once again quarter-past *something*.

The next night we decided to cover Grandfather with an old sheet at night, like we would a touchy parrot. I thought that we had solved the problem nicely until our daughter ran into our room in the middle of the night.

"There's a ghost standing in the downstairs hall," she shrieked, "and I can hear his heart beating."

October 6

It must be fall. Not only are my friends more relaxed because the kids are back in school but I find myself seized with my annual urge to clean under the refrigerator.

I know it's all psychological. When I'm beseiged on every side with the sight and smell of burning leaves and the sounds of muffled activity as robins pack to leave their nest in our chimney for their trek South, I suppose that it's only natural to feel guilty that the part of our nest that lies under the refrigerator hasn't been cleaned for a year.

The best cure that I've found for this fall-time attack of guilt is simply to lie down with my feet up and a cool cloth on my forehead and murmur, "This, too, shall pass." In addition, it helps to ask myself two pertinent questions:

Q: What exactly do you propose to do?

A: I propose to court a severe rupture by attempting to move a three-hundred-pound refrigerator in order to wipe up six ounces of ick that has accumulated underneath it. Unless I succeed regarding the rupture, I then propose to move the refrigerator back so that "ick" can collect underneath it again.

Q: For whom do you propose to do this?

A: Obviously not for my family. My family is concerned only with what is *in* the refrigerator; I could store dead frogs underneath it for all they care. Even if I were to tell them about the hideous job I had cleaning it, and about the rupture and all, the only accolade I could expect from them would be a rather disinterested "Uhhuh," if that.

By the time I have finished answering those two questions, I find that my pangs of conscience have vanished. Better to let another year or two of ick accumulate. By then we'll probably be moving, and the moving men can haul the refrigerator out while I stand poised with a damp cloth, ready to swoop upon the refuse making little "Tsk, tsk, how did *that* get there?" noises. As if I didn't know.

October 9

Every modern child psychology book will tell you that it is important to instill a sense of responsibility in your children.

Tell them that along with the obvious benefits, being a member of a family entails certain obligations on their part. They will express delight at the prospect of being allowed to assume a vital, active role in the family. If they don't exhibit delight, simply threaten to cut off their allowances and leave them out in the forest to be raised by wolves.

No matter how old he is, any child is capable of helping around the house. Different ages have different capabilities.

Children three to five years old are sobbingly eager to help you do everything from baking brownies to putting on your girdle. All they need is a bit of direction.

They can:

1. *Run simple errands*. Just as jet engine manufacturers employ midgets in assembly lines, children this size are invaluable for crawling under beds to determine whether that dark blob is a missing navy blue sock that must be washed or simply a banana skin.

2. *Empty the ashtrays*. At this age, you owe it to your children's sense of responsibility to smoke. How can they empty the ashtrays if you don't smoke? Of course, they will empty half the contents of the ashtray into the paper bag under the sink and the other half onto the kitchen floor, but it's the thought that counts. Besides, the kitchen floor needs washing anyway. Well, doesn't it? Of course it does. It has cigarette ashes all over it.

3. *Put their toys away*. While you are busy filling the ashtrays, your children will be busy emptying the toy box. If they start at 2:00 P.M. picking up the building

blocks under the dining room table, the toy cars under the sofa cushions, and the marbles on the stairs, they *may* finish by bedtime. At this rate they will have no time for the ashtrays. On second thought, you'd better stop smoking. Not only will it be better for your lungs, but you won't have to wash the kitchen floor nearly so often.

Children from six to nine lack the enthusiasm exhibited by the three-to-five-year olds, but still can be persuaded to:

1. *Feed their pets.* Unless his pet is vocal enough to meow or bark while pointing to his mouth with one paw, the child may very well forget this chore. It is therefore necessary for you to badger him to feed the goldfish, as the only way the goldfish can remind him is to begin floating belly-side-up in their bowl.

2. *Pick up the dirty clothes and throw them down the laundry chute.* This is one thing that a child really *likes* to do. In fact, he may get so carried away that when he finishes with the dirty clothes, he will begin flinging down all his clean clothes, his baseball cards, the alarm clock—and the cat. This makes for quite a clutter in the basement, not to mention a decidedly neurotic kitty.

3. *Make their beds.* This involves simply pulling the spread up over all the things he sleep with; at this age, two teddy bears and a basketball. When questioned, he will argue that since he is going to be getting back into the bed in just twelve hours, having the blanket already turned down and the teddy bears and the basketball in there will save time. Besides, nobody ever sees his room except him, and he likes it that way. Personally, I've never been able to come up with a reasonable argument to refute this logic.

The only solution is to keep the door to his room closed and tell yourself that he will do better as he gets older.

While not necessarily true, it's a consoling thought,

rather like imagining that a pastel mink coat would only make you look fat.

Unfortunately, large-sized children (from ten to thirteen) do not have much time for chores. But in the odd moments when they are not practising the bassoon or determining how long it will take an airplane flying six-hundred miles per hour into a fifty-mile per hour head-wind to fly from Cedar Rapids to Bombay, they may be induced to:

1. *Mow the lawn.* Regrettably, the only children who are really keen to mow the lawn are middle or little. Letting a middle or little struggle with the lawn mower will cause the neighbors to report you to the welfare authorities as being unfit parents. But by the time a child reaches a size where the neighbors begin to say, "Why doesn't that big lout of a kid next door do any work?" he will be completely disenchanted with the thrill of mowing. He will insist that he is not big enough to mow the lawn and will lop off his big toe just to prove it.

2. *Set and clear the dinner table.* While this may work admirably if your cuisine lends itself to plastic plates and jelly glasses, I would be a bit loath to entrust a handful of heirloom Limoges to anyone who has been known to trip over a piece of lint on the carpet.

3. *Take out the garbage.* To be absolutely safe, it's best to add "and put it into the trash can." If your son is anything like mine, he may very well absentmindedly take the garbage to school and stuff it into his desk until lunchtime, when he will bring it home and deposit the bag in the kitchen again.

4. *Climb up on the roof and pry the Frisbee out of the chimney.* Of course, if you didn't have a large-sized child, you wouldn't *have* a Frisbee in the chimney. But at this age, a chore is a chore.

October 12

I am admittedly an astonishingly gullible person. The following, however, is a list of phrases that even I tend not to believe:

Child: "So what if this is the last turnpike exit for fifty-seven miles. I said I don't have to go."

Husband: "Of course I'm not going to fall asleep. I'm just going to lie here for ten minutes and rest my eyes."

Friends: "Listen, any time you're in the neighborhood, be sure to drop in."

Husband: "He'll grow out of it. He's only two."

Man at the door: "I'm taking a survey in your area."

Husband: "Don't call a repairman. I can fix the toaster blindfolded."

Mother-in-law: "He's still in diapers? I had his father completely trained when he was six months old."

Husband: "He'll outgrow it. He's only seven."

Child: "And I promise that I'll clean his cage every single day."

Neighbor: "There's no hurry to get her neutered. She's not old enough to have kittens."

Husband: "He'll outgrow it. He's only twelve."

Pantyhose package: "One size fits all—95 to 165 pounds."

Husband: "What do you mean, it's six o'clock and you want to stop already? Why, I'm just hitting my stride. Don't worry, there will be lots of motels with vacancies at nine o'clock."

Child: "He followed me home."

Husband: "Of course I don't need glasses. It's just that this wise guy publisher is trying to save money by using microscopic print."

Friend: "Take it from me. Soybean futures are nothing but a license to print money."

Husband: "I mean it. I don't want anything for my birthday."

Child: "And I promise that I'll practice an hour every day."

Husband: "He'll outgrow it. He's only eighteen."

October 14

In response to several magazine articles exhorting me to enjoy the incomparable autumnal exhilaration of an October picnic, I would like to offer the following first-hand observations:

Granted, there is a crispness in the air when it's twelve degrees above freezing that effectively eliminates the mosquito problem while keeping all the food nicely chilled. Except the lemonade, which inexplicably remains at approximately body temperature and contains a dozen mosquitos who threw themselves in simply to get warm.

Of course, by the time you have finished hauling a picnic hamper, playpen, baseball bat, blanket, radio, four folding chairs, and a cooler that alone weighs more than a four-year-old child to the last empty picnic table (which is invariably located beside the comfort station), you are quite warm, especially under your arms where your woolen sweater has begun to scratch unmercifully.

Within ten minutes a chill northern wind will come whipping through the trees, sending sixteen dried oak leaves into the potato salad, whereupon someone will suggest that we throw the old ball around a bit before eating to get the blood stirring.

Now even though I take care to hold my hand correctly, just before the old ball reaches me I succumb to some primordial urge and throw both hands over my face, crouch with my head between my knees, and begin whimpering. Whereupon the old ball knocks three pounds of potato salad, not to mention sixteen dried oak leaves, into the playpen.

Of course, the one jolly thing about October picnics is that you eat all manner of things that you wouldn't dream of eating at home where you are warm and toasty. Children who normally go all pale and trembly when confronted with a carrot stick at lunch, on an October picnic will proceed not only to down thirteen carrot sticks and six deviled eggs that they find buried in the sand under the picnic cooler, but scrape off and eat all the leafy potato salad from the playpen pad.

October 15

Dear Mrs. Hall,

I am terribly sorry that I didn't reply sooner to the note you sent me last Tuesday, but I didn't find it until I washed Eric's brown corduroy school pants this morning.

It certainly was a long note. By the time the washer finished spinning, I found so many pieces of paper that I had to wash the entire load over again.

I know that it was an important note, too. I mean, what with molding character and teaching long division, you certainly don't have time to write long notes for pleasure. Besides, one piece (the one stuck to a navy blue stretch sock) said "Urgent."

Since it was obviously so important, I picked all the pieces out of the lint filter and off the clothes and tried to put them together. I'm sorry that the school board gives you such inferior paper; most of the note had turned into a sort of slimy goo, even with the machine set on "Gentle." Unfortunately the only piece I could read, besides the one that said "Urgent," said "Show."

The only show I can think of is a school production like the one I made eighteen Bluebell costumes for in 1973. That was the same year I was room mother, cookie chairman for the PTA, and drove six little girls to hula dancing lessons every Tuesday afternoon.

I don't do that sort of thing now, Mrs. Hall. I mean, "for everything there is a season," and between my bursitis and hot flashes, I'm just not in season anymore. It's no great loss, actually; I put all the Bluebell sleeves in backwards.

There is one other possible interpretation, but somehow I can't imagine that you conduct Show-and-Tell in the sixth grade. Of course we know that they still tell. Heaven knows he's told us a lot about you. And I want you to know that we don't believe even half of it.

But if he's showing anything he shouldn't, I certainly hope you'll phone me immediately.

October 16

In these times of domestic and foreign turmoil, many readers find themselves unable to decide between the two major political parties. With the election only a few weeks away, the dilemma has become particularly acute. As more and more writers are endeavoring to aid the public in this momentous decision, perhaps it is time to muddy up the waters with my own political observations of how Democrats differ from Republicans.

—When Republicans mention "my club," they mean their country club. Democrats mean Book-of-the-Month Club.

—Republicans get tennis elbow and ulcers. Democrats get heartburn and sties.

—Republicans play golf. Democrats bowl.

—Democrats drive six-year-old green Pontiacs with roof racks. Republicans drive six-month-old Cadillacs with bumper stickers that say "I Like Ike."

—Republicans own horses. Democrats bet on them.

—Republicans drink Drambouie and Cafe Capuchino after dinner. Democrats drink creme de menthe and Sanka.

—Republicans get face lifts and hair transplants. Democrats get nose jobs and silicone implants.

—Republicans have nannies for their children. Democrats have grandmothers.

—Republicans hire good cooks. Democrats marry them.

—Republicans read *Vogue* and the *National Review*. Democrats read *The New Republic* and *Photoplay*.

—Every three weeks, Democratic women make an appointment to have a manicure and get their hair shampooed, cut, and blown dry. So do Republican men.

—Republican men wear monogrammed silk pajamas. Democrats sleep nude.

October 17

In these days of high-pressure salesmanship, an unwary consumer can easily find himself agreeing to purchase unnecessary items. Test your own sales resistance in the following situations:

1. A salesman calls at your door contending that he is taking a survey of selected, intellectually advantaged families in your area. You would:

(a) Express delight at being part of such an obviously exclusive group. Explain that first you simply must get the garbage cans moved out front or you will miss the pick-up. Ask if he would mind moving the cans while you put on coffee. While he is thus occupied, sneak out the door and go to a movie.

(b) Invite him in, but warn him that the survey will have to be short as you are expecting the exterminator to arrive momentarily to rid the house of lice.

(c) Express relief that he is, in fact, taking a survey, rather than attempting to sell you anything. Confide that you were released from prison last Tuesday after having served six months for setting fire to an encyclopedia salesman.

2. A woman on the telephone informs you that you have won three free dancing lessons. You would:

(a) Express your appreciation and sincere desire to accept her generous offer—if and when you get out of your iron lung.

(b) Laugh heartily. Explain that you have recently been named choreographer for the June Taylor Dancers. Mutter something about "coals to Newcastle."

3. Handling your hair as if it were a particularly revolting strain of tropical fungus, your hairdresser informs you that your whole appearance is drab and lifeless and strongly suggests a forty-five dollar hot oil treatment followed by a color rinse. You would:

(a) Point out to your hairdresser that she's not so great looking herself.

(b) Buy a wig.

October 19

Psychiatrists assure us that fear is normal, that the human animal is beset by one anxiety after another from birth to old age. The following is a catalog of common fears:

A very small child fears that the stopper will come out of his belly-button while he sleeps and that he'll deflate like a beach ball, or that he will fall through the toilet seat and drown.

A twelve-year-old boy is afraid that his teacher will ask him to name the capital of North Dakota.

A girl of twelve is afraid that her classmates will be able to tell that she is wearing a bra. At fourteen, she fears her classmates *won't* be able to tell she is wearing a bra.

A boy of fifteen is afraid that he will fail his algebra test. At nineteen, he fears he'll fail his Wasserman test.

Although people in their twenties are relatively free from anxiety, irrational fears return by age thirty.

A thirty-five-year-old man is afraid that the government will audit his 1976 income tax return, and that someone will erect a motorcycle scrambles track in the vacant lot next door.

At forty-five, he fears that he is the only man in the world who doesn't taper, and that the pain in his arm will turn out not to be tennis elbow, but arthritis.

Women are not free from anxiety during adulthood. A thirty-five-year-old woman is afraid that her son is growing a moustache; a forty-five-year-old is afraid that *she* is growing one.

A forty-year-old woman fears that the lovely green plant her daughter gave her last Mother's Day is really marijuana.

A thirty-year-old woman is afraid that her children will grow up and leave her. A forty-year-old woman is afraid that they *won't*.

October 20

All too often, an otherwise memorable dining experience is ruined by the supercilious attitude of a wine steward who appears smugly certain that you wouldn't know Chateau Rothschild from Sunsweet Prune Juice.

It is necessary to intimidate such an individual immediately.

Shake your head wistfully over the wine list, flick a forefinger deprecatingly at three or four items, and sigh "a passable selection. Barely passable. But none of my favorites."

"What wine would you desire?" the steward, who is clearly nonplussed, will stammer.

"For one, Chateau Beaulieu, 1943."

"Chateau Beaulieu?"

"That amusing Tuscany wine. Surely you've heard of it?" Of course the steward hasn't, as you just made the name up on the spot, but he'd sooner swallow his key than admit it.

"Ah, monsieur," he will sigh. "We served our last bottle an hour ago." Extract a small leather notebook from your pocket. Murmer sadly, "no Chateau Beaulieu. What a pity," as you inscribe a large check mark.

The steward will beg to be allowed to bring a bottle of their finest wine.

Eventually he will get around to uncorking it and pouring some into your glass. Ignore it. After two minutes gaze at the glass speculatively, as if wondering how it got there. Raise it to the light. Squint at the color. Raise one eyebrow skeptically. Inhale the bouquet (or whatever it is one is obliged to inhale). Bring the glass slowly to your lips, allowing no more than one teaspoon of liquid to enter your mouth. Do not swallow. Let it just sort of sit there in a puddle on your tongue for twenty seconds, then close your eyes and slowly slosh it over your bridgework.

Sigh deeply and admit that while acceptable, even vaguely amusing, it's no Chateau Beaulieu, 1943.

October 21

Faced with the prospect of inflation, it seems that food is the only flexible item in our household budget.

After all, even though my daughter is so low on school supplies that she has to submit an in-depth report on dealing with the social customs of New Zealand aborigines written on paper towels from the girls' washroom, I can't simply write a letter to the trust company and lop ten dollars off the October mortgage payment.

And I have discovered through bitter experience that the electric company becomes extremely petulant when they receive a whimsical note stating "I.O.U. 357 kilowatts."

As children are notoriously undiscriminating, I expected no resistance to my recently instituted Culinary Austerity Program.

"Why," my son sighed last night, while staring pensively at the chicken leg I had fashioned out of ground beef, "do we always have to have hamburger?"

"What do you mean 'hamburger'?" I countered. "That looks like a chicken leg to me."

"Watch." He picked up his chicken leg, which fell apart in his hand.

"O.K., Smarty," I retorted. "But five nights a week isn't 'always.' Besides, it's not as if I always fix it the same way. What about the hamburger kabobs, the roast suckling hamburger, not to mention the hamburger slice with raisin sauce?"

"How can I forget?" he shuddered. "Why don't we ever have steak any more?"

"As a matter of fact, we *are* having steak tomorrow night."

"Wonderful!" he whooped. "What kind? Porterhouse? Sirloin? T-bone?"

"Salisbury."

October 22

One of the sad facts of my life is that there are not many things which I do well.

But if there is ever an Olympic event to determine proficient sleeping, I am certain to be awarded at least a bronze medal.

I am always amazed at people who declare that once they wake up in the morning, they are completely unable to go back to sleep. One of the chief joys of my life lies in waking up and going back to sleep every fifteen minutes from 6:00 A.M. to 7:30 A.M. In fact, were it not for pressing commitments, I could conceivably drift in and out of consciousness every fifteen minutes until it was time to peel the potatoes for dinner.

Once up, my proclivity for sleep does not diminish. Whenever I attempt to read anything to do with the Boer War, the balance-of-payments deficit, or any type of poetry written in blank verse, my eyes glaze, my chin drops to my chest, and I take on all the alluring charm of an old man on a park bench.

Bus rides never fail to render me half-comatose. Eight stops before I must get off, my eyelids become leaden. Four stops before mine, I must begin biting the sides of my cheeks and driving my fingernails viciously into the palms of my hands to stay awake, a process which gives me the alarming appearance of one who is about to go off into some sort of violent seizure.

Two seconds before the bus reaches my stop, my subconscious wrenches me awake and I leap up, begin yanking feverishly at the bell, and bellowing "Now! ME! Off!"—thus confirming my fellow-passengers' suspicions that they are sharing transportation with one who, far from being a bronze-medal winner, is dangerously deranged.

October 25

While there is a growing tendency in this country for a couple to limit the number of children they have to only one, I feel that there are several distinct advantages to having two.

A younger child is perfectly suited to acquire that size two, fur-trimmed Eskimo parka that set you back $47.98. In fact, with a modest degree of foresight in buying unisex clothing and an unlimited amount of iron-on patches, one needn't buy the second child a stitch until he is sixteen or so.

Remember, too, that if one child is ill, there is always a healthy one to throw into the breech should the trash want taking out or the dog need to be walked.

Besides, two children create a nice balance in the family.

Rather than having to face the tedious frustration of constantly having to function in a solely adult world, a brother or sister proves to be a valuable ally, a cohort in the magical world of make-believe, a partner who will join him in unraveling the mysteries of childhood. Someone to help him pour Ovaltine down the hot air register.

Occasionally, a certain degree of sibling rivalry is bound to occur. Although this is an integral part of their social development, a parent wonders when to step in. While it is definitely advisable to interfere before one child performs a frontal lobotomy on the other with the electric frying pan, it is equally permissible to interfere simply because you are rapidly reaching the point of braining *both* of them with the electric fry pan, just to get a little peace and quiet.

October 27

This is the time of year when I truly envy people who live on farms.

How jolly it must be to stomp out into the back forty in search of your own Halloween pumpkin. Especially since, with a bit of forethought, you can manage to have forgotten to plant any, thus relieving yourself of the bother of finding a round one, not to mention the loathsome duty of gutting it.

For us city-folk, pumpkins are like Christmas trees; they grow in supermarkets. Ideally, one should prop a prospective jack-o'-lantern up on a stack of canned lima beans and walk around it for ten minutes or so, determining what potential, if any, it has. Unfortunately, by the time I reached the pumpkin display last week, the entire contents of a half-gallon carton of butter pecan ice cream had begun dribbling down my left arm, and I involuntarily grabbed an orange football which gave distinct promise of falling over at 7:00 P.M. Halloween night and setting the verandah on fire.

When I arrived home, I placed the pumpkin on the kitchen counter As the four of us watched, it toppled over into the butter dish. "*Anyone* can have a plain old *round* pumpkin!" I asserted.

"Anyone but us," my husband observed glumly.

While the children ran outside to tell all the neighbors how their pumpkin mashed the butter, my husband began carving the face. Half an hour later the children returned to survey their father's efforts.

"Keen!" declared our daughter. "But what's all that red stuff in the eye hole!"

"Blood," snarled Daddy, licking the stump of his left thumb.

"Daddy bled all over our punkin!" she wailed.

"Don't worry," I assured her. "Nobody will notice in the dark."

"I've got a suggestion," said my husband. "How about we forget the whole thing next year and just put up our Christmas decorations early?"

October 31

When I was little, Halloween costumes never posed much of a problem. If you couldn't afford to be a storebought skeleton, you simply grabbed the top sheet off your bed and went as a ghost.

These days, children start agonizing in January over their Halloween costumes. And they never want to be anything simple. By November, they generally have it narrowed down to going as either the Marquis de Sade or a typewriter, either of which is a bit of a challenge to whip up out of crepe paper.

One year I decided to enter into the spirit of the season and dress up as a witch. I bought a grotesque rubber mask, a black wig, and wrapped myself in a pair of gangrenous green drapes. Our first caller was a three-year-old, out for the first time. After one look at me, he wet his Donald Duck costume and ran straight home, quacking all the way.

Aside from the costume problem, there's the question of what type of candy to give out. I've learned to buy good quality candy. Otherwise, if there is a blizzard on Halloween night, you may be stuck with 375 of those horrid chewy caramels wrapped in orange paper and end up paying $78.50 to get your bridgework rebuilt.

I must admit that I dislike Halloween intensely. I mean, it took me six weeks and $7.68 worth of heavy-duty aluminum foil to turn my son into the Tin Woodman of Oz. (Actually, he looked more like a leftover meatloaf, but I would cut my tongue out before I told him so.) And for what? Sixteen circus peanuts, fifty-seven pieces of candy corn, and three Chiclettes which I belatedly discovered were actually Feen-a-mint.

Of course, on Halloween night I myself am always wildly extravagant until 7:30, when I realize that I have only three Kraft caramels left. From 7:30 to 7:45 I part with three slices of Italian salami, five dimes, and eleven anchovy olives. At 8:00 I am reduced to either turning out the porch light or distributing a roll of Tums.

The only person I know who avoids this problem is our dentist. Realizing that giving out candy would strike people as being decidedly self-serving, our dentist chooses instead to distribute toothbrushes.

While many youngsters grumble over this heresy, my children profess delight. My son even went so far as to announce to the dentist that he had never had his own toothbrush.

"You told him *what*?" I gasped.

"Well, you didn't want me to hurt his feelings, did you?"

By 10:00 the children had finished their circus peanuts, candy corn, and (unfortunately) their Feen-a-mint. Announcing that they were ready for bed, they grimaced widely to show me their sparkling teeth.

"I even brushed the dog's teeth!" my son confided.

"Not with your new toothbrush?!"

"Of course not. I used yours."

November 1

One of the difficulties with the original concept of equality for women was the fact that the woman who viewed homemaking as a viable career was regarded as either dangerously subversive or mentally deficient.

"Why should anyone," the argument ran, "disdain the inherent challenge of executive decision making in favor of defrosting the refrigerator?"

Those in the vanguard of The Movement neglected to point out that few of us, men or women, ever succeed in scaling the corporate heights. For sheer managerial autonomy, nothing equals the role of homemaker. As there is no higher-up to whom she must report, the homemaker enjoys complete freedom in such situations as the following:

1. The living room windows are covered over with a nasty, yellowish-brown film in which someone has traced the words "Wash me." The homemaker can: (a) Clean the windows with paper towels soaked in ammonia and water; (b) wipe them with a vinegar solution and bath towels; or (c) draw the drapes.

2. Someone has given her a bright magenta sweater with orange reindeer on it. After searching carefully, the homemaker can find no washing instructions. She can: (a) Wash the sweater by hand separately in cold-water soap, roll it gently in a bath towel, and blow it dry with

her hair-dryer; or (b) boil it for ten minutes, then throw it over the hedge to dry.

November 2

Last week our son announced that he was bringing home a "Very Important New Friend."

That afternoon I met them at the door wearing my best Mother-of-the-Year-type smile, waving a batch of home-burned peanut butter cookies. Before he left, I even recited "Casey at the Bat" and gave him my autograph.

The next morning, New Friend arrived to walk to school with Eric.

"Is that your mother?" he gasped, pointing to a lump of frayed terry cloth attached to a cup of reheated coffee.

"Yep," answered Eric.

"She sure looks different in the morning!"

"That's because of her face. She isn't wearing it."

After they left, I ran to the bathroom and peered at myself through the toothpaste specks on the mirror. The regulation number of eyes, lumpy nose, prominent ears, all stared back at me. Actually, I looked much the same as I did at twenty. It just takes longer.

I got my lipstick and dug around in the nearly-empty tube with a bobby pin. Rats. This meant a trip to the cosmetic department.

Later that morning, after skulking around the shoe

department for an hour, I got up enough courage to approach the lipstick counter, feeling like a candidate for a complexion improvement test. The salesgirls saw me coming and quickly drew straws. A striking redhead undulated over to me, crumpling a very short straw in her fist.

"May I help you?" she asked in a pitying voice.

"I'd like a lipstick."

"What color would you like?"

"Red would be nice," I suggested.

"Let's see, coral would only make you look more sallow," she mused, then suddenly she gasped and began wringing her hands. "We haven't been using our night cream!"

"But when we use our night cream, our husband sleeps on the sofa," I protested.

"Ah, but this night cream is extracted from the tail feathers of male Himalayan bald eagles and is guaranteed nongreasy," she crowed.

"Our husband will be so happy," I murmured. Before I got away, we had spent two weeks' grocery money on enough creams, oils, and extracts to assure the immediate extinction of Himalayan bald eagles. At least we got a lipstick. Unfortunately she gave us Certainly Coral by mistake. It does make us look even more sallow, but when one can recite "Casey at the Bat" like we can, no one really cares.

November 5

Ignoring the outraged screams of our next door rose fetishist, we bought a dog last year. His mother was a pedigreed poodle. Judging from her son's present physique, the putative father must have whinnied.

When we first saw Adolf he was six weeks old, furry, wet-nosed, and cuddly. The fact that his feet were five inches in diameter and he cost $1.50 should have warned us that he would grow up to be a "Big."

We attributed his owner's hysterical joy as we left to his elation that Adolf was going to a good home. I know now that it was shameless relief that he finally unloaded his canine Quasimodo.

After arriving home, Adolf immediately sized up the situation. Taking the lay of the land, he sniffed every chair, table, bed and chest, then squatted on the Oriental carpet and christened it. Satisfied that he had thus made our casa his casa, he crawled into the lazy susan and went to sleep beside the potato chips.

While I blotted up his Mark, my husband went out and bought a $10.98 wicker bed and a large bottle of vinegar. (To those who are uninitiated, applying vinegar to carpeting neutralizes previous indiscretions.)

One hour later, we confidently put Adolf into his wicker bed and called it a night. Before I could turn out the light, Adolf was howling like a banshee. He was trembling violently, obviously miserable and terrified. Not realizing that I had witnessed a performance that qualified for an academy award, I did what all mothers do; I brought him into bed with us "just for tonight."

Every day for four months I would follow Adolf around the house, ready to scoop him up as soon as he started to squat. I'd rush outside with my leaking dog, and if he had any left for the lawn, I'd praise him as if he'd meant to go there all along.

At the end of five months, Adolf was seventy pounds heavier. His errors were of heroic proportions. The Oriental carpet was a mildewed marshland of vinegar. One memorable day, however, he lugged his ponderous bulk to the door and smugly barked his desire to go out. Our neurotic child was trained. Victory was ours.

Now if I can just get him out of our bed.

November 6

Few magazine articles annoy me quite so much as those entitled "How We Manage Our Money," featuring young couples like Babsie and Pudge and their four offspring who get along beautifully on Pudge's salary of $412.76 a month.

I would simply ignore these bits of folklore completely, if my husband didn't insist upon taping them to the bathroom mirror and complaining "What do you *do* with all our money?" possibly implying that I smother it with A-1 Sauce and have it for lunch.

In reading the article, one discovers that Babsie and Pudge pay $128 a month for a twenty-two-room Georgian mansion with hand-hewn beams which was once Millard Fillmore's carriage house. They discovered it one crisp autumn afternoon while tramping through the New England countryside searching for musket balls.

"Certainly it needs work," cried farsighted Babsie,

plunging her thumb through the rotten siding, "but you're ever so handy, Pudge."

After persuading kindly old Mr. Scrubbs at the bank to sell them the house for $15,000 and the promise of their first-born child, Pudge armed himself with $27.58 worth of hammers, nails, and a big ball of twine. Within a fortnight, Pudge hung the finishing touch, an exact reproduction of the chandelier in Mount Vernon, which he had fashioned out of two-hundred lids of discarded Maxwell House coffee cans.

Another formidable item in their budget is food, which runs to a whopping $105 a month. "Babsie can make hamburger taste like filet mignon," the article quotes Pudge as saying. Of course, Babsie grows and cans her own vegetables. They evidently don't have problems with weevils and gophers; if they do, resourceful Babsie presumably cans them, too. They're probably what Pudge mistakes for filet mignon.

Naturally Babsie sews, and when she isn't putting up gophers, she's fashioning Dior copies out of sugar sacks and old bedsheets.

"Of course they manage on $412.76," I announced after reading the article. "Their children's teeth came in straight."

November 8

Undoubtedly one of the most difficult adjustments in a marriage is learning how to breathe.

Of course, breathing during the day is relatively simple, even for newlyweds. The problem arises only at night when one attempts to breathe in a double bed.

Unison Breathing: Initially you attempt to breathe in unison. You soon discover that, although otherwise you are perfectly well-suited to each other, you breathe at wildly divergent rates. Some find that to retain a semblance of unison they must pant like an exhausted Great Dane; others, married to deep breathers, turn blue.

Tandem Breathing: Besides involving all the timing problems of union breathing, the carbon dioxide exchange occurring during face-to-face tandem breathing (otherwise known as inhaling each other's exhale) is not beneficial unless one of you is a plant.

Regular Breathing: Eventually, about 2:00 A.M., you resolve to revert to regular breathing. Unfortunately, although you have been regular-breathing successfully for over twenty years, you find that suddenly this automatic reflex has become a strangely foreign exercise. "In goes the good air," you murmur, "out goes the bad air." It invariably feels as if you're doing it all wrong.

By now your bed partner is blissfully asleep, completely unaware that you have lost a vital bodily function. He is not only asleep, but snoring. Isn't that cute? Just like a saw. "Ah-whoof, Ah-whoof." Such a regular rhythm. "Ah-whoof, Ah-whoof. Ah." The sudden absence of a corresponding "whoof" jolts you from semi-consciousness, and you leap to all fours, certain that he has experienced a cardiac arrest. Just as you begin to attempt mouth-to-mouth resuscitation, he "whoofs" into your nose.

It may help to console yourself with the fact that, given ten or twelve years, you may become accustomed to breathing in a double bed. While not necessarily true, it may help you get to sleep.

November 11

As I remember, it all started when I refused to let him eat lunch with his hockey helmet on.

The situation deteriorated rapidly during a lecture entitled "I'm Fully Aware that Creamed Chip Beef on Toast is Not Your Favorite Meal, But This Doesn't Happen to Be the Army, and Don't You Ever Call It That Again."

An hour later, wearing blue ski pajamas and his hockey helmet, he confronted us in the living room.

"You don't have to pretend any more," he announced gravely. "I know."

"He *knows*!" I gasped, icy fingers of panic clutching at my heart.

"Omigosh!" my husband replied, his face ashen. We sat in stunned silence for thirty seconds.

"Do you have any idea what he's talking about?" I finally asked.

"Not the slightest," my husband admitted.

"I'm adopted, ain't I?" our son said.

"What ever gave you that idea?"

"If I were your own little boy, you wouldn't pick on me all the time."

I was momentarily tempted to remind him that if he weren't our own little boy, we'd have given him back five years ago.

"Of course you're not adopted," my husband replied. "I'll show you your birth certificate to prove it."

"Besides," I reminded him, "being adopted doesn't mean that your parents don't love you. Being adopted means being chosen by two people who want that particular baby more than anything else in the world. They choose him out of all the other babies to take home with them and love."

"See," added his father, who had finally located our son's birth certificate in a folder containing the warranty on the blender. "You weren't adopted."

To our surprise, our son took one look at his birth certificate and burst into tears.

"If I were your chosen child," he sobbed, "you wouldn't pick on me all the time."

November 12

Last week our daughter announced that she would like to have a party.

"How about a Thanksgiving party," I suggested. "The girls could come as Indians or pilgrims."

"I want to have a mixed party," she replied.

"What do the girls come as at a mixed party?" my husband asked me.

"About half of them come as boys."

"Boys!?" he gasped.

"You know, snips and snails and puppy dogs' tails."

During the week before the party he took to wandering aimlessly around the house murmuring "Boys!?" in a stricken voice, as if we were about to be visited with an incurable disease.

For safety's sake, we held the party in the basement, where the only vulnerable antique is the furnace.

"For heaven's sake, can't you quiet those kids down?" my husband bellowed at 9:00 P.M. "What in the world is going *on* down there?

Not wanting to appear obtrusive, I quickly stripped three beds, gathered up the not-very-dirty sheets, and stomped down to the basement, whistling loudly. A hush descended on everyone, even Sam, who had been using chopsticks to drum out "Bridge Over Troubled Waters" on the water heater.

"Just going to wash out a few things," I explained. "Try to hold the noise down a bit," I added casually as I disappeared into the laundry room.

Fifteen minutes later my husband began frowning.

"For heaven's sake, now I can't hear a thing!"

"Neither can I," I mused. "I hope the washing machine isn't broken."

"What in the world is going *on* down there?"

"What could possibly be going on? They're only thirteen years old."

"I *know* they're only thirteen, but they've had all those sex education courses!"

Just then our daughter bounded upstairs.

"What a great party!" she exclaimed. "I'm so glad I invited boys. They're teaching us to burp at will!"

November 19

A difficult problem in any family lies in how to handle breaches of discipline.

As one of the manifestations of sibling rivalry is the delight of seeing your fellow sib get the tar swatted out of him, most children take perverse pleasure in reporting any and every questionable activity in the vague hope that it might turn out to be a punishable offense.

The acts reported during a typical day are as follows:

"Jimmy said *that word* again!"

"Debbie blew bubbles in her milk!"

"Jimmy ate paste!"

"Debbie took *three* Kleenexes to blow her nose!"

"Jimmy left the seat up again!"

At which time, mother, who by now wishes she'd stayed single, delivers a lecture entitled "Nobody Likes a Snitch."

Things are blissfully quiet for two days until a blue flame shoots across the living room, Jimmy loses his eyebrows, and the entire house is plunged into darkness for three hours.

Whereupon another lecture is delivered, entitled "Although Nobody Likes a Snitch, If Jimmy Is Sticking Bobby Pins in the Electric Outlet, *Tell* Me!"

November 21

I am sure that somewhere there are married couples who can enjoy successful husband-and-wife projects.

Actually, I am not all that sure, but I prefer to start on a note of optimism, however unlikely and far-fetched.

One of the major difficulties a husband and wife face is the question of pace. While one views a project as a sort of random activity which one can turn to during an odd hour or two every third Tuesday if "Three's Company" is a rerun, the other is frantically dedicated to seeing the entire project completed by 4:30 that very afternoon.

Consequently, observing that they have no sandpaper, the former is given to solemnly intoning nauseating homilies such as "Anything Worth Doing Is Worth Doing Well," before absently wandering out into the kitchen for a cup of Ovaltine and a jelly bun.

The other half, meanwhile, is grimly determined to scrape paint off the darned rocker, no matter what, and tackles the job with a nail file.

The more casually-inclined of the two will wander back periodically, while munching on his jelly bun, to deliver his considered opinion that the other is going about the project *all wrong*, running the obvious risk of being impaled on the pointy end of a nail file.

Of course, one is forever reading articles about a couple named Charlie and Mibbs who have a joint workshop in the basement where they hole up every night and have a splendid time tie-dyeing lamp shades.

If the truth were told, I'm certain that they loathe every minute of it, and as often as not spend the greater part of the evening smacking each other with sheets of wet batik.

November 22

"I can stay by myself," my daughter declared. "And for one dollar an hour, I'll even take care of 'It,' " she added, gesturing toward her brother, who retaliated by smashing her kneecap with a croquet mallet.

"If I leave you alone, there will be no eye gouging, hair pulling, or hitting below the belt. You will retire to neutral corners, refrain from spitting out of the upstairs windows, and there will be peace in the valley when I return or I'll belt you!"

The first time I left them alone, I carefully wrote down the telephone numbers of the police, ambulance, fire department, doctor, dentist, veterinarian, the Suicide Prevention Center, and Alcoholics Anonymous.

"Now, I'll be at the Bennetts," I concluded. "Call me if there's an emergency."

When I arrived at the Bennets' house ten minutes later, they informed me that the children had called three times, saying it was urgent. I raced to the telephone.

"Whatsthematter?" I shrieked.

"Can I have a Popsicle?" my son asked.

They called twelve times during the next four hours, imparting the vital information that we were all out of bread, that Archie Bunker said "damn" and that the bathroom light had burned out, and asking a variety of questions ranging from what is a cesarean section to what was for dinner tomorrow night.

"Look," I said to them the next day. "Call me for emergencies, not just to ask what Grandma's middle name is."

"What's an emergency?" my daughter asked.

"Blood, fire, explosion, rape, pillage—that sort of thing."

The next week I left them alone again. I had just arrived at the party when I received a phone call.

"Boy, what an explosion and fire!" my son began.

"What!?!"

"Yeah. I bet that Edith and Archie Bunker don't even have insurance!"

November 23

I remember Fred Allen. I remember Studebakers. I remember white washbowls with two faucets and two taps marked "H" and "C," when washing up involved whisking your hands rapidly between the two and having them alternately parboiled and frozen.

Fred Allen is dead. Studebakers are out of production. And last night I found myself alone in a strange bathroom, staring blankly at a washbowl with no faucets or taps, only a single chrome wheel.

I considered seeking assistance from my hostess who, presumably, had mastered the art of procuring water from a wheel. But, noticing the distinctive aroma of three dozen burned crab puffs, accompanied by the anguished wail "What do you mean, we're *out* of *ice*?!" I decided that my hostess had problems enough.

By resting my head in the washbowl and peering up, I discovered that there was an opening under the wheel for the water to flow through. A bit more assured, I stood up and pressed the center of the wheel gingerly with my index finger. Nothing.

Next I grasped the wheel firmly and pushed. Still nothing. Finally I attempted to turn it. In desperation I pulled the wheel, whereupon a torrent of scalding water dashed into the bowl and began ricocheting onto the bathroom mirror, the front of my dress, a box of facial tissues, and a paint-by-number picture of the Lord's Supper.

My hostess, possibly reasoning that we were her husband's friends and a shifty lot at best, had hidden all her bath towels, providing instead three tissue paper hand towels—featuring pictures of purple mice peering out of martini glasses—which disintegrated immediately upon contact with water.

Fortunately I have resourcefulness. I also have ingenuity. I have everything, in fact, but a cotton half-slip to replace the wet one I left in their tub after using it to wipe up the bathroom.

November 24

Winter driving is tricky.

The following are some typical winter driving problems and their logical solutions.

Problem: You have gone to the veterinarian to get the dog's worm medicine. When you return to the car, you find that the plow has been past and there is nine inches of snow behind each rear tire. You attempt to back out, but your wheels spin helplessly.

Solution: You must put something under the back

wheels to add necessary traction. An ingenious solution is to use your coat. An even more ingenious solution is to use someone else's coat.

Problem: You are twenty miles from home in a raging snowstorm, returning from the hairdresser who Mildred claimed was a magician, wearing a red woolen ski hat pulled down as far as it will go. The engine begins to go "Plick-plick-plick."

Solution: Pull into a gas station and knowledgeably explain to the attendant that you in all probability have an icy piston. After inspecting the car, he will reply that you have a Popsicle stick caught in the fan belt. He will snicker. Do not tip him.

November 25

I find that as we are approaching Thanksgiving, I have many things for which to be thankful. Having to cook a twenty-pound turkey is not among them.

Though normally they rank fairly high on my list of blessings, my children are no help at Thanksgiving, as they tend to hang about the kitchen all morning demanding freshly-squeezed orange juice and blueberry waffles when all I am able to concentrate on is wresting a bag of frozen giblets from a turkey that I had believed was completely thawed.

The distressing fact of the matter is that you simply cannot roast a turkey which still contains a cellophane bag full of liver. Even if you fully intend to throw the cellophane bag and everything in it down the garbage disposal, it still must come out of the turkey if you're to have any room for the stuffing.

The stuffing, of course, is another problem.

There is something infinitely pathetic about watching someone whose eyes are glued shut with last night's mascara standing over a hot cutting board at 8:30 A.M., chopping onions. You would think that at such moments any child with a shred of human decency would resist the temptation to bound around the kitchen, demanding to dissect the turkey's heart.

Once the children are breakfasting on hastily poured bowls of Rice Krispies, I reluctantly force down a sample of dressing, trying, usually unsuccessfully, to avoid the oysters.

"Is the stuffing good?" they demand.

"Super," I shudder, washing it down with a glass of prune juice.

"Gee, I wish we were having hamburgers instead."

December 1

For two children who can never seem to recall where they've left their shoes, my offspring have remarkable memories for personal injustices.

It isn't as if I haven't tried to be fair. Anyone who spends twenty minutes measuring the one cherry in a bowl of fruit cocktail with a micrometer, so that she can cut it into two exactly equal halves, can hardly be accused of playing favorites.

Over the years I have come to the sad realization that being a mother is just like being a Supreme Court justice, only the pay is worse.

It is all I can do to decide what to fix for dinner, without having to act as the final authority on who gets to open the can that it's in.

"We've had the electric can opener for four days, and I've never *once* gotten to use it," my daughter complained.

"So what?" countered her brother. "Mom let *you* dissect the turkey heart last week."

"When we were little, you were always the one who got to ride in the grocery cart."

"Yeah, but she let *you* take the dog's baby teeth to school for Show-and-Tell."

"Maybe so, but Mom always gave *you* the rubber bands from the morning paper."

"That's not because Mom loves me best. That's because whenever she gave you one, you ate it."

December 2

I don't know the practice in your school district, but where we live, approximately twenty days out of every year are given over to Professional Development Days.

As the teaching staff obviously cannot develop professionally while simultaneously grappling with square roots, iambic pentameter, and the principal exports of Uruguay, everyone under eighteen is afforded a holiday.

While children eventually adapt to prolonged lack of regimentation during their summer vacation, they are ill-equipped to deal with a sudden one-day break in routine.

As a public service, I would like to offer my children's list of "What to Do on Professional Development Day."

1. Get up at 8:00 A.M. and watch your mother do her Bend-and-Stretch. Ask her how she got those wiggly red lines in the backs of her knees.

2. Wash your hair.

3. Start a batch of cardamom cookies.

4. Have Mom drive you to the store to buy cardamom.

5. Vacuum your guinea pig.

6. Watch "As the World Turns" and make retching noises.

7. Wash your hair again.

8. Count the number of raisins in a box of Raisin Bran.

9. Hold a Kiss Rock Festival.

10. Make an Evil Potion of milk of magnesia, Hawaiian Punch, and Clearasil.

11. Try to get your brother to drink it.

12. Paint your shoes.

December 3

One of the distressing aspects of an otherwise festive season is the inevitable necessity of choosing a Christmas card.

Somehow I find that I must choose between the following types:

Nostalgia Cards: A typical nostalgia card features a two-hundred-year-old stone house with a wisp of smoke rising from the chimney. Nostalgia cards are based on the dubious premise that there was something essentially festive, even ennobling, about plucking a bullet-ridden goose while snowbound in an isolated cottage.

Symbolic Chic Cards: A typical symbolic chic card is white cardboard emblazoned with a stark sprig of holly embossed in fourteen-carat gold. The sentiment inside is a Spartan "Seasons Greetings" above a printed name, evoking the same good cheer as an announcement of a corporate merger.

Cutesy Cards: Cutesy cards invariably feature pictures of white mice wearing Santa Claus suits climbing out of empty martini glasses, reindeer with kegs of brandy around their necks, or three rabbits peering into a manger at the Christ Child, who bears a startling resemblance to a Chatty Cathy doll.

Folksy Cards: Folksy cards are preprinted with color photographs of the senders taken in July while standing in front of their twenty-foot sloop, 1978 Lincoln Continental, or a quaint little shop on the outskirts of Istanbul. These cards are especially depressing when received by a person who spent July driving a ten-year-old Dodge back and forth to a son's trombone lesson.

Old Masters Cards: An old masters card features a sloe-eyed Virgin Mary holding a chubby Jesus whose eyes have been printed off-center. The card, printed in old English script, reads "May the Peace of Jefuf live in your heartf."

December 9

I took my children to Chicago to visit my mother and all my relatives, an event, I fear, rather like casting swine before pearls.

"You can do your own packing," I said to my daughter. "But I don't want to see any green nail polish, bleached jeans, or sweatshirts that say 'I Like Being a Sex Object.' Don't you have anything with puffed sleeves and smocking?''

"I thought you wanted us to be ourselves," she complained.

"Of course not! Are you out of your mind?" I exclaimed. "And you," I said, turning to my son. "In Chicago you wear pajamas to bed, not your underwear. Here, take these," I added, handing him seven monogrammed handkerchiefs.

"What are these?" he asked.

"They're for blowing your nose."

"Cloth Kleenex!" he exclaimed. "What will they think of next?"

Early on departure day, we frantically distributed house keys, African Violets, and gerbils to semiwilling neighbors, arriving at the airport an hour early for our flight. My son decided to while-away the time by sitting between a pair of skis and a green two-suiter. I wouldn't have minded, but they happened to be on a luggage conveyor belt at the time. I plucked him off smartly as he went past.

"Why don't you go watch TV?" I suggested, a note of desperation creeping into my voice.

"What's on?"

"An award-winning drama called 'Arrival and Departure Times.' You'll love it," I assured them.

"Now for heaven's sake," I cautioned them as we finally boarded the plane, "watch your language at Grandma's house!"

"You mean we can't say %!&N or **$&?"

"*Especially* not **$&," I exclaimed. "By the way, what's that bulge in your pocket?"

"A gerbil," he admitted.

"Oh **$&" I sighed.

•   •   •

"I certainly hope they've corrected the basic structural fault that they discovered in these planes last month," my daughter remarked in the tone of voice one normally reserves for calling hogs, as we boarded the plane.

A blanket of silence fell over the entire economy class, followed by a rustle, as morning newspapers (whose owners realized might be final editions) slipped from nerveless fingers. Seventeen people ordered double martinis on the spot. Six others demanded that the stewardess baptize them.

"What do you know about basic structural faults?" I whispered to my daughter.

"Nothing," she grinned. "But I sure got them going, didn't I?"

The flight passed uneventfully, except for us each getting five lunches, thanks to an inexplicable lack of appetite among the other passengers.

Now, seeing them every day, a parent tends to forget how very much children can change during one year. We arrived at O'Hare Airport to find my mother anxiously peering through the arrival gate.

"Where are my babies?" she demanded, after giving me a decidedly perfunctory kiss on the cheek.

"Do you see those two enormous girls following me?" I asked.

"Yes."

"Well, the girl with the shorter hair is your grandson."

"Hi, Grandma," he said. "I'm hungry."

"You'll have to excuse him," I explained. "We had rather an exciting flight, and he hasn't eaten for two hours."

Being exposed to a large, urban metropolis like Chicago is an exhilarating experience for a child. Unfortunately, in a ninth-floor, one-bedroom apartment, two exhilarated children are approximately as welcome as a fungus infection. It becomes a question of keeping them occupied. My children solved the problem of potential boredom by jamming pins in the emergency-stop button on the elevator, throwing pennies down the incinerator, and telling each other dirty jokes over the intercom.

After this paled, they began rummaging through Mother's refrigerator.

"What's to eat?" my son asked.

"You can't eat now!" my mother exclaimed. "We're going out to dinner in a restaurant in an hour. If you eat now, you'll spoil your dinner."

"Mother!" I protested. "That's the whole idea!"

During the next four days, the highpoints for the children were the hot-fudge sundaes we had after touring the Natural History Museum, the foot-long hot-dogs we ate before going to the Science Museum, and the barbecued beefburgers we smuggled past the guard and ate while touring the aquarium.

"I want this trip to be something you'll never forget," my mother said to the children. "Chicago is just full of fascinating educational attractions. What else would you like to see?"

"The Playboy Club," suggested my son.

"How about the scene of the St. Valentine's Day Massacre?" my daughter offered.

"Look, if we visit one more tourist attraction, I'll burst," I complained. "Besides, we leave tomorrow. I have to pack."

"I sure hate to see you go," my mother said.

"Don't think of it as losing your grandchildren. Think of it as getting your refrigerator back."

December 12

A great deal has been written about the loss of the true meaning of Christmas. As an aid to those of you who are disgusted by crass commercialism, I offer the following step-by-step instructions on "How to Have an Old-Fashioned Christmas."

1. December 10—Buy a live goose. Call him Sylvester. Tie him to the water heater in the basement. Encourage the children to play with him and teach him tricks.

2. December 15—Choose a day when it's thirty degrees below zero to go out and cut your own Christmas tree. Don't cut the first tree you see. Tromp through the whole forest looking for a better one. *Then* come back and cut the first tree you saw.

3. December 16—String popcorn and cranberries to decorate the tree, using heavy thread and a very sharp needle. Try to bleed only on the cranberries, where it won't show.

4. December 17—Invite both of your entire families to spend the holidays with you. Even Uncle Frank, whom no one has mentioned since he voted for Roosevelt.

5. December 18—Give the milkman and the paperboy shiny dimes for Christmas. The look of wonder in their eyes will reflect their sincere intention of giving you truly unbelievable service during the coming year.

6. December 19—Organize a skating party on the river. Be careful not to trip over the raw sewage.

7. December 23—Kill Sylvester. Pluck him and make a pillow.

8. December 24—Turn off the furnace before you go to bed, ensuring that Christmas morning will find everyone blue with cold and unable to use the bathroom because the pipes are frozen solid.

9. December 25—Arise promptly at 5:00 A.M. Stuff the goose. Cook it in an iron stove with faulty dampers. Later, give each of the children a pair of too-large handknit mittens and an orange.

December 16

Call me a slave to tradition, but each year I insist upon having a real Christmas tree. The kind that gets sap all over your hands and drops long needles that clog up the vacuum cleaner.

To me there is nothing very festive about assembling a boxed Christmas tree. I know that they are fireproof, more perfect than nature, and a savings in the long run, but they don't *smell* like Christmas trees. It's the sap that smells. Of course, sap gets all over your hands and we're back where we started.

My family humors me in this harmless idiosyncrasy as one might a senile uncle who saves toothpaste caps. I'm not really bothering anyone, and my little fetish does provide lots of laughs:

"Your Christmas tree is all sticky."

"That's sap."

"What's 'sap'?"

"Ask my mother."

Humoring my hang-up doesn't include assisting with the purchase, however. After all, no one helps senile uncles look for toothpaste caps. As soon as little forests start sprouting around the shopping center, I whip on

my longjohns for another lonely quest. My system involves starting with the Boy Scouts ten miles away and
working back toward home, past the Women of the
Moose and the Baptist Church.

Last year the routing was similar, but the temperature
was zero when I set out. Six lots and two hours later, the
mercury had tumbled to ten below, and the only might-
do-in-a-pinch trees were three dollars a foot. My
eyelashes were frozen together by then, and I'd lost all
feeling in my left foot. Ending up at my last hope, the
Baptist Church, I had to decide finally whether to get a
twelve dollar Douglas fir that was tall enough but
shaped like a mushroom, or a gorgeous seven-foot
Scotch Pine that was twenty dollars. Impetuously, I
bought the Scotch Pine, wondering vaguely how I'd
serve the Christmas meatloaf.

By the time I got home, my family had evidently given
up hope of seeing me alive again and were getting ready
to go out to dinner.

"Well, I got one."

"Another sticky one?"

"That's sap."

"What's 'sap'?"

Ask your mother, she's one.

December 26

While a vast amount of literary effort and advertising promotion has been expended in extolling the

merriment of Christmas Eve and Christmas morning, very little, if anything, has ever been written about Christmas afternoon.

But, yes, Virginia, there is a Christmas afternoon. It exists as surely as does a second day of school, a fifty-first wedding anniversary, and the day after two glorious weeks in Acapulco.

December 27

Friday, December 14
My Dearest True Love:
Along with the orthodontist's bill for $75.50 and three Christmas cards from total strangers, I received your pear tree today. You shouldn't have. I mean, every time I look at it (which of necessity is fairly often, as it takes up half the living room), I think of you. Oh, yes, I almost forgot to mention the enchanting little Cornish hen perched on one branch. Absolutely charming. A little stringy, perhaps, but a welcome change from hamburger.

Saturday, December 15
My Dear True Love:
Gosh! Another pear tree. Another stringy Cornish hen, too. Have I ever mentioned how badly I need a new steam iron? Until our son builds a coop for the pigeons, I'm keeping them in the coat closet.

• • •

Sunday, December 16
Dear True Love:

We couldn't coax today's Cornish hen out of the tree; he just sits there on the top branch and throws pears at us. Thank heavens the coop is finished; you should see what those pigeons did to my hat. By the way, those three chickens you sent are terribly high-strung. They leaped out of the box, shrieked "Mon Dieu!" and ran under the sofa.

Tuesday, December 18
Dear T.L.:

I'm sorry that I didn't write yesterday, but since our son has lost interest in pigeons, I had to clean the coop myself. I was delighted with the five rings. I didn't know that there was such a thing as two-carat gold.

Wednesday, December 19
Hi:

We chopped today's tree into kindling, which so frightened the Cornish hen that he flew through the picture window. The geese have made themselves quite at home, so much so that they follow us around, nipping at our heels like puppies—big puppies! Big untrained puppies! I finally understand what is meant by the phrase "loose as a goose."

Thursday, December 20
My Dear True Love:

Today the post office delivered seven swans. They have been temporarily billeted in the bathtub, where they are unsuccessfully attempting to mate with the rubber duck.

Friday, December 21
Dear T.L.:

I was ecstatic today to be greeted by eight maids. Unfortunately they refused to deal with the mess that the birds have created. They insist on milking. In view of the fact that good help is so hard to come by, could you see your way clear to sending us a cow?

Saturday, December 22
My Dear Sir:

I was puzzled and dismayed today to receive nine members of British nobility, when what I really needed was a cow. When they aren't busy bounding over the furniture, they are engaging in an unseemly amount of slap and tickle with the maids, who are not remotely interested in milking anymore.

Monday, December 24
Sir:

Regarding your gifts of the past two days, the last thing I need is thirty-one additional houseguests. Especially since the bathtub is full of swans. Besides, I am not overly fond of bagpipes, believing in fact that the only good bagpipe is a dead bagpipe. It is impossible to concentrate on the morning paper with eleven pipers marching around the breakfast table, followed by twenty girls frugging to "Loch Lomond."

Tuesday, December 25
Now Hear This!

With the arrival today of twelve bongo players, there are now 140 people drumming, piping, dancing, leaping and not milking. Not to mention 184 birds (less the two we ate and the one that flew through the picture window), doing birdlike things such as picking lice out of their tails.

I am returning all forty golden rings. The engagement is *off*! Do you hear me? *Off!*

New Bestsellers from Berkley
The best in paperback reading

___**IMPERIAL NIGHTS** 04233-2—$2.50
Olivia O'Neill
___**THE LAST CONVERTIBLE** 04034-8—$2.50
Anton Myrer
___**LEAH'S JOURNEY** 04430-0—$2.50
Gloria Goldreich
___**THE LEGACY** 04183-2—$2.25
John Coyne, based on a story by Jimmy Sangster
___**MOMMIE DEAREST** 04444-0—$2.75
Christina Crawford
___**NIELSEN'S CHILDREN** 04111-5—$2.50
James Brady
___**NO BED OF ROSES** 04241-3—$2.50
Joan Fontaine
___**NURSE** 04220-0—$2.50
Peggy Anderson
___**PURSUIT** 04258-8—$2.50
Robert L. Fish
___**THE SIXTH COMMANDMENT** 04271-5—$2.75
Lawrence Sanders

Berkley Book Mailing Service
P.O. Box 690
Rockville Centre, NY 11570

Please send me the above titles. I am enclosing $_____
(Please add 50¢ per copy to cover postage and handling). Send check or
money order—no cash or C.O.D.'s. Allow three weeks for delivery.

NAME_____

ADDRESS_____

CITY_____STATE/ZIP_____

1 C

The Best of Berkley's Nonfiction

____AIR TIME: THE INSIDE STORY OF CBS
NEWS   04190-5—$2.95
Gary Paul Gates

____DOLLY   04221-9—$2.50
Alanna Nash

____FAT IS A FEMINIST ISSUE   04035-6—$2.25
Susie Orbach

____IT TAKES A LONG TIME TO BECOME
YOUNG   04121-2—$2.25
Garson Kanin

____NOBODY ASKED ME, BUT...THE WORLD
OF JIMMY CANNON   04100-X—$2.95
Ed. by Jack Cannon and Tom Cannon

____NURSE   04220-0—$2.50
Peggy Anderson

____THE POSSIBLE DREAM   03841-6—$2.25
Charles Paul Conn

____PURE AND SIMPLE   04167-0—$2.95
Marian Burros

____RECREATIONAL DRUGS   04142-5—$2.50
Lawrence A. Young, Linda G. Young,
Marjorie M. Klein, Donald M. Klein,
Dorianne Beyer

____REFLECTIONS WITHOUT MIRRORS
Louis Nizer   04637-0—$2.95

____A TIME FOR TRUTH   04185-9—$2.50
William E. Simon

Available at your local bookstore or return this form to:

B **Berkley Book Mailing Service**
P.O. Box 690
Rockville Centre, NY 11570

Please send me the above titles. I am enclosing $_____
(Please add 50¢ per copy to cover postage and handling). Send check or
money order—no cash or C.O.D.'s. Allow three weeks for delivery.

NAME_____

ADDRESS_____

CITY_____STATE/ZIP_____

2 b

P9-DGN-550

Praise for the novels of

JODI THOMAS

"One of my favorites."
—Debbie Macomber

"Packs a powerful emotional punch....
Highlights the author's talent for creating
genuinely real characters.... Exceptional."
—*Booklist*

"Jodi Thomas is a masterful storyteller. She grabs your
attention on the first page, captures your heart, and
then makes you sad when it is time to
bid her wonderful characters farewell."
—Catherine Anderson

"Fantastic... A keeper!... A beautiful story about
unexpected love. An exceptional storyteller, Thomas
has found the perfect venue for her talent, which is as
big—and as awe-inspiring—as Texas. Her emotionally
moving stories are the kind you want to go on forever."
—*RT Book Reviews*

"Jodi Thomas paints beautiful pictures with her words,
creates characters that are so real you feel as though
they're standing next to you, and she had a deliciously
wry sense of humor... Thoroughly recommend it."
—*The Book Smugglers*

"A fun read."
—*Fresh Fiction*

Also from Jodi Thomas and MIRA Books

The Secrets of Rosa Lee
Finding Mary Blaine

JODI THOMAS

The Widows *of* Wichita County

STAFFORD LIBRARY
10 Levinthal Run
P.O. Box 100
Stafford, CT 06075

MIRA®

If you purchased this book without a cover you should be aware
that this book is stolen property. It was reported as "unsold and
destroyed" to the publisher, and neither the author nor the
publisher has received any payment for this "stripped book."

MIRA®

Recycling programs
for this product may
not exist in your area.

ISBN-13: 978-0-7783-1256-7

THE WIDOWS OF WICHITA COUNTY

Copyright © 2003 by Jodi Koulmalats

All rights reserved. Except for use in any review, the reproduction or
utilization of this work in whole or in part in any form by any electronic,
mechanical or other means, now known or hereafter invented, including
xerography, photocopying and recording, or in any information storage or
retrieval system, is forbidden without the written permission of the publisher,
MIRA Books, 225 Duncan Mill Road, Don Mills, Ontario M3B 3K9, Canada.

This is a work of fiction. Names, characters, places and incidents are
either the product of the author's imagination or are used fictitiously, and
any resemblance to actual persons, living or dead, business establishments,
events or locales is entirely coincidental.

MIRA and the Star Colophon are trademarks used under license and registered
in Australia, New Zealand, Philippines, United States Patent and Trademark
Office and in other countries.

For questions and comments about the quality of this book please contact us at
Customer_eCare@Harlequin.ca.

www.MIRABooks.com

Printed in U.S.A.

A special thank you to...

My two coffee drinking buddies at the donut stop
who told me tales of the early oil days and set the
background for this story. Thanks Norman Dysart
and Bob Izzard. I love you both.

Thanks to a wonderful professor and nurse at
West Texas A&M University who spent
one rainy afternoon teaching me about burns.
Thanks, Debra Davenport.

To Jay Wilson, a friend and a pharmacist
who answered endless questions. Thanks Jay.

To Natalie Bright and the wonderful ladies of the
Desk and Derrick Club. Thanks for your support.

A special thanks to my cheerleaders in Houston
who've been with me from the first as I told stories of
books to come. Thanks TESA ladies.

To the Panhandle Plains Historical Museum and to
Cornette Library on the West Texas A&M University
campus. Thanks for giving me a home.

Stafford Library

Adopt-An-Author
Donated
2011

Prologue

The last day of August
Clifton Creek, Texas

Randi Howard pressed the fold in the marriage license with one long ruby-red fingernail and slipped it into her huge leather purse.

"Good luck with this one," the clerk said without smiling. "Sorry we misspelled your name and you had to come pick up another copy."

Randi waited for her to add, "see you again in a few years," or "I'll remember it's *i* next time around." But the clerk moved away without another word.

Suddenly in a hurry to leave the aging courthouse, Randi pivoted on the heels of her red boots, letting the fringe of her jacket fly. The place gave her the creeps; everything echoed off the scrubbed floors and pale marble.

"There won't be a next time," she whispered to herself as she patted the license hidden away in her purse. "I swear on my mother's grave—if she has one by now."

She hit the latch on the door at full speed, letting her long legs carry her straight into the wind and toward Jimmy's truck parked half a block down at the café. He would be her salvation this time. He would live with her long enough for the glue of marriage to stick. She would be thirty in two years and she planned to be married, not looking for husband number four. At best, Jimmy would make her happy. At least, he would stay around.

Which was more than she could say for the last two good old boys who had also swept her off the bar floor and into a wedding bed. By the time she'd changed the sheets, they were gone.

But Jimmy had promised to give it a good try. He owned his own trailer home outright. He had a good job and a rich uncle. No one in town had a bad word to say about him and, in the three months they had lived together, he had not hit her once. That, for Randi, was some kind of record.

She closed her eyes against the sting of the wind whirling dust devils across the West Texas parking lot. This time, if the marriage failed, she would have no one to blame but herself. Jimmy was solid and kind. He married her even after everyone in town tried to talk him out of it. He drank a little, but then she usually finished at least two beers by the time she spread on her makeup. And he loved her. At least she thought he did. He told her so once and once seemed enough.

Randi slowed as she passed the long windows of the town's only bank. Her image reflected back at her from the smoky glass. Wild red hair, too much eye liner for daylight, Western clothes cut tight to show off her endless legs and square shoulders. Randi smiled. She was a bar light beauty and she knew it.

A woman inside the bank stepped to the window. For a moment, their images blended and both looked through the other. They stood, the smoky glass separating them, seeing only themselves.

Randi blinked, almost crying out as the fine young woman's expensive clothes and regal carriage mingled with her own frame. She wore breeding and grace for the first time in her life. For one instant, she saw another Randi, one that might have been or maybe one that might yet be. She saw a lady, not a throw away cowgirl who had to fight sometimes just for the right to keep breathing.

Finally, Randi raised her gaze to the beautiful woman's huge dark eyes.

Truth delivered a solid kick in her gut.

The lovely woman in the expensive clothes had looked at Randi and must have seen the same blending of images. She saw what she might become if she continued to live in Clifton Creek. Only unlike Randi's pleasure, the lady appeared horrified.

Unable to stare a second longer Randi ran toward the café, wiping tears she blamed on the dust away from her cheek. "What's wrong with me?" she swore under her breath. "I'm married to Jimmy Howard now. I'm going to be happy. Ain't no sense in wanting what you can't have."

She kicked at a dandelion fighting its way through the crack in the sidewalk. "I should have been born a plant. I wouldn't care if I was a flower or a weed. Plants don't care if they're wanted or loved, they just grab ahold of the earth and grow."

Opening the café door Randi straightened to her full height. Without caring that folks watched, she ran to Jimmy, straddled him like he was a kitchen chair and kissed him long and hard.

She would survive in this town even if she had to grow through the cracks in the sidewalk. Nothing better was coming along. Tired of wandering without a compass, she planned to take root right here in Clifton Creek.

* * *

Half a block down the street Anna Montano stepped out of the bank and walked toward a waiting Range Rover. Even her tailored clothes and grace of movement could not hide the doubt coursing through her body as she regarded her new hometown.

Clifton Creek, Texas, had to be the ugliest place on God's planet. The very air smelled of cow manure. She had left a beautiful country villa in Italy surrounded by rolling land rich in color and entered a world painted only in brown hues. A Coming Soon Wal-Mart sign was the most colorful thing in this place named after a creek that had dried up years ago.

Her new husband had described his home in Texas as a place with wide-open spaces and an endless sky. But he forgot to add that the countryside and air were dusted in dirt so thick Anna could not tell where the land ended and the sky began.

As if the flat brown country was not ugly enough, the people of this place had dotted the landscape with monstrous drilling rigs for oil production. She had not seen Davis's ranch yet, but the farther she got from the airport the more homesick she felt. At twenty-one she suddenly was not ready for the changes she had thought were so romantic only days ago. The whirlwind courtship, the huge wedding, all the gifts and well-wishers had been replaced with silence, and she felt more alone than she ever had in her life with her new husband sitting only a few feet away.

"Clifton Creek," she whispered trying to become familiar with the words. But they felt foreign on her tongue, as alien as everything around her.

She smiled slightly, her mood shifting for a moment when she remembered something her mother said once.

"When all are strangers around you, you are the one in the wrong place. You are the foreigner."

Anna had wanted to come to America slowly, by boat, with the horses Davis had brought from her father's ranch. But Carlo, her brother, had traveled with the fine animals while Anna had flown alone with her new husband. Rocketed into a world she did not understand beside a man she hardly knew.

The change had been too abrupt. She felt like a freshwater fish splashing down in the ocean and expected to survive. She could not breathe.

Anna slipped into the car and reached for her husband's hand, but he only brushed her fingers away as he turned a page of the local paper. "Don't worry." He gave her a quick glance. "You'll get used to it here. Before long you'll love it. This place settles in your blood."

Anna wanted to scream. No, this place would never be a part of her. When she had agreed to marry Davis, she thought she would be flying away to freedom. She had no idea freedom would look this desolate.

Old-timers say that in the oil fields trouble rides the wind, but death explodes in the silence of routine.

The chrome streetlights rocked with the rhythm of the dawn wind as Meredith Allen crossed Main and headed toward Clifton Creek's only elementary school. She was an hour early. She always arrived an hour early. It had become her routine over the dozen years she had taught school.

Meredith told herself she needed to be up and out of the way to allow her husband, Kevin, to dress without them constantly bumping into one another in the bedroom and bath of their tiny house. She refused to admit her leaving early might be because they had little to say to one another in the morning. After a day apart, they would talk of the news and who they saw or the changes in the weather. But at dawn, conversation had somehow grown as stale as morning breath. She told herself it was to be expected. After all, they had grown up together, and after a decade of marriage they were bound to run out of things to say from time to time.

Parking in the empty school lot, Meredith stared through the cracked windshield of her old Mustang. The sunlight sparkled off the grain silos just beyond the Wal-Mart store and the city limits sign. When she had been a child her father told her the silos were the castle of an evil king who had been forever banned from Clifton Creek.

Meredith smiled. He also told her the oil rigs were dancing to a tune they heard deep in the earth. The huge rigs kept dipping to the beat, trying to pull the melody to the surface so that all could hear.

Her father had been a dreamer. The rigs were no more than ugly mosquitoes, sucking the earth's blood. But that blood had built the town and had kept it alive when many other small communities in West Texas had dried up like wild gourds and blown away. Clifton Creek had survived amid the rocky soil just as she had. This was not just her hometown, this place was a part of her. She belonged here, as native as the cottonwoods and coyotes.

Meredith collected her school bag and purse then climbed out of the Mustang, excited as always. She would have plenty of time to get everything organized before the first student arrived. Her house might be a mess— sometimes her life seemed disjointed—but in her class-room everything had its place. There, a magic happened that only teachers understood.

If her existence were an art gallery, teaching would be shown with colorful brush strokes and her home with careful line-drawn prints.

Not that she hated home. Home was just home and Kevin just Kevin. She could never hate her small town or him; they were both as much a part of her as bone or blood.

At first Kevin had told her how lucky she was to be his girlfriend, and then his wife; as though she needed reminding from time to time. Lately the words had changed; now she should count herself fortunate if he stayed around. As if there were other places he might go. Meredith would just laugh and remind him they belonged here, together. They always had, they always would.

As she walked to the school building she wondered what he was thinking, for he had been moody for weeks. The only blessing she counted each day was the twenty-three smiles looking up at her inside the sanctuary of her second-grade classroom. Kevin would work through his melancholy state, he always did. In the meantime, she had the children.

She waved as Helena Whitworth passed by in her long white Buick, driving toward downtown. The older woman looked every inch the queen in her small kingdom of Clifton Creek.

Helena Whitworth did not wave back. In fact, she didn't even notice Meredith or the grade school. With the precision of a general about to go into battle, Helena organized her thoughts, rehearsed her orders and prepared her defense on several fronts.

She had dreaded this day all week. Talking to the city council about increasing the budget would be not only boring, but time-consuming. She needed her wits sharp and alert. Her husband, J.D., had already made her late by joking about what he would like to do this Thanksgiving instead of going over to one of her daughters' homes and being assaulted by grandchildren. He told Helena over eggs Benedict that he planned to take a weed whacker instead of a cane this year. Maybe that would keep the little devils away.

For the hundredth time, Helena wished she had married J.D. first, or even second. Then, maybe they would have been young enough to have children together. Everyone in Clifton Creek thought of him as The Colonel, a hard, career Marine, who married the richest widow in town. But J.D. had taught her to laugh and to love. Despite all her duties and projects, J.D. was her core, the center that made everything else worthwhile.

Helena patted the wheel of her Buick as though the horsepower would respond to her touch. If she planned to get anything accomplished in the council meeting today, she had better stop thinking of J.D. and his jokes and start concentrating on what she planned to say about adding roadside parks at both ends of town.

Another year, maybe two, and she would turn loose her civic responsibilities and travel with J.D. They would go to places she did not know how to pronounce, eat food she had never heard of, and make love like they were still in their fifties.

For the past year J.D. had tried his best to get her to reduce her workload, but he did not understand. Helena needed work like she needed air. She was a workhorse, loving the challenge of each day. She had not slowed down in the forty years of running her own business and today was not the time to even start thinking about it. Maybe tomorrow she would watch the birds a little longer, or take a walk with him hand in hand. Maybe tomorrow there would be more time.

Helena forced her thoughts back to the problems of the day. The meeting should be over by noon. She could still do the final buying for the holiday season if she ate lunch with her secretary in their office above her store. *Helena's Choice* had not become a quality dress shop by neglecting details. The last of the Christmas orders needed to be placed, and soon.

For almost forty years, she had a motto; buy for

Christmas before the first frost and for summer before the trees bud. Helena prided herself on being a woman who lived by timetables. With practiced diligence everything in her life had an order to it. The clock, the calendar, the seasons measured out her days in predictable patterns. And the patterns brought a peace to her aging. These were all things she could count on just as surely as she always counted on J.D.

By the time she pulled into the lot between the courthouse and the post office, Helena felt the weather changing, along with her mood. The day would be long and tedious. It would probably be after dark before she got back to her home that J.D. laughingly called Pigeon Run. There would be no twilight time for them this evening.

One of the Montano Ranch pickups had parked sideways in the lot, and the horse trailer it pulled completely blocked her reserved spot. Helena waited, irritated but not surprised. Ranchers in these parts thought the wide-open spaces extended into town. She had seen them park loaded cattle trucks in the center of Main Street while they ran in for an hour-long cup of coffee.

Helena watched as Davis Montano's young Italian wife hugged her mail and ran for her pickup. Helena could not help but wonder where the stylish woman bought her clothes. For once, the older woman had no idea. All she knew was that Anna Montano did not buy them at Helena's Choice, and they certainly had not come from one of the local discount stores.

"Sorry," Anna Montano shouted, jumping into her truck. "I—I was just picking up the mail."

Anna did not expect the older woman to respond. Most of the people in this town acted as if they could not quite see her, even when she bothered to speak to them. In their eyes she was an outsider and therefore not a real person. The five years she had lived in Clifton Creek might as well have been a month to them.

Anna watched the thin, well-dressed woman park her Buick and hurry into the courthouse. "Helena Whitworth," Anna said aloud as if her own voice could somehow ease her loneliness.

"Hello, Helena," Anna added as she started the truck. She had long ago accepted the fact that these Texans were not being rude, just unobservant. If she had been from New York, or L.A. they might have passed the time of day, but Anna was from Europe and, for most of them, that might as well be the moon.

Anna gripped the three letters from Italy lying beside her. The first year she had come to Texas as a bride, she found several letters from her family unopened and crushed in the floorboards of the ranch trucks. Unsure of what to say to her husband, she solved the problem by getting a post office box. Whenever she made a trip to town she stopped by, knowing her letters would be waiting. If her husband Davis noticed, he never commented.

That small inconsiderate act made her think about leaving him and going back home where she knew she belonged. But she hesitated with indecision in the same halting way that she stuttered in speech. No action was less frightening than action. It seemed every time she acted on impulse or emotion, she had chosen the wrong path. She always had to remind herself to think before she acted, just as she had to think before she spoke. It was her bad luck that her husband was a man deeply involved in his own agenda and who had little time or interest in her problems.

If she had told her family about her thoughts of leaving Davis because he did not deliver her mail, they would have said she was a pampered fool. They would have suggested she stay and grow to love him while learning to overlook his flaws. After five years, Anna sometimes felt as if all her energy had been spent on swimming through the rocky shoals of her marriage. If she did not act, and soon, it would be only a matter of time before she drowned.

Driving past the five buildings that framed the college grounds, Anna took a deep breath and tried to convince herself one more time that everything was all right. She was letting her thoughts run away with her. But she was no longer the schoolgirl Davis brought home to Clifton Creek.

This part of town always welcomed her with its large trees and neatly trimmed grounds. Davis had told her the locals started the college when one of Clifton Creek's first settlers donated his huge home. For years the entire teachers college had operated out of the one building. Dorms, a gym, other classrooms designed in the same aging brick structure, had grown up around the old home.

Anna thought the campus was the only place for miles that anyone might call pretty. She would like to put the area on canvas, a view peeping through the colors of fall to the hundred-year-old home that must have been a mansion in its time.

She slowed. Maybe she would paint it in the violets of sunset, if she could catch the twilight just right. Here, its beauty tiptoed quickly, never overwhelming as it had back home. She would have to work hard to catch the uniqueness of the mansion on canvas.

As Anna passed, a few students hurried from their cars to their early classes, paying little more attention to the traffic than the squirrels did. She noticed a long-legged woman dressed in Western clothes crawl out of a Dumpster with a box in each hand.

Anna did not need to hear the woman's words. The look of someone swearing was the same in any language. Anna turned away, not wanting to be a part of another's troubles.

"Damn, damn and double damn," Randi Howard mumbled as she tossed the boxes in the back of her Jeep. She'd fought like a warrior inside that Dumpster to claim the boxes and both of them smelled like cheap whiskey and hot sauce.

Any clothes she packed in them would reek of the same, but at least she would be seeing this town in her rearview mirror. She thought briefly of packing all her junk in trash bags, but somehow boxes seemed more dignified. She should have invested in some of those fine packing boxes sold by moving companies. As many times as she had moved over the years, she would have worn the boxes out.

Randi climbed into her Jeep and headed back to the trailer park. The sky clouded up as if it might rain, but she planned to be long gone before she got caught in a storm.

She waved as she passed Frankie's Bar thinking of the good times and the bad times she had had there, and wondered about the times she had forgotten to remember the next morning.

She thought of the old adage that said we only regret the things we didn't do. Randi knew it wasn't true. The possibility of regret usually fired her into action. She recalled how she could not wait to get a tattoo on her ankle so she could talk about how sorry she was for doing such a foolish thing. The remorse had been so complete she had added a butterfly to her butt.

When Randi drove by the Y she noticed Crystal Howard jogging around the track on the roof. In days past Randi might have honked, or yelled, but lately she seldom talked to Crystal. Even though they were married to kin, they didn't travel in the same circles anymore.

There had been a time when Frankie's Bar didn't come to life each night until Randi and Crystal stepped through the door. Most evenings they wouldn't have to buy a single drink.

But that was before Crystal had married Shelby Howard, an old oilman with a huge house just outside of town and the dozen oil wells pumping nothing but money. A few weeks later Randi had married his nephew, Jimmy, settling for the younger, poorer Howard. He'd been a good husband and, for a while, a good lover, but like everything else in Randi's life, she figured it was time to run before he yelled, "Last call."

The thought of starting over at thirty-three was frightening and she wasn't getting any younger. It was time she left Jimmy to follow her dreams.

That was one thing Randi decided she was proud of—no man had ever left her. She'd never given them the chance. When Jimmy got home tonight, he'd wonder where she was for a while or, more likely, where his supper was. Then he'd check the closet and notice she'd moved on.

She doubted he'd even try to find her and knew he wouldn't take off work to come after her. In a few years, if they crossed paths, they'd remember the good times and laugh. It hadn't been a bad marriage, just one that had ended, as everything does. Seems like most folks thought their relationships were going either forward or backward. Randi felt hers and Jimmy's had just got stuck in neutral. They had some good times. They had some bad times. Now was just the goodbye time.

Randi glanced in her rearview mirror at Crystal. She would have liked to have said goodbye, but that would just complicate things, and Randi had to get busy and untangle her life.

Crystal Howard watched the familiar red Jeep turn into the trailer park gate as she circled the west end of the running track. She lifted her hand to wave, then reconsidered. It was almost eight o'clock. Randi must be running late for work. If Crystal had caught her attention and she had backed up to talk, even for a few minutes, there would be trouble with her boss at the plant.

Slowing to a walk, Crystal began her cool down. Randi would only have told Crystal how lucky she was, no longer having to punch a time clock. Crystal would agree, letting Randi believe that at least one of them was living the dream of marrying rich. Randi didn't need to know about the pain of the cosmetic surgeries, or the two-hour workout each morning, or the overwhelming feeling of living in a world where she didn't belong.

Crystal grabbed her water bottle and sat down on the club's only lawn chair. She told herself that Shelby made her life bearable in this town. Shelby would pick her up and dance around the room with her, yelling that he had the prettiest girl in town. Then, she would forget about the surgeries and the workouts.

He might be thirty years older than she was, but he knew how to make her feel special. He told her once he didn't care about all the other men she had in her life just as long as he was the last.

A breeze cooled the thin layer of sweat on her skin.

Crystal shivered. She would be glad when this day was over. There was an uneasiness about it. Shelby would laugh at her if she mentioned her feelings, but she sensed calamity rumbling in with the upcoming storm.

In the early oil boom days of Clifton Creek, Texas, a bell was erected on the courthouse porch. When an accident happened in the oil fields the bell sounded and, within minutes, was echoed by churches and schools. Silently, the children would pack their books and head home...past the clanging...past men rushing to help.

They did not need to be told. They knew. Someone's father, someone's husband, someone's son was dead amid the man-made forest of rigs.

October 11
9:45 a.m.
Montano Ranch

Anna Montano cleared away the breakfast dishes and poured herself the last of the coffee. She collected the letters she had picked up a few hours before and relaxed, finally having time to read. From her perch on a kitchen bar stool she could see all of what Davis called "the company space" in their home. The great room with its wide entry area at the front door and ten-foot fireplace along the north wall. An open dining room filled with an oversize table and ornate chairs, never used except when Davis paid the bills. And the breakfast nook, almost covered over in plants, where she ate most of her meals, alone.

Carlo's familiar honk rattled the morning calm. In the five years they had been in America, Carlo had become more and more Davis's foreman and less her brother. She had grown used to him walking past her to speak to Davis, or inviting her husband to go somewhere without including her.

Anna heard Davis storm from his office, hurry down the hall, and bolt out the front door. She knew by now he would not bother to look in her direction, or say goodbye. She was no more visible to her husband and brother than a piece of the furniture. He did not bother to inform her why he had returned to the house after leaving almost an hour before. She had not bothered to ask.

She watched as Shelby Howard's truck plowed down the road toward the oil rig he was building on their land. She had only met the old oilman once, but he drove like he owned the land he leased. Another car followed in his dust, but Anna could not see the driver. From bits of conversations she had heard Davis having over the phone, Anna knew they needed more money to drill deeper for oil. She guessed the men were having a meeting this morning on the site.

She finished her cup of coffee, enjoying the quiet of the house once more. The sun had been dancing in and out of clouds all morning, making it impossible to trust the light in the back room—the only room in the house she dared to call hers.

Soon after she had arrived as Davis's bride, she began to paint again just as she always had during her lonely childhood. Between the horses and her painting, Anna continued to pass the hours.

Anna watched the horses in the north corral for a while before climbing off the bar stool and washing her coffee cup. When she turned to put away the cup a sound, like a hundred rifles firing at once, thundered through the house, shaking the walls with fury.

By the time the cup had shattered on the tile floor, Anna was at a full run toward the door. Nothing in nature could have made such a sound.

She fought with the latch on the heavy front door, her heart pounding in her throat. When the door finally swung open, yelling came from the barn and bunkhouse.

Men raced toward trucks and pickups, shouting at one another to hurry.

Anna held her breath, watching them, trying to figure out what had happened. The very air seemed charged with panic. Then she saw it. Black smoke billowed from the oil rig site that earlier had been no more than a dot along the horizon.

Carlo's pickup sprayed gravel as it swung around the drive. "Stay here!" he yelled at her.

Anna stared at the smoke blackening the white-clouded sky, like ink spilling onto a linen tablecloth. "Where is Davis?" she whispered as Carlo raced away. He did not bother with the dirt road that ribboned toward the site. He bobbed across the open pasture directly toward the rising fury.

Anna huddled on the first step of the porch and watched the flames dance in the smoke as every hand on the ranch rushed to the fire. She did not need an answer to her question. She knew Davis must be there, somewhere in that smoke. Somewhere near the fire.

In her mind she painted the scene, closing her thoughts away to the tragedy unfolding before her eyes.

10:24 a.m.
Clifton Creek Courthouse

Helena Whitworth stared out the second-floor window of the Clifton Creek courthouse conference room, watching the Texas wind chase autumn into winter. She had seen pictures of places in New England where fall blanketed the landscape with brilliant hues and piled color in vibrant heaps like haystacks on an artist's palette. But here, as the leaves began to turn, gusts ripped them from their branches and sent them northeast toward Oklahoma before the metamorphosis of color was given a chance to brighten the gray landscape.

Clifton Creek was rich in oil and cattle and sunny days, but sometimes, when the scattered patches of green dulled to brown, she felt washed out all the way to her soul.

The town of six thousand reminded her of a mesquite tree spreading out over the dry land, offering little in comfort or beauty. Even the streets were drawn out like points on a compass, north to south, east to west. No curves, no variance and no tolerance for change. She had lived here all her life, sixty-three years so far, and she always dreaded autumn.

Slowly, Helena straightened bony shoulders beneath her tailored suit and faced the rest of the city council members. "Gentlemen, it may be years, maybe even beyond our lifetimes, before we see the importance of building even a few small parks. But, mark my words, we will see it."

Not one man dared argue. They could have been made of the same mahogany as the bookshelves lining three of the walls. To say Helena Whitworth was a thorn in their sides was as understated as calling skin cancer a blemish.

"J.D. and I talked it over." She softened her blow by including her husband so the members would not look on her idea as simply a woman's way of thinking. "And we've come up with a plan...."

"Mrs. Whitworth," a plump woman, with a hair bun the size of a cow patty, whispered from the open doorway, "I hate to interrupt, but you have a call."

"Not now, Mary. Please take a message." Helena unfolded a chart, dismissing her assistant without another glance.

"No, Helena." Determination hardened Mary's normally soft voice. "It's the hospital. Something about J.D."

Helena placed the chart on the huge table, moved through the doorway and into the reception room before Mary's voice settled in the air. In the almost forty years she had been in Helena's employment, Mary had called her boss by her first name only twice.

As Mary handed Helena the phone, the two women's stares locked. The men in the adjacent room would have been surprised at the sympathy in the secretary's gaze and at the fear in Helena's.

"Hello?" She hugged the receiver with both hands. "Yes, this is Mrs. Whitworth."

A long pause followed. No questions. No denial of information. No cries. "I understand." She forced her voice to steady. Years in business served her well. Emotions were a luxury she could not afford to wear. "I'll be right there."

Helena's shoulders were rod straight now, as if her jacket were still on the hanger. Her voice brittled with forced calmness, for she knew full well the men labored to listen from just beyond the door. They couldn't see her grip Mary's hand. They heard no cry as her lips whitened with strain.

"There's been an accident on the oil rig J.D. and Shelby Howard are investing in. The nurse said five men were badly burned. Some died before the crew got them to the hospital."

"Five?"

Helena nodded once.

"J.D.?" Mary whispered.

"One man's burned too badly to identify, but he's still alive." Helena shook her head. "The odds are not with us."

Mary cried in tiny little gulps that sounded like hiccups. Helena opened her arms to her employee, her friend. Helena had buried two husbands already. Mary had sobbed each time. But, for Helena, there was too much to do, too much to think about for tears.

She handed Mary a tissue. "Would you go to my house and tell the girls, when they arrive, to stay put until I get back to you? I know as soon as they hear, they'll come by, and I don't want them laying siege on the hospital with all their children in tow. Tell them I need them at my house to answer calls. I'll phone as soon as I know something."

"They love J.D. like he's their father," Mary lied, as always, trying to be kind.

Helena pulled her keys from her purse and smiled, thinking J.D. hated her forty-year-old twin daughters only slightly less than he hated bird poachers. If he were burned and near death, Paula and Patricia were the last two he would want at his bedside.

"He's got to be the one alive," Mary mumbled and blew her nose. "He didn't survive thirty years in the Marines to come home and die in an accident. Three Purple Hearts prove he's too tough for that."

"Before you go, inform the men inside that the meeting is over." Without another word, Helena turned and marched down the hallway, her steps echoing like a steady heartbeat off the drab walls lined with colorless pictures and maps.

She was not a woman to make a charade of being dainty or falsely feminine, but she would not wear grief lightly for a third time in her life.

"Be alive," she ordered in more than a whisper. "Be alive when I get there."

She hurried through the deserted courthouse. The

alarm bell from years past hung in a glass case reserved for memorabilia. "Not today," Helena said as she remembered her childhood during the oil boom. "I'll hear no bell today. Not for my J.D."

In a town marinated in secrets, hinted at but never told, Meredith Allen played Alice, innocently lost in Wonderland. At thirty-four, she still wore her hair long with a ribbon and faced life as if all she saw made sense.

Her path would not have been so tragic if she had wandered blind, but she knew...she knew and she still pretended.

When pulled from the refuge of teaching her second-grade class to report to the office, Meredith saw a lie in the principal's eyes. Something he refused to say. Something he could not reveal as he told her she was needed at the hospital. Kevin had been involved in an oil rig accident.

She asked no questions as they walked back to her classroom, brightly decorated in a papier-mâché autumn. Principal Pickett offered to read the students a story while Meredith gathered her things and organized her desk, putting markers in order and papers in line. She was in no hurry. The lie in what he had not said could wait.

Meredith compiled lies, organizing them, ranking

each, but never confronting any. Her father had been the first master of the craft. Her first memories of Christmas echoed with stories and half truths. "Things will be better next year." "This is just as good as what you wanted." He kept up the falsehoods until finally he told his last, "Don't worry, princess, I'm not going to die and leave you."

As Meredith left the school, she thought of how Kevin had fallen right into the shoes of her father with his lies. Only last week he had sworn he no longer left the bank except to eat lunch. He must have lied, for oil rigs did not spring up over cafés. He was probably still leaving the office every chance he got, still staying away too long. His boss would be furious if Kevin lost hours of work or was hurt bad enough to have to take sick days. He might even be fired.

Ten minutes later, Meredith parked in front of the twenty-bed hospital, straightened her sweater appliquéd with the alphabet and lifted her head, carefully erasing all anger from her face.

County Memorial Hospital stood exactly as it had since the early '70s when Meredith had played on the grass out front while her father died inside. The trees had grown larger. A slice of lawn had been paved over in the '80s to allow for three handicap parking spaces. The eaves, built without any thought of architectural style, now sported aluminum siding and gutters. All else, even the putty-colored door frames, remained the same. Twenty beds available for a town that had never needed ten.

As a young girl, she had tried to imagine a big city hospital where people rushed about shouting orders, and groups huddled in corners speaking in foreign tongues. The busiest night at Memorial had probably been three years prior when the Miller triplets were born. Memorial was not much of a hospital. Even the name, Wichita

County Memorial Hospital, that had once been lettered across the front had been shortened to simply County Memorial. It was mostly where the people of Clifton Creek came to give birth and die. If anyone needed surgery or faced a long stay, they drove the hour to Wichita Falls.

Meredith slammed her aging blue Mustang's door three times before it stayed closed. Kevin had promised to fix it a month ago. But he had not, just as he had not done a hundred other things. Or was it a thousand by now? Things had been piling up since they started dating at sixteen and married five years later.

It must be at least a thousand, she thought: the car door, the front lock, the garbage disposal…their marriage. Not that their marriage was crumbling, only cracked, Meredith decided. She had no doubt they both still loved one another. But sometimes, it felt uneven, like a table with one short leg, never in danger of falling, but irritating all the same.

Meredith fought the wind as she hurried into the emergency entrance. She glanced back at the bank of dark, boiling clouds forming to the north. The storm was moving in quickly. She should be in reading circle, not standing in a tiny foyer with the smell of bleach and antiseptic death thickening the air around her.

A swirl of dried leaves charged the automatic door as it closed behind her. She arranged her sweater once more and touched the ribbon that held her natural curly auburn hair away from her face.

Shaking her head, she tried to figure out what Kevin had managed to do now. With all his sports activities and weekend drinking, the hospital was a familiar place. As a junior officer at the bank, he had no business being out at an oil rig. If he had ruined another suit, she would say something this time.

Last summer, she had sat quietly as Kevin told his latest adventure to his friends. He had been looking over land near the south fork of the Red River when an old football buddy begged him to catch one more long pass.

In the end, the buddy got his loan from the bank, and Meredith used half her paycheck for stitches across Kevin's forehead and the other half to replace the three-piece suit he used as "game clothes."

I'm already working two jobs to keep us out of bankruptcy, she reasoned. Every year Kevin found more football buddies who remembered the great games over beer, and every year he found another job after he fumbled.

Amid it all, he somehow managed to remind her of how she had been the lucky one to catch him. Right now she did not feel lucky. She felt frightened and tired to the bone of worrying about money…and guilty for even thinking about it when the only man she had ever loved might be hurt.

"Morning, Mrs. Allen." A candy striper greeted Meredith where three short hallways merged. The center passage doorway had been closed and a sign, No Unauthorized Personnel, taped across the seam.

The girl had that do-you-remember-me? look in her eyes.

"Good morning, Kimberly." Meredith forced a smile. Kimberly had not changed in ten years. She had been a timid second-grader who grew into a hesitant woman. Her age and bust size were well beyond her youthful uniform, but the girl's insecurity clung to one more year of childhood.

"I'm looking for my husband." When Kimberly did not answer, Meredith added, "Kevin Allen."

Meredith glanced at the reception desk but, as usual, it was deserted. Paperwork was usually handled at the

nurses' station, or in an emergency room while waiting
for one of the town's three doctors.

"This way." Kimberly hurried down the hallway
marked with a number 3 above the entrance. Her head
low. Her hair curtained her face.

"Has Kevin been admitted?" Meredith hoped not.
They could not afford a hospital stay. If he was laid up,
she would take a few days of emergency leave and take
care of him. Lately, everything in her life boiled down
to how to save money, nothing more.

Kimberly did not answer.

"Has he seen the doctor yet?" With the center doors
closed maybe the doctors were busy with a birth or a car
wreck, and had not had time to get to him yet. "Were
there others hurt in the rig accident?"

The timid girl seemed to have gone deaf as well as
mute.

Meredith stopped her with a touch. "What is it?" The
thought that Kevin might be behind the No Unauthorized
Personnel sign worried its way into her thoughts.

Kimberly shook her head. "I don't know nothing. I was
just told to ask the widows to wait in the break room."

"Widows," Meredith whispered.

Kimberly shoved open a door at the end of the third
hallway and waited for Meredith to step inside a room
lined with vending machines.

The blood in Meredith's head sought gravity, leaving
her brain suddenly light and airy. She felt nothing, absolutely nothing, as she peered into the cavelike room at
the other women who, with one word, had become her
clan, her tribe. Widows.

Black mascara tears trailed down Crystal Howard's tanned face as she stepped into the break room. She looked around with a watery gaze. In a town the size of Clifton Creek, everyone knew everyone. They might never have spoken, but Crystal had seen pictures in the paper, or passed them in a store, or stood behind them in line at the bank. Strangers were people with out-of-state license plates, the women before her were home folks.

"Shelby's been in an accident!" Crystal said to no one in particular. She ran a thumb beneath the stretchy material of her watermelon-colored body suit that fit her curves like a second skin and tried to pull the garment lower over her hips. "He may be dead already, and they're not telling me. I've a right to know. I'm his wife."

"We understand." A tall, silver-haired woman's low voice seemed to fill every inch of the room. "Our husbands were also in the accident. We're all waiting to hear something from the doctors."

"Only one survived," added a woman a few years older than Crystal. "I'm Meredith Allen, Kevin's wife, and this is Helena Whitworth. J. D. Whitworth and my Kevin were at the oil rig when it exploded."

When Crystal just stared the woman continued, "Helen's husband, J.D., planned to invest in the rig. For some reason, my Kevin went along for the ride this morning."

Crystal looked down at Meredith's offered hand. People in Clifton Creek were never friendly to her when Shelby wasn't around. She knew what they said about her, marrying a man thirty years her senior. She'd been a waitress with nothing to her name, and he was a rich engineer, newly widowed. No one would believe they married for love even if Shelby had been willing to shout it from the courthouse roof.

Crystal took the hand. Meredith Allen did not look like the type to listen to gossip, much less spread it. She probably hadn't heard any of the colorful stories about her and Shelby. Crystal found it hard to imagine this woman walking into Frankie's Bar, wearing an ABC sweater, and sitting down to have a drink.

"I'm Mrs. Shelby Howard," Crystal said, daring anyone to comment. She'd been married five years, had her hair bleached blonde at a fancy salon and bought her clothes in Dallas. She had endured three surgeries to mold her body to perfection, but she still felt like street trash. She was prepared to fight every time she met someone new.

"I know your husband." The silver-haired lady stepped forward. "Though he was a few years younger, I went to school with him. He's friends with my husband, J.D. I'm Helena Whitworth."

Crystal tried to pull her jersey jacket closed across her workout clothes. She suddenly wished she'd had time to change. The gym fashion didn't belong here. She swiped a palm across her cheek and stared at the makeup on her hand. Not only was she dressed improperly, if she didn't stop crying she would be without makeup. Shelby was sure to yell at her.

A third woman, Crystal hadn't noticed before, moved away from the shadows. She was tall, but then everyone towered over her five-foot-two-inch frame.

The woman pulled a cloth handkerchief trimmed in lace from the velvet folds of what looked to be an English-style riding jacket. She held the linen square out to Crystal.

Refusing the offer, Crystal added, "Oh, no. I couldn't."

The woman didn't lower the handkerchief. When Crystal met her gaze, she was struck by the natural beauty before her. Huge dark eyes. Long black hair. Breeding that came with generations of old money.

Crystal took the handkerchief and stood up straighter, wishing she had her four-inch heels. "You're not from around here, are you?" The question was out before she knew she'd spoken, but no one looking like this woman ever grew up in Clifton Creek. She reminded Crystal of a picture of Snow White she had seen in an old children's book.

"I—I am Anna," the woman said in a way that made the words sound foreign. "I—I am the wife of D-Davis Montano. The oil rig was being built on our land. I—I have been told Davis was there when the accident happened." Her words stumbled over each other. "A—a nurse said they found his wallet in the pile of burned clothes collected from the emergency room floor."

Crystal nodded, trying not to say anything else to the foreigner. Everyone in the county knew Davis went all the way to Italy for a wife, but few people had ever seen her. Several of the single girls around town were upset when he married. Davis raised racehorses on the good pasture land he inherited. He had traveled to Europe for a new bloodline and had come back with a stallion and a woman.

Wiping her face with the linen of Anna Montano's handkerchief, Crystal decided she might be little better than white trash, but at least she was from around here. Pretty Snow White Anna wouldn't belong here if she lived to be a hundred. In fact, when she died and was buried in the Montano plot, she'd still be the foreign wife Davis had brought home.

Pacing to the door, Crystal crossed her arms over her ample chest. "My Shelby's still alive. Isn't he? They didn't tell me he was dead. They just said to come to the hospital. They wouldn't have said that unless he was still alive." She looked at the older woman she'd seen in the paper a hundred times. Shelby had always pointed her out and called her "one fine lady." "Isn't he, Mrs. Whitworth? My Shelby's still alive? Don't you figure?"

Helena visibly softened, as if responding to a child. "We don't know. All we've found out so far is there were five men on the rig when it exploded. Four are dead. One is badly burned, and I don't think his chances are good."

Crystal looked around. "You mean all of us are widows except one?"

"That's right, baby doll," came a husky voice from the doorway as a fifth woman entered the room.

Randi Howard closed the door to the tiny room and
leaned against it with all the drama of a breathless hero-
ine in a B movie. "The newspaper and a TV station from
Wichita Falls were pulling in when I parked. They say
it's hailing between here and the city, but those folks are
like roaches, they can live through anything."

When no one commented, she continued, "There's also
more cowhands and oil field workers than I could count
hanging around in the lobby. It's busier than Frankie's Bar
on payday. I had to fight my way through, then convince
some nitwit girl dressed like a peppermint that I'd been
told to show up here." She brushed raindrops from her
Western-cut jacket. "We're in for one hell of a storm, gals.
This hospital is probably a good place to wait it out."

She scanned her audience of four and shrugged off
any acting she might have planned. "I guess folks dying
in this county from anything other than old age is big
news."

"What are you doing here, Randi?" Crystal's tone held

an edge that was not entirely unfriendly. "I thought you were working the day shift now."

"Didn't anyone tell you? My Jimmy was with your Shelby on the rig." Randi twisted her dyed, gypsy-red hair into a braid.

Crystal frowned. "I should've guessed he'd be there. He's always shadowed his uncle Shelby. Jimmy knows more about Howard Drilling than either of Shelby's kids. If there were problems on the rig, Shelby would have wanted Jimmy right there with him, learning all he could." She glanced at the others. "Shelby says Jimmy's been at his side since he was a boy."

Randi nodded and took a seat, propping her red Roper boots on an empty chair. She pulled out a pack of Marlboros, looked around and reconsidered. So, she thought, these are the newly widowed. An old woman, a foreigner, a Pollyanna who had to be a schoolteacher and darling Crystal who was almost thirty and her husband still called her baby doll.

In truth, she envied Crystal more than disliked her. They had been friends in their single days, sharing everything including boyfriends. The bubbly bleached blonde snagged the rich old Howard while Randi only caught the poor nephew. Oh, old man Shelby always made sure Jimmy was paid well, but Shelby's kids treated her and Jimmy worse than hired help. Which, she had to admit, was better than the way they treated their daddy's second wife, Crystal.

Randi looked directly at Crystal, catching only a glimpse of the girl she had once thought of as a sister. "I might as well tell you, you'll find out soon enough in this town. I was packing to leave Jimmy when the sheriff stopped by our trailer. I quit my job and sold everything

I couldn't fit in the back of my Jeep. I've got to get out of here while I can still breathe. I was meant for something more than singing a few songs once a week during talent night. There's a whole world out there that thinks of more than oil and cows. There's got to be. What was it we used to say, 'so many men, so little time'?"

Crystal smiled with lips a little fuller than they used to be. "I thought it was so many margaritas, so little time?"

"Well, either way, it's time I moved on. I don't want to grow old and die here, still thinking about what might have been if I'd only been brave enough to go take a look."

Crystal knelt beside Randi, taking both her hands. "You can't leave, Randi. Shelby says Jimmy is doing real well. He'll be in charge of all the drilling soon. You know Jimmy's crazy about you, girl."

Randi shook her head. "I swore nothing would stop me from leaving this time. I'm aging by the hour in this town." She glanced at the machines, hoping one said Coors across the top. "Jimmy loves me, I guess, but that ain't enough. No one in this place seems to understand… life here is sucking the marrow from my bones." She closed her eyes, fighting back tears. "God, I hope he's dead."

Silence crystallized, as though speaking her thoughts had somehow made it possible. The four other women in the room forgot to breathe.

Randi opened her eyes. "If he isn't, I won't be able to leave him hurt and burned," she mumbled, more to herself than anyone. She was not a woman who thought of apologizing for anything she said. "And I won't survive much longer here, just sitting on the porch waiting for sundown."

She raised her head, knowing her words were cruel, but realizing they were true. "If Jimmy's alive, this accident just signed my death warrant."

2:55 p.m.
County Memorial Hospital

Anna Montano sat quietly at the table, watching the women before her. The rain rattling on the roof provided background music to her thoughts. In Italy, women in crisis would be crying and wanting the family close. A priest might be sitting with them, and their hands would hold prayer beads. In Italy, worry and grieving were emotional passings, shared with family. But these Americans only talked and waited. Unlike Anna, they had not seen the fire and the smoke filling the sky above the oil rig. They still held hope close to their breasts.

She closed her eyes and tried to forget what she had seen this morning. Black smoke rising, polluting the morning sky with tragedy's omen. The ranch hands, hurrying to the scene, would not allow her to come with them. But when the first ambulance had left the ranch, Anna followed in her car. She knew her brother Carlo would be upset that she had not told him she was leaving. He considered watching over her part of being Davis's foreman. But today she had not cared and, besides, he had all he could handle putting out the fire.

She could have waited at home. She knew the news would only be bad. But for once, Anna had not wanted to be in her private world at the ranch. Now, curling into herself in the uncomfortable plastic chair, she realized that for the first time in a long while, she did not want to be alone.

Loneliness was nothing new to her. She rode alone each morning, helping to train the horses. Since childhood, horses were as much a part of her life as family, sometimes more so. She worked alone in her small studio and, more often than not, ate alone both noon and evening while Davis and Carlo went somewhere on ranch business.

Anna thought of herself as no more than a bird in a cage filled with toys. One day someone would leave the door open. The only question haunting her thoughts was would she be brave enough to fly away?

She and Davis had run out of anything to say to one another after their first anniversary, when she still was not pregnant. If it had not been for her love of horses and his love of the money they brought, he probably would never have spoken to her at all. But, from time to time, he needed her advice. He needed her skill. Carlo might know horses, but Anna had an instinct about them. Over these past five years Davis Montano had learned to trust that instinct even though he valued little else about her.

Davis was not unkind. He was never unkind. But, she realized after the first year that he had married her to breed children, and she had failed him. Honor and duty were words that described her marriage, not love.

To her surprise, no tears came as she faced the possibility of his death. She married Davis the week after she had turned twenty-one, and they had been little more than strangers. For her, he provided an escape from an overprotected life in Italy. She arrived in Texas with her big brother, who was hired as foreman. Between Carlo and Davis, Anna found little freedom in this land of the free. Even the trips she had taken with her mother to hear the great symphonies of Europe were now gone.

"Would you like a soda, dear?" The older woman broke into Anna's thoughts.

"N-no, thank you." Anna liked Helena Whitworth. She wore honesty like a tailor-made garment.

"I could use a beer," Randi grumbled. "How long are they going to keep us waiting?" She and Crystal had been talking about the days when they had spent most of their nights boot scooting at Frankie's. "Surely this place has a happy hour." Randi laughed to herself and began another story that started as the others had, "Remember that night at the bar…"

Anna knew little of such a life, but from the way they talked, their times were more sad than happy. Out of habit, Anna began logging in new words as the women talked. She had learned both English and French before she left for boarding school, but it was the words that were not in the dictionary that fascinated her most. Randi's vocabulary was richly painted in bold strokes.

"M-maybe you would rather be with your f-family?" Anna suggested when Randi and Crystal finally ran out of stories.

Randi shook her red hair. "I don't have none to speak of. My mother ran off with a salesman from the farm and ranch show at the Tri-State Fair the year I was three. My father hasn't called me since last Christmas." She laughed to herself. "He'd probably call on my birthday, if he could remember it. I'm sure he misses kicking the shit out of me every time he gets drunk. The bastard was meaner than the devil's brother and so dumb I'm surprised his sperm knew how to swim. With a father like him, you got nothin' to do but pray you're adopted."

"I'm pretty much the same," Crystal added. "My step-dad booted me out when I was sixteen and told me not to ever bother knocking on their door again. Mom had to sneak me out a bag of my clothes after dark. She gave me forty bucks and wished me well in this life before telling me not to bother calling to ask for money or anything."

Crystal rubbed her hand along her workout suit, smoothing away memories with the wrinkles. "I only have my Shelby. Sometimes, when he's busy doing something, he'll give me forty dollars and tell me to get lost, but before I can leave the room he always laughs and says I'd better not be gone long." Tears tumbled down a face long free of makeup. "His two grown children hate me, though. If he's dead, I'll be lucky to get my clothes out of the house, even in paper bags, before they bar me from the property. Shelby's all I have. All I've ever had."

"You're not in Shelby's will?" Randi pulled the tab on her diet drink.

"I mentioned it once, and Shelby said his son told him that's the reason I married him, to get all his money. I guess Shelby wanted to prove them wrong, 'cause he never changed the will and he kept all of Howard Drilling out of community property. I never asked him about it again."

"You poor thing." Randi draped her long arm around Crystal's shoulder and squeezed. The gesture offered more discomfort than sympathy, but neither woman noticed. "I always figured when you hooked up with him, it was your lucky day."

"I do love him," Crystal cried. "No one understands, but I do. I'd love him if he didn't have the money or the big house. I can't think about what it would be like without Shelby."

Helena lowered herself into the chair next to Anna, directly across from Crystal. "We know you love him." The older woman patted Crystal's arm. "J.D. told me many a time that you must love Shelby to put up with his drinking and pranks."

Anna thought Crystal suddenly looked far younger than her years as the tears ran down her face. She and Randi had to be close to thirty, but Anna felt a lifetime older. They might have lines forming around their eyes, but Anna felt like she had them on her heart. Maybe people who never got involved in life aged faster on the inside. Anna felt sorry for Crystal, the kind of blind love she had for Shelby seemed far sadder than the cold, routine love she had for Davis.

"Shelby isn't so bad." Crystal sniffed. "Oh, he gets crazy and makes me do things that embarrass me something terrible in front of his drinking buddies. But then he says he's sorry and can't live without me. He's always buying me stuff after he hurts my feelings."

"Jewelry?" Randi leaned closer, looking genuinely interested in her friend's whining. The lines on Randi's face reflected years of answering to last call.

"Sure. Lots," Crystal said proudly. "But it's all locked up at the office. Trent won't get it for me unless his daddy tells him to." Crystal blew her nose. "I don't care about the money or the jewelry. I just want Shelby." She sniffed loudly once more. "I don't want to be out on the streets again. I want to be close to him and he feels the same. He says his heart doesn't start each morning until he looks at me."

Anna watched as Helena pulled the crumbling group

back under control. "What about you, Meredith? Is there family you'd rather be with?"

The schoolteacher raised her head. She had not said anything in half an hour. The size-too-small sweater she wore was hopelessly twisted, once more making the letters tumble together. "No," she answered. "My mom moved to Arizona to live with her sister when she retired. I have no siblings, or kids of my own. I guess I always figured Kevin is enough of a kid to keep me busy. Since I can't go back to my classroom, this is as good a place as any to wait." She lowered her head, returning to the thread she had been twisting off her sweater.

"Well, I have enough kids for us all." Helena smiled. "I had two girls by my first husband. Twins, though they look nothing alike. My second husband had four children I helped raise, but none of them live close any longer. I was fifty when I married J.D. but if it had been possible, I'd have had his child."

"You're kidding." Randi gulped her drink. "You'd be on Social Security before the kid got out of high school."

Helena laughed. "It's crazy, but I wish I could've done that for him. He's my third husband, and the only man I ever really loved. If he's dead, he'll also be my last. God only made one man like J. D. Whitworth."

"I—I have tried," Anna said slowly, trying not to stutter. "T-to have children, I mean. But there have been no babies."

"Not me." Crystal shook her head. "First, a kid would ruin thousands of dollars of surgery. Second, I might have a brat like Shelby's others. I can't see going through all that to bring someone like Trent Howard into the world."

"That kind of thing is not for me," Randi's low voice was added to the group. "I don't mind running the plays, but I sure don't want to make a touchdown. Western clothes are hard to find in maternity sizes."

Suddenly the talk turned to life, and living life, and making choices all women have to make. Their conversation became real. No need for social barriers or polite lies. Somehow, the accident, on the rig miles away, made them all the same. All equal. All sisters. The fear they shared brought them together, making each stronger because of their bond.

They talked of the joys in their lives and the changes they wished they had made. Helena, as the oldest, perhaps felt she could be the most honest and her honesty cleared the table of all pretenses. She told of marrying young the first time and losing him in Vietnam, a month after the twins were born.

For a while she had been a single mother trying to start a business and rock two babies at night. After five hard years, she'd married a man ten years her senior for security.

They'd found babysitters and housekeepers to manage the children and he'd taught her how to build her small dress shop into Helena's Choice.

When he'd died years later all she could say about him was that he had been a good accountant.

Randi talked of deeds done and regretted, Meredith talked of thoughts she harbored, and somewhere in the confessions the cowgirl and the schoolteacher were the same. The difference lay only in degrees.

Anna mostly listened and smiled to herself. In the strange room so far from Italy, she suddenly felt very much at home. She even told the others of her art, something Davis would never approve of, and, to her surprise, the women were interested.

The room finally grew silent, except for the low rumble

of the vending machines. Each woman knew they were opening, showing themselves as they never would have done under normal circumstances. Their honesty bred a calmness that floated like a current through the room, washing away worry and fear.

Helena leaned across the table and touched Crystal's manicured hand with her wrinkled one. "No matter what, we'll survive, dear. If no one else, we have each other. I'll be there for you, if you need me. I swear."

"Helena's right." Meredith added her hand brushing the older woman's. "We can get through this."

Randi joined the covenant. "Oh, well. Hell, why not. I'll help where I can, if any of you need me."

Slowly, Anna's hand finished the circle of fingers in the center of the table. No one said a word, but a pact wove its way around them. They silently agreed to stand beside one another. Women from different worlds within the same small community.

Whatever lay beyond the door did not seem so terrifying knowing someone stood near. They were silent, thinking of what was to come, realizing the news would be bad for some, if not all, in the room.

The door opened with a slight swishing sound. All hands retreated slowly, yet the covenant remained. Invisible. Strong. In the passing of a few hours they had put aside their masks and accepted one another. The world's intrusion would not alter that acceptance. For the first time in her life, Anna did not feel so alone.

"Ladies." A retired doctor shuffled into the room on shoes that never lifted from the floor. He was stooped with age and looked well into his seventies, but intelligence shone from his eyes. "The staff called me in to help right after they sent the ambulance out to the Montano place. I was here by the time the men started arriving.

Because I know most of you, I was asked to speak to you."

He nodded a greeting to Helena and Crystal, and then touched Meredith on the shoulder. When his watery gray eyes met Anna's, he said, "I'm Dr. Hamilton." Before Anna spoke he added, "Mrs. Montano."

Randi turned toward him, lifting her Coke a few inches. "Doc."

"Randi," he answered with an honest smile.

"We've been waiting." Randi sat up in her chair. "Hope you can tell us something."

He cleared his throat, trying to be professional. "As I'm sure you know, all five of your husbands were on a rig Shelby Howard built that stood on Montano land. The way I hear it from a few of the crew being treated for burns, J.D. planned to invest extra money in the rig so one of the bank officers, Kevin Allen, had to come along for the ride."

He glanced at Randi and added, "Jimmy was there with Shelby. Helping out as always."

"And how many workers were on the rig?" Helena asked, needing the details.

"None," the doctor answered. "Jimmy had offered them a beer from the cooler in his trunk. From what I understand that is pretty much routine."

His eyes bubbled with tears. "Only your husbands were standing on the rig when a box of explosives, that never should have been near the place, exploded."

The women waited, knowing Dr. Hamilton had said the easy part of his tale. He stared just above their heads as he added, "Four were killed. The man still alive is hanging on by a thread. We tried to get a helicopter from Parkland, but the storm's preventing that. I did get a specially trained nurse to drive over from Wichita Falls. She arrived about half an hour ago in her car packed with much needed supplies."

The sheriff slipped into the room and stood behind the doctor. He was tall and solid in his tailored uniform. He stood at attention, official.

Hamilton continued, "I asked Sheriff Farrington to join us in case you have any questions. He's here to help in any way he can. He'll also see you make it past the reporters if you don't feel like talking to them."

Randi was the only one who glanced in the sheriff's direction. The others waited for the doctor to continue.

Hamilton's sorrowful gaze darted from one woman to the other. "I don't know how to say this easily." He clenched his jaw, forcing tears not to fall. His hand shook so badly he had to grip the lapel of his coat to keep his fingers steady.

Anna stood and folded her arms, hugging herself as tightly as she dared. Her riding jacket seemed to offer her no warmth now.

Randi pulled Crystal against her.

Meredith moved close to the door, looking as if she might bolt at any moment.

Only Helena faced the doctor directly. "We've waited long enough, Simon. Say what you have to say and get on with it. Bad news doesn't get any better with age."

The doctor nodded and turned to Meredith. She looked like a firing squad had just drawn aim on her. She did not move.

"I'm sorry, Meredith. We determined Kevin's body by size and blood type. He was a good three inches taller than the others and the only O positive among the men."

Meredith opened her mouth to scream, but no sound came out. She would have slid to the floor, but Sheriff Farrington's arm encircled her and held her up. He seemed a cold man and his hug felt cold now, as though he were only doing his duty, nothing more.

"Kevin," Meredith cried. "I want Kevin. We've been together since we were sixteen. How can he be gone?"

"If it's any comfort, Meredith, he didn't suffer. We think the blast killed him, not the fire that followed." The doctor swallowed hard. "I signed his birth certificate so I asked if I could sign the death certificate."

The sheriff held Meredith steady. She turned her face into his shoulder and sobbed.

Dr. Hamilton looked at Helena. "I'm sorry, Helena. J.D. fought for life all the way into town but died before we could get him stabilized. He was a soldier to the end."

Helena nodded but did not move. She sat like a statue at the end of the table. Not a hair out of place. Not a wrinkle to be seen on her clothing, but her heart crumbled inside.

"The other three men were almost the same height and build. All B positive. They were burned so…" The doctor stopped, not wanting to tell more.

He stared at the center of the table.

"The one still alive only has a slim chance and, if he makes it, it will take months, maybe even years, of care and therapy. He wore a plain wedding band. We had to cut it off."

A single tear rolled down Anna's face. "D-Davis wore no wedding band," she whispered in a blending of English and Italian. She took Helena's hand as she joined the growing ranks of widows.

The doctor raised his fist and slowly opened his palm. "This will tell us who's alive, I guess."

All the women stared at the ring. A plain gold band, badly beaten and twisted, tarnished to black. It belonged to one of the Howard men, either Shelby, Crystal's husband, or his nephew, Jimmy.

Tears streamed, for the first time, down Randi's face. She choked in one deep breath. No one moved.

Anna raised her gaze to meet Randi's terrified stare, then she thought she saw Helena nod slightly to Crystal. The movement was so small no one else but Crystal seemed to notice. In the length of a heartbeat Crystal nodded back, first at Helena, then at Randi.

Meredith's wide-eyed look was unreadable as she stopped her sobbing and watched.

Crystal glanced around at each of the women, then straightened slowly. Her stare locked with Randi's, not on the ring in the doctor's hand. Understanding and sympathy passed between the two women.

Not a woman in the room breathed as Crystal slowly raised her hand and took the ring. She buried it into a white-knuckled fist and closed her eyes. "Shelby's alive," she whispered. "Shelby's alive."

Randi pulled her hands off the table, covering her left hand with her right. She huddled into herself as though the room had grown suddenly cold.

Among the riggers in the early days of the Clifton Creek oil boom the question wasn't *if* you'd be hurt, but *when*. It was often said, after an accident, that fire climbed the rigs with lightning speed and no one within a hundred feet would be left untouched.

October 12
Just after midnight
County Memorial Hospital—A makeshift ICU room

Pain materialized one inch at a time into his mind until it filled every pore, every cell of his body. He couldn't move. He wasn't sure he was even breathing on his own. There was nothing but fire seeping into his skin where it continued to smolder, burning all the way to his bones.

The weight of the sheet pressed agonizingly against him, while a tube choked past his swollen vocal cords, holding back a scream. Fighting with a strength borrowed from the deep recesses where life struggles to survive without consciousness, he pulled at tubes clawing their way into his arms. But his fingers had been individually wrapped with fine gauze and cupped, as if to hold a can, around a soft mass. The gentle splint rendered his efforts to touch anything useless.

Figures moved around him. Shouting. Ordering. Begging him to stop resisting.

He stilled, more from a need to conserve his last bit of strength than from cooperation. He tried to open his eyes but couldn't tell if they were bandaged or swollen closed.

"Please don't move, Shelby," a soft voice cried close to his ear. "You'll only hurt yourself more. Skin is coming off each time you move. Please be still."

He couldn't make sense of the madness.

"They're giving you morphine for the pain," the woman whispered between sobs. "It won't hurt so bad in a few minutes. Hang on, darling."

The fight to stay conscious was lost before he could tell her no one had ever called him darling. He drifted on an ocean of turmoil so constant it became commonplace, a part of him.

"Shelby?" the soft voice came again. "Shelby, can you hear me? They're changing the bags of saline on each arm. I know you hurt, but hang on, darling. Hang on."

He tried to open his mouth to tell her she was wrong. Somehow there had been a mistake. He didn't want to hear, or think, or feel. A dark void finally lulled him into numbness. Her words pulled him back to the surface where the horror stayed vivid. He wanted his suffering to end.

Let me die! he tried to beg. But he could not make words form. *Let me die! Please, God, let me die!*

Pulling at his bindings, he fought to take flight. If he could run fast enough and hard enough, he could outdistance the pain. He was surrounded once more by shouting and movement and machines. As he fought, he realized he couldn't feel his legs.

Let me die! his mind screamed. What did it matter? He was already in hell.

The woman was there in the chaos, begging him to live. She didn't understand. If she knew his torment she would not keep asking.

The sound of her crying finally eased him back into the blackness where his mind could rest even if his body still throbbed.

When he awoke the third time, the pain was too familiar to be shocking. Drugs had taken the edge off of hell, nothing more. This time he heard the drone of machines forcing him to breathe. He cursed the technology that kept him alive.

He drifted, trying to make his lungs reject each breath. Trying to force his heart to stop pounding. People moved around him, whispering like gnats in the night air. Nobody heard him beg for death.

Someone must have understood a fraction of his suffering. He heard her near, crying once more. He no longer resided alone in fiery hell. She stayed at his side. Unwanted. Unbeckoned. Unneeded.

Time lost all meaning. He would wake and force himself to take the blast of agony before his captured screams drove him mad. Then he'd hear the voices, and the woman sobbing softly at his side.

Sometimes, she would talk to him, low and Southern. For a second, he'd remember life before the pain. Moments, frozen like photographs, but real with smells and sounds. A ball game played on fresh-mowed grass. Drinking cold beer on a hot day. He felt the chill slide all the way to his gut. Sleeping on the porch in summer, with music from the house competing with crickets outside.

He forgot about his pain and tried to move. Volts of fire sliced through him. All thoughts vanished when the drugs dulled his mind once more.

Time passed, others came and went. The light grew softer, then brighter with an electric glare. Once, in the moment between blackness and agony he was aware. He made no effort to open his eyes, but listened to the sound of rain on the windows and a conversation hovering near.

"Look at the bastard," a man mumbled. "He can't live much longer. That special nurse said it was a miracle he's hung on this long. She said there's a rule, age plus percentage burned equals chance of death. The old man's fifty-eight with a sixty percent burn. That equals no chance in my book."

The male voice laughed. "The staff wants to move him to a burn unit in Dallas, but Crystal's following Daddy's orders and keeping him here. He'd already be there if they could have gotten the helicopter from Parkland Hospital through the storm the first few hours after the explosion, before they knew who he was."

The man's low voice grew closer. "Now he has next of kin. It's Crystal's choice, and she's not likely to forget his ravings every time he got drunk and talked about never being taken out of the county to die. He used to swear the big city hospital killed Mom. Too bad they couldn't do the same for him."

"Stop talking about him, Trent. He might hear you," a woman's sharp tones answered. "The hospital is doing what they can. They've turned this room into an ICU, and equipment from the city is coming in by the hour. He's got as much chance here as anywhere. Stop talking about Daddy as though he's already left us."

"He can't hear. Hell, he wouldn't even be breathing if it wasn't for this machine. All I'd have to do is reach up and…"

"Stop it, Trent! You don't have the guts to kill him."

"Or the need. What the rig explosion didn't do, the old man's stubbornness about being transferred to a real hospital will. He may have blamed the Dallas hospital for killing Mom, but I'll be able to thank this little place for not having the ability to keep him alive. In a few hours, I'll be running Howard Drilling. Even if he lives, he'll be a vegetable, and I'll take over."

The woman's tone was cruel. "And our dear little tramp of a stepmother will be back to waiting tables where she belongs. I'd feel sorry for her if I thought Daddy ever loved her. But she was just his toy. I'll always believe he married her just to irritate you."

"He did a good job of that."

The woman laughed. "Wait till you see what I brought her as a change of clothing. I find it hard to believe she had the guts to even ask me to do such a thing. She hugged me as if she could comfort me and asked if I'd do her a great favor. She even said it didn't matter what I brought, she just needed a change because she wasn't leaving the hospital until Daddy did."

"All she'll have left is guts as soon as the old man dies." Trent laughed.

A door opened. The conversation ended. He drifted with the pain for a while before he heard someone crying again.

"Don't die, darling," the soft Southern voice whispered over and over. "Please don't die."

Her fingers pressed lightly over the bandages on his hand. She willed him to live with a determination stronger than his need to die. Whoever she was, she wasn't giving up. She wasn't letting go.

Through the pain he realized he didn't want her to give up on him. She was the only hope he felt he had ever known.

Sleepy little farming towns flooded overnight with thousands of oil field workers, teamsters and speculators. Gambling houses, saloons and shacks called parlors offered entertainment for a price. Small-town sheriffs from Borger to Port Arthur called in the Texas Rangers to help maintain a modicum of control. When the boom died, the local law stood alone as the towns drifted back to sleep.

October 12
1:45 a.m.
Frankie's Bar

The bartender leaned as far over the bar as his huge belly would allow and whispered, "We're closing, Randi, you want another one?"

Randi Howard stacked her last shot glass beside the others and shook her head. "Can't seem to drink enough to feel it tonight, Frankie."

The old boxer behind the bar nodded. "I've been there, kid, believe me." He used two of the glasses she'd emptied to pour them each a shot of tequila. "Jimmy was a good man and he'll be missed. Here's one to him."

Randi didn't down the offered drink. She just nodded. "He was a good man. Best damn husband I ever had." She looked up at Frankie. "He never beat me. Did you know that? Not once."

Frankie moved down the bar to the next customer; sympathy and advice were doled out like whiskey, in short shots. He'd been a boxer and a biker before settling down to tending bar. Randi guessed he'd heard every hard luck story over the years, and hers was just one more.

She lifted the last drink to her lips. "To you, Jimmy. I might not have been able to stand the boredom of living with you any longer, but I'm sure going to miss you now I know you're gone and I can't come running back."

Blinking away a tear, she remembered how he once told her that she was a one-woman wrecking crew leaving broken hearts wherever she went. He always said things like that to her before they married. Afterward she swore sometimes he looked right through her. He worried more about his uncle Shelby's business than he ever did about her. If the accident hadn't happened, he probably wouldn't have noticed she was gone for at least a week or two.

Randi closed her eyes wishing she could write the kind of sadness that settled in between them into a song. But singers don't sing about love dying by inches or how it feels when there is nothing to feel anymore. None of the sad country songs she knew could ever make her hurt as badly as watching Jimmy slowly stop caring.

She hadn't lost him in an oil fire. She'd lost him a fraction at a time…the day he stopped calling her name when he entered their trailer…the first morning he forgot to kiss her goodbye…the night he rolled away even though he knew she wanted to make love. She hadn't known how to say goodbye then. She wasn't sure she knew how to say goodbye now.

Maybe she should have had a farewell song ready the day she married. Then, every time something cut off a piece of her heart she could have turned up the volume a notch. Eventually, he would have heard it and then her leaving wouldn't be a surprise.

The only thing she could think to do now was to stick with the plan she'd come up with less then twenty-four hours ago. She felt like she'd wasted most of her life trying to figure out what to do. She had been leaving him, heading to Nashville to give herself a chance at a dream she'd had all her life. She would just pretend Jimmy was back here waiting for her. That he still cared. It shouldn't be much of a stretch really, she'd been pretending someone cared about her most of her life. Pretending was easier than believing. Believing could get her hurt, but pretending could go on forever. But now that she had finally decided on a direction, she would cut and run.

"It's time to face the champ!" Frankie yelled from the end of the bar as he raised his fist and tapped the set of boxing gloves hanging above his head.

A young cowhand a few stools down leaned toward Randi. Long past drunk, he smelled of smoke. "What's he talking about, ma'am?"

Randi smiled, wondering how many times she'd explained Frankie's last call. "It's time to face the champ. When anyone says that to a fighter, you can bet it is your last round for the night."

The drunk nodded as if he understood.

Randi lifted her purse along with his hat off the empty stool between them. "Come on, cowboy. I'll walk you to your pickup."

"How'd you know what I drove?" he said as she turned him toward the door.

"Lucky guess."

Parking lot of County Memorial Hospital
2:15 a.m.

"Can you drive home, Meredith?" Sheriff Farrington knelt beside the open Mustang door as he helped Meredith Allen into her car.

She worked summers and holidays at the county clerk's office just down the hall from his office, but she could never remember him using her name. Funny, when you are a schoolteacher in a small town everyone calls you by your last name. First students, then their parents. Even the other teachers in the building referred to one another as Misses or Misters. Slowly, the town knows you that way.

Meredith knew what people thought of her. When she had been in school, she had been a "good girl," the type boys remembered to open doors for. She figured she would grow into middle age and become a "fine woman." Then her hair would turn from auburn to light blue and she would take her place up front in church with all the other widows and become "a sweet old dear."

Only now she was already a widow, and not one hair of her curly mass had turned gray. Something had gone wrong with the order of things.

"I'll be fine, Sheriff. Thanks for sitting with me." She took a long breath and leaned back against the headrest. "I just didn't want to leave until the funeral home picked up Kevin. It didn't seem right somehow to leave him alone."

"I understand," he said, his voice still cold but less formal than usual. "Restlawn would have been here faster if they'd known you were waiting. I guess they didn't figure it mattered, so they sat out the rain."

She looked up at him. "They will take good care of Kevin?" She knew she was making no sense, but she had to ask. Restlawn was the only funeral home in town. Kevin was dead and far too burned to have an open casket. What difference could the care make?

"Of course they will." He played along with the fantasy. "Those boys have known your Kevin all his life. They'll be taking care of one of their own."

Meredith nodded.

"You call me if you need anything," he offered.

"I will," she answered, knowing she never would.

He stood and closed her door. She watched him walk back into the hospital as she pulled out of the parking lot. It was good of him to sit with her even if they had not said more than a handful of words to one another.

Meredith drove through deserted streets, trying to make herself believe Kevin was gone. Even after the long day at the hospital, it seemed impossible. She had loved and worried about him for more than half her life. He had always been there, through high school and college. Even before they married, every action, every thought, every decision had Kevin factored in. Then, today, for one second she blinked and the world changed. He was gone.

How could the town, the people, look the same? Didn't they know the earth had tilted? Crystal Howard said she had felt something in the wind, a shifting. She was right. After this day, life would change for them all.

But the grain elevators still loomed like a miniature skyline behind the old depot. Main Street still ran in front of the courthouse with store fronts sliced in between vacant buildings, just as they had that morning when she drove to school.

Several years ago, a senior class had taken on a project to install displays of the history of Clifton Creek in the empty store windows. The undertaking was a great success but, as the years went by, sun and dust faded the efforts until they matched the dilapidated buildings that housed them. Tonight they loomed through the fog like ghosts of the past.

Meredith fought back tears, forcing herself to maintain control. Kevin always says getting emotional doesn't help.

Kevin always said she corrected, as if a red pen sliced through her thoughts.

He could always tease her into smiling, no matter what happened. Only Kevin was no longer here. He would never be here again. Not to tease, or to gripe about the town, or to speed down Main when he thought he could get away with it.

He was gone. Not for tonight. Not for a few days. But for forever.

Breathe, she instructed. Breathe. Drive. Think.

The town Kevin swore never changed, had done just that. It was no longer small and welcoming, but cold and drab. The foggy air that hung on after the storm left Clifton Creek's streets as colorless and as empty as her heart.

Meredith focused her eyes straight ahead. She was afraid if she turned to look at any place in town, she would see a memory. Kevin may have died, but she didn't want to turn and catch a glimpse of him sitting on the bench outside the café, or walking across the grass on the square, or watching her pass from his office window at the bank. He loved to wave as she passed and then run out the back door of the bank and beat her home.

Meredith blinked hard and stared at the shiny black road. She had to think. She had to plan. This time he wasn't racing home to greet her.

Where was she going to get the money for a funeral? The last time she checked, she had forty-three dollars in her savings account and even less in checking. She had called her mother and aunt a few hours ago. They told her they doubted they could afford to come. She could not ask them for a loan.

Tears bubbled over, blurring her vision until the streetlights were starbursts. She hated thinking about money now. She hated that she had to.

As she opened the door to their one-bedroom house, she caught herself almost shouting, "I'm home." The place seemed quieter than she ever remembered it.

The living room was a mix-match of furniture they had either been given or had bought in garage sales. The couch was Mission, the chair Early American, the coffee table Modern. The tiny kitchen was cluttered, with a colorful plastic flower arrangement covering the burned spot on the counter.

"Our starter house," Kevin had called it. Something they had bought right out of college, planning to move up in a few years when Kevin's college loans were paid off. But the years passed and up never happened. Not that she minded, she told herself. This was home, easy to clean, close to school.

Meredith put her purse and the tote bag that served as a briefcase on a bar chair. She wiggled out of her sweater and straightened the cotton blouse she wore beneath. It's ruined, she thought, as she folded the sweater. She had picked at loose thread ends so often today that several of the letters were now missing. The *L* had rolled up like a retracting tape measure. What good is an alphabet sweater with twenty-one letters and a curly *L?*

She pulled out a lesson plan book and tried to think of what to tell the substitute to do for the next week. She told Principal Pickett she could come back the day after Kevin's funeral, but he insisted she take some extra time off.

Walking to the kitchen, she pulled down a mug and coffee canister. Why was it people thought teachers got a day off when they were not at school? she wondered.

The substitute's plans were harder to do than showing up for class.

She opened the canister and smelled the aroma of coffee then remembered the coffeemaker lay upside down on the tiny kitchen table. Parts were scattered among tools. Kevin had promised he would fix it last night before he came to bed. But, as always, he had not even tried.

Meredith calmly put down the mug and walked to the back door. On the screened-in porch, she found two mops, a dust pan and the hatchet Kevin had borrowed from the neighbor a month ago. He had planned to trim a branch that kept scraping the bedroom window.

She lifted the hatchet, ran her fingers over the handle and tromped back to the kitchen. The first blow hit the broken coffeemaker with enough force to send parts bouncing off the ceiling. Whack! Whack! The fourth strike cut deep into the linoleum tabletop.

All the anger she had bottled up for years exploded with each swing. "He...never...fixed...anything!" she said almost calmly between attacks.

Like a lumberjack discovering the power of the ax, she widened her stance and lengthened her swing. Pieces of plastic and cord and metal flew around her.

Just as a chunk struck her on the cheek, the doorbell rang.

For a moment Meredith stood, hatchet ready, like a crazed killer seeking the next victim. Then slowly she wiped a drop of blood from her face and walked to the door.

"Yes," she said, trying to hide the hatchet behind her.

"Are you all right?" Sheriff Farrington's voice sounded from the shadows of the unlit porch.

Meredith calmed her breathing. "I'm fine. I was just fixing the coffeepot."

There was a long pause. Meredith guessed she should say something else or turn on the light, but she made no move. It would be better if he could not see her face.

Finally, the sheriff cleared his throat. "I forgot to ask you what you want me to do with Kevin's car."

Meredith could not fight down the smile as she gripped the hatchet. "I'll take care of it tomorrow."

She could almost see the sheriff raise an eyebrow. His hand went out as if to touch her, then he pulled back. "Meredith, are you sure you're all right? I could call someone. A friend or relative."

"No," she answered, surprised at the sheriff's concern. She had passed him in the halls of the courthouse for years and he had never said more than a few words. He was like her, an observer, not a participant. Two onlookers rarely have much to say to one another.

"Where is Kevin's car?" She had no intention of telling him how few friends she had. She knew almost everyone in town, but could think of no one to call to be with her.

"It's in a two-hour parking spot at the bank," he answered. "He must have ridden out to the Montano place with Shelby or Jimmy. I saw both Howards heading into the bank yesterday morning."

She nodded. Everyone in town knew the sheriff observed folks passing on Main Street from his window with the same intensity that a sailor studies the sky.

"Don't worry about Kevin's car," Farrington finally mumbled. "I'll see it doesn't get ticketed. You can deal with it after you've had some sleep."

"Thank you." Meredith slowly closed the door, thinking maybe she could sell the car to help pay expenses.

Kevin wouldn't want anyone to know money was tight. Over the years she had seen him insist on paying, or throw money into a pot even when he knew it would run them short for the month. Once he had given a hundred dollars to help send the extras on the basketball team to the state tournament. The boys made it to Austin, but Meredith and Kevin ate macaroni and cheese for three weeks. That was the year they were so broke they got religion. The Baptist church had a young couples' dinner every Wednesday. For all couples under thirty there was no charge, the church's way of helping young folks get started.

She could continue to play the game alone. Meredith closed her eyes and reminded herself one more time to keep breathing.

"Our money is nobody's business but ours." She could almost hear Kevin saying.

"But *mine*," she corrected.

October 12
After midnight
The Whitworth home—Pigeon Run

Across town, money also pestered Helena Whitworth's mind. She wrote two checks to her daughters. Since she had got home from the hospital, they had worried about little else except the fact they had nothing black to wear to J.D.'s funeral.

Paula and Patricia were fraternal twins born to Helena when she was still in her teens. Paula was the brightest of the pair. If one can compare the brightness of flannel. She managed to fail two years of college before dropping out. Patricia quit her first semester because the books were too heavy to carry across campus.

"You don't have to do this, Momma." Paula blew the ink dry on her check. "I could have charged what I needed at Sears. I know how important it is for you to have us dress properly and there is never anything in Helena's Choice in our size."

Patricia fidgeted impatiently. "I'm sorry I have to run, but Bill's home waiting up. He says he can't sleep without me beside him in bed. You know how it is." She took her check then glanced up at her mother. "I'm sorry, Momma. I didn't think. I'll get someone to keep the baby tomorrow and come over and help you."

"That won't be necessary." Helena tried, as always, to keep her words kind, not out of fondness, but out of self-preservation. When the girls were upset, whining leaked into every word they communicated.

"Oh, Momma, I don't mind coming to help." Patricia lifted the three-year-old she still called "the baby." He'd had a plug in his mouth so long Helena sometimes wondered if it were a birth defect.

"You need to get rid of J.D.'s things, Momma, as soon as possible. It's not healthy to keep them around making you sad and all. Bill could probably wear some of those golf shirts on his Saturday runs. They're not real strict about the uniform then."

"Harry is J.D.'s shoe size," Paula interrupted. "Don't go giving his shoes away until Harry tries them on. We'll be over first thing tomorrow, too."

Helena closed her eyes, thinking of something J.D. used to say. "Even the bottom of the gene pool rises after a rain." It must have flooded the day she conceived. Though she loved her daughters dearly, they were a trial. Paula forever bossy, Patricia forever needy.

Both always wanted to help her. They meant well, but Helena hated discussing decisions that were hers to make. J.D. understood that about her. She was a woman who knew her own mind and did not need to take a poll to determine her actions.

"What are you going to do with all those hats he's got?" Patricia shook her head. "They're not even proper to give the Salvation Army—the ones he wore in the Marines. You know, the ones he always made us call 'covers' instead of hats."

Paula snorted a laugh. "Can't you just see the home-less wandering the streets wearing a colonel's hat? And the old things he wore to watch birds wouldn't be fit for fishing."

Helena had had enough. She headed toward the door.

Like puppies hearing the paper being rolled, both girls looked suddenly guilty. "We're sorry, Momma," they chimed. "We didn't mean to hurt your feelings."

Both opened their arms to hug Helena, but then decided it would be safer to hug each other. Between ample bodies and ample breasts, they looked like huge Humpty Dumpty toys trying to dance but only succeeding in wobbling.

"I'm really going to miss the old guy," Paula cried on her sister's shoulder. "He wasn't so bad once we got used to the sin of Momma marrying him."

Paula never missed a chance to remind Helena that she and J.D. were first cousins. Everyone in town seemed to have forgotten except "One-track Paula."

"I'll miss him, too," Patricia added, but from the con-fused expression in her eyes, she couldn't remember any sin. "Even if I didn't understand what he was talking about half the time. He was always naming some place I never heard of like it was important and I should drop everything and go home and look it up on a map."

"Good night, girls." Helena held the door open as her offspring hurried out. They were her flesh and blood. The only part of her that would live on in this world. But they did not hold her heart. No one had until J.D.

Both daughters stood on the front step when she spoke again. "No one...I repeat, no one, touches J.D.'s things."

They looked at her as if they felt sorry for their mother's inability to face the facts.

Helena tried to keep her anger in check. "If either of you do, you will never be welcome in this house again."

"Oh, Momma, you don't mean..."

"I mean every word. J.D.'s things stay untouched." Helena closed the door, wishing she could talk to her daughters without getting angry.

She walked slowly up the staircase to the bedroom that had been hers and J.D.'s for over ten years. His things surrounded her. Welcomed her. She closed her eyes and relaxed for the first time since the call from the hospital.

His robe hung on the door, his reading glasses were on an open book, his running shoes lay between the chairs by the window. He couldn't be gone. She could still smell him near. Still feel the warmth of his gaze watching her. Sometimes when they were sitting side by side, paying no attention to one another as they read or watched the birds, Helena would match her breathing to his. If she were still enough she knew she could do that now.

"Don't leave me, Cousin," she whispered across the shadows. "Don't leave me alone."

Helena closed her eyes and forgot about all that happened. The nightmare of reality ended. Need brought in the dream.

In the stillness of their room she heard him whisper, "I'm right here. Waiting. Come here, Hellie."

Helena slipped beneath the covers and into the arms of the only man she ever loved. His chest was bare and hair tickled her nose as it always did. His arm was strong about her. The smell of his aftershave blended with his favorite brand of pipe tobacco.

"Don't go just yet," she pleaded. "I couldn't bear it."

She felt his gentle kiss on her forehead. "I'll be right here as long as you need me. Remember when I came back? I gave you that silver dollar your mother had given me to take to war for luck. I promised I'd never leave you alone. Let the storm come, Hellie, let it come. You'll always have my arms to protect you."

There were folks who believed God put oil in Texas because it was the only place on earth where the rigs could be seen as an improvement on the landscape. On a windy day tumbleweeds would blow into the eaves of a rig making it look like a skeleton Christmas tree covered in huge, hideous ornaments.

The next few days had passed in a haze for Anna Montano. The road to their ranch became a highway of cars and trucks traveling back and forth from the site of the explosion. Most were on official business but a few were simply sightseers, wanting to get closer to the spot where four men had died.

The sheriff stopped by saying he needed to talk with her, but Anna felt she had nothing to say. Carlo told her the explosion was just an accident and no matter what someone tried to make of it, that was all to be said.

Anna asked Carlo if he would handle the sheriff and he agreed. She did not want to talk to anyone.

The rig, now twisted and black, appeared to still smolder thanks to the clouds of dust from cars circling it. Anna swore the smell of the fire lingered, seeping into everything and everyone on the ranch. Or maybe the whiff of oil afire and men burned had stained her lungs, and she would forever taste the odor with each breath.

Her brother Carlo made all the funeral plans. Davis had no relatives who sent flowers, but cards from the people of Clifton Creek filled the mailbox each morning. Businesses closed for the funerals and church bells from all denominations sounded during the processions to the town's only cemetery.

As an outsider, Anna watched in amazement while a town grieved. She saw the first signs when she and Helena left the hospital the day of the accident. Randi stayed behind with Crystal for a few minutes and Meredith waited in the hospital hallway for the funeral home, but Helena and Anna walked out together. Men lined the sidewalk from the door to the parking lot. Oil field workers and cowhands stood silent. It did not matter that the rain pounded. As the women passed, the men removed their hats and stepped back into the muddy grass. No one said a word, but the respect they paid would linger forever in her mind.

By dawn, business doors along Main wore wreaths of black. From the courthouse to the café, Carlo informed her, no one talked of anything except the accident. Anna may have lost a husband, but the town lost one of its wealthiest oilmen in Shelby Howard. Even if he lived, he would never make it back to running Howard Drilling. Everyone agreed over coffee that Jimmy Howard was probably the brains behind the old man's success over the past few years, but Shelby had been a wildcatter. Carlo quoted what he had heard, saying they did not make oilmen like that anymore.

The folks relived all the highlights of Kevin Allen's football games and decided his years on the team were the best they had seen. J. D. Whitworth moved from retired soldier to town hero and several wondered why they had never recognized him as such. There was talk of putting up a memorial.

And Davis Montano, Carlo would tell Anna over and

over, was like a son to them all. Fifth generation in the town. And that is as deep as roots go in Clifton Creek. Not just four men died in that fire, Carlo would say, but a part of the town's heart burned that day, as well.

Anna rode the fringes of the ranch in the sunny mornings that followed, but the memory of steel-toed shoes and cowboy boots washed over with mud remained in her thoughts. She found it odd that she could not remember a single man's face.

In the afternoons Anna escaped, as always, to her tiny studio that had once been a sunroom. There, amid neglected plants, she painted. She caught herself still hiding her work as if expecting Davis to stop by and criticize her at any moment. He hated the dark mood of her paintings. Now the mood seeped off the canvas and into her life.

Shelby Howard's son, Trent, was among those who came to see the ruins of the rig. He stopped at the house to tell her how sorry he was about Davis. Carlo insisted she talk to the man. After all, Trent was Shelby's only son and the two families were forever connected by the tragedy.

Trent opened the conversation by informing her that the explosion and fire were not related to anything Howard Drilling had done. He implied the sheriff suspected no foul play, but when she questioned him about the reasons for the fire, he did not seem to have enough information or knowledge to say more.

Trent reminded Anna of a buzzard with his thin frame and long nose. She played a game she had found helpful around most American men. Anna acted as though she did not understand the language, so he had to spend most of his time talking to her brother. In truth, except for a slight stutter, Anna had spoken four languages fluently by the time she was eighteen, but by then she had discovered that most men were not worth talking to.

The few men her father had allowed her to date while she was home on school vacations were usually the sons of old friends. They talked of horses and little else.

Only two people called before Davis's funeral. Randi Howard, to say she would be leaving town sooner than expected. She planned to stay until all the husbands were buried, but she'd heard of a job offer in Memphis and did not want it to slip away.

"Everyone knows Memphis is as good a place as Nashville to become a star." She laughed a little too loud. "I'll sing my way across the state."

Anna agreed with her just to be kind.

Randi had Jimmy cremated the morning after the accident. He wanted no service, and since he always talked of traveling someday, she put his ashes in the glove compartment of her Jeep and figured she would take him to Memphis with her.

Anna promised to keep in touch, but she had a feeling she would never see Randi again. Randi was a cowgirl who had probably never ridden a horse, and Anna was a horsewoman who had never danced the two-step. A stranger might think them alike, but here in ranch country they were polar opposites.

Helena Whitworth was another story. She called every morning. Anna attended J.D.'s graveside service at dawn two days after the accident. The ceremony carried full military honors. Half the town surrounded the tent staked over a grave where the dirt and the grass were the same color. Many cried, but Helena sat so still and silent she could have been one of the statues in the cemetery. Not a white hair out of place. Not the hint of a tear on her cheek.

The next day, Helena returned the kindness by sitting behind Anna at Davis's funeral.

It amazed Anna how many people came to Davis's service. In the five years she had been here, she had met very few who called him friend, yet the townspeople missed work to pay their respects.

Flowers lined the small Catholic church, making the air heavy and damp. The incense and candles reminded Anna of the smell of the fire. She fought not to gag as she waited for the service to be over.

Carlo sat beside her, weeping openly during the entire funeral. She might have lost a husband, but he lost his brother-in-law, friend and boss. Being ten years older than she, Carlo slipped easily into the father role. Anna let him, glad to have someone take care of details.

Though he saw no need to tell her of ranch business, he did mumble complaints about Trent Howard as they waited in the family room. Carlo said Trent didn't want to bother with a full investigation. Accidents were just a part of the oil business, he said.

In Italian, Carlo ranted about how he would insist on the sheriff looking into every detail. After all he would not allow Davis's name to be smeared in any way. If the sheriff found someone responsible for the deaths, Carlo swore he would see that they paid even if he had to kill them himself.

Anna was pleased when Helena lingered after the service, for she dreaded the ride back to the ranch with Carlo. Though the women were almost forty years apart in age, they bore their grief in the same way. Silent. Without tears.

Anna had parked her car downtown in the bank's garage so after the graveside service, she rode with Helena to the hospital to visit Shelby. Carlo offered to go with them, but looked relieved when Helena stepped in and said she would look after Anna. He quickly backed away, mumbling about all the work that had to be done before dark. Funeral or not, he had a ranch to run.

As they crossed the town, Helena talked of how nice Kevin Allen's funeral had been in the big, new Baptist church. Every student Meredith had ever taught must have been in attendance. The bank employees were all pall-bearers. His old high school football team sat together.

Anna barely remembered Kevin's funeral. She and Carlo had arrived a few minutes late because Carlo insisted on driving her. They sat at the back of the church, unable to hear. Anna was glad to know the funeral was nicer from Helena's view near the front. She had a feeling doing everything right might be important to Meredith Allen.

When they entered the hospital ten minutes later, Helena straightened her shoulders and walked right past the No Visitors sign. Anna followed, her head down.

Two nurses watched from the desk, but did not say a word.

A middle-aged woman in white met them at Shelby's door. Anna knew the moment she spoke that the woman was not from Clifton Creek. Though she had the same accent as Helena, the nurse did not know the town's great lady. No one, not even Anna, who kept to herself, could live in Clifton Creek and be unaware of Helena Whitworth.

The nurse introduced herself as Marge Landry from Parkland's Burn Unit. She explained that they could stay only a moment and must not pass a curtain dividing the room unless they planned to put on masks and scrubs. Her disapproval was evident. "No one...no germs can be allowed in," she ended. "There should be a glass, not just this thin curtain."

They walked silently into Shelby's room. Crystal slept in an old, armless recliner pulled close to a curtain blocking most of the area from view. Her hand held the cotton divider like a child holds a security blanket.

The nurse cleared her throat, and Crystal jumped awake. "Any change?" she asked as she blinked sleep away.

"No," Nurse Landry answered with a great deal more kindness than she had shown Helena and Anna. "You have company. I'll get back to the patient." She disappeared behind the curtain.

Crystal stood, rubbing her eyes. "Shelby's been so quiet, I must have fallen asleep."

Anna almost did not recognize Crystal. Her eyes were puffy and black-rimmed, her hair dull and dirty, her clothes wrinkled gray rags. It seemed impossible that a woman could change so drastically in four days. The day of the accident Crystal could have been a model for workout clothes in her brightly colored outfit. Now, the sweatshirt and baggy pants she wore looked as if they belonged to someone several sizes larger.

"Thank you for coming." Her voice sounded hoarse. "We've seen very little change in him, but he's still alive, thanks mostly to Nurse Landry. She came in from Dallas by car when the storm delayed the helicopter. When she learned he wouldn't be moved, I talked her into staying a few days. She got us tons of equipment and special private duty nurses coming in for twelve-hour shifts. She may look all starch and proper, but she's an angel for sure."

Helena hugged Crystal for a long while without saying a word.

Anna could do nothing but stare at the glimpses of

Shelby through a break in the curtain. Tubes came out of him in several places. The exposed skin was the red of a horrible sunburn. Some places looked black beneath the light covering of cotton and others as white as ash. A thick tube ran out of his mouth past lips swollen several times their normal size.

"I can't leave him," Crystal moaned as she noticed Anna watching through the tiny slice of light. "The hospital lets me sleep out here since this is a makeshift ICU room. As long as I stay out of their way while they check on him, I can remain."

Helena moved closer and whispered, "He's so swollen. I can't even tell it's Shelby. His eyes look completely shut."

"W-will he live?" Anna asked, as gently as she could.

Crystal nodded. "Nurse Landry says as long as there's a heartbeat, there's hope. There may be damage to his spine, but right now he has more serious problems to worry about. The doctor thinks he may have had his back turned to the explosion. But the fire burned both sides.

"One of the workers from the rig stopped by yesterday. He'd been burned on his face and hands trying to help after the explosion. He said Jimmy ordered all the field workers to take a break. They had headed for the cooler of beer in Shelby's trunk when the accident happened.

"Of the five men left on the platform, Shelby's the only one who survived, but there could have been more killed if the workers had been close by."

She lifted her head forcing words out. "He's been resting quietly since they degloved him. They must have finally given him enough drugs to let him sleep."

"He was wearing gloves?" Anna asked a moment before the horror of what Crystal meant sank into her mind. They had removed dead skin as completely as if they pulled off a glove.

Panic climbed up Anna's spine. None of this was real. Not the fire she had watched in the distance. Not the hospital wait. Not the funeral. It was only part of a play she had been acting in for years. She knew all the parts: act happy, act interested, act as if you are loved. But the man dying only a few feet away made everything real. She spent a lifetime not feeling and suddenly, with this stranger, she knew his pain. She smelled it in the air, heard it in the drone of the machines, saw it in the agonizing way he fought not to move as he breathed.

Anna concentrated on Crystal, staring at the young woman's shaking hands, memorizing every detail as only an artist would. Slowly, like water trickling through her body, she forced the horror of the fire and Shelby's burns to the side and once more stepped onto her own private little stage. The whispers of the pain that circled in the corners of her mind threatened to come forward and haunt any peace proclaimed. The thoughtful scenes she painted in her imagination grew cloudy.

Crystal took a long breath. "I have to be here when he comes to. 'Course, he can't talk with that ventilator down his throat, but I figure he'll know I'm close."

"I understand," Helena whispered. "You do what you think is right, child. Don't let anyone push you around, even this nurse."

Crystal smiled. "Thanks. I needed someone to say that. But Nurse Landry has been great. She's about the only one who seems to know I'm here. The others just walk around me."

While they watched, Shelby's fingers twitched, as if feeling along the bed for something.

Crystal grabbed her scrubs. In seconds, she had put on

all the gear and rushed to his side. "What is it, honey?" she whispered close to his ear.

His bandaged fingers found her hand and closed around it slightly.

"I'm right here." Tears filled her eyes. "I'm right here."

She looked back at Helena and Anna. "He likes to hold my hand when the pain's bad. It calms him if I talk to him. Funny, before the accident, I don't remember him ever more than half listening to anything I had to say, but now he seems to want me to talk."

Helena glanced around the private room with eyes as sharp as a health inspector. "You'll need a more comfortable chair. If the hospital doesn't have one, I'll send one out."

Crystal's eyes widened. "Thanks," she mumbled. "Will they allow that?"

"Of course they will. You can't be expected to sit in this all day." Helena touched the broken-down recliner Crystal had been using as a bed, then looked back at her. "I'll call my hairdresser and have her come by later this afternoon. She can wash and curl your hair in the hallway if nowhere else is available. And give you a manicure, too, while you're close enough to listen for Shelby."

Tears rolled down Crystal's face and soaked into the cotton mask she wore. To many women, Helena's offer would have seemed frivolous, but Anna saw that Helena offered Crystal a gift she would treasure.

Anna knew to follow suit. "I-if you like, as soon as the special clothes are not needed, I could stop by your house and pick out a few outfits for you."

Crystal broke into a full scale cry. "Oh," she wailed. "Would you?" She hid her face in gratitude. "Colorful clothes and a real nightgown. Tasteful, of course."

"O-of course." Anna doubted Crystal owned anything that could be worn at the hospital. "I-if I can not find your gowns, I will buy one for you, if you will allow me."

"Nothing low-cut," Crystal added. "And only shoes with soles that don't make noise."

Anna smiled. "I will bring several outfits and a selection of night wear. As soon as you are able, they will be waiting for you."

"Wonderful." Crystal wiped her face as she moved away from Shelby's bed. The nurse carefully elevated his arms.

"I probably sound selfish, but you're the first people to visit me and not just Shelby. I can't tell you how good it is to see you."

"I'll be back tomorrow," Helena announced as she straightened formally. "In fact, I'll be back every day until that husband of yours wakes up and realizes what a jewel of a wife he has."

Crystal stood a little taller. "No one's ever called me a jewel before."

"Well, it's about time someone did," Helena said matter-of-factly.

Anna guessed Helena was a woman who made up her mind about who was friend or foe within minutes of meeting someone. For some reason, Helena decided she cared about Crystal. And for Helena, that was like signing on to a campaign.

After Helena made a few phone calls and had a short visit in the hallway with one of the nurses, the women said goodbye. Anna did not need to hear the words or even understand the language. She knew by the nurse's movements things would be easier for Crystal from this point on, or Helena Whitworth would see that heads rolled.

When oil rigs first spread across the land, labor was hard to find. Many of the farm boys were pulled from the cotton patch to work in what they called the "oil patch."

Helena and Anna stopped off downtown at the Randell House for a late lunch. Neither wanted to end their time together.

Back in Italy, Anna would have left the funeral of a loved one to go home to a house full of company. Here, there was no one. She longed for relatives to cook for and clean up after. Somehow, keeping busy seemed a kinder way.

The two women walked into the empty restaurant arm in arm like old friends.

Davis once told Anna that during the 1890s the Randell House had been a huge home. The town had grown up around it. At some point, the house lost its first floor to commerce. Now, it stood like an architectural mutant with a top-floor restaurant of old grace and charm and a main floor filled with offices and bank tellers. The Victorian decor had been further humiliated by the joining of a parking garage at the back.

As they sat at the table surrounded by dark mahogany

and leaded glass, Anna saw nothing but the beauty that
had somehow survived a hundred years.

Anna found Helena surprisingly easy to talk to. An
unconditional acceptance between them crossed the barrier of age and made friendship possible.

From the second-floor windows, they watched shadows
grow long across Main Street, elevating the town from
dilapidated neglect into classic mystery. Helena ordered
a third cup of coffee and asked to see the dessert menu.
Although neither woman commented, both realized that,
for once in their lives, no one waited for them to come
home.

Half an hour later, Anna sipped her coffee and watched
Zack Larson walk into the restaurant. He looked as out
of place among the ferns and bookshelves as a bull in a
deli. His usual work shirt and jeans were gone and his old
Stetson had been replaced by one without a sweat stain.

"That your neighbor?" Helena asked as she sampled
her coconut pie and tried to peek through the foliage.

"H-he was at the funeral." She guessed Helena knew
who Zack Larson was, but she continued anyway, "He
has the p-place to the north of us." She only remembered
speaking to the man a few times when Carlo or Davis
could not be bothered to deliver a message. Larson had
not been friendly. Once, she told him what she thought
of the horrible barbed wire that fenced his cattle in, and
once she had complained about the cattle trucks using
the back road between their property lines. The constant
roll of dirt had dusted her sunroom windows on the north
side for two weeks.

"He hasn't been home to change out of that ghastly
suit," Helena added. "Must have had business in town
after the funeral. Word is his ranch is struggling, but
then what ranch hasn't at some point? I would like to see

him prosper enough to buy new clothes and maybe get a decent haircut. I hate to see a nice-looking man ugly himself up. I swear he wore that suit to his wedding."

"He is married?" Anna lowered her voice even though Zack Larson could not have overheard them.

"About eight years ago." Helena usually limited her gossip to the facts and comments about clothes. "His wife left him before the first year was out. He's kept pretty much to himself since then, not that he was particularly friendly before. He must be real tired of his own cooking to stop in here."

The waiter directed Zack to the table behind Anna. Even though plants separated them, Anna heard him ask the waiter if the place served beer.

"I got a headache the size of Oklahoma," he mumbled bumping both the table and chair as he tried to fold his six-foot frame.

Anna turned back to Helena, Zack Larson forgotten. She watched Helena order another slice of pie. "You are very hungry?"

Helena laughed. "J.D. swears I can put away more than a field hand. I guess I just enjoy eating. Good food, good company." Helena raised her thin shoulders. "Well, that's not altogether true, though I've enjoyed your company. I eat just as much when I'm home alone. Give me a good movie and I'll finish off a bag of Oreos along with the popcorn."

"I—I do not mind eating alone," Anna admitted, as she wondered what Oreos were. After meeting Helena, she guessed they must be something fancy ordered in only the best shops. "Davis was gone most of the time, anyway. It is nice to eat in silence watching the day come to an end."

"I know," Helena answered. "With my two daughters

setting up camp at my place this week, I long to be alone. They're masters at making trivial conversation. We've had entire meals with nothing talked about but a thirty-minute TV program from the night before. We could have all watched the rerun in less time." Helena waved at the waiter and pointed at her coffee cup. "Now, my grand-children are a little better. If we ever get their volume controls fixed, I might listen to them."

Anna laughed. "Y-you know what I miss most?"

"What?" Helena leaned forward.

"I—I miss something I never have had, really. But at least when Davis was alive, there was a chance of it."

"Oh? What's that?" Helena thanked the waiter with a nod as he delivered her pie.

"I miss…" Anna sighed. "I miss those huge, warm, all-encompassing hugs men sometimes give women. I would like to disappear into a man's arms and forget about ev-erything but being safe. It is a fantasy I know must only exist in the movies."

"I know what you mean. My J.D. gives me those hugs. He has since we were in our twenties. I remember the first one when Paula and Patricia's father died in Vietnam. I was a young mother with two little girls to raise and no skills. I thought it was the end of the world."

Helena smiled, looking more into the past than out the windows as the town lights flickered on. "J.D. was back in the States for training of some kind. He'd already been to Vietnam once. He came home for a short visit. The minute he saw me, he hugged me like he would never let go and told me everything was going to be all right."

"Did you love him, then?"

Helena shook her head. "Not the way you think. Though I've loved him all our lives, folks don't marry their first cousins. So, I thought the love was more brotherly than anything. I'm a few years older than him. We were great friends as children, our mothers being sisters and all. When he came back years later for the funeral of my second husband, we figured we'd wasted enough time with the brotherly love. We expected all kinds of trouble after we got back from tying the knot in Mexico, but most people thought since he'd been gone for years; he wasn't really a close relative anymore."

Anna laughed again as they stood to leave. Helena had managed to give Anna a quiet sense of peace in their hours together. As they passed Zack Larson's table, Anna noticed he had tossed down a few bills and walked out behind them, leaving his drink untouched.

At the elevator, Helena said goodbye to Anna with a motherly kiss on the cheek, while Zack politely held the door.

When Anna entered the elevator alone, she tried not to look at him. She wanted the feeling of peace to last just a little longer before the world stepped in.

"Garage?" he said.

"Pardon?" Anna glanced his direction, but Zack stared straight ahead as if looking at another in the elevator was strictly forbidden.

"Are you heading to the garage?" His voice sounded rusty as if he talked little.

It was a dumb question, she thought. Everyone who ate at the restaurant parked in the garage in the basement. Except maybe a few folks like Helena Whitworth who had bank-front parking. The first floor housed the bank and a few lawyers' offices that were long since closed for the night.

"Yes, please," she answered formally. "Th-the garage."

"You make it sound like some place I'd like to visit." He smiled, but still didn't look at her.

As the old elevator jerked in movement, they both swayed and waited.

"Mrs. Montano," Zack said. "I'm sorry to hear about your loss. Davis was a hardworking man and a good neighbor."

"Th-thank you," she answered, staring at the seam in the silver door.

Zack closed his eyes and continued, "I overheard what you said a few minutes ago in the restaurant. I want you to know if you ever need that hug, I'll leave my porch light on." Words tumbled out of his mouth as if he had no control over them. "I imagine you can see it from your place, 'cause I can see your lights from mine. No strings, no questions, just a hug if you need it."

The elevator tapped bottom, and the doors slid open. He waited for her to exit first.

Anna reacted without thinking. She took a step forward, then swung back suddenly and slapped Zack Larson hard across the face.

She walked away, shaking with anger knowing he had listened in on her conversation with Helena.

Just as the elevator closed with him still inside, she heard him mumble, "Or…maybe not."

In the 1920s wagons carrying nitro to oil sites would occasionally blow up while crossing railroad tracks or deeply rutted dirt roads. The railroads were *not* happy, nor were the widows of the drivers.

October 18

Meredith Allen curled into the shadows of her living room and watched as Sheriff Granger Farrington climbed out of his patrol car. He tossed his hat on the seat and headed toward her door. She glanced at the clock glowing from her VCR beneath the TV. Nine o'clock. Probably time for his final rounds, she decided. How did she get on his list? It must read something like "lock up office, check on fights at bars, drop in on pathetic widows."

Everyone in town knew his routine. Since being elected sheriff, he started each day at his office by seven and ended every shift by driving through town just after dark. On weekends he was on call, but most folks knew they could find him at his office on Saturday mornings and checking out the bars around midnight without taking the time to order a drink. Sunday was slow and he was a little harder to locate.

Meredith always thought he deserved his Sundays alone. Surely one of his deputies could handle things. But, in a small town you are what you do. Not just during work hours, but all the time. She had seen the town pharmacist cornered at church about a prescription and heard last week the home economics teacher was called at midnight because the Methodist Women's League had a canning problem.

The only unlisted number in town was the home phone of Hank Wilson, the TV repair shop owner. He figured in his line of work other folks' emergencies were never his. Rumor had it that the unlisted number made some people so mad they would buy another set rather than give Hank their business.

Just guessing, she would say Granger Farrington loved what he did. The paper had reported he worked ten years on the Houston Police Department and three with the highway patrol before running uncontested for sheriff. Most folks felt he had done a great job for the past four years.

Once, when Meredith had borrowed his copier at the courthouse, she noticed his rules posted on a wall beside his desk.

Farrington's rules
One: Know what's going on in town.
Two: Be professional.
Three: Never get involved personally.

As far as Meredith knew, he had followed every rule to the letter. He never dated any women in Clifton Creek, nor made drinking-buddy friendships with anyone in town. Some said he limited his friendships and his women to Sundays in Wichita Falls.

Meredith thought of his third rule as he knocked on her door. This was a professional call. Nothing more. The principal at the grade school probably phoned him, reporting no one had seen her since the funeral. Principal

Pickett might be worried and influential enough to ask the sheriff to take action.

Meredith curled back into her chair. She was not interested in talking to anyone. No amount of talking would change anything. She just wanted the world to go away and let her be unhappy all by herself.

The sheriff knocked again, then tried the doorbell as if it would make any difference.

"Go away," she whispered. "I don't want to get involved personally." From now on she planned to take the sheriff's third rule to heart. A week had passed since Kevin's death and she could not stop the hurt inside. If she learned anything, she had learned caring is not worth the pain that follows. From now on no one would come close enough to be more than a "Hello" friend.

After waiting a few minutes, he finally stepped off the porch. He took a few steps down the walk, then noticed the old Mustang parked in the garage. The same car that was usually parked next to his at the courthouse when she worked on holidays while the county clerk's office was closed. On those days he would stop by to let her know someone else was in the building. She always passed his office and told him she had locked up when she left. That had been the extent of their communications before the night at the hospital when he held her tight to keep her from falling.

But, he had only been doing his job as he was now and Meredith did not want to be part of his duties.

They were considerate strangers, she thought. Saying hello to one another at work. That was enough.

She heard him step onto the back porch and knock at the rear door. The sound echoed through her little house.

"I'm not answering," she whispered once more. "I don't

want to see or talk to anyone, Sheriff. Not even a considerate stranger like you."

To her shock, he ventured further without probable cause of crime. He tried the doorknob. She had seen enough cop movies to know he was not following the rules.

She closed her eyes, pretending she did not hear his footsteps coming inside her house.

"Meredith?" he called. "Are you home, Mrs. Allen?"

Don't make a sound, she thought.

The sheriff swore beneath his breath as he tripped over the mop just inside the back door.

"Meredith," he shouted as he moved through the cluttered house. "You've got to be in here. No one would leave the heater turned up so high. It has to be eighty in the place." He caught his foot on one of the kitchen chairs. "You must be alive. If you were dead, you'd smell in this heat in no time."

He drew a deep breath. "As it is, it smells like dying potted plants in here."

She wondered if he always talked to himself or if he was keeping a running dialogue so that she would hear him coming and not be afraid.

He rounded the bar and entered the shadowy living room. For a moment, he did not see her hidden within the furniture. She sat perfectly still hoping he would yet go away.

"Meredith?" His feet crunched atop dead leaves as he moved around crumbling sprays that had filled the church a week ago. White mums, limp and brown-tipped, were all that clung to the wiring of once beautiful arrangements. "Meredith!"

She did not move.

Slowly, he neared. Crouching beside her chair, he touched her arm.

She finally looked up at him.

"Evening, Sheriff Farrington," she said in a voice that sounded dry.

"Evening, Ms. Allen." He smiled out of relief. "How are you tonight?"

"I'm fine," she answered, "and you?"

"I was a little worried about you." He moved so he could see her face better in the pale light coming through the Venetian blinds. "Folks seem to be having a little trouble reaching you. You're not answering your phone."

"I haven't heard it lately." She glanced at the phone on the table beside her. The cord was wrapped around it. The plastic plug that should have been in the wall reflected the streetlight's glow.

The corner of Granger's lip lifted once more. "Got tired of the ringing, did you?"

She nodded. "Everyone kept calling, saying how sorry they were that I lost my husband. I didn't lose Kevin. I buried him."

"I know. I was there. It was a real nice service." He patted her arm awkwardly. He looked as if he would rather be handling a bar fight than be here talking to her.

Meredith smiled up at him. "I planned the service all by myself. I figured it was the last thing I'd ever do for Kevin."

"You did a good job," Granger said. "You had anything to eat today, Meredith?"

She glanced down as she tried to remember. The area surrounding her chair looked like a snowbank made of tissues. Her legs were curled inside a huge jersey of Kevin's. She touched her long hair, now matted and plastered against her scalp.

"I had some of Mrs. Pickett's pie yesterday, I think." She closed him out and settled back into the folds of the chair. "I've been so cold. So cold."

Meredith folded into her own world, turning her face away from him. All she wanted was to sleep and make the world go away. She had been too tired to even think about her class. In truth, she felt too tired to even sleep.

Without warning, Granger grabbed her by the arms and pulled her to her feet in one quick jerk. "Meredith!"

For a moment she remained limp, like a gelatin doll. He tightened his grip, as if willing her to respond. "Meredith! You are not one of those wilting mums. Come on. Snap out of it. Kevin is the one who died, not you."

She took a deep gulp of air as though he had pulled her from beneath water. Awkwardly, she stiffened, bones straightening. Her legs took her weight.

She tried to pull away from him. How dare he come into her house and remind her that her husband had died? Did he think for one minute, for one second, that she had forgotten? She gulped in air wishing she knew how to fight. Never in her life had she wanted to hit someone, to hurt someone, so much.

He backed away a few feet and watched her. "Sorry. I didn't mean to startle you." He tried to brush away the pain he had inflicted from her arms. "I didn't hurt you, did I?"

"I'm all right, Sheriff." Rubbing her arms she tried to decide if she hated him or needed to thank him. "You don't have to worry about me. No one has to worry about me." She suddenly wished she knew all the words to tell him to go away. Who did he think he was, breaking into her house, shaking her, reminding her she did not die with Kevin?

"Stop staring at me that way. I didn't mean any harm,

Meredith. To tell the truth I don't even know what got into me, shaking you like that. I just couldn't stand seeing you curled up, giving up. Not you." He looked like he wanted to run, but he forced himself to face her. "How about I go pick up something for supper? Maybe if you ate something you'd feel better."

She stared at him thinking he might just be the strangest man she had ever met. She would bet he never planned to touch her and the fact he did bothered him more than it bothered her.

"I thought, if you'd join me, I could be back in thirty minutes with some food. You'd have time to take a shower while I'm gone." She did not answer. "The hot water might warm you up and save a little off your heating bill."

When she did not comment, he unlocked the front door.

"If I come back and the door is locked I'll know your answer is no to my offer for dinner." He walked out without waiting for an answer.

Thirty minutes later he was sitting at her kitchen bar with hamburgers and malts when she walked out of the bathroom.

"I feel better." She admitted as she pulled her robe tighter and tossed her wet hair back. "What did you bring?"

He stared at her as if he'd never seen her before. Surely her thick robe was not that different from the sweaters she usually wore. But he seemed to be studying every detail about her.

"You did bring food?" she asked, as she moved around him and opened the sack.

"I didn't know what you liked," he finally said. "I picked up a couple of cheeseburgers from Jeff's."

Meredith climbed onto the stool beside him and waited.

He handed her a cheeseburger, then a malt. They ate without conversation. She had no clue about what to say to a sheriff. If she had ever committed a crime, she might confess. It did not seem polite to ask about his job. She was not sure she wanted to know who in town had been arrested lately.

When she finished, she went to the refrigerator and returned with a cake someone must have brought over. Funeral food, her grandmother used to call it. Friends and neighbors in small towns always baked their favorite dish and brought it to the house. It did not seem to matter that "the house" only contained one person who could not possibly eat a counterful of sweets and ten pounds of chicken. It was tradition.

She cut them both a slice and returned to her chair.

He pushed the dessert around with a fork without tasting a bite. Finally, he looked at her, and seemed to be studying her face with great interest. He lifted his napkin, leaned over and wiped the top of her lip.

Chocolate malt stained the white of his paper napkin.

She could have written the action off to instinct, but she guessed the sheriff had never done such a thing to anyone in his life.

"Thank you," she said.

For a moment, he did not say anything. He seemed to realize what he had done. He was not a man who touched easily and he had touched her twice in less than an hour. The cake forgotten, he stood.

"Anything else I can do before I leave?" he said awkwardly.

Meredith yawned. "No. I think I'll go to sleep now. Thanks for the dinner."

With him still standing in the middle of her kitchen, she walked the few steps into the bedroom. She lifted the covers and crawled into bed, still wearing her robe.

She heard him shoving food wrappers into the trash. Since he showed himself in, she figured he could show himself out.

"I'll lock up when I leave," he said, the same words he had said to her many times when they both worked holidays at the courthouse.

When she did not answer, she heard him step to her door. She snuggled into the pillows too exhausted to care what he talked about.

He pulled the quilt over her shoulder. "Good night, Meredith."

"Good night, Sheriff," she mumbled, too near sleep to say any more.

A hand was dealt in a no-name saloon in '27. Three oilmen passed the time playing poker with a local farmer. Money centered on the table. Cards were shown. Guns were pulled from both boot and vest.

When the smoke cleared all four were dead, bleeding across the five jacks facing up from the deck. The deaths were ruled an accident.

October 28
9:00 p.m.
County Memorial Hospital

He felt her presence even before the perfume that was always Randi penetrated his consciousness. She said she wore it because it was the only one she had ever found that could survive in bar air.

Through the thin bandages he saw her tall, slim, cowgirl shadow moving toward him. She made his blood warm from the first day he spotted her in the middle of a line dance at Frankie's Bar. He wished he could move closer to her, now. He needed to touch her. She was the kind of woman who drew a man's hands.

"Hello, Shelby," she whispered in a voice that was made to sing country-western songs. "I'm not supposed to be in here, but I had to drive back to pick up the rest of my stuff. I figured, what the hell, I'd stop by and see you on my way out of town."

She stood just out of his reach.

"I don't know if you can hear me, but I need to say something. I won't feel right until I do." She crossed and

uncrossed her arms. The plastic of her leather-look jacket
made a popping sound.

He smiled. Randi was all pretend, always had been.
Pretend leather, pretend fur, pretend love songs. She had
probably pretended with half the guys in town, making
every one of them believe he was the first, or the second
anyway.

Back years ago, when she and Crystal were running
wild and single, every man in the bar knew the party had
started when they walked in. Crystal, with her baby-blue
eyes, may have had her beaten on looks, but when a man
danced with Randi, he left the dance floor feeling like
the foreplay was about over.

Her low voice whispered over the machines. "I need
to tell you about that first day, when the doctor brought
the ring in. I couldn't be sure if it was yours or Jimmy's.
You both wore that plain band Taylor's sells to just about
every man. It was so out of shape, it didn't look much like
a ring at all. With you and Jimmy looking so much alike,
you being kin and all, it was impossible for the hospital to
tell. You two even had the same blood type. Folks always
said he seemed more like your son than Trent ever did.
He even told me once he thought he'd been following you
around since he could walk."

She rocked from her toes to her heels. "I guess what I'm
trying to say is the hospital thought it would be easier if
we just identified the only husband alive. Crystal wanted
you to be Shelby so bad, and me..."

He relaxed, guessing what she was about to say.

"I was never meant to take care of an invalid, much
less be stuck in a small town. We don't even have insurance to cover any hospital bills." She clicked her nails
along the metal frame of the fancy bed. "I was packing
to leave when the accident happened. Healthy, Jimmy

wasn't worth much. If he was hurt bad, I don't think I could..."

He closed his eyes, no longer wanting to look at her. Randi was a woman who always divided the pie in her favor. The most important person in her world lived in her skin. He could never hate her for that. With Randi, it was like instinct. Self-preservation. She would never change.

"Well..." She sounded nervous. "I just came by 'cause I've been thinking. What if there was a one in a million chance you were Jimmy and not Shelby under all those bandages and burned skin? After all, once Crystal took the ring, there were no further checks and everyone knew Shelby had a thing about never going to a big hospital. So there was no thought of transferring him."

She pulled a pack of cigarettes from her pocket, hesitated, then put it back. "If you are Jimmy, I figured I should tell you the score. You've got a chance to come back from this as Shelby Howard and do a lot of good for yourself. You could be like the old legend of that bird and rise up out of the ashes to fly. If you're Jimmy and anyone finds out, you'll probably spend the rest of your life in a welfare hospital. But Crystal says she's already ordered thousands of dollars worth of stuff to take Shelby home and give him the best of care."

She glanced at the door. "I got to go. There's a sign outside that says no one but family. If you're Shelby, I wish you the best. If you're Jimmy..."

Sniffing, Randi dug a balled tissue from her jeans pocket. "If you're Jimmy, keep your mouth closed and do us all a favor. You weren't a bad husband. I just couldn't love you like you wanted. It ain't nobody's fault."

A rattle sounded at the door. She slipped into the blackness. A nurse came in to pull the blinds and shift his position.

"Looks like a storm is moving in, Mr. Howard." She straightened his arms, making his body mold to the airplane-looking splints. "Now don't you worry, that little wife of yours will be back in a minute. The only time alone she gets is when she takes her bath, and we want her to take her time and enjoy it."

He hated it when the nurses talked like that, as if he were a child, as if they knew how he felt or what he thought.

The nurse checked the machines. "Hope the rain don't keep you up, Mr. Howard. We're supposed to get a storm tonight. The wind's already whirling around so bad even the weatherman can't make up his mind which direction it's coming from."

She left the room without expecting him to comment.

A moment later, the door opened enough for a thin cowgirl to pass through.

He closed his eyes and wished himself dead for the hundredth time since the accident.

Old-timers used to swear that if a sane man settled on the plains, he would be driven mad by the wind before he made it through his first winter.

October 28
Midnight
Montano Ranch

Thunder rumbled across the land in low angry bellows. Anna Montano wrapped her arms around her waist and tried not to jump each time she heard the sound. Pacing back and forth across the wide living room, she wished the walls of her ranch house were not constructed mostly of glass. At sunrise and sunset she thought the view beautiful, but now, with lightning flaring, all she could think was that the windows might crash in on her at any moment.

The reverberation reminded Anna of her childhood when her father's voice often echoed with rage off the tile walls of their villa. His solution to all disagreements was a swift and physical reaction. He would draw his belt with the precision of a gunfighter brandishing his Colt. The sons were trained to stand and take their punishment. But Anna learned to hide away, to remain silent, to become invisible. It was the way she, as the only daughter, survived.

As she grew older, she realized her father knew she

was tucked away just out of his sight, curled in some shadowy corner. His pride would not allow him to pardon her but, silently, he permitted the game.

Her brother Carlo's storms of rage were nothing compared to their father's, but Anna feared that by the time Carlo fathered children he would mirror the generation before. Since she and Carlo had been in America, her brother turned his anger more on the hired hands and less on her.

In fact, he had fired a ranch hand the morning before the rig exploded. Anna watched from the window as Carlo not only ordered the former employee to leave, he half dragged, half beat the man all the way to his car.

The man swore he would be back to even the score, but Carlo only laughed, welcoming a rematch. The threat made Anna shiver, not from fear of the stranger, but from how far her brother might go if the man set foot on Montano land again.

On the few occasions she had been the target for Carlo's anger, her husband, Davis, had done nothing to interfere. He allowed Carlo to yell and swear at her in two languages with little more interest than a bystander watching a parent discipline a child. She had been so young when they married, she knew he and Carlo saw her as little more than a child and probably always would.

She wanted Davis to stand up to Carlo, to protect her, to take her side in the argument. But Carlo was Davis's friend and foreman. She was only his wife.

She stared out into the night. Her brother would laugh at her if she called and told him the storm frightened her. He probably would not venture the hundred yards from his place near the barn to check on her. Anna thought of Helena, but it was too late to call. She must face the storm alone.

Then, in the blackness between flashes, she saw it. One lone light to the north. It had been two weeks since the rancher had offered a hug any time she needed it.

It is ridiculous. Do not think about it, she fretted. *Men do not offer hugs to women they do not know, not even in this strange country.*

But the light shone steadily in the ever changing sky.

It is half a mile across the prairie littered with mesquite trees, she reasoned. Halfway between was one of those barbed wire fences she hated so much. They might be fine for hemming in cattle, but she had seen how it had cut a horse who had accidentally raced into it. Her father never allowed wire to border his fields. But Davis did. He told Carlo to keep the broodmares in the north pasture. They were not so rambunctious and, if the barbs cut one a little, it would not matter. Only the colts were important as far as looks were concerned.

Anna paced the shadowy room. Long ago she had begun to call it her cage and not her home. The heavy leather furnishings. The architectural blending of iron and beams criss-crossed over her head like bars to a cage. Even the paintings reflected Davis's taste, not hers. Only the classical music drifting around the leather and iron mirrored her taste.

In the days since the funeral, she had found it more and more difficult to remember any happy memories with Davis. She tried to think of the first time she had seen him at her father's ranch. He had stood almost a head taller than her brothers as he examined one of her father's finest horses. He was strong and silent, just like a hero in an old Western. She had mistaken coldness for shyness. Indifference for strength.

Thunder rattled the windows as a Texas wind blew across the land, bringing Anna back to the present.

Walking to the glass, she pressed her hand against the window where the single light shone from the north. The glass was cold, but she imagined the warmth from the tiny light. Slowly she pulled away, hating her foolishness. She was not a desperate woman hungry for attention. Her life was adequate. She did not need another man to complicate it. Her husband had been dead less than a month. What kind of woman even thought about another man holding her after such a short time?

What had Zack Larson said in the elevator that day? No questions, no strings. Just a hug.

Thunder shook the walls again.

Grabbing her coat, Anna was out the back door before she had time to think any more.

She took long strides across the muddy ground until she reached the barbed wire. Carefully she climbed over it at the post, but even her long legs could not quite make the swing. A wire caught on her pants just above her boot, ripping the material.

Angry now, and frightened, she stormed ahead, almost daring the neighbor to be a liar.

Reaching the edge of the porch light's circle, she saw him. He sat in a wooden swing on his wide porch watching the storm as if the show had been staged for him.

Anna quickly took a step backward. He would probably rebuff her for slapping him, or he might laugh at her. Or he would think he could take liberties.

She retreated another step. She had been an idiot. She knew little about this Zack Larson. Davis said once that he had been a troublemaker in school, but Davis liked few people. And Larson was more than ten years past school.

Just as she turned to go, he stood. "Anna?"

Like an animal hearing the first crack of gunfire,

she ran. Her long legs carried her across the blackness between the houses. Icy rain pelted her and the wind whipped around her like a huge belt.

Within minutes, she was home. Her entire body trembled with cold as tears chilled against her cheeks.

Unable to stop crying, Anna pulled off her clothes and crawled into bed. She shook with sobs and loneliness. For a moment, she had been a fool. She had forgotten she was Anna Montano, widow and owner of a huge ranch. She was no longer a dreamer. There were no arms for her to run to. There never had been.

In 1905, Frank Phillips drilled for oil on tribal land leased to him, with her grandparents' permission, by an eight-year-old Delaware girl.

On September 6, they hit a gusher and AAI roared, making Phillips and one little girl rich overnight.

Yet, Texas and Oklahoma ranchers still considered themselves ranchers and not oilmen, many times refusing to lease oil rights to their land at any price.

October 29
North of the Montano Ranch
On Larson land

Zack Larson wasted his time trying to sleep. By dawn he felt as though he had personally wrestled the storm and lost. About the time his coffee was ready, Bella had showed up in her broken-down Ford pickup.

"Morning, kid," Bella grunted as she dragged her aging Hoover through the side door of his kitchen. "You sleep last night with all that racket the Irish were making?"

Zack grinned and poured a cup of coffee into her old pink mug she kept on his windowsill. Bella had been his mother's housekeeper and friend since before he was born. He might be thirty-four, but she still called him kid. And she still defined thunder as the dearly departed Irish throwing potatoes in heaven.

When his mother died, Zack kept Bella on even though his place was hardly big enough to demand much care. Folks told him she once had a drinking problem and had no steady job, so he figured she needed the work.

Regular as clockwork, once a week, she cleaned. Of course, her eyesight was fading and her joints were stiff. Nothing got dusted above her head or below her knees. It didn't matter that he'd bought a new lightweight vacuum; she only trusted her Hoover. She cleaned the old-fashioned way with ammonia and water, vinegar for spots and bleach settling in the sinks long after she left. For days after the spring cleaning, Zack's eyes would water every time he entered the house. Luckily, she only felt the need to spring clean every third year or so.

He handed her the cup as she made herself comfortable at the tiny dining table crammed into a small kitchen. The yellow linoleum tabletop was covered with Zack's efforts at bookkeeping.

Bella showed no sign of being in a hurry. After all, she worked by the hour. Zack's house took her all day, no matter what she cleaned or how long they talked.

"Storm kept me up," he finally answered. "How's the road from town?"

"A little muddy, but not bad." Bella's chubby fingers gripped the mug. "Why?"

"I thought I'd go in after a few supplies. You need anything?"

She shook her head. Hair that had never known a style wiggled around her wrinkled face. "I learned a long time ago, kid, to bring what I need when I come all the way out here. No sense driving into town for something you should have remembered. When I was young, we only went to town once a month and that was plenty. Folks nowadays think the Farm-to-Market Road is the interstate."

"Now, don't give me a hard time—" Zack fought down a grin "—or I'll get married again on you."

Bella snorted. "Oh, please, not that."

Zack remembered the hell his wife had put Bella through. From the moment they married, Bella could do nothing right. The only time his wife stopped complaining about the housekeeper was when she started picking on him. It took Zack only a few months to discover he did everything wrong, then a few more months to decide not to change. By the time he got around to telling his wife the bad news, she was packing.

He smiled at Bella, the only woman he needed in his life. "You want me to bring back some of that Chinese food for lunch while I'm running my needless errands?"

Bella acted like she pondered the question. "It's hardly fit to eat." She scratched her chin. "'Course, I'll be mighty busy today. Don't know if I'll have time to stop and eat, much less cook anything."

Zack cut her brainstorming short before she did any damage. "Extra egg rolls and extra sauce, right?"

"You talked me into it. But I'll still make you a batch of brownies for dessert. Them Chinese places never have fit desserts."

He nodded as if they'd struck a bargain. "I'll be back in a few hours, and we'll eat. Then, if the ground's not too wet, I'll work on the fence that borders the Montano spread."

Bella sipped her coffee slowly. "Sad about the accident. That poor beautiful woman left all alone. She's not stuck-up like some folks claim. I go over now and again to help her clean."

Standing slowly, Bella reached into the canister on the counter and pulled out two cookies from her stash. "Not that her place needs cleaning. You could eat pudding off the floor and not get a flea's-weight of dirt."

She dipped a cookie into her coffee.

Zack knew better than to interrupt. He scooted the canister closer to her.

She munched as she continued, "Her husband would

call me and insist I come. She didn't say a word when I'd show up. He'd tell me to clean the place, and she'd just stand there. Then he'd leave, and I'd sweep spotless floors and mop like I was doing some good."

"Odd," Zack mumbled. He stood and put his cup in the sink. He had no intention of gossiping about Anna. But shutting Bella up once she got started was harder than delaying birthing after a heifer took to ground.

Bella shook her head. "Not so strange. He was wanna-be rich. Thinking he needed a housekeeper, too proud to consider his wife *was* one. He'd brag about my work and ignore hers. I felt sorry for her. She's a real lady, better than Davis Montano deserved. And she can paint, too, real good. Pictures that make your heart sad to look at them. In a movie I heard a man once describe a painting that brought out feelings like hers do. He said the artist's tears must have blended with the colors. Her work's like that."

Zack stared out the window toward Anna Montano's place. He could imagine her painting. But he also remembered the slap she gave him the last time they met. A slap that should remind him she was not interested in even speaking to him.

She was a proud, now rich, rancher. He had to fight to keep the loans paid when they came due. She came from Europe, a place he would spend his life only dreaming about. He had never been farther away than Oklahoma City. Enough people in town remembered the trouble he got into the year his folks died that they probably told Anna Montano she would be better off if she never spoke to her neighbor for the rest of her life.

He grabbed his hat and nodded toward Bella. "Wash that old quilt on the porch swing, would you?"

"The one your grandma Larson made?"

"Yeah, and put it back beside the swing."

Without waiting for the questions, he headed out, telling himself he was crazy for losing sleep over what he *thought* he saw standing in the rain last night.

Three hours later, he stood knee-deep in mud, trying to install a stile over the barbed wire fence between his ranch and Anna's when he sensed her again, just as he had last night.

Zack looked up. She was riding full-out from the west. Her body moved in long, fluid movements, a part of the horse. Zack watched her as she spotted him and reined her mount.

He lifted one gloved hand to the brim of his hat and tipped his Stetson slightly in greeting.

Her only response was to turn and ride away.

Zack smiled as he tugged off his glove and reached in his pocket for the scrap of material he had found in the very spot where he was now installing a walkover. She might never set foot on his land again. But if she did, she would have a place to get over the fence without ripping her clothes—a place well hidden by thick brush and the roll of the land from anyone who might be watching from the Montano buildings.

October 31
Memphis, Tennessee

Randi Howard paid her money and maneuvered her large purse around the pimple-faced roly-poly teenager taking tickets.

"Third one to the right," he mumbled as she passed.

"You're welcome," she answered back, then hurried down the carpeted hallway to the last theater door on the right. She almost laughed at the excitement rushing her blood. This was a big-time theater, not some small local place that smelled of mold and age. She was in the big city now.

She'd been in Memphis for three days and was batting zero on working on her great plan to become a star. No apartment. No job. Her motel was the right price, but noisy until after midnight. Tonight, being Halloween, there was no telling how long the parties would last. Of all the holidays, Randi hated this one the most. People were frightening and mean enough without getting dressed up.

She had spent the day rubbing elbows with all kinds

of creeps, being nice, putting her best foot forward, and now all she needed was a little downtime.

Falling into the first plush theater seat she found, she decided life wasn't all bad. This place was dark and cool, and the chair rocked. Here she wouldn't have to worry about being hit on or told to look somewhere else. At one place she had applied they asked if, while she was singing, she would mind taking off her clothes. He didn't see why she was offended. He offered to pay five bucks more an hour.

She relaxed, breathing in the popcorn-flavored air. This had been a good idea and it even came with a movie.

She rocked back as the previews started with a volume high enough to push anyone still standing into a seat. The place darkened and music surrounded her.

Randi tried to let go of the day but she was too sober to stop thinking.

The bad thing about job hunting in bars, she decided, was going into them in daylight hours. A bar might look great after dark, but in the sunlight most looked seedy. There were no shadows to hide the stains on the welcome mat or the blood splattered in some long-forgotten bar fight. The people found in a bar before dark were also different. A few were just in to drink their lunch, but most looked like they lived around the clock in the smoky air. They were like the strange little bugs and spiders found in caves. They'd lived in the environment so long their skin had become translucent, their eyes blind to light.

Randi pulled one of the beers from the six-pack she'd stuffed in her huge purse, thinking she wanted to just forget the day and have some fun. She rocked back and forth trying to think of the name of the movie she was about to see. Not that it mattered, she'd be too far gone to remember by halfway through.

She thought of calling Crystal and checking on Shelby. Or Helena. Both had made her promise to call. The old lady had even insisted on giving Randi a phone card before she left Clifton Creek. "A phone card." Randi laughed out loud. "Who do I have to call? Next thing you know she'll be getting me a cell phone for Christmas."

"Hey, lady!" someone yelled from a few rows back. "You going to talk or watch the movie?"

"I haven't decided!" Randi yelled back, noticing for the first time that the movie had started.

"Well, make up your mind before I call you and tell you to shut up!"

Randi gulped down a long draw. There was something exciting about arguing with someone in the dark. "How about I come back there and show you what I can do with my phone card?"

"Come on back and bring your doctor. You'll be needing him."

Randi twisted around hoping to tell which one of the shadows was her advisory. All the heads looked the same. "And you bring your mother," she shouted. "Because you'll be crying for her like a little boy."

"Shut up and watch the movie!" a deep voice declared from somewhere on the left. "I didn't pay money to listen to you two exchange mating calls."

Several other people joined in, adding their two cents.

Randi swore and straightened back into her seat. She'd ended up in the middle of a damn choir.

She finished off the first beer and let the bottle clank its way along the floor to the front.

"That beer you drinking, calling card lady?" Her original harasser was back.

"That's me. If you were old enough to drink I'd give you one!"

"I'm old enough!"

Randi held up two beers and yelled, "Well, come on down!"

Ten minutes later she was sitting on the curb in front of the theater she'd just been kicked out of. Her harasser sat beside her offering her Milk Duds while he drank one of her beers.

"How old are you?" She looked at six feet of mostly arms and legs.

"Twenty-three," he answered. "How old are you?"

"The same," she lied. "And in all the years I've been twenty-three I've never been kicked out of a theater for drinking."

"Sorry about that." He tapped his bottle against hers. "Better luck next time."

He didn't sound any sorrier than any other man she had ever heard. But Randi forgave him anyway. Holding something against a man was no better than keeping a grudge against a dog. They may wet on your carpet and look real sorry when you yell at them, but that doesn't mean you won't be stepping on another damp spot soon.

"How about I buy you a plate of the best barbecue in town, lady?"

Randi smiled. "And I buy the beer, right?"

"Right," he smiled. She almost expected to see braces on his teeth.

Two hours later, after they'd eaten and drunk their fill, the kid did her a big favor. He introduced her to his cousin, the owner of a bar, who needed someone to serve drinks. The cousin even agreed to let her sing a little on slow nights.

Randi returned the favor. She kissed the kid good-night

at her car. He might want more, but he was too young. The fantasy of what might have been between them would give him far more pleasure. When he really was twenty-three, he'd think of tonight and wish, and when he was forty-three he'd probably remember the night and laugh. And, if she were lucky, when he was sixty-three, he'd look back and regret missing out on what might have been.

She returned alone to her hotel room. Most of the noise had stopped. Her brain was too clouded with beer to think. She stumbled around the small space pulling off her clothes. When she finally landed in bed, Randi grabbed her pillow and screamed into it with pure joy.

She was living her dream. The big city. The big time. Tomorrow she would be one day closer to being discovered.

Settlers watched from a dugout as the oil teams moved in. One young daughter stared in wonder at the endless line of supply trucks and wagons rolling by.

"Who are they, Mother?" she asked.

"Not anyone you'd want to know," the mother answered. "They're just oilmen."

November 3
County Memorial Hospital

Crystal Howard stood beside her husband's bed and
watched the line of suits file into the hospital room. The
first man in line was in his late twenties and carried a
colorful plant in full bloom. But the others looked as if
they were coming to a funeral.

The nurse took the plant from him before he could step
past her. "No live plants allowed," she said simply.

The young man smiled. "I'll bring dead ones next
time."

She didn't acknowledge the joke, but Crystal had to
glance at Shelby to keep from laughing.

Her husband looked more like a mummy in an old
movie than Shelby Howard. Parts of his skin were beginning to heal in patches, parts were covered in thick cream.
Though his head was bandaged, the swelling had gone
down, leaving only blisters and charred deposits where
his hairline had once been. He'd mumbled few words
since the accident, but she could feel his pain when she
touched his hand.

Trent Howard was the last to step through the door,

and he closed it behind him. He was convinced Shelby had suffered brain damage from breathing in too much smoke, and today would mark the showdown at the OK Corral as far as he was concerned.

Crystal had tried to tell Trent that morphine made Shelby's mind fuzzy. Trent paid her no mind. She guessed Shelby's only son saw her as filler packed around the important people in life. She was no more valued than that curly foam that fills a packing box. People like her: the waitresses, clerks, construction workers, doorman and hundreds others were no more important to him than a machine.

The men crowding into Shelby's room might wear business clothes instead of Western gear, but Crystal knew they would be shooting from the hip today. All the power Shelby had so carefully guarded was about to shift from father to son, and there was nothing she could do to stop it.

She smoothed the linen of her dress that almost passed as a businesslike suit, knowing she couldn't protect Shelby or herself from what was happening. How could she even talk to this group? She'd dropped out in the tenth grade and gone to work when her stepdad kicked her out of the house. Half the time she didn't know what Trent was talking about and, today, he'd brought his lawyers. She was so unimportant, Trent didn't even bother to introduce her to the group.

Crystal slipped her fingers onto Shelby's, wishing she could reassure him. Since the accident she sensed fear, as well as anger in his slight grip. She felt both now.

"Gentlemen, thank you for coming so late in the day. I felt we could delay no longer on what must be done. I'd like you to say hello to my father." Trent made a grand sweep of his hand as if he were a barker showing off the newest freak in the circus. "His condition and the hospital reports will confirm the urgency in taking action today to transfer the reins of Howard Drilling to me."

One man opened his briefcase over the tray-table and asked, "Does your father concur?"

"My father hasn't said a word in almost a month. He's awake, but he can't communicate. One ear was burned completely off, the other damaged. The nurses tell me he can see light and dark, but we're not sure how much else. The damage from the fire and the tubes thrust down his throat would make it hard, if not impossible, for him to speak."

Trent moved impatiently. "We can't wait any longer. I'm sure he would want me to take charge. After all, I'm only following the orders laid out in his will, nothing more."

A gray-haired man migrated closer to the bed. "But as long as he's alive, the will doesn't take effect."

Frustrated, Trent added, "I understand. But the company can't run itself. There have been questions about the cause of the fire on the Montano Rig. Someone needs to be there to answer them before investors on other rigs get nervous. As his only son, I have to take the reins. At least until he recovers."

Three of the men appeared uncomfortable. The oldest advanced another step. He glanced at Crystal, nodding a silent greeting, then looked at the bed where she held Shelby's hand.

"May I touch his hand?" he asked politely. "I promise not to shake it too hard."

"The doctor said that his left hand wasn't burned so badly." Crystal tried to press against the wall as he moved beside the bed. She couldn't remember ever seeing the man, so he wasn't one of Shelby's drinking friends. He had kind eyes and a soberness about him that made her think most folks probably trusted him more than the other suits.

"Shelby?" The man touched the lightly bandaged hand, sliding his fingers into a handshake. "It's Elliot Morris. I don't know how much you can hear or understand, but I'd like you to know how sorry I am about all the suffering that has found you."

"He won't respond," Trent snapped. "I've tried to talk to him every day since the accident. Nothing. My father may be little more than a vegetable, gentlemen. I am forced to take charge to see that his company stays intact."

"Shelby? It's Elliot. Can you hear me?" The old man wasn't listening to the younger Howard. "I've been doing legal work for you for thirty years. I'm dreading like hell to draw up the papers your son wants."

Crystal swore she saw a tiny tear fight its way down the old man's face.

"Shelby?" he whispered. "Shelby, is the wildcatter who walked into my office all those years ago beneath those bandages and burns?"

Crystal stared as the old friends touched. Slowly, Shelby's fingers closed around Elliot's hand.

No one in the room breathed.

Elliot straightened. "Shelby, can you hear me?"

The bandaged hand closed slightly again.

"Can you understand?"

Shelby's head rose an inch and nodded once.

Crystal broke into tears. She didn't care that makeup streamed down her face and puddled onto her good clothes. She hadn't been imagining that Shelby was somewhere beneath all the pain. Sometimes, late at night, she thought maybe she was just wanting him to know she was there, to need her when he really was too close to death to care. But now she knew. Everyone knew.

Elliot chuckled. "Well, wildcatter, you sure had everyone worried. Appears it takes more than a little explosion to slow down Shelby Howard."

Everyone except Trent laughed as Elliot continued, "Since I'm here, do you want to turn over the power of attorney to your fine son? That way, you can recover without worrying about the company."

Crystal read the lie in the honest man's face as easily as she used to spot an undercover cop at the bars.

When Shelby shook his head slightly, she saw Elliot's grin. The old man tested Shelby, and her husband just proved his sanity.

"This is insane." Trent finally recovered enough to attack. "He can't run a business from this bed. I'll bring lawyers from Dallas if I have to. The man is too far gone to do anything. In a few weeks, he'll be looking at months of surgeries. For his sake, I have to take charge." He moved to the end of the bed, a gambler covering his bet. "I'm doing this for your sake, Dad. When you do get better, I'll step down from the helm."

It was obvious that no one in the room believed him.

"I'm sure the company ran just fine when Shelby took a few days off." Elliot's voice was calm, almost as if he were going over facts to himself. "I remember he and Crystal went to Vegas for a month last year. The payroll still got made. The bills got paid."

"That's because of my cousin, Jimmy Howard. Some say Jimmy knew more about Howard Drilling than my father did. He ran it most of the time even when Dad *was* in town," Trent offered. "He's the only one who could write checks on the business account besides Dad. He was killed in the accident."

"Can't you sign?" Elliot looked directly at the son.

"No. Dad never got around to authorizing anything but an annual salary for me. I'm rarely at the office. I have a great many other responsibilities."

Elliot's forehead worried into a hundred tiny lines. "Someone must be able to sign on the account. It doesn't make sense that a man would have so many holdings and not trust more than one person."

Crystal didn't miss the slight emphasis on *trust*.

"I can sign checks," she whispered.

"We're not talking about the household account," Trent grumbled.

His reaction came fast, like an invisible slap. She braced herself, expecting to hear him tell her to keep her mouth shut.

Elliot ignored Trent. "Is that true…Mrs. Howard? You can sign checks on Howard Drilling?"

She smiled at the way he called her Mrs. Howard. No one ever called her that, though everyone in town knew she was rightfully married to Shelby. Mrs. Howard was Shelby's first wife, the mother of his children. She was just Crystal, the tramp he'd married one weekend in Dallas.

"After we got married, Shelby would always bring his work home. To finish his work faster he had me write the checks out." She saw no need to tell them that Shelby's eyes were weakening, and he'd been too vain to wear glasses. "He said he'd learned a long time ago never to let a bookkeeper sign checks. 'A man handles his own money,' he'd say, then he'd tell me what to write and I would."

Elliot nodded toward one of the younger men. The silent soldier pulled out a cellular phone and stepped to the door.

"Dad never mentioned such a practice to me." Trent glanced at her as if she were bothering them by talking. "You would've cleaned out the liquid assets and been long gone if you could sign on the corporate accounts."

Crystal shook her head. "I didn't need any money. He gave me plenty for spending. All I ever wanted was to have a home with Shelby. I don't care about the business or how much he's got."

Trent huffed in disbelief. Silence grew in the room like bindweed.

The young man stepped back inside. A nurse's warning about using cell phones drifted through the open doorway, but the man answered directly to Elliot. "It appears, Mr. Morris, there are two names on the signature card for Howard Drilling other than Shelby Howard. James Howard and Crystal Howard. The bookkeeper told me most of the business checks that come through each month were signed by one Crystal Howard."

Trent paled.

"Well." Elliot grinned. "It seems we have no problem after all. While your husband is recovering, you'll be able to keep the cash flowing."

He looked directly at Trent. "I assume you'll be taking over the running of the company while your father's ill."

"I guess I'll have to."

"Good." Elliot motioned for the others to leave. "I'd like to offer my assistance, Mrs. Howard. I'll be happy to look over the accounts each month, answer any questions you have about expenses." He handed her his card. "Call me any time."

"Thank you, but I don't know if I can—"

"Of course you can. Howard Drilling has a bookkeeper and a few secretaries that I'm sure will be made available to you." No uncertainty echoed in Elliot's voice. "Shelby really needs your help now. I know you won't let him down."

Crystal wiped mascara from her cheek. "I'll do my best."

Trent left after Elliot Morris without saying a word. Crystal lowered her face to Shelby's hand. "I'll try real hard, Shelby. I'll do the very best I can. I won't let you down. Mr. Morris will look over everything I do, just to make sure. He can explain things to me, and as you get better, I'll be able to talk with you."

Nurse Landry came in to close the curtains and tell Crystal she could use the whirlpool tub at the end of the hall if she wanted. Visiting hours were over. Since that day Helena had first visited the hospital, a folding bed with clean sheets had been delivered every night at nine for Crystal.

During her bath, Crystal thought about how she was a real wife now, not just some bracelet on a rich man's arm. She'd be helping, working with Shelby, not just signing checks. She could feel a good wind blowing in her direction. A wind that would give her a chance to prove she could be somebody important. Somebody worth loving.

By the time she dressed for bed, she decided she would call Anna and Helena. Maybe one of them could go shopping with her for proper clothes. She'd have to go to the bank now, and Mr. Morris's office. She had responsibilities.

Sitting gingerly on the side of Shelby's bed, she whispered, "I'll do the right thing, darling. You can count on me."

Shelby's bandaged arms had been taken from the splints. He lifted his hand to her face.

"I'll go to your office and find out all I need to do. I

can type. I took a semester before I dropped out. Maybe I could get someone to teach me how to use your computer to check on stocks, like you always do."

Bandaged fingers lowered to the V of her nightgown.

"Oh, no." She giggled and gently pushed him away, still lost in her thoughts of becoming a businesswoman. "I could find a book at the library on the stock market so I could talk to you about it, too. You always said it was the biggest poker game around, but I never understood what you meant."

He reached again, hooking the material with curled fingers.

"Shelby?" Crystal tried to pull his hand away. "I don't want to do that. Not here. Not now."

He tugged again.

"But Shelby, I want to think about all I got to do. Surely you don't want me to—"

"Yes!"

His voice was so low and hoarse she didn't recognize it. Any joy over his first word vanished as she realized what he wanted.

Slowly, Crystal unbuttoned her gown and bared her breasts. Big, beautiful, perfectly formed breasts he'd bought for her the second month they'd been married.

Tears floated in her eyes, but she knew he wouldn't notice. She'd played this game for years. When he was drunk, he'd say, "I got my own peep show." He wanted her to sit still as he touched her. Since the day she came back from Dallas and the surgery, he'd bragged about her breasts to any man who would listen. Demanding his feel of them even before the bruises healed.

As he brushed a bandaged hand over her bare flesh, she remembered how one night he got drunk and bet a feel of her breasts in a poker game. He'd lost, and she'd had to unbutton her blouse and kneel down beside the winner's chair while the stranger fondled her.

Shelby touched her nipple. A tear bubbled over and rolled down Crystal's face, but she didn't move. She knew he saw, not only her breasts, but her whole body as his. He had since the night he'd taken her from the bar to his hotel room and left five hundred-dollar bills on the nightstand. She'd never gone back to work. From the morning she'd picked up the money, she'd been Shelby's. When he married her, she'd thought things would change between them, but it hadn't.

He lowered his hand. When she moved to close her robe, he stopped her with a wave. Crystal straightened, knowing she'd have to wait until he had his fill of viewing.

It didn't matter that she could sign checks or that Mr. Morris had called her Mrs. Howard. Crystal knew who and what she was. Shelby had just reminded her.

She closed her eyes and waited. She had learned there was no use trying to make him hurry. Once he'd told Jimmy over breakfast that he was tired because he'd had her strip and stand in front of him until after midnight. Claiming he never got tired of staring at perfection, he continued with the details. Jimmy had looked uncomfortable and she'd been too embarrassed to say a word.

A moment later, the feel of his bandaged fingers brushing her tears away startled her. She leaned away and buttoned her top, watching him carefully. He'd never noticed her crying before. He'd never cared.

The legend goes that God ran out of plans for landscaping when he got to Texas, so he thought it easier to just make a people who liked the barrenness.

November 4
Pigeon Run

Helena Whitworth lived in a big, rambling two-story house in what everyone referred to as "the historical district," though no one quite knew why. As a joke, the first day he saw the place, J.D. called her home "Pigeon Run." The name stuck, at least in hers and J.D.'s minds. No one else dared to call the Whitworth House, bought and paid for by Helena herself, anything so crazy.

Her favorite room was the master's quarters she'd had enlarged after she married J.D. She had taken in the bedrooms on either side and made small studies for each of them. Between the studies was an open area with floor-to-ceiling glass where they spent endless hours reading and watching the birds in the backyard.

Every morning, Helena started her day with coffee at her desk. Today was no exception.

"Well, I'll be," she whispered as she replaced the receiver. "You'll never guess who that was."

"Who?" J.D. sat in his favorite chair by the windows. She could only see his profile in shadows, but she knew he was there. She might have attended his funeral, but he was still very much alive to her.

"Crystal Howard." Helena stood and poured herself another cup from the coffeemaker behind her desk. "She wants my advice."

"She needs it," J.D. answered. "I always felt sorry for her. Shelby treated her like a hunting dog, paying all kinds of attention when he needed her and ignoring her when he didn't. She must be lost now, poor thing."

"But she stays with him. No matter what Shelby does, or how bad off he is, she stays. There's glue in that girl's blood."

"My guess is she doesn't have anywhere else to go." J.D. shrugged. "Plus, I think she really loves the bastard. Hell, we all do. There's something about Shelby."

"Plain ornery," Helena decided. "Pure and simple. From his school days, Shelby was the most ornery person I ever met. That kind of trait endears him to men, but drives women crazy."

J.D. laughed, and Helena thought of how dearly she loved the sound. He had a contagious laugh, always luring others to join him. When he had been in the service he barely let himself smile, but once he retired and married her, she watched him learn to laugh all over again. The boy she had played with and the gray-haired man were the same to her. The changes in their bodies were like changes of clothes. Inside, loving was the only thing that altered through the years. And it grew and grew.

A pounding shook the bedroom door. "Momma, you up?"

Helena did not answer.

"Momma, I heard you in there. I know you're still home. Don't try to fool me."

Slowly, Helena crossed to the door and threw the bolt,

wondering when her daughter had started talking to her in such a way. "Morning, Paula." She tried to smile at her offspring. "You're here early."

Paula hurried into the room like an overweight, middle-aged, SWAT team commando. "I thought I heard you talking to someone."

Helena did not look in the direction of J.D.'s chair. She knew he was no longer there.

"I must have been thinking aloud," Helena finally offered as explanation, and returned to her desk. "I was trying to arrange my schedule today." She frowned at Paula's unisex clothes. Both girls had no regard for the fact that their mother owned a dress store. You would think they would at least try to dress in fashion colors if not styles.

"Oh, Momma, you shouldn't talk to yourself. That's the first sign of a weak brain."

"I doubt that, honey." Helena laughed. "Or half the people in this town would be babbling day and night."

A sense of humor had been left out of Paula's makeup. She fidgeted like a freshman debater being challenged. "I didn't mean nothing personal, Momma. I just came by to see if you want to go to lunch with me. I'm worried about you being all alone and I know you're not eating like you should."

"Sorry, but I made plans for lunch." Helena noticed relief more than disappointment cross Paula's face. "Crystal Howard needs my advice about a few things. I promised to meet her at the hospital."

"You're not going to lunch with *her?*" Paula circled the desk. "She's nothing but a lowlife, Momma. Folks say she was old Shelby's mistress even before he was widowed."

"Be careful," Helena warned. "She happens to be the

wife of one of J.D.'s friends. If she needs help, I'll do what I can."

"Yeah, but J.D.'s dead, Momma." Paula whispered the words as though she could lessen the blow as their impact reached Helena.

"Not in my heart." Helena lifted her chin. "He'll be with me always."

She reached for a silver dollar she kept in the organizer at the corner of her desk. "When he left for the army, my mother gave him this. Told him it would bring him home. When he came back the last time and we married, he slipped this silver dollar in my hand during the ceremony promising he'd never leave me again. He said it took him through the valley of the shadow and back to me."

Paula looked like she was fighting to keep her eyes from rolling to the back of her head. "Oh, all right, Momma. If you want to think he's still here, Preacher Wayne said it's understandable for the first few months."

Helena made no comment. Preacher Wayne was quoted so often in this town, she would not have been surprised to see him come out with a quote-of-the-day calendar.

Paula changed the subject. "Can't someone else help Crystal Howard? Or maybe you could just talk to her, give her advice. But don't go to lunch. At least not where you'll see anyone we know."

Helena was disappointed in her daughter, but somewhere deep down she knew that a part of the blame for what Paula had become lay with her. When the girls were small, she had left them in someone else's care most of the time. Helena told herself that, as a single mother she had to make a living but, in truth, she'd always felt like an outsider. Almost from birth, the twins bonded with one another, treating her as a stranger. She had built a success-

ful business by working day and night. The twins were
passed from day care to babysitters to housekeepers.

"I need to help Crystal," Helena answered. "For her
sake and mine."

"Oh, I understand." Paula's whole body relaxed. "You
do need something to keep you busy. A project. Everyone
will understand that."

Helena did not argue. She finished dressing, listening to Paula remind her to take her heart medicine as
though she had ever forgotten a pill in her life. She left
two hours before she planned to meet Crystal. Paula was
still there when she came downstairs, talking with the
housekeeper about things that needed to be done. Paula
seemed convinced her mother would forget such details.
Helena overheard her, but made no comment. In her way,
Paula was just trying to be helpful.

Helena thought of returning to lock her bedroom
door, but decided that would spur too much curiosity.
Paula might rifle through the desk, or help with cleaning,
but she would never sit in the chairs by the window as
Helena had done for an hour yesterday. She would never
notice the beauty and color as the last few leaves fought
to remain on the trees. She would never see how the bare
branches seemed to thicken and knot like thin aging fingers stretched toward heaven. Her daughters would never
witness the wonder she saw each day simply sitting beside
J.D. in their worn leather chairs.

Ten minutes later, Mary looked surprised when Helena
walked into the small office over the dress shop. Though
Helena could well afford a suite of offices for herself and
Mary, they both enjoyed the quarters they had started
with almost forty years ago. Helena remembered an old
saying her father liked to quote: Having money doesn't
always have to breed gluttony.

"Morning, Mrs. Whitworth." Mary stood at attention. "We weren't expecting you." Mary used the plural as though there was more than herself in the office.

At four feet eleven inches, Mary looked frail and washed out with her gray hair and eyes, but in all their years together she had never taken a sick day or asked for more than her two-week vacation.

"Morning." Helena smiled. "I wonder if you might call Elliot Morris and ask him if he's got a little time free for me this morning?"

"Of course." Mary never asked for explanations. "Right away."

She followed her boss to the other end of the office where a long window looked down on the finest dress shop between Dallas and Oklahoma City. *Helena's Choice.*

"Mrs. Whitworth?" Mary whispered.

"Yes?" Helena continued to watch a few customers moving about the store. When Mary did not say anything, Helena glanced at her friend. "What is it, Mary? Don't tell me we've had another manager quit?"

"No." Mary looked tortured.

Helena waited. Mary always bore the burden of every problem on her shoulders as though it were her fault. The wiring could spark, and Mary would start apologizing.

"It's about your daughters. They've both been in asking all kinds of questions about the running of the store. Paula even asked to see the books."

Laughing, Helena patted Mary's arm. "I'm sorry, dear. It's my fault. They've felt the need to smother me since the accident and in truth, I've been more tired than usual. Out of desperation, I asked them to check on the store just to allow me some peace. I hope they didn't pester you."

"Oh, no. I just wasn't sure how much to tell them."

Mary was a woman who always needed to know exactly where to stand. If she had been on the *Titanic,* she would have been looking for her place card as the ship submerged. "Paula's got a head for numbers, I can tell. She likes everything in order, like her mother."

Helena never thought of either girl as being like her and guessed Mary was, as always, being kind.

"Tell them whatever they're interested in knowing. Someday, they'll have to run the place. Let them take care of any last-minute Christmas ordering, if they like. Any mistakes they make can be sold in the January clearance sale."

Helena closed her eyes, trying to imagine what the store would look like if her daughters took over. Grays, blacks and browns would be the colors for all seasons and a blue-light special would flash every hour. Handbags would all be huge and shoes practical. Animals and cartoon characters would likely dance across the hem of all the blouses.

She straightened. She was only sixty-three. Retirement was still years away. She felt so good lately, she had not bothered to take the atenolol her doctor thought she needed twice a day. Her blood pressure had not been high for years, and it was time to stop bothering with at least one of the many pills he always insisted she take.

There was nothing wrong with slowing down a little and just enjoying the sunsets with J.D. She was old enough to know what her body needed and fewer pills seemed right.

Thirty minutes later, Helena walked into Elliot Morris's law office in a royal-blue wool suit that flattered her white hair. She said simply, "How can I help Crystal Howard?"

Elliot offered her a seat and asked his secretary to bring a fresh pot of coffee. Both knew this would take some time.

They came to the oil fields on horseback, by train, by wagon and in Model T Fords, all loaded down with what they owned. They came unprepared and untrained, but with their pockets full of dreams.

November 4
Dusk
Randell House Restaurant

By the end of the day, Crystal's head whirled with excitement. Helena not only helped her select several new, professional-looking outfits, she gave Crystal suggestions on how to handle Shelby's business. Helena knew the insides of running a company and shared her knowledge freely.

Anna Montano joined them at the restaurant for drinks and dinner. As before, her speech was halted, almost a stutter at first. But by the time the salad arrived, her words flowed smoothly with only a hint of accent. There was an intelligence about Anna, a grace that Crystal knew she would never have no matter how many people called her Mrs. Howard.

There was also something fragile about Anna that frightened Crystal, for she was not sure her foreign friend would stand to face the winds of change. A few of the oil workers had said Anna refused to talk to the sheriff or anyone else investigating the fire. They commented it was almost like she was afraid of the law. So far her brother had been answering all the questions, claiming that when she had to make a statement she would.

Crystal worried. Anna seemed too fragile, like a hot-house flower that had never had to face the real world. She wasn't sure what it would take to make Anna stand on her own.

Some folks are fighters, and some aren't. Crystal saw herself as a fighter, scraping her way since her teens. But Anna? Anna didn't have a scar on her.

Crystal noticed a few gaps in the conversation, but they weren't uncomfortable. It was grand to sit in such a nice restaurant and eat a meal with her new friends. Helena looked stately, as she always did, and Anna's beauty was timeless. Crystal found herself sitting up straighter and watching her manners carefully.

After all, she did know how to eat at a restaurant that didn't have a drive-up window. Shelby used to joke that she'd never had a meal she didn't have to pay for first until she married him. Crystal could hardly wait to tell him about tonight.

She made it through the meal with only one mistake. She stacked the plates after each course. When the waiter frowned at her and picked up the dinner plates, Helena told him to bring several desserts. They were still starving she said, and might eat until they had the plates stacked a foot high. All three women laughed and Helena, thin to the point of being bony, ate three desserts before she gave up the challenge.

As they hugged goodbye in the parking lot, Crystal knew they all felt that invisible bond that had formed in the nurses' break room the day of the accident. It had grown stronger with time.

Thirty minutes later, Crystal could still feel it, like an invisible hug. She sat on the edge of Shelby's bed, telling him every detail about the meal and everything Helena and Elliot said.

As usual, she had no way of knowing if Shelby was listening. Maybe he was already asleep, or maybe he was in too much pain to care about her day. It didn't matter. She talked to him anyway. "We'll get you out of here as soon as the doctor gives the okay. I talked to Nurse Landry and she said she'd contact a nursing service that will provide the best round-the-clock care. We'll convert a few of the spare bedrooms into nurses' quarters, so they will be with us all the time."

The house they'd built on the north edge of town always seemed so huge to Crystal. It had wide marble floors and gold doorknobs just like a palace. With the new plans it was shrinking by the minute. "Everything you'll need will be upstairs. I'll move your office staff to a few rooms downstairs so I can work with them and still be close to you. Helena says they shouldn't mind coming over if I have the cook prepare them lunch every day."

Crystal brushed her hand over his. "Oh, Shelby, you're going to be so proud of me. I've thought of everything— even a lift for the stairs. I'm going to help you get well."

He didn't respond.

"I can do this, Shelby." Tears welled in her eyes. "I promise I can. You'll see. You'll be so proud of me."

"Mrs. Howard?" A nurse had slipped in silently. "Is it all right if I bring your bed in now? Visiting hours are over."

Crystal straightened. Things were changing, she could feel it as surely as she'd felt the north wind chill her bones when she'd walked in from the parking lot. She just wasn't sure if they were changing for the better or worse.

Shelby was still alive. She was still his wife. Yet fear choked her. Some days Shelby seemed to be barely

hanging on to life, and if Trent had his way no one would
see Crystal as part of the Howard family. At first Trent
told everyone she'd run the first time she got ahold of any
real money. She had already written checks for thousands
of dollars and she was still here. She didn't blame him
for hating her; she'd probably feel the same way he did if
their positions were reversed.

Crystal smiled at the nurse. It didn't matter what Trent
said or thought, people were starting to respect her.

"Bring the bed in." Crystal smoothed her new clothes
as she moved off Shelby's bed. "I'll hold the door so it
doesn't bump and wake Shelby."

The nurse nodded. As she worked, she whispered,
"He's stable now. You should go home and get a good
night's sleep yourself."

Crystal shook her head. "I'll go home when my husband does." Smiling, she swore she'd show all those
people who wouldn't give her the time of day. She wasn't
some tramp Shelby picked up. She was his wife, and she'd
be a good one if it took her twenty-four hours a day.

She wasn't the nobody her stepfather had predicted
she'd be. She was somebody and, for the first time since
she married, she had friends to prove it. Helena had even
said she was a jewel and Helena Whitworth wasn't the
kind of woman to say something that wasn't true. Also,
Anna cared about her for no other reason than they were
friends. Even Meredith Allen, a schoolteacher everyone
respected, came by to visit almost every other day.

When Shelby got better, he would see the change. Her
clothes had class. She was learning and growing. He'd see
it in the way she walked and talked and in the way she
knew to let the waiter stack the plates.

Then he could take her back to the Randell House

Restaurant, and they would sit right in the middle of the place. And maybe when she told him she loved him, he'd say it back to her...just once.

Thunderstorms have a habit of whirling across the prairie without warning, but snow rolls in like the tide bringing layers of winter. Before man settled the land, buffalo roamed by the millions. The buffalo is the only animal that faces the wind no matter how cold it blows. Some say the wildcatters were like that, always facing their problems head-on.

November 6
Streets of Clifton Creek

The weather turned ugly a few hours before dawn, coating the streets with what the locals called "Satan's Ice." A sheet of ice so thin it was invisible on the highway, but if you hit it, you might slide right into hell.

Meredith crept toward school in her old Mustang with the bald tires. Almost there, she passed Sheriff Granger Farrington. He stood beside his car parked behind a van that had slid off the road and taken out the school crossing sign and ten feet of an old chain-link fence.

Waving at him, Meredith moved past. When she glanced in her rearview mirror she noticed him watching her.

She felt sorry for him having to work in the cold. It usually took a few hard freezes before the college kids wised up and slowed down.

As the day progressed, Meredith thought of Granger when the snow moved in on top of the ice. She doubted he would have time to go home for a set of dry clothes or even have time to eat. The thought of him out in the weather made her shiver even in her warm classroom, for she knew he was spending the day pushing people out of ditches, jumping cars with their lights left on, and directing traffic.

At four, with most of the school empty, Meredith borrowed the office phone and finally called the sheriff.

"Sheriff Farrington's office. This is Inez. How can I help you?" Inez sounded official and bored.

Meredith smiled into the phone. Inez usually only worked mornings. Whenever Meredith was at the courthouse on holidays Inez always found the time to stop in for a visit. She seemed to think her breaks lasted until someone from the sheriff's office yelled her name down the hall.

"May I please speak to the sheriff?" Meredith kept her voice formal not wanting to have to explain why she was calling.

"Sure, Meredith. I'll put you right through. No problem at school, I hope?"

Meredith closed her eyes. Of course, Inez would have caller I.D. and from there it would be no mystery to figure out who was calling. "No problem at school. I just have a question about the weather."

"It's ringing," Inez said, a moment before Meredith heard a click.

"Yes!" Granger almost shouted. "What's the next problem?"

Meredith almost hung up the phone. He sounded busy.

"Go ahead," he snapped.

Meredith glanced around the tiny office to make sure no one was listening. "Sheriff Farrington, this is Meredith Allen."

There was a silence on the line and she wondered if she had lost the connection.

His voice finally came, slower this time. "Are you all right, Meredith?"

The concern seemed more than just professional, but she could not be sure. "I'm fine," she answered, knowing his question was not just a way of passing time. "And you?"

Granger laughed. "I'm standing knee-deep in snow and mud trying to dig a car out right now. I'm cold, wet and hungry, but other then that I'm just fine, Mrs. Allen. Maybe we could talk…"

"I understand this is not a good time to visit." Meredith knew she had to hurry. "I called to ask if you would like to come to dinner tonight. I want to pay you back for buying me dinner and I thought tonight you might like getting off work and having a meal ready."

The silence lingered so long she was sure he was thinking of how to turn her down, but then he answered, "What time?"

"I'll have it ready at seven but I can leave it on warm if you're late."

"I'll try, but I can't make any promises."

"I understand." She could almost hear him trying to think of an excuse to get out of coming.

The connection ended. He obviously was not a man who wasted time with goodbyes.

Meredith gathered her bags and headed home. She had a great deal to do before seven. She hadn't cooked a meal in a month. During lunch she had made a list of what she needed from the store, but there was still the house to clean.

Rushing like a madwoman, Meredith had everything ready by seven and then she relaxed. She was glad as the minutes ticked away giving her time to rest. But by nine o'clock she knew he wasn't coming and the disappointment surprised her.

As she stood to put the food away, a tap sounded at the door.

The sheriff had already backed away to the steps when she answered. "I'm sorry I'm so late." He looked tired. "If you'd like to try it another night, I'd understand."

"No." She motioned him in. "I put supper in the oven. It won't take me but a minute to set it on the table."

He removed his hat and coat before following her into the kitchen. "We could make it another time." He tried again. "I know you've got to teach tomorrow."

He looked tired. She almost changed her mind. But she had cooked the food. They might as well eat. Plus, she had been looking forward to seeing him all day. Now, she was not sure why. "Please, Sheriff, sit down."

He watched her, studying her. But he did not make her nervous like most people did.

After a few minutes she had to ask, "What is it?"

He grinned. "I guess I've never seen you wearing anything but boxy sweaters that are usually wallpapered in nursery rhymes. It seems strange to see you wearing jeans and a T-shirt."

"Do I need to change to make you feel comfortable?"

"No. Of course not. I didn't mean to make you feel uncomfortable. You look great just the way you are. I'll just have to get over missing the nursery rhymes."

He leaned against the bar and continued watching her. They both seemed to have run out of anything to say, and she was still setting the table. The sheriff was no good at small talk, and all she usually talked about was school. The greeting they paid one another in the hallway of the courthouse was about their limit.

The warmth of her house seemed to help him relax. Finally he talked of his day, but it sounded more like a report than conversation. When she did not add much he went back to watching her. She could almost read his thoughts. She wasn't his type. He looked like he counted the minutes until he could say good-night.

"Help yourself to a beer," she said with her back to him as she pulled food from the oven.

"Beer? Mrs. Allen? Are you telling me teachers are allowed beer?"

She glanced in his direction. "Do I need an ID?"

He smiled. "Wearing that Texas Tech T-shirt you look almost young enough to card. But no, you're old enough." He reached for two longnecks and leaned back against the counter as he opened them.

Meredith walked past him delivering food to the table. He closed his eyes, and took a deep breath. "Smells good."

She almost asked if he was talking about the food or her.

"And peaceful here," he added. "Or maybe it's not the place but you that makes everything seem in order."

She knew what he meant. They were not playing games; they were simply becoming friends. They were just two people about to have a meal. Then he would go on his way and the next time he saw her in the hallway at the courthouse, they might talk a little longer than before. Maybe they would ask about more personal things than the weather, like "Did you have a nice weekend?" or "Hope you haven't caught the flu going around this season."

"I made barbecue." She broke into his thoughts. "I hope you like it."

"Sounds fine," he mumbled before taking a drink of the beer.

She watched him run his hand though his hair, as if pushing memories aside and relaxing.

Meredith reached into the oven for the pan of rolls. The crocheted pot holder slipped in her hand. She jumped backward, trying to avoid the pan hitting her legs and feet.

A second later, her elbow struck the beer in Granger's hand. He let it fall as he grabbed her around the waist to steady her.

Beer and dinner rolls hit the floor, splattering and tumbling everywhere. He pulled her close, leaning back against the bar as they watched the mess collect at their feet.

It took her a moment to realize she was in his arms. Her body pressed against the length of him, warming him after his cold day. He suddenly felt better than he had in a long time.

All she had to do was step away. His hands at her waist only steadied her. She was not the kind of woman to flirt, much less come on to a man. But she did not want to move away. She wanted to stay if only for a few more minutes. She could feel his breath and his heart pounding.

The beer slowly dripped on the floor, but neither reached down to clean it up.

Move, she shouted inside her mind, but her body didn't cooperate. Step away and act like this didn't happen. But to the very core of her being Meredith knew she did not want to move away. She wanted to be even closer.

The sheriff also seemed to be struggling. All he had to do was say "Pardon me" and walk to the other side of the bar, then they could both pretend she had not been so close. They could avoid each other's eyes and act as if they had never touched. In time, maybe they would forget.

But to start the process of forgetting, one of them had to move.

She felt his fingers pressing against her shirt. The need to touch must be as strong inside him as it was in her.

He moved his hand down her body and took her hand. Lifting her fingers up, he whispered, "Are you burned?"

Slowly, he turned her hand over.

"No," she answered. She moved her fingers into his hair as she had seen him do only moments before. "I'm all right. Don't worry about me."

Granger spread his hands along her middle. The feel of her seemed to feed the hunger of a lifetime. "You are far more than all right, Meredith."

She heard the evening news coming from the small set in the living room. The smell of beer blended with the barbecue aroma. Yet everything seemed faraway except her sense of touch.

He slipped his hand beneath her shirt and brushed the band of her jeans and the skin just above.

This could not be real, she told herself. Nothing like this had ever happened before in her life. He was not the kind of man who flirted or who women talked about. And she was a good woman no one ever spread rumors about.

And right now, the good woman was silently telling him what she wanted. They might have trouble talking, but he had no problem understanding what she was trying to communicate.

She wanted to be touched.

He moved his hand to the warmth of her middle, and

she leaned her head back against his shoulder. With trembling fingers, she guided his touch higher.

Her brain pounded with all the reasons why she should stop as his fingers pushed aside her bra and closed around her breast.

"Are you sure you want this?"

"I'm sure," she whispered as she stretched and let his other hand slide down the front of her jeans. "And you?"

"I—I'm not a big enough liar to tell you I want to stop, Meredith. If your wanting to be with me is just a stage of the grief you are going through, I'll still be here, but I'd like to know from the first. Because my wanting to be with you has nothing to do with anyone else but you."

Meredith smiled. "I'm not sure what you are, Sheriff, but you're not some therapy I'm taking." She leaned closer and pressed her lips against his throat.

He undressed her slowly, then led her into the bedroom. She felt him watch her as she climbed on the bed and lay down atop the covers. There was no fear or doubt or hesitation in her, only need. He undressed and folded his clothes on the room's only chair.

He pulled the thin white ribbon from her hair and twisted it in his hand. Somehow the action was more intimate than removing her clothes. His hand, half-covered in white satin, slid over her full hips.

"I don't like to be touched when I'm making love," he said as his hand stilled, waiting for her response.

"All right," she answered.

He moved his fingers down her body.

She kept her arms at her sides making no attempt to reach for him.

His hands brushed over her, boldly caressing. There

was no need to kiss her, or to say anything. They had gone
beyond any game of seduction in one move.

She closed her eyes and grinned as he explored her
curves. For the first time in her life lovemaking was all
about her. And the knowledge of it being so made her
almost explode with joy.

"Say my name," he insisted above her. "I need to know
that you know it's me here with you."

"Make love to me, Granger." She read his mind. "No
one but you."

He made love to her more completely than she ever
imagined a man could make love to a woman. He treated
her as a gift that had been handed to him. He could not
get enough of her. He was gentle and kind and starved
for the feel of her.

She kept her hands at her sides, but moved with him,
gently pressing close. Without any words, she knew what
he wanted, what he needed. She made no sounds of passion. The air was warm and still and quiet around them as
if brand-new. No mood music, no candles. Only Granger's
arms.

She never tried to be shy or coy. She offered her body
to him, honestly, completely. And he took her in the only
way he knew how, completely.

It was after midnight when he moved his hand along
her body, damp with perspiration. "I have to go," he whispered against her ear.

She did not answer, and he slipped away from her side.
She fell asleep listening to him dress.

November 7
Clifton Creek Elementary

Meredith did not allow herself to think about what had happened until midafternoon the next day. She got up late and rushed to get to school before the students. Her tardiness was easily explained away by the weather. Then, from the moment she entered her classroom, she was too busy to think of anything but her job.

Finally, when the students were all wrapped in wool and sent home, she sat behind her cluttered desk and stared out at the snow swirling across the playground equipment. She had never done anything in her life as crazy as what she did last night with the sheriff. She hoped people would not see it on her face. She would not have been surprised if the school billboard had announced her affair, instead of next Tuesday's PTA meeting. It should have said something like Second-Grade Teacher Has Wild Night With Town Sheriff. Details To Follow.

People do not just go around bumping into one another and making love. Or at least until last night, she never thought they did. She had never even had a conversation longer than a few sentences with the man, and last night she had let him touch her all over.

At the thought, Meredith blushed. All over, she repeated in her mind.

She had wanted to lose all control, or maybe hand it over to someone else for a change. That must have been her plan, only she could not remember thinking it. And he certainly took control, leaving her free to float. She got what she asked for, but more than she had known to expect.

She put her head in her hands. Nothing made sense. What if he told someone? Gossip like this would spread so fast. They would be pointed at, talked about in whispers, joked about.

Meredith reconsidered. Of course, he would never tell anyone. They were not in high school.

The vision of Granger sitting around the Pancake House with all the old farmers swapping stories made her laugh.

Ridiculous, she thought. People have affairs all the time.

Affair.

Her forehead hit the desk. This was not an affair.

Oh, God, it was a one-night stand. She had been a one-night stand. She thumped her head once more on the desk, thinking it was too late for her to do any brain damage. One night too late.

"Meredith?"

She jumped, almost toppling out of her swivel chair.

Granger stood at her door with his hat in his hand. If possible, he looked as confused as she felt. "I noticed your car was the only one left in the lot. I stopped by to make sure you weren't having trouble getting it started."

He took a step into the room and appeared even taller

than usual with the small desks scattered around him. His hair was damp with snow, and from the dark lines under his eyes, he had clearly not slept for some time. He was the kind of handsome no twenty-year-old could be, gray salting his short, curly hair and not an ounce of fat on the man.

Meredith fought to keep from giving her head one more rap against the desk. Here he was checking on her, making sure her car would start, and she was staring at him thinking about—no remembering—details about his body.

"I'm leaving." She stood and hurried to her closet, thinking she was almost always the last one in the building since the principal's wife had had twins last spring. Granger had never stopped by before.

He waited just inside the doorway, looking nervous and out of place.

She gathered her things, trying to think of something to say. Finally, when they were walking down the hallway, she asked, "Are the roads bad?"

"Not too," he answered. "I'll follow you home if you like."

"No. I'll be fine." She felt she should call him Sheriff Farrington again. How could it have only been hours ago when she had called him Granger? She did not even know how old he was. Five years older than she? Ten? No, he could not be ten. Not with that body. Maybe three or five.

Meredith wrapped her scarf around her throat. The way her thoughts were running she might never be able to speak to the man again.

He must have been in the same fix, for he did not say anything as he took her arm and helped her along the slippery sidewalk to her car. He waited until the Mustang started, then knelt beside the open car door.

"I was thinking," he said slowly. "Maybe we shouldn't see one another for a while."

She just stared at him for a long moment, waiting for him to say more…letting his words soak in…wishing she had misunderstood…knowing she had not.

"All right." She wanted him to move so she could close her door and get away. But he just stood there as if they were making small talk.

"You understand? I don't want there to be any talk about us."

"Of course," she lied.

He touched the brim of his hat, pulling it lower as though the weather had suddenly grown colder.

"Evenin', Mrs. Allen." He moved away.

"Evenin', Sheriff." Her words traveled on frost. She shoved her car into gear, realizing he had done it again. He had taken control. This time to end whatever there might have been between them.

When the rigs went up fitted with multicables climbing to the tower, men were always aloft. A single cable ran from the highest point on the rig and was tied to the ground several feet away from the base of the rig. If an accident happened, the man up top would lace his gloved fingers over the emergency cable and ride to safety.

November 11
Montano Ranch

Anna watched the snow whirl in drifts on the land between her ranch and Zack Larson's place. She had not been off her land in days and wondered if he had. The horses she worked with were inside the barns, and exercised in the huge indoor arena Davis had built a few years ago.

She told herself she was just restless, needing the exhilaration of a long ride, but she knew it was more. It made no sense, but she missed seeing Zack. Or rather, she missed the slim possibility that she might see him working along his fence line, or checking his mail in town, or working his cattle, or lifting his housekeeper's vacuum into her truck.

Anna's sightings of Zack Larson were pure chance, nothing more. Only she had seen his housekeeper, Bella, sliding along the frozen road to his place a few hours ago. If the old woman was out, surely everyone but her had given up waiting out the weather.

Anna paced the wall of windows that faced his house. She was acting the fool, she told herself. If she knew the man she would probably dislike him. She had not given him a second thought until he offered to give her a hug if she ever needed one.

What kind of man makes such an offer?

"Not any man I have ever known," she answered, wondering for the hundredth time what it would be like to fold into his arms.

She wasn't sure she even wanted to talk to him. They would probably have nothing to say to one another. "If I could just have the hug," she whispered to herself. "Then I could stop thinking about him." But of course, that was impossible. She could not just walk up to his place and demand her hug. "But he did offer."

Anna circled the house once more. The remains of the half-burned oil rig sat low along the horizon. Now, covered with snow, it looked harmless, almost like a sculpture.

As Anna stared, Bella's old pickup rattled down the road from Zack's place. The old Chevy was almost to her drive before she realized it had intentionally turned off the road to her house.

She pressed her palms against her face, trying to erase signs that she had been crying as she rushed to answer the doorbell. No one ever came to see her except her brother, and he never rang the bell. He used to knock as he opened the door, but since Davis died he had even forgotten that formality.

"H-hello." She tried to smile as she greeted the housekeeper standing on her porch. The old woman wore a bright green parka and snow-white earmuffs.

"Hidy." Bella nodded. She crossed her hands in front of her, ignoring the way her huge purse flapped against her ample stomach. "I thought I'd stop by and see if you needed anything, Mrs. Montano. You out here all alone and me making a trip right by your place every week. I would be happy to stop by and pick something up for you if you have a need."

Anna held the door open wide. "P-please come in." She fought down her nervousness and made herself say each word slowly. "It is very kind of you to come."

"Oh, it weren't no trouble. I clean for Zack Larson ever' Wednesday." Bella looked around as if hoping to find something amiss that needed her special touch. "Got that pretty music playing, I see."

"It is the London Symphony Orchestra. I heard them once when I was a child. My mother took me."

"Oh." Bella nodded as if Anna were speaking Italian. "I see you hung your pictures. It looks real pretty in here."

Anna did not meet Bella's eyes. "I was just trying them in a few places. I was about to take them down."

"Don't see no need. They look fine. Add a lot to this room if you ask me."

"Thank you." Anna motioned toward the kitchen. "I am stopping for tea. Would you like to join me, Miss Bella?"

"Just Bella." The older woman held her chin high. "And I'd love some tea."

Anna led her to the kitchen, floored with huge Saltillo tiles framed by dark wood cabinets and walls bricked to the nine-foot ceiling.

Motioning for Bella to sit at the breakfast table, Anna finished brewing the tea as she watched the housekeeper out of the corner of her eye. Silhouetted against the bay window, overlooking the barren land, Bella appeared totally in her element, almost as though she were bred from generations born to this open space.

Bella's purse rested in her lap as if she planned a quick getaway.

Anna pulled down a tin of cookies, then smiled. "Call me Anna, please. And make yourself comfortable."

"All right. Anna it is." Bella set her purse at her feet and pulled off her earmuffs. After all, she was about to have tea. Real English tea, from china cups.

She stroked the white fur. "I won this at bingo in town one cold night last year. Zack always kids me and tells me I'm wearing my mink. They're real mink, too, said so right on the front of the box they came in."

"They are very nice." Anna sat a cup in front of Bella.

"Oh, before I forget, Zack Larson says to give you his regards and hopes you're weathering this storm without any problems."

Before Anna could answer, Bella added, "I told him I wasn't going to pass along that. I ain't one for passing notes. Told him if he wanted to hand out his regards he needs to do it in person."

Anna grinned. "And what did Mr. Larson say?"

Bella smiled back. "He said he might just do that sometime."

They sat by the windows and talked about the weather and horses. Bella knew very little about fine horses, but she knew how to ask questions. Anna could not remember having such a delightful tea. From the look on Bella's face, neither could she. Anna had been raised on a horse ranch and Bella on a dryland farm, but the two had many things in common.

Eventually, the conversation settled back on Zack. Bella was not a gossip, but her motherly love for the man was apparent. She bragged about him. "He might be a loner, set in his ways, but he's honest. And he loves his land. He's got a sense of humor that'll tickle your funny bone all the way to your liver."

Anna listened.

"He's had his share of trouble, but ain't many who get through this life without taking their full slice. His mother died while he was still in school, and he had to watch his father drink himself to death within the year. Most thought he'd lose the ranch after that, him not even being eighteen and all, but he's a fighter."

"He is lucky to have you as a friend." Anna patted Bella's hand.

"I'm the lucky one. He's as near to family as I got, I reckon."

Bella stood to leave.

Carlo suddenly plowed his way through the front door. He still wore clothes like he had worn in Italy, making him stand out even more among the cowhands. He might be short, but his stocky build and quick movements made him appear menacing even when he was not angry.

Anna stepped in front of Bella.

Carlo was halfway across the wide living room waving papers before she spoke. "B-Bella, I would like you to meet my brother...Carlo. He takes care of the ranch."

Carlo remembered his manners. He made a quick, slight bow. He had the same coloring as Anna, but his dark hair and eyes made him look sinister.

"This is the woman who cleans?" he snapped.

Anna fought to hide her embarrassment. His English might be broken, but she knew Bella understood every word. "Yes. She stopped by to check on me."

"Well." He switched to Italian. "Tell her we need her to come and clean every week, but we will pay no more than Davis did."

"I can do it," Anna answered in her native tongue.

"No! Everything is to remain the same as before. I will do that for Davis." His words came fast and sounded even more furious in Italian. "You will not disgrace him by having people believe you are too poor to afford a housekeeper."

Anna nodded as he turned and walked out without saying another word to Bella.

Anna faced the older woman. "It was kind of you to come. I am sorry about my brother. He is displeased with me, not you. Back home, the women left the workings of the ranches to the men. He is a little old-fashioned. He resents me always asking questions."

Bella huffed. "I could figure that out without understanding the language. What got him so thorny today?"

Anna smiled at her use of words. She could study language in school forever and never be able to add that kind of color in her vocabulary. "He does not like me hanging my paintings in this room. You see, my husband and he were best friends and Carlo knows Davis would not have approved."

"Tell him you don't give a bootlegger's snort." Bella put on her earmuffs.

"I am afraid I have never been able to tell a man in my family anything." She looked at her painting. "Bella, could you come back next week? Maybe every week for a while?"

"Your house don't need cleaning," Bella answered. "It wouldn't be fair to take your money."

"Would you consider coming to sit for me? I would like to paint you. I will pay you the same as I did when you cleaned."

"What? I never heard of such a thing." She rubbed her face as if she could scrub off the blush. "I wouldn't have to take off my clothes or anything, would I?"

Anna laughed, truly laughed for the first time in months. "Oh, no. I want to paint the character in your face. I want to try to capture a little of your spirit on canvas."

"Well…" Bella looked as if she had been asked to try on a two-piece bathing suit. "I guess it would be all right."

"We could have tea while I work," Anna offered.

"With some of them butter cookies you called biscuits?" Bella asked.

"Of course. It will be such fun for me to paint something besides flowers and landscapes."

"Well, all right. I could come when I finish with Zack's place ever' week."

When Anna closed the door, she smiled. It would not be so sad that she had to take all her paintings to the back room now that Bella would sit for her. She could clean her own house, and Carlo would never know.

Just after dark, she took all but one of the paintings down before Carlo returned to the house. He looked as if he had been drinking, but Anna knew better than to say anything. Davis's death and the extra responsibility had weighed heavily on her brother.

Carlo wanted her to sign some papers. When she asked about them, he angrily replied, "It's just the payroll!" Then he changed the subject to the remaining painting.

She signed the papers in frustration and stood, planning to tell him this was her house and the painting would stay.

Only a few words were out before she felt the broad side of his hand against her face. The blow would have knocked her off her feet if she had not grabbed the table.

Anna stepped away from him, shocked. Despite all

their arguments, he had never struck her. The sting on her face was nothing compared to the blow against her pride.

He seemed as shocked as she. "I did not mean to do that," he mumbled and headed toward the door. By the time he stood in the doorway, he had regained some of his control. "Have the painting gone before I return. Davis would not have wanted it there. Whenever he talked of your work, it was always to joke."

Anna stared at the closed door for several minutes. How could she have ever hoped her life might be better without Davis? Carlo moved into power one step at a time. And she had let him, Anna realized. She stood by silently, as always, without fighting. She hid away. Even before Davis was in the ground, Carlo had taken the reins of running the ranch and her life.

Anna walked the house for hours trying to think of some way out. But in the end, she knew she could do nothing. First her father, then Davis and now Carlo. All her life she had been trained to stay in the background and say nothing. And now, when she might have stood alone, she realized she was too weak.

As the night aged, Anna felt more anger against herself than Carlo. The thought that he would now control her frightened her more than she wanted to admit. She would fight him in little ways that he would never know. Her mother had done the same thing with their father. Anna never saw her challenge him directly, but she moved behind his back, cutting away at his authority, sabotaging his plans.

Anna stared out into the night at the lone light shining from the north. Carlo would not repress her. Not completely.

She grabbed her coat and walked out the patio door.

The ground was frozen, but the moon offered enough light to see. Silently, she moved toward Larson's ranch.

When she reached the walkover, she was almost running. Tonight, she would move into the light of his porch and demand the hug he had offered a month ago.

Snow crunched under her feet as she crossed the road and stepped into the light.

Zack Larson leaned against the door frame with a cup in his hand. She knew he watched her even when she moved in the shadows.

Anna waited. Ready to run.

He did not look surprised. If he made fun of her, or made a joke, her soul would shatter into a million slivers. If he asked her one question, she knew she would stutter too badly to answer.

He leaned inside, and when he straightened, his hand held a coat instead of the cup. He walked onto the porch, putting his coat on as he neared.

Anna did not move. It was too late to turn back. Too late to explain her many reasons for being here.

She expected him to walk toward her, but he just stepped off the porch and waited.

Her heart tried to break through her ribs. She narrowed the distance between them, trying to think of something to say. Wishing she had not come. Wishing he had not been waiting.

"I…" When she was four feet from him, she shoved her hands in her pockets. Warm tears stung her icy cheeks.

"I know," he whispered and opened his arms.

Anna was not sure how she crossed the last few feet. Had he moved? Had she? All she knew was that suddenly she was in his arms, and he was hugging her against him as if their lives depended on it.

Tears came then. She leaned her face into his suede jacket and cried as he circled her with his warmth.

He did not say a word when he lifted her up and carried her to the wooden swing on the porch. With a quilt wrapped around them both, he held her close.

She cried for a while, then rested her head against his damp jacket and closed her eyes, enjoying the slow motion of the swing. The whispered sounds of the wind made it seem like they were totally alone on the planet. Their breath was smoky with frost but she was not cold. Off into the night, she heard the breeze cracking ice from the branches of mesquite trees.

She cuddled closer.

When finally, she stood to leave, he made no protest, but kept his arm across her back as he walked her to the fence.

"Th-thank you," she said as she climbed up the ladder.

"Anytime," he whispered.

She was almost home when she turned around and saw him still standing at the walkover. His outline was tall and lean. She could not help but smile. Zack Larson had kept his word. No strings. No questions. Just a hug.

A hug that warmed her still.

Most of the time he felt like an alien life-form that had crashed to earth and primitive humans were trying to discover what to do with him. Their methods were painful and heavy-handed at best. At worst, the marrow in his bones still smoldered from the long dead fire.

His vocabulary increased to include words like *eschar*. He'd heard one of the nurses explain to Crystal that eschar is a nonviable tissue that forms after a burn injury. It has no blood supply therefore antibodies can't reach it. So, *eschar* makes a fertile breeding ground for bacteria.

He was lost in the hell of an old *Twilight Zone* episode. Before long, they'd stash him in the basement and grow mushrooms off his charred skin.

Even the spray baths they gave him weren't called baths, but *wound debridement*. Twice a day a nurse would up his pain medicine enough so he could endure the process, then she'd clean him, removing dead tissue. Only, she called the black infected skin *devitalized tissue,* as if calling it *dead* might be too personal.

His bodily functions became the small talk of the

people around him. Folks used to ask about the weather or
the news, but now they told each other of his urine output
for the day. The constant risk of hypothermia loomed
like the plague and worried everyone until he wanted to
scream.

He longed to escape, to run away where the talk was of
other things. But even when he dreamed, the nightmare
of his reality crept in, just beneath the surface, waiting
to shatter any peace he might find.

Crystal was always around, asking questions until he
wanted to jump from the bed and choke her, even if it cost
him his last thread-hold on life. She started a notebook of
details, so every time a bag was changed she was there,
like a reporter, recording amounts and dates.

Sometimes he ignored her completely, acting as if he
didn't hear her talking to him or touching his hand. Sometimes she possessed the only sanity in the chaos. He'd
hold her fingers long into the night.

When his mind cleared enough for him to think of anything but the pain, he let his thoughts wander to the way
her breasts looked. Crystal had the most beautiful round,
full breasts. He had always considered himself a leg man,
but no man could help but worship such perfection.

He hadn't asked her again to open her blouse. Not that
he hadn't thought about it. But with his bandaged hands,
he knew he wouldn't be able to feel her, even if he did
touch her. And the tear he'd seen slide down her cheek
the night she'd sat there with her top wide open…the tear
bothered him more than he wanted to admit.

"Shelby?" She broke into his thoughts. "Shelby? Are
you awake? I'm sorry I was gone so long."

He had not even noticed. Time was no longer measured
in minutes and hours, but by injections.

"I had to go see Mr. Morris again. He had lots of

papers he wanted me to look over. I wasn't sure if I should read each page or just glance at them, so I stared at the words until Elliot asked if I was satisfied."

He did not open his eyes. *She was calling Morris by his first name. That was fast, even for Crystal.* The bed shifted slightly as she sat by his side.

He was not dead yet and she was already looking for husband number two. Elliot wouldn't be a bad choice if Crystal could snag him.

"I signed all the places where he'd marked, and Elliot told me this increase in salary should make Trent happy."

When he groaned, she patted his hand. "Now don't worry. The office girls say Trent has showed up for work every day since the accident. Sometimes he doesn't get there until ten-thirty and leaves for lunch by eleven, but at least he's trying. He even put a hard hat in the back window of his BMW. The girls think he's planning to visit the other drilling sites."

Trent would look ridiculous at a site. Tiptoeing around so that he didn't get oil on his Italian-made shoes.

Crystal chatted on about stopping in to buy two more dresses from Helena. The older woman was quickly becoming Crystal's best friend. Helena Whitworth was always dropping by the hospital but usually only talked to Crystal or one of the nurses.

The few times she'd talked to him, he noticed that she still spoke of her husband, J.D., as if the old soldier were still alive. No one else seemed to notice that Helena had yet to bury J.D. in her mind. In Southern towns, a little craziness was tolerated as a character trait. Some said only the insane settled in West Texas, so most folks around here must be descended from crackpots. Helena

Whitworth talking of J.D. as if she'd had supper with him the night before drew little attention.

Crystal buzzed around him like a fly. Making sure he was comfortable, she said. But in truth, the state no longer existed for him.

He closed his eyes and walked the rig in his mind once more, as he had that morning, seconds before it blew. Every detail was still fresh in his mind, from the way the wind whistled across the land kicking up dust in little whirlwinds, to the sound of the drill as steady as a heartbeat.

Howard Drilling had needed another investor, so he brought J.D. and a young banker named Kevin Allen out. Nothing worked like a meeting at the site. The rancher, Davis Montano, stood in the center explaining the workings of a rig like he knew something about the industry. No one stopped him. As long as they were on Montano land he could talk all he wanted.

The crew had found the beer and were all leaning against the car enjoying a long break. They were too far away to say thanks, but one lifted his bottle in salute. A moment later the whole world seemed to explode.

He went over the scene again, repeating every detail. There must have been something amiss—something different about that morning that he should have noticed. He had been standing several feet from the others, feeling a difference even if he could not pinpoint it. The blast knocked him off the rig and sent him rolling across the dirt. He hadn't seen the others die, hadn't heard a sound, only the blast, and then the silence when the rig stopped. Moments later the wind caught the fire.

In that one moment of total nothing, he knew he was dying. He was above the pain. But for some reason, he dove back in, letting the agony of it all take him full force.

Why hadn't he stayed in the calm? That one question haunted him and might yet drive him mad.

Thanksgiving
November 26

Some holidays are meant to be enjoyed, others endured. Helena had always thought Thanksgiving fell more into the endured category. It was too close to Christmas to really be excited about seeing everyone, and the weather often hampered, though rarely canceled, the event. For her, the only good thing about the day was that with its passing came the busiest shopping season of the year.

She spent an hour trying to convince J.D. to come along with her to Patricia's annual spread. But, as he had for years, he insisted the day belonged to her family. He would only be an outsider, unable to relate to the husbands, who called a rifle a gun, or the children who thought Martin Luther King was a general in the Civil War.

Helena laughed as she drove down Main, past stores already decorated for the next holiday. J.D. was her family, her world. How could he think otherwise? He just wanted her to go so that she could return with stories. They would open a bottle of red wine and watch the sunset as they laughed at her tales of the twins and their families.

Then, as they always did on holidays, they would make love. Maybe not wild and abandoned as they had in their fifties, but with no less pleasure. J.D. had a way of making her feel young and loved as no man ever had. While they were still breathless and wrapped around one another, he would whisper "Happy Thanksgiving" or "Merry Christmas" or "Happy Birthday," like their lovemaking was what made the day special.

Glancing over at the courthouse, Helena noticed Meredith's old Mustang parked near the side door. She had asked the little schoolteacher to dinner at Patricia's. Both of her daughters had had children in Meredith's class, so Helena knew they would not mind the extra company.

Meredith refused, saying she planned to work on the filing system over the break. She had been working at the courthouse part-time for as long as Helena could remember.

Helena made a mental note to call Crystal as soon as she got to Patricia's house. Shelby's cook was making a feast and having it delivered midafternoon to everyone who worked the Thanksgiving shift at the hospital. He could easily drop a plate off at the courthouse for Meredith.

She almost wished she had taken Crystal up on her invitation to join them. It would be a nice change from enduring Thanksgiving with her daughters. Randi was driving in from Memphis for the weekend. And as far as Helena knew, Randi had no family of her own—that she still claimed, anyway. Her former in-laws hadn't bothered to invite her. After all, now Jimmy was dead, she was not really a part of them anymore. But Crystal had remembered her, even wiring her the money for gas.

Randi's career as a singer had not taken off as expected, but Crystal swore it would only be a matter of time. Randi wrote that she had met a manager in a bar where she worked. He was now handling her bookings. She had told Crystal the bar also sold boots along one wall.

Helena shook her head. She was only a small-town businesswoman, but she would always be able to recognize a snake. She hoped Randi could. In her opinion, a man who never went in a bar wasn't to be trusted any more than a man who called it his second home or office. And a Western-wear store that had a dance floor and bar was too wild for her taste.

She pulled into the drive of her daughter's house. Patricia had a way with flowers in the spring that made the place look bright and welcoming, but in the winter the untended beds made the house look like it was sitting on a huge brown nest.

There was the usual menagerie of bikes and toys scattered along the drive and in the grass. But at least in the winter the brown circles in the grass, left by the plastic pool, did not show.

Helena's three oldest grandchildren came running out to meet her. She loved them dearly but rarely had time to see them. When the twins had been small, Helena had fought night and day to get her business going. Even when she had been home, she was usually slaving over the store's books. She had missed their childhood just as she was missing her grandchildren's—but only with a passing regret.

Climbing from the car, she reached for the bag filled with toys Mary always prepared for her. Helena might not cook, but she never showed up empty-handed.

J.D. teased her that Mary secretly hated buying the gifts and got her revenge on Helena by always including at least one toy that made noise. Last Easter, she'd found huge eggs for the boys that contained harmonicas, and plastic chicks for the girls that made chirping sounds.

It had taken J.D. and two bottles of wine to calm Helena's nerves that night. Harmonica-playing chickens even haunted her dreams.

Today, Helena was happy to find books about juggling with bags of soft balls attached. She handed them out and made her way past the husbands, who were glued to a football game on TV as though hypnotized. They were a nice pair, but Helena could not remember having a conversation with either of them in years.

"Momma!" Both daughters hurried from the kitchen.

"Momma, you look so nice." Patricia wiped her hands on her apron.

Paula touched the wool of Helena's suit. "That's a real fine suit on you. The color makes you look younger. No one would ever think you were a day over fifty."

"She doesn't look old enough to be our mother as it is now," Patricia bragged. "When we were little, our friends used to think Momma was a model, remember?"

For the hundredth time, Helena wished her daughters could wear the sizes in her store. They had open accounts but only charged a bag or a scarf now and then. Helena felt she had a lifetime of knowledge about clothing and no one to pass it down to.

"Mary tells me you both have been helping out at the store."

They grinned, proud of themselves.

"We think you'll be pleased, Momma. We've been trying, hoping to take some of the load off your shoulders." Paula took Helena's coat and umbrella and put them by the door. "Is it raining?"

"Not yet," Helena answered. "But you know I like to be prepared."

Paula led Helena toward the kitchen. "Mary even let us do some of the ordering. We had a great time."

Helena wanted to ask more questions, but she saw that the table was already set. She was always a little surprised at what good cooks they had both become. Paula made breads and pies better than any bakery in town. Patricia managed to set a pretty table even though the napkins were paper. Holidays were important to them and therefore Helena always tried to be on her best behavior.

She surprised herself by enjoying the dinner. Nowhere in town had a better meal than the one her daughters cooked. They were both pleased when she asked for not only seconds, but thirds.

Two hours later, as they stood side by side in the kitchen doing the dishes, Helena said almost sadly, "I've had a wonderful time, but I need to start back."

Paula leaned over the sink and stared out the window. "If it rains, it might freeze after dark, but you've got a few hours yet, Momma."

Helena pulled off her apron and laid it across one of the kitchen chairs. "You outdid yourselves today, girls. This was the best Thanksgiving dinner ever. I'm sure J.D. would enjoy a plate. I'll make him one."

Neither daughter said a word as Helena filled one of the plastic plates with food. When she finished, she kissed them both and headed toward the door.

At the tiny table in the front entrance, she set the plate down and slipped on her coat. The noise from the TV would have drowned out any goodbye she wanted to make to her sons-in-law, and all the children were watching a movie in the back of the house.

As she lifted J.D.'s plate, Paula's voice drifted from

the kitchen. "Don't worry about it, Pat. She's just dealing with his loss the only way she knows how."

"She's not dealing with it at all. She hasn't removed anything that belonged to him. The other day I was in her bedroom, and his reading glasses are still on the stand beside his chair."

"I did like old Doc Hamilton suggested. I've told her several times that J.D. is dead when she starts talking about him. But she doesn't seem to hear." Paula sounded like she was about to cry. "There is nothing more we can do. Our mother is taking her dead husband a plate of food and we're all acting like that's just fine."

Helena ran out the door before she had to listen to more of such nonsense.

By the time she got home, Helena felt a little out of breath. She put J.D.'s food in the kitchen and hurried up the stairs to change out of her dress clothes and into something more comfortable.

Once in her bathroom, she pushed a full bottle of blood pressure medicine, atenolol, aside, thinking her blood pressure must be low, not high, since she felt so tired lately. Tonight, she would not bother with the captopril pill, either. She really could not remember why the doctor had suggested she take it in the first place. All she needed was a glass of wine and she would feel fine.

She went back downstairs for the warmed meal for J.D. but climbing back up the stairs, Helena moved at a slower pace than usual.

"I'm tired," she whispered. "It has been a long day."

The door to their bedroom was open and she smiled, knowing J.D. was already waiting for her.

"I'm back," she yelled, and as she entered the room she could hear the cork on the wine popping.

Meredith Allen sifted through the files. Cora Lee Wilson, the county clerk, had left her plenty to do during the four days the office would be closed to the public. In most small towns like Clifton Creek, the clerk's position resembled the Pope's. Once elected, the term stretched for life. Cora Lee had started passing jobs off to Meredith when she worked summers during her last two years of high school. At first it was filing, then record keeping. Now Meredith was not sure the clerk even remembered how to do some of the reports that had to be kept.

But Meredith didn't mind. She enjoyed the silence of the work. It was so different from teaching, and it offered her the extra money she needed.

Thanksgiving passed faster at work than at home alone. The cold marble and brick of the courthouse were familiar to her. She had danced in the empty halls while her father cleaned the place years ago. When she had been five, the building was her palace with huge windows that reached the sky, and wooden railings that shone as if liquid glass had been poured over them. She knew where every light switch was, every back door, every hidden cove where a little girl could hide and pretend.

She glanced out the windows she once thought were the tallest in the world. Sheriff Farrington's car was parked next to hers on the otherwise empty lot. He arrived first, but Meredith didn't stop in to let him know she was here.

In the past five years, they had developed a pattern. Whoever came in last or left first always checked in at the other's office to let them know someone else was in the building.

Only she did not want to face him this morning. Meredith knew he was here. He was always here. Sheriff Farrington once told her that he worked holidays because both his deputies were family men. In truth, she guessed he was more like her now and did not want to be at home alone.

Meredith tried to keep busy, but she could not concentrate on filing while thinking about him, only a few doors away. She probably had not crossed his mind. One-night stands were no doubt his specialty.

Closing her eyes, Meredith decided she must be the worst lover in the world. Or at least the worst Sheriff Farrington had ever known. That was why he told her they should not see one another again. Or maybe he didn't like the way she looked, or felt, or smelled. Who knows? She had spent most of her life trying to understand Kevin. It seemed far too much trouble to start over with another man now. There wasn't enough lifetime left to make any progress.

Kevin had been big. He loved hugging and cuddling. Even when they were arguing, usually about money, he would always pull her close at night, like she was a part of him.

Granger's night with her was totally different. He touched her, but she didn't feel a part of him. He knew how to please a woman but, before and after, he did not seem to have any idea what to do with her. For him, the loving was something he did *to* a woman, not something they made together.

Meredith decided she would just become a monk, or whatever women are called who have no sex in their life. Feeling great for a short time was not worth the hours of worrying about him afterward.

He had probably been right to end their affair the day after it started. Where could it lead, anyway? Neither were the type to sneak around which, in this town, was nearly impossible. He obviously liked being a bachelor; he'd avoided several attempts to be matched up with single ladies in the area.

The last thing she needed in her life right now was a man. It would be a long time, maybe never, before she would be able to set herself up for the possibility of marrying and then losing another husband.

He'd been wise to end it, but that didn't make it hurt any less. She felt like the only girl dumped at the prom.

Granger paced in his office down the hall. He circled his desk for the tenth time, thinking of crossing the distance to Meredith. He was glad the dispatcher, Inez, wasn't there to watch him acting like a squirrel in a cage. Inez would have laughed at him. She'd probably stop making fun of Adam, the oldest deputy, and start picking on him.

He thought of trying to call Anna Montano again. Eventually she would have to talk to him. She couldn't just send answers care of her brother, even if Carlo seemed to consider himself some kind of guard dog over his little sister. There were still questions about the accident.

Granger glanced at the hallway. Maybe he should ask Meredith about the Montano woman. At least that would give him some way to start a conversation.

He reconsidered, realizing he was acting the fool again, thinking about Meredith as if there weren't a hundred more important things for him to concentrate on. He couldn't help wondering why she hadn't stopped by when she came in this morning. It wasn't like her not to follow the rules. Even unwritten ones. He didn't even like her all that much he reminded himself. She wasn't his type, and he was far too old to let any woman get under his skin.

She was cluttery. He required an order about everything in his life. Half the time he saw her, she looked like she'd gotten dressed in the car on the way to school.

She was too short. Her legs would never wrap around his waist. He liked a woman who could do that. And her breasts were too large. Far too large, he told himself. Any more than a handful is a waste. And she wore her hair like a little girl. A damn ribbon. She had to be in her thirties, and she still wore ribbons.

He opened his bottom desk drawer and pulled the sliver of satin through his fingers. He had no reason for keeping the thing he decided as he shoved it back in the drawer.

Something his father used to say drifted through his mind. A man is pestering an idiot when he tries to fool himself.

Granger closed the drawer and headed down the hall. It was time he shook this interest before she became an obsession.

Meredith's appearance did not surprise him as he entered the county clerk's office. She wore a boxy sweater that had turkeys lined up along the border and sleeves. She had pulled her shoulder-length hair back in a loose knot at the base of her neck so that the tiny turkeys dangling from her ears would show. Her skirt was too long and her shoes too practical to ever have been in fashion.

She looked ridiculous, he decided. Not a second-grader in sight and she still wore the uniform, like a clown who smeared on face paint even on his day off.

Stepping down from the chair she'd been using as a step stool, she watched him walk toward her as if she were watching a total stranger heading in her direction. He almost expected her to ask, "May I help you?"

Granger tried to think of something to say. He had been hoping that she was three doors down thinking about him all morning, but from the looks of things, she had been working.

He tried to focus on the turkeys on her sweater. "I thought I'd go down to the truck stop for coffee and a burrito. You want anything?"

"Coffee would be nice." She reached for her purse. "The pot in the back is broken."

He almost told her he had a pot in his office, but somehow that seemed too personal.

She handed him fifty cents and he took it. From the beginning, she would never let him pay for anything. He did not even try to now. Men buy one another coffee or meals in a haphazard rotation, but women always want to keep everything even. Teachers were the worst. He had seen them get out their calculators and figure tax and tip down to the penny.

"With cream, no sugar. Right?"

She smiled. "Right."

He stood there for a few seconds, waiting for her to say more. When she remained silent, he walked back to his office, grabbed his keys off the corner of his desk, and his pager from the wall, then headed out into the cold. If a 911 call came in, which it rarely did, the pager would sound.

The gray day suited his mood.

The truck stop on the interstate was busy as always. You'd think people would settle down for one day of the year he thought, but the highway still flowed like a stream of ants. He circled the lot once before parking, taking note of the out-of-state license plates. Nothing looked amiss.

In ten minutes he headed back with two large coffees and a burrito that had been frozen less than an hour before. He didn't bother to stop at his office but went straight to hers.

He almost expected her to be gone, but she was still there, working at her desk in the back corner. When he set the coffee down, he noticed the sandwich she must have brought from home. Times were tight for her he bet, wishing he'd insisted on buying her coffee.

Without a word, he pulled up a chair and sat down at the corner of her desk. He unwrapped his burrito and pulled off the lid to his coffee without looking at her. If she did not like him staying long enough to eat, she was going to have to say something. Neither of them would get over their night together hiding in separate rooms. And it might only be a burrito and a sandwich, but they might as well have Thanksgiving lunch together.

"Think it will snow?" She opened her coffee and poured in both the creams he had brought, then looked around for something to stir with.

It occurred to him that he might be the only one trying to get over anything. She did not even look like she remembered their night together. Maybe she had forgotten it. Maybe she thought it was a dream. Who knew about women? He'd been seeing one of his Sunday ladies off and on for two years, and she still got mixed up and called him George now and then.

"I doubt we'll see snow. Might get rain later tonight." He tried to sound as casual as she did. Leaning back, he took a drink and frowned.

"Something wrong?"

"I can never get the coffee back here while it's still hot," he mumbled.

She pointed with the fork she had found in her desk drawer and had been using as a stir stick. "There's a microwave next to the sink over there." She pointed with her head toward the corner.

While he waited for his coffee to warm he said, "The only thing that seems to work around this place is you. The janitor told me the other day that if Cora Lee Wilson didn't move a little faster, he was going to have to start dusting her."

"I like to keep busy."

The microwave dinged and he reached for the thin cup. As he lifted his drink, the bottom of the cup caught the lip of the tray and splashed coffee across his hand.

Granger swore, tossed his cup in the sink, turned on the water, and plunged his right hand into the cold stream.

Meredith rushed to his side, pulling at his arm, trying to see if he was hurt. "Let me see where you're burned!"

"It's nothing," he said between clenched teeth. "Only a scald."

He rolled his sleeve up with one hand as water splashed over the cuff of his uniform.

She moved closer.

He jumped away, as if her touch burned deeper than the coffee.

Before she could react, he put the length of the desk

between them. "It's not important." Granger fought to keep his voice calm. "There's no need for you to worry over it."

"Let me..." She reached toward him.

"No. Don't touch me."

Meredith stopped in midstride. She didn't say a word, but stood perfectly still, staring at him as though she had no idea what kind of creature he was.

Granger left the office in a hurry, no longer aware of his throbbing hand. He had told her it was nothing. Why did she have such a problem listening? What was wrong with the woman? Couldn't she understand that some people do not like to be fretted over, smothered with patting and pampering?

He rushed out the side door and walked to his car. Without a backward glance, he drove off the parking lot and headed toward the campus. There would be no one there today. He would cross through the streets of town until he calmed down and forgot about the way Meredith's face looked, all hurt and disappointed.

She was not his type. Not tall, not long-legged. Cluttery. Not what he liked. She was mothering. The kind who would tie strings around a man until he could not move.

After an hour he turned into the truck stop and told them the burrito was so good, he'd come back for a full meal. He took his time eating and visiting with the manager. When he returned to the courthouse, Meredith's blue Mustang was gone. He made himself finish his paperwork and, about nine, finally figured he was tired enough to get to sleep without thinking about her.

But despite his plans, he circled by her house on his way home. A fog had moved in, and he needed to see that she'd got home safely. With that piece of junk she drove it was always a question.

Every light in her place was on. The air, thick with rain, made her windows fuzzy against the dark wood of her house.

He pulled up and waited for ten minutes before he finally turned off the engine and climbed out of his car.

He knocked twice before she answered.

She opened the door and stepped back, letting him in without a word.

As always, her place was warm. He took a deep breath, wondering what he would say.

She walked to the center of the living room and crossed her arms over her funny-looking bedspread robe. "How's your hand?" she said calmly. He saw slippers with bunny rabbit heads peeking out from beneath her robe.

"Fine." He held up his left hand. "I drove around with it hanging out the window for a while." That was not what he had come to say. He had no idea why he had come, but talking about his hand was definitely not it. He should have just circled Frankie's Bar and headed home as usual.

"I have some lotion that might help." She did not move to get it.

He didn't want to talk about his hand or lotion. She was not one of his Sunday girls; she deserved better. "Look, I'm sorry."

"So am I," she answered.

He smiled. "What the hell have you got to be sorry about, Meredith? I'm the one who swore and bolted out of your office." It made him mad that she was slicing off a piece of his "I'm sorry."

Walking to the bar, he deposited his hat and noticed the counter was as cluttered as ever. "I'm not some kind of pervert or anything." He shifted, not wanting to discuss the subject but knowing he had to. "I just don't like people touching me. I hate it when someone slaps me on the back or shakes hands longer than necessary." This was not a topic up for debate; it was just the way he had always been.

He faced her. She hadn't moved. The woman stood so still she must have grown roots.

"If you're waiting for some sad story of me being slapped around by my old man or something, you're out of luck. No deep-seated short circuit, just a preference. My parents are normal people. My dad's an accountant who might bore someone to death one day with his love of numbers, my mother keeps a spotless house and plays bridge."

"What about you touching others?" She tilted her head slightly.

He saw where she was headed. "I never offer a handshake first, but in my line of work there are times I have to handle folks." He thought of the night at the hospital when she had crumbled and he held her to keep her from falling.

"Look, Meredith, this is more than you probably care to know about me. I just came to say I'm sorry about blowing up like that in your office. I know you were only trying to help." He picked up his hat, absently dusting it off.

"What about me?" She asked directly. "Did you like touching me or was it just one of the things you have to do sometimes 'in your line of work'?"

"I enjoyed the other night. Better than I've enjoyed anything in a long time. I felt like you were the first real person I've been around in years." He remembered the softness of her body, the way she was rounded with curves. He liked the feel of her more than he wanted to admit. She was different from other women—she did not act as if she had been handled by many men. With her it was pure feeling, not just some way she had learned to behave.

"So this isn't a two-way street with you? You like touching, but you don't like being touched."

He did not even try to follow her logic, but he nodded. He had never really thought about it. Most women just accepted his terms, without trying to define and analyze them.

"What about kissing?" She took a step toward him. "Where do you stand on that?"

"Kissing's all right, but there are better things to do."

"And holding hands?"

"A waste of time. I'd never bother with such a thing." He thought of adding something like "A lawman needs to keep both hands ready to reach for his gun," but she was far too smart for that corny rookie line. She deserved more.

Problem was, the "more" was more than he wanted to give.

She moved to within a few feet of him. "Thank you for explaining things to me, Sheriff."

He watched her as she played with the belt on her robe.

"I have a plate of food Crystal Howard's cook brought over just after you left." She did not meet his eyes. "I could warm it, if you're hungry."

He set his hat back on the counter, not the least interested in the offered meal. "How do you feel about shaking hands, Meredith?"

She finally looked at him. "It doesn't bother me."

"And kissing?"

"I could use a little more of that in my life."

"And touching?" He hooked his finger around the belt of her robe and pulled her a step nearer.

"That, too," she answered.

He tugged at the belt and the robe parted slightly. Leaning down, he pressed his mouth against hers. Dear God, she tasted of hot cocoa.

It had been so long since he had just kissed a woman, he was afraid he had forgotten how. He felt her bottom lip tremble.

"I want you." He whispered words that had never failed.

No line, no sweet talk, just honesty. His hand slipped beneath her robe and felt the fullness of her breast.

She stepped away so quickly, he swayed forward a few inches.

"And I want more." She gulped the words as she pulled her robe together.

Granger was more shocked than angry. He straightened as he retrieved his hat. She was turning him down. The little schoolteacher with the too short, too rounded body was turning him down.

"Good evening, Mrs. Allen," he said as if he were just checking on her safety.

He was at the door when he heard her say, "I want a man who'll hold my hand in front of God and everybody."

"Grow up, Meredith," he mumbled as he closed the door behind him.

He barely heard her whisper, "I'm through settling in my life."

In the early days of cattle ranching, cowboys were hired for "forty and found." Forty dollars a month and what they found on the table to eat.

Thanksgiving Night
Montano Ranch

Anna Montano made it through the time called Thanksgiving without feelings, as she had for five years. She cooked for the ranch hands who did not leave for the long weekend. This year, scattered among the men who cared for the horses were rough oil workers who came to clean up and restart the drilling on Montano land.

Anna seldom talked with the ranch hands, except to ask about a particular horse that was having trouble. Most mornings her mount would be saddled and waiting for her when she reached the barn. When she finished her ride, she would brush the horse down and put up the saddle herself. If she chanced to pass one of the men, he would be polite, but never friendly.

The oil workers were different. They were louder. More sure of themselves. More full of themselves.

Davis had an old fellow who cooked for the men in the bunkhouse. He made pies and breads before he flew home every holiday, leaving Anna to prepare the rest of the meal. She then loaded dinner in the back of her car and drove to the bunkhouse on the other side of the barn fifty feet farther away from the house than Carlo's quarters. Thanksgiving was the only day she wished the buildings were closer. Anna enjoyed the walk to the barn each morning for her ride, but she could have never carried the dozen dishes there and back without the use of her car today.

The first year she tried Thanksgiving dinner, it had been a disaster. Davis had not complained though, he just called the hotel in town that boasted of the best buffet on Thanksgiving and ordered twenty deluxe dinners. By the time he drove to town, twenty take-out boxes were waiting for him.

He gave her a cookbook for Christmas, and the next year she did everything right. She remembered how proud she had been of herself and how disappointed that he had not said a word about her efforts.

This year the usual twenty men had grown to thirty-two with the addition of the oilmen. The hired men lived in a long building they called "the bunkhouse." But the oilmen did not stay in the quarters provided. They moved ugly little trailers onto Montano land and parked near the site of the burned rig. They all drove huge pickups with wheels that looked twice the size needed. The grassland around their trailers was now chewed up by the tires.

The newcomers tried to talk with her as she served the dinner, but Carlo quickly told them not to bother because her English was "not so good." He knew she was nervous and would not prove him wrong. One of the young hands who had helped her deliver a colt last spring glanced up at her. She smiled, knowing he knew the truth. The young man opened his mouth to argue with Carlo, then thought better of it and became totally interested in his food.

By six o'clock, Anna was exhausted. She finished washing the serving plates and pots. Now it was time to make sandwiches from the leftovers and deliver them to the bunkhouse door. Then, her job would be over. Tomorrow the men would make do with cold breakfasts and delivered pizza for lunch. Friday night dinner always started the weekend where each man was on his own. Most ate in town. A few rummaged for food in one of the bunkhouse refrigerators. By Monday morning they were always glad to eat the cook's meals no matter what he prepared.

Anna made sure the small kitchen in the bunkhouse was stocked with snacks and beer, plus all the basics should one of the hands get the urge to cook. She doubted it. When she delivered the sandwiches, the men were playing poker in the long main room, while a football game blared on TV. Beer cans already littered the floor and no one except Carlo seemed to notice she brought supper.

"Good night, Anna," Carlo said without bothering to add a thank-you. He did not wait for her to answer before he turned back to his card game. The stress on running the ranch was starting to show on him. Though they were making money nothing seemed good enough.

He had had his hair cut short like most of the hands and, for the first time, Carlo had switched to American clothes. He was becoming Americanized, she thought, though he probably would not know the word.

As she walked the hundred yards back to her house, she noticed the light came on at Zack Larson's place. She had not repeated her journey to his porch. Told herself she never would. But the sight of the light made her smile and remember.

She wondered if he had spent the day alone. Maybe as alone as she had been surrounded with people. She could still feel the warmth of his arms around her.

The music of Chopin greeted her when she stepped back into her house. Nothing in the place was hers except the music. The thick leather furniture, heavy wooden tables and iron lamps were only necessities in her prison.

Anna lifted an afghan from the footstool by the fireplace and curled up in the huge chair Davis had always called his. He had been cold and distant, but she missed him. Or more accurately, she missed being able to hope that life might get better, that someday he would come out from behind all the papers and work and see her. Now, there was no more hope for that day.

She drifted in sleep until Carlo opened the door wide, letting in the cold damp air. He was halfway across the room before she was awake enough to take flight.

He caught her in two steps.

"I saw you flirting with one of the men." He did not bother to even try English.

Anna choked on the smell of beer as he pulled her close and glared down at her.

"You are Davis's widow. You should have more pride."

"I—I—"

He tightened his grip on each arm. "You will not shame the family." He shook her so hard she felt sure he would break the bones in both her arms. "I will see that you do not!"

Anna sobbed trying to get a word out, wanting to tell him that she did not even know what he was talking about. But he never stopped swearing and calling her names.

He released one arm and she swayed trying to keep her footing. Her hands flew to her face to shield herself from the blow she knew would come.

Carlo hesitated, swearing at her cowardice, then he threw her against the brick of the fireplace as though he could not stand to look at her any longer.

A moment later he was gone, leaving the door open.

Anna leaned against the rough brick and slowly lowered her hands from her face. Tears came in gulps of fear. As a girl, she had lived in dread that one day her father might find her when he raged. Carlo was a childhood nightmare come to life.

She staggered to the door and pushed it closed, locking it for the first time since she had lived at the ranch.

Watching through the thin glass slit in the door, Anna saw Carlo disappear behind the barn. It must be almost midnight, but there were always men who would be willing to drink with Carlo, just as they used to drink all night with Davis when he was in one of his melancholy moods.

Anna rushed to the kitchen, fighting tears. She glanced out the back windows. There it was. Zack's light. A tiny dot in the fog.

Determined to control one moment of her life, Anna slipped on her raincoat over her silk blouse and walked out the back door.

Tonight, she did not hurry. Her blood pounded double-time through her veins, fired by anger and hurt, thick with fear. For she knew Carlo was getting worse, and the next time he might put her in the hospital—if he did not kill her first.

With slow steady steps she crossed the muddy distance between her house and Zack's. She had no idea what she would say. She hoped she did not have to say anything. She needed to feel safe, if only for an hour. She needed to think.

The fog cloaked any view until she was within twenty feet of his place. He was not outside on his porch tonight, but sitting at a table by one of the huge windows that ran along the front of his place. He leaned over a stack of papers, frowning.

She moved closer.

He ran his hand through hair the same color as the mud around his place. When he reached for his coffee mug, he glanced up and spotted her standing a few feet from his porch.

Zack was out the door before she had time to react.

"What happened, Anna?"

She saw his worried eyes and realized she must look a fright. Her hair was wild and wet. Warm tears blended with the rain.

"M-my—" How could she tell him? Her mother's voice echoed in her mind. Only the family's business...a family secret...no one else needs to know.

Once her father had blackened her mother's eye during an argument. When he thought she had gone to the police, he'd beaten her so badly it had taken a week before she regained enough strength to climb out of bed. The first night she had been able to dress and come down to dinner, Anna's father had invited the police chief to join them. Anna watched as her mother slowly ate her meal in silence and she never forgot the lesson. Some problems in the family must remain in the family.

Anna closed her mouth, shook her head and took a step backward. She should not have come. No one else needed to be involved.

When she lifted her hands to warn him not to follow, she heard Zack's abrupt intake of breath.

For a moment, she had no idea what could have startled him. Then, she saw. Her hands were covered in blood.

"Anna," he whispered as he neared. "Anna, what happened?"

Pain hit her like a bullet. She had been so frightened,

so angry there was no room to feel physical pain. She stared at the crimson droplets being watered down with rain. Anna crumpled.

Zack caught her just before she hit the ground. He carried her carefully to the porch swing and wrapped her inside the quilt he always left there. "Where else are you hurt? Anna, answer me!"

Kneeling in front of her, he examined her hands. A layer of skin had been scraped off both hands from the fingers to the wrists. Scratched deep enough to bleed, but not so deep to be dangerous.

She did not say a word. She was here. She was safe. That was all that mattered.

He helped her remove her raincoat and ran his hands along her body. When he touched her upper arms, she tensed.

"What's wrong?" he asked, as he felt for broken bones. "Tell me what happened?"

Anna could not bring herself to tell him. Some secrets must be kept. It had been an accident, nothing more. Carlo had not meant to hurt her. He was not like their father.

Zack covered her with the blanket, not caring that blood stained the beautifully made quilt. "I'll be right back." He pushed the hair away from her face. "You will stay until I get back?"

She nodded. There was no place else she wanted to be.

He returned a few minutes later with water and the first-aid kit. He knelt on one knee in front of the swing and slowly cleaned the broken skin.

Her hands shook when he touched her, but his gentle words calmed her.

"Don't be afraid Anna. No one is going to hurt you.

I don't know what you are running from, but I want you to know you can always run to me."

By the time he had cleaned the blood away and spread antiseptic on all the tiny cuts, she had stopped shaking. He wrapped both hands in gauze then gave her a flask of whiskey he kept for emergencies.

She took a sip, made a face and handed the flask back to him.

Zack chuckled. "There were times in my life when I couldn't get enough of this stuff, then I realized I was following in my father's footsteps. A few months after my wife left me, I threw away all but this flask and decided to look at the world, no matter how bad, without the haze." He offered her another drink but she shook her head.

"Pretty awful, huh?"

Anna nodded. She started to wipe her mouth, then stopped at the sight of her fingers wrapped in white.

Zack leaned in and brushed his thumb across her bottom lip, catching the moisture the whiskey had left.

The simple action was the most loving thing anyone had ever done for her. She felt as if he had made love to her in an instant.

"Feeling better?" His voice was unsteady, and she knew he had felt it also.

She nodded once more and raised her hands. "Th-thank you."

He waited for her to explain, but she did not.

Finally, he leaned back against the swing and gingerly placed his arm around her shoulders. She relaxed against his side, curling her feet up beneath her inside the quilt.

"You can tell me what happened. Or you can tell me nothing. It doesn't matter. I'm still going to be here."

Her slender arm slid around his chest, right across his heart.

The rain fell in sheets off the edge of the porch, but they barely noticed. After a long while, he whispered against her hair, "I swear, I'll never tell anyone you come here, Anna. I swear on my life."

The promise and his arms around her were all she needed right now. She would worry about Carlo later; tonight she just wanted to be with Zack.

They rocked back and forth on the old porch swing until the rain stopped. Then, he walked her back through the mud to the walkover.

She took the first step and turned to face him.

After a moment of silence, he said, "Remind me to tell you sometime when we're talking, how much I like your hair down and all wild."

She leaned forward and kissed his cheek, then took the next step.

"Take care," he said as he helped her over.

She nodded in answer and headed toward her place. When she reached the back patio, she turned and waved, knowing he would still be watching.

Oil field workers often put a six-pack in the water can as they come to work. At quitting time everyone has a cold beer.

Saturday, November 28
Montano Ranch

Anna slowly unwrapped the gauze Zack had placed around her hands two nights ago. There was no bleeding, but her skin looked raw and covered in long thin scabs.

She trembled, realizing if she had not covered her face when she fell, the scabs might be across her cheeks.

"What's wrong with you?" Carlo asked in Italian from the kitchen doorway. He saw no need to use English when they were alone. Neither did he bother to close the door. He was truly a man more comfortable in barns.

"Nothing." Anna guessed Carlo must have slept Friday away and finally recovered enough from his holiday drunk to make an appearance. He would not really be interested in anything she said as he rummaged through her cabinets for the bottle of aspirin she kept there.

"I noticed the front door was locked." He opened the bottle. "Not a bad idea with all the extra men around the place." He helped himself to coffee as if nothing had happened between them two days ago. "If you do not feel safe, I could move over here into the other bedroom until the drilling is finished."

"I—I am fine." Anna fought down panic. "Y-you need to be near the horses." She and Carlo were from the same blood. They had been taught since birth that horses were more important than people. If he really thought there was any danger on the ranch, he would stay near them, not her.

She had to convince him she was not afraid to be alone. If he saw fear, or weakness, he might start moving in. "I scraped my hands on the fireplace wall when you pushed me Thursday night. I am not worried about the extra men you hired. I am worried about my brother who comes over here drunk to yell at me."

Carlo looked confused for a moment, and a little guilty. He quickly recovered. "I hardly remember coming over. I wanted to warn you to be careful." He played his big brother role now, the one she had loved so dearly when she was a child. "You are Davis's widow, Anna. You can not be smiling at the employees. It would not be proper. You are lucky to have me here to guide you."

No matter how old she got, he would always be ten years older. Ten years wiser in his mind.

She raised her hands seeing the scratches and imperfections in their sibling bond as well as the ones on her flesh. "You call this lucky?"

"You probably fell wandering through the great room in the dark. Do not blame your problems on me." His eyes told her he did not believe his words, but he continued, "I am working day and night to keep this place making money. I have no time to hear about your scratches."

Anna found no argument in his last statement. She also knew the discussion was pointless. At best, they would go in circles, at worst he would get angry. She decided the safest choice was to change the subject. She continued in Italian. "Speaking of money, I may need some today.

Helena Whitworth called and asked if I could have lunch with her and go shopping."

Carlo's mood changed. "Of course. Whatever you need. I will put extra in the box." He switched to English. "It is good that you become her friend."

The box was a leather case on Davis's desk in the den. He always left several hundred dollars in it for Anna in case she needed household funds. A checkbook with her name on it rested in the bottom of the box for emergencies.

"I—I may be gone most of the day."

Carlo nodded. "I will have someone exercise the horse you are training. Do not worry about it." He seemed almost in a hurry to be rid of her.

Anna watched him go, then collected the money. As she twisted her hair in a long braid and circled it at the back of her neck, she thought that in her country it would have been the proper style for a woman in mourning. She also wore black, but broke with custom by adding a multicolored scarf.

An hour later, she pulled into the garage beneath the bank and the Randell House Restaurant. She was early, but she planned to enjoy a cup of tea before Helena arrived.

As she stepped from her car, she saw Zack Larson walk out of the elevator and start across the shadowy parking lot toward her.

He walked in long strides to his pickup with his head down.

Anna was not sure what to do. If she stood perfectly still, he probably would not even notice her. If she moved, he might speak to her. She was not sure which would be worse.

Words lodged in her throat preventing all possibility

of calling to him. Her hands shook. Her purse fell to the concrete.

Zack looked up and froze. His troubled frown lifted slightly as he held her gaze.

They were both aware of other people rushing from the elevator to their cars.

He took a few long steps and knelt at her side, picking up her purse. "You dropped this, ma'am."

"Th-thank you." Her hand brushed his as she took the purse.

He touched his fingers to his Stetson and walked away without another word.

Anna forced herself to turn and walk toward the elevator. She did not breathe until the door closed and she stood alone. By the time she reached the second floor, Anna was once more in complete control. No one who saw their brief exchange would suspect anything.

She sat enjoying her tea, thinking of how once more Zack Lawson had kept his word. When Helena joined her, Anna was a little surprised to see how tired the older woman looked. Helena explained that she had not been sleeping well.

"We have much to do," she whispered as if she and Anna were planning a great crime and not just having lunch.

Before she could add more, Meredith Allen joined them and a moment later, Crystal Howard.

The widows are assembled, Anna thought. All except Randi. Meredith was dressed in a Christmas sweatshirt that had a Santa Claus head made from yarn sewn on it. She apologized for having only an hour for lunch before she had to be back to work at the clerk's office.

Crystal also looked tired, but there was a grace about her that had not been there months ago when Anna first met her. Crystal was growing. She looked comfortable in her clothes and at home in this restaurant.

"Now, we're all here." Helena opened the luncheon as though it were a board meeting. "We have a problem."

The three younger women leaned closer. If Helena had a problem they were all three there to help.

Helena took a deep breath and got right to it. "Randi got arrested last night."

"What?" Crystal shouted, shattering her new image. "She was with me until ten when I drove her back to her hotel." Crystal looked at the others and added, "What with Shelby coming home yesterday and all the nurses moving in, Randi said she would rather stay at a hotel and get a good night's sleep before she headed back this morning. I figured she'd be halfway to Memphis by now. How did she have enough time to get into trouble in the past few hours?"

"What happened?" Meredith directed her question to Helena.

The senior woman among them shrugged and continued her report, "From what I've been able to piece together, she must have driven over to the bar for a nightcap. She took out one of the light poles at Frankie's place when she left. I phoned Sheriff Farrington about it this morning after my daughter notified me. Her husband works for the electric company and was called in early to shut off the electricity going to the pole. I swear, nothing happens in this town that I don't hear about before the newspaper even has time to report on it.

"Anyway, that is beside the point. The sheriff told me Frankie was fighting mad at Randi and wanted to file charges. He claims she did it on purpose. Sheriff Farrington thinks that might be the case since she wasn't legally drunk, and she's spent most of her time this morning calling Frankie names when he finally woke her up at the motel. He said there is a pole-size dent in her bumper, so there is little chance of her pleading innocent."

Meredith was not following. "Why would she do such a thing?" In her world, accidents happened, not intentional destruction.

"You don't know Randi." Crystal sounded suddenly depressed. "She's got a temper and old Frankie loves to push her buttons. Which isn't hard to do when she's been drinking. She never mentioned it to me, but someone told me once that he's always telling her she married the wrong Howard. Giving her a hard time about how she didn't get rich like I did."

Anna knew the reason did not matter. The problem still needed to be solved. "How can we help her?"

Helena took a long sip of coffee before she answered. "One of us has to see the sheriff about making her bail, and one of us must go into Frankie's place and talk him into dropping the charges. Maybe we could even offer to pay for new lights around the parking lot. Money usually makes this kind of situation seem a little better."

Everyone at the table nodded in agreement.

Anna spoke first. "I—I will pay for the lights." Contributing money was far easier than talking to someone she did not know.

"I'll talk to Frankie," Meredith volunteered.

Helena and Crystal both looked surprised. They had expected her to choose talking with the sheriff. After all, she would be working a few doors down from him all afternoon.

"That leaves me to discuss the matter with the sheriff." Helena nodded once as if finalizing a deal. "Crystal, you've got your hands full with Shelby right now."

Crystal frowned for a moment, then brightened. "I

could have one of the mechanics who works for Howard Drilling check on her car. By the time you all get her out of jail, I could have it gassed up and ready to make the trip back to Memphis."

"That would be a good idea," Helena agreed. "This place has nothing but bad memories for Randi. Maybe she needs time away."

Helena did not have to say more. Anna and the others understood. Each dealt with grief in their own way. For Randi, maybe it was drinking. At least in Tennessee, she would not be reminded of her Jimmy every place she turned.

The women talked on of other things. An hour later, when they parted, they were all soldiers with a mission.

Anna had already figured out where she could get the money to buy the new lights for Frankie's bar. She would tell Carlo she wanted to make a donation to a charity Helena Whitworth supported. He would never question it.

Along muddy, tent-lined streets, boomtown joints served a crude alcoholic drink made popular during Prohibition. They were open round-the-clock to accommodate all shifts from the oil fields. Roughnecks who drank cheap liquor sometimes lost workdays because the alcohol produced a paralysis of the feet and legs.

Saturday, November 28
5:00 p.m.

As Meredith walked down the courthouse hallway, the bells at the Catholic church chimed for Saturday evening mass. They reminded her that this place had once been her palace and she had danced across the marble floors. She knew every corner of the first two stories as if it were her private playhouse.

Her father had never allowed her to climb the stairs to the third floor, just in case a prisoner was being held in the small two-cell holding unit. Once in a while, a man would be brought in for trial early in the morning and transferred out that night to the main jail six miles out of town. She had seen the small elevator in the sheriff's office that only went to the third floor, but doubted it still worked.

She could not help but glance over near the back door when she stopped at Granger's office and told him good-bye. The elevator was still there but the county clerk said Granger, or one of the deputies, took prisoners straight to the main unit nowadays. They did not have the manpower to assign someone to the third floor as a guard.

Granger looked up from his spotless desk and stared at her as if he had forgotten she was in the building.

She did not give him time to say anything. She wanted to get to Frankie's Bar and complete her mission. She was several feet down the hall when she thought she heard him answer, "Evening."

Kevin and she had gone to bars a few times during their college days. She guessed it was still the same—no one ever came early to a bar. So, five o'clock would probably be a slow time if Saturday had a slow time. She could talk to the owner, Frankie, get her business done, and be home before dark.

Clifton Creek once boasted thirty saloons, but when the oil boom slowed, the bars eroded into dilapidated buildings, storage garages, and quick-stop gas and grocery stores. Somehow, like the last dinosaur, Frankie's had survived. It had changed owners several times. In the sixties it was a biker bar, a beer and barbecue stand in the seventies, but since the early eighties, Frankie's place was pure country-and-western music and longnecks.

When she pulled into the parking lot, Meredith breathed a long sigh of relief. Only three cars huddled in front of the shack. Since lunch, she had been planning what she would say and now wanted to get it over with before she forgot her speech. She would use logic on Frankie. Even a bar owner would respond to that.

The wind whirled a caliche cloud around her car as she parked. White powder settled on her old Mustang, dirtying the already dull blue to Confederate gray. Clumps of dried weeds fought their way through broken sidewalks to serve as landscaping. Shattered bottles that had been tossed at the building framed the foundation like colorful crystal in the afternoon sun.

Meredith rushed inside, telling herself she did not care

if someone saw her. She was on a mission. But she knew she would rather not have to explain. Thirty years ago a teacher patronizing such an establishment would have been grounds for dismissal. Today, it would probably only be frowned upon. She did not want to find out for sure.

As she walked in a heavyset man, with a beard half-way down his biker shirt, looked up from the bar he was cleaning. Meredith glanced around. A young waitress talked to a cowboy in the corner, but other than that, the place was empty.

She quickly crossed to the man behind the counter. "Mr. Frankie?"

He stared at her as if he was trying to identify a new species never before seen in this environment. "Who wants to know?"

Meredith extended her hand. "I'm Meredith Allen, a friend of Randi Howard."

He did not take her hand and she could not help wondering if he had caught Granger's disease. "Lady, you may be Meredith Allen, but I'd stake what's left of my hair that you're not a friend of Randi's."

The barmaid moved closer, suddenly more interested in Meredith than the cowboy. "Where'd you get that sweater, honey?" She raised one eyebrow that looked to have been painted on with a first-grade crayon. "I'd like to have me one of them Santa shirts."

"A friend made it." Meredith held up the bottom of the shirt so the Santa shone in the bar lights. "You can buy the sweatshirts at Wal-Mart, then all it takes is a little yarn and a pair of eyes. She glued these on, but you could use buttons."

Meredith glanced up to see them laughing at her. She fought the urge to run. She was not used to having her kindness met with sarcasm. She did the only thing she could think of, she continued.

"It has to be washed by hand or the yarn tends to come out." She held her head high and stared at the barmaid's forehead like she had been taught to do when she first started teaching. "I could leave it here for a few days if you want to use my shirt as your pattern."

The woman was taken back by Meredith's kindness, but was too jaded to believe. "What planet did you drop from, honey?"

Meredith smiled as if she understood the joke. "I grew up here but went away for a few years during college. Took over Mrs. Helderman's second-grade class when I got my degree."

The barmaid smiled. "I had Mrs. Helderman. She was so old we all believed she dated Robert E. Lee. She still have that picture of him hanging behind her desk when you got there?"

"Of course. I don't think she ever threw anything away. You should have seen her files. She kept toothless, second-grade pictures of most of the people in this town." Meredith leaned closer so she could read the name tag. "I don't remember seeing a Barbi, though."

"It's Barbara. Barbara Coleman. I think I was in the fifth grade when you came. I kind of remember seeing you around."

"Yes, of course." Meredith patted Barbi's arm. "You're Molly and Jake's big sister. How are they doing? I heard Molly got into A and M."

"That's right. Another few years and my baby sister may be an engineer."

"I'm so proud. She was such a sweet little girl."

Meredith glanced at Frankie. He looked like he might throw up.

The cowboy sauntered from the other end of the bar, his beer in hand. "I had Mrs. Helderman. She used to turn her ring around and thump us with the stone if we caused trouble. I still got dents in my head to prove it."

Frankie groaned. "I'm calling the cops. You stay much longer, teacher, and there's bound to be trouble. Who knows, all the customers will probably start getting out their old annuals and we'll sign 'See you when the summer's over.' We can have a regular grade school reunion."

Meredith ignored Frankie and looked at the cowboy. "You're Smiley Weathers, aren't you? Mrs. Helderman used to tell stories about you when she'd come up to have lunch in the teachers' lounge."

"She remembered me?" He seemed touched.

Meredith added, "She showed the newspaper clippings of you making it into the rodeo finals in Las Vegas."

Smiley took a swig of his beer. "She did, huh? Well, I'll be."

Frankie had had enough. "You'd best be ordering a drink or stating your business, teacher. I can't stand much more of this."

Meredith folded her hands and leaned her elbows on the bar. "As I said, I'm a friend of Randi Howard, and I'm here to see if you'd be willing to drop any charges against her if she had the light pole fixed."

His eyes squinted like he was trying to see a lie. "And how might you be friends with Randi?"

Meredith forced out the words she hated to say. "My husband was killed with hers on the oil rig that caught fire a few months ago."

Both Barbi and Smiley drew closer.

"Ohhh." Barbi sighed. "I'm so sorry. It was horrible, wasn't it? They say old Shelby Howard is little more than a vegetable. Had one of his ears burned completely off, too. No telling what else. Maybe it's lucky your man died."

Meredith did not answer. She had grown used to such insane statements.

"I've got friends who played ball with your husband." Smiley made a slight toast with his beer. "They say he was one of the best who ever played in this town."

Frankie glared at the pair of crybabies. "Now don't get started again. So you're friends with Randi because of some accident. That don't make you her keeper. She got into trouble last night, and this time she's going to pay."

Smiley and Barbi looked at him like he had thumped a puppy.

Frankie picked up the rag and wiped the bar, trying to ignore their disapproval.

"Randi's not alone," Meredith added. "Helena Whitworth is posting her bond and Anna Montano as well as Crystal Howard will stand behind her with any money needed to make the repairs."

Frankie snorted. "Crystal, I believe. She and Randi used to run this place on busy nights. Haven't seen her for a while. Don't know Anna Montano, but everybody's heard of her. Cowboys from the Montano spread who come in here say she's a looker."

"Look but don't touch," Smiley added. "I hear tell her brother threatens to cut the nuts off anyone who talks to her." He glanced at Meredith. "Pardon my language, Mrs. Allen."

Frankie rolled his eyes. "So Randi's got her some friends. So what? That don't fix my pole."

Meredith played her ace. "We'd be willing to put up a string of light poles that look like old fashioned streetlamps if you'd drop the charges. We have every intention of squaring up with you."

"Wouldn't that be swell," Barbi chimed in. "Think of it, Frankie. This place would finally have some class. Maybe folks could find their cars if we added more than one light pole."

"More poles would just be more for them to run over." He wasn't giving in so easily. "Besides, the pole hit the building when it fell. Scratched the paint off the left side."

"You've got to be kidding." Smiley laughed. "How could you tell that scratch from the hundred folks made trying to leave the parking lot? Some nights it's like bumper cars at closing time."

"But if we got a string of new lights, folks would notice the paint job," Frankie reasoned.

Meredith remembered Helena's words to offer whatever she had to in order to get the charges dropped. "Would you call it even if we had the building painted?"

Frankie slowed his cleaning. "I might. I always liked Randi. If she hadn't killed my pole I'd say we would still be friends."

"Blue!" Barbi giggled. "The building has to be blue."

"Blue's not a good color for a bar." Smiley took another drink. "Black, maybe with a red roof."

"Both of you shut up. The two of you sound like those interior decorators on TV." Frankie looked like he needed a drink. "It's a deal, lady. I'll let you know what color. Now get out of here or order, I don't have time to chat."

Meredith offered her hand again, and this time Frankie took it.

As she turned to hug Barbi goodbye, the door swung open with a pop, letting in a wide slice of late-afternoon sun.

Sheriff Farrington stood with his feet wide apart and

his hand resting easy on his gun belt. Meredith almost laughed. He looked every bit the lawman stepping into a saloon in the badlands.

When he saw Meredith, she didn't miss the way his whole body relaxed. He closed the door and walked in as if finding her in the local dive were an everyday occurrence.

"Evenin', Frankie."

"Evenin', Sheriff. You off duty and drinking tonight, or like half my business lately, just come to talk?"

"Any problem?"

"Not unless you call arguing over what color to paint the place a riot."

Granger looked at Meredith. "You having car trouble, Mrs. Allen?"

"No," she said. "I was just leaving." She hugged Barbi again. "Now, tell Molly hello for me."

Barbi promised, then added, "I'd really like that pattern from your sweatshirt. They'd make real neat Christmas presents."

Meredith wiggled out of the sweatshirt and then straightened the white blouse beneath. It was wrinkled and hopelessly covered in tiny red balls. "I'll pick the sweatshirt up in a few days when I come back."

"You're coming back?" Granger looked away as if there was a possibility she thought someone else had asked the question.

Meredith saw no need to answer. This was none of his business.

"I've got to go. Bye, Barbi. Take care, Smiley." Meredith moved toward the door. "Bye, Frankie. I'll return with some paint samples."

"Bye!" Frankie drew the word out as he wiggled his fat fingers.

All three on the other side of the bar glared at him.

Meredith ran to her Mustang, in a hurry to get home.

On the fourth try to start her car she noticed Granger standing beside her driver's side window.

"What?" she snapped, angry that he had followed her again.

"Let me try."

She got out of the Mustang, shivering. "What makes you think it will respond to a male foot pumping the clutch any better than a female foot?"

He pulled off his uniform jacket and dropped it over her shoulders. "Just let me give it a try."

The second time he turned the key, the engine kicked to life.

"Luck," she said as he climbed out.

"Does this thing have a heater?"

"No." She offered him back his coat. "But I won't freeze in the ten blocks to my house."

He refused to take the coat. "Keep it. I know how you hate to be cold. You can bring it back tomorrow, if you're working at the courthouse this Sunday."

"I have to get finished with some reports. How about you? Are you planning to be in your office tomorrow?" Everyone in town knew the sheriff did not work Sundays.

"I'll be there," he snapped as if they were having an argument and not simply a conversation. "I have some end-of-the-month paperwork to catch up on."

He walked away without saying another word.

Meredith drove home wrapped in his warm coat, wondering how he knew she hated to be cold.

Farmers and ranchers supplied the need for oil field workers in the early days. They were used to hard, backbreaking work in all kinds of weather.

Anna waited for Bella to take a drink of tea before she continued painting. The old housekeeper loved to talk while Anna worked.

"So," she started once more. "I was doing Zack Larson's laundry. It is never much, he takes his shirts and good jeans to the cleaners in town. He kids that he doesn't trust me with white shirts after seeing what I do to white socks."

Anna smiled, enjoying the music of the woman's words even though she talked of nothing important.

"I don't mind the laundry, which probably makes me a candidate to be committed in most women's minds. But for me, it means an order to the day. I always washed the sheets first, so I could make the bed. Then the towels. By the time they are done, I'm cleaning the bathroom and kitchen. The laundry is a timetable, a clock that ticks away the hours to the beat of Zack's country-and-western music."

Bella popped a cookie into her mouth and continued while she chewed. "Only today, hidden among the dirty clothes was a real puzzle. One old blanket he always keeps by the porch swing and the only two good guest towels the man owns were stuffed in the bottom of the hamper. All three were spotted with blood and Zack standing there, not a Band-Aid on him. If he had cut himself, he would have had to search past two stacks of ordinary towels to find the two fancy ones. Why would a man use his favorite blanket and two good towels to clean up blood?"

Anna had stopped listening. She was remembering.

"I would have asked, but I'm not one to pry. He's a man who guards his solitude. In his teens, when he was wild and out of control, he gave up trusting people." Bella shook her head, forgetting she was the model. "I'll never forget the day, fifteen years ago, when his mother was not long dead. I spent half the morning sobering up Zack's dad enough to drive him down to bail out his son. No one in town would give the boy the time of day after that, not even when he buckled down and worked the ranch after his father died."

Bella sipped her tea and ate another cookie. "I do love these things. I told Zack I was going to get some for his place."

Anna did not miss Bella's gaze resting suddenly on her bandaged hands.

"Did you take a tumble riding?" Bella asked.

"Oh, no." Anna tried to not meet Bella's stare. "I fell against the fireplace trying to cross the great room in the dark."

Bella smiled and Anna knew the old housekeeper had figured out her puzzle. Neither said a word.

Anna worked the rest of the day on Bella's painting, but when darkness fell, she watched for the light from the north. Carefully, she waited. It would not do to go to

Zack's too early. She did not even want to think of how Carlo might react if he saw her crossing the land.

The night was still and cold when she finally climbed the walkover and headed toward the porch light. Zack sat on the swing. He stood when he saw her walking toward him.

He offered her his hot cup of tea when she reached the porch. Anna cradled the mug in both hands and curled into the blanket he offered.

"T-tea?" she asked after taking a sip.

"My housekeeper seems to think I need to drink the stuff, but can't say I care for it much. I'm sure glad you showed up to take it off my hands."

She smiled and took another drink.

"I don't know how long you can stay tonight, but it wouldn't be long enough."

They talked of the tea, and Bella, and the construction of a new rig on Anna's land. Her words were hesitant and shy. He wanted to tell her to slow down, relax. He would wait. He liked hearing her voice as she told him the fire had finally been ruled an accident and how Carlo was taking care of all the details.

It was too cold to be outside, but he did not invite her inside. Maybe he thought he might frighten her. So he brought out another blanket when he went to turn up the music and the lights.

They finished the pot of tea and opened the English cookie tin while looking at a travel book of places she knew well. She laughed at him when he popped one of the cookies in his mouth whole. Bella forgot to tell him they were for nibbling on.

Anna could not help but wonder how long Bella had known about the two of them meeting.

As they talked of her home, her words finally began

to flow. Zack was careful not to ask any questions but to let her lead with anything she wanted to tell him. She liked that about him, more than he would probably ever realize.

When she told him, she added, "Now tell me something you like about me."

"I like watching you move. There is a grace about you that fascinates me. It almost makes me forget how much I hate the taste of tea."

They laughed; the night aged. She snuggled close against him and leaned her head on his shoulder. As they rocked, she slept.

He held her for a long while, then drifted to sleep.

They awoke in the stillness just before dawn.

"Anna?" he whispered as she tried to move closer and go back to sleep.

She turned her ear away, not wanting to wake.

Zack laughed and tried again. "Anna, it's almost dawn."

She finally looked up at him thinking he was handsome with a day's worth of beard along his jaw.

"You'd better go." He moved his hand over her hair. "I hate to say it, but in a short time you won't have the aid of darkness to cover your journey."

She stretched and nodded.

He kissed her forehead. "Funny thing, I slept better on this swing last night than I have in weeks on my bed."

"I also." She pushed on his shoulder. "Only my pillow is not very fluffy."

"I'll start gaining weight."

"If you do, you will break the swing." Pushing herself away from him, she stood and looked down for her boots.

He let the swing drift away with her shove and then

back again to catch her on the back of her knees. She tumbled atop the blankets and back into his arms.

They both laughed, then he helped her put on her boots. He reached inside his house, grabbed his coat and, as always, strolled with her to the walkover.

The sky was just starting to gray as she stepped on the first step and turned. "Good night."

"Good morning," he corrected.

She leaned as before to kiss his cheek. On impulse, her lips shifted at the last moment and pressed against his mouth.

Zack took the kiss like a blow.

He stepped back, almost stumbling. With her at eye level, he stared for a moment, then closed the distance between them and returned the kiss.

He slid his hand around to the small of her back, pulled her against him as if starved. They had been touching for hours, but this was different. Before this kiss they could have written off everything between them as friendship. This kiss changed everything.

Finally, he broke the kiss and forced himself to move away. "There is no time," he said out of breath.

She touched his jaw with the tips of her fingers wishing they had another hour of darkness.

Zack closed his eyes. "It's so real with you, Anna. So real it scares the hell out of me."

She laughed, knowing what he meant. She sensed it, too. A part of life that had never been there before. A hope of a future. They had both been walking through the world in a dream state and now, with one another close, every cell was fully awake.

Before he could say anything more, she was gone, running to beat daybreak. Running before her heart exploded with the pure joy of knowing he was in the same world as she.

When she was almost home, she turned to see him still standing beside the walkover. There might never be more than the one moment they just shared, but somehow it was enough. For the first time in her life, Anna was alive.

Mesquite seeds traveled from South Texas in the bellies of cattle during the cattle drives of the 1880s. They were planted along the trails, stomped into the ground, and today mesquite trees clutter the plains of the state.

Helena Whitworth sat in her favorite chair by the windows, drinking her third glass of wine. She had had a busy day and now wanted to enjoy every moment of the evening with J.D. "You wouldn't believe the way Randi looked when Crystal handed her the keys to her BMW. Oh, J.D., I wish you'd been there."

He smiled at Helena, seeming to enjoy the hearing of her story as much as she enjoyed the telling.

"Everyone did their job. Meredith somehow persuaded old Frankie to agree to drop the charges. Anna said she got catalogs for the lamps and color samples for the paint. She even checked the city codes on outside lighting." Helena laughed. "As if we had any. I talked until I was blue convincing Judge Lewis that Randi was no threat to anyone. Only Crystal faltered."

J.D. told her a story of his army days when one of his young lieutenants hadn't carried through with a field maneuver and almost got them all killed.

Helena had never loved the war stories, but she did love listening to his voice. Sometimes she would beg to hear a tale again just to enjoy the rhythm of his words. Some men have a knack for telling stories. Her J.D. was a master.

"Crystal did try," Helena added when J.D. finished. "She had the mechanic lined up and even a body man on standby to fix that tank Randi drives. But Trent Howard got wind of it, and all of a sudden he needed every hand out on the Montano place. Like they were going to re-build that rig in a day. That young Howard is nothing but a bother. He's doing all he can to keep Crystal from making everything run at Howard Drilling. Thank good-ness Elliot is keeping an eye on everything. Trent may think he can get away with something, but my guess is Elliot will stop him every time."

She took a drink, feeling warm despite the cold outside. She had taken to perspiring lately, even on the coldest days, just like she had done when she went through "the change." Maybe she should take J.D.'s advice and slow down a little.

"Is it warm in here?"

J.D. did not answer.

Wiping sweat from her upper lip, she continued, "Crys-tal didn't have a choice. She knew how badly Randi wanted to get out of town. The poor girl can't even stay with Crystal and Shelby. It's like every time she sees Shelby, she thinks of her Jimmy, all burned. Randi may have talked about leaving Jimmy because he bored her, but if truth be known he was good to her. That's how it is with some women...no man's ever good until he's gone."

Helena shook her head. Hard times all around. "Crys-tal's changing. I'm not sure a few months ago she would have turned loose that toy she calls a car. But this morning she handed over the keys, and told Randi to keep it until she came back at Christmas."

Helena poured herself another drink. "Oh, I know you think she was trying to guarantee Randi comes back at Christmas. It must get lonely in that big house with all those people around and no one to cuddle with or talk to. Randi needs to keep in touch, as well. She and Crystal were friends long before they were both married to Howards. Now they seem even closer."

Helena leaned back and relaxed as J.D. talked of doing something for Randi. The cowgirl was not getting any younger, maybe they could jump-start her career. He had a few old army buddies around Nashville, and Helena knew most of the independent store owners. Randi said she had lost yet another job in Memphis. There was nothing keeping her there.

It was after midnight when Helena crawled in bed. They had discussed every option. Finally, they arrived at a plan to help Randi.

Helena lay her head next to J.D.'s arm and fell asleep knowing she had something important to do tomorrow. Her store would have to wait another day. For the first time in forty years, she had not been there to open the Christmas season, thanks to Randi's problems. But she left it in Mary's capable hands. It would be all right for one day more.

At ten o'clock the next morning, Paula called to see if Helena was all right.

"Of course, dear." Helena tried to sound as if she had been awake when the phone rang. "I'm just a little tired. I thought I'd take it easy today. J.D. is always telling me to take a day off now and then."

"That's good, Momma. You rest. I'll watch after the store. Pat and I have been helping out where we can."

"That's nice." Helena could think of little else except hanging up and going back to sleep. The wine must have made her drowsy, and she did not dare tell Paula that she had felt dizzy when she sat up to answer the phone. Her daughter would insist on making an unnecessary doctor's appointment.

"You are taking your medicine, Momma?" Paula asked. "You've been a little absent-minded since—"

"Of course," Helena lied before Paula could finish her sentence. "I always take my medicine right after I brush my teeth. I never forget."

"I'm just worried about you. How about I bring you a plate over for your supper? I'll let myself in and leave it in the fridge."

"That would be nice." Helena had given up on trying to talk her daughters out of feeding her. If they had their way, she'd be fat as a bear. She had not been eating a great deal lately, but her appetite would come back. "Thank you, Paula," she said, making a mental note to throw away their previous offering before Paula made another delivery.

"I love you, Momma."

Helena rarely said those three words to her children. Somewhere over the years, she had stopped and just did not know how to get started again.

"I love you, too," she finally said, hearing J.D. in the background telling her there was no time like the present to get started on a habit.

Helena hung up the phone and relaxed onto her pillow. She would dream a few more hours, then she would set Randi's surprise in motion.

During the early days of oil, change was the only constant from boom to bust. One sign taped to a window in a former boom town read, Don't Bother To Unpack.

Many men traveled with wives and families. Women worked just as hard trying to build homes at each stop as the men worked to build the rigs. Sometimes the money a wife made as a secretary or doing laundry would cover expenses for getting to the next town.

December 6
9:53 p.m.
Howard House

Crystal Howard sat alone in the shadows of Shelby's room. The whine of machines blocked out all other sounds. She closed her eyes and dreamed of silence. The odors no longer bothered her. They were now the scent of Shelby. He had gone from having the aroma of cigars and whiskey and oil fields, to smelling of antiseptic, bleached cotton and dying flesh.

Her life with Shelby before the accident had been a roller coaster, high highs and low lows, but never boring. They would decide to fly to Dallas over breakfast, or have a party at sundown. No matter what the whim, their days and nights were exciting and unpredictable.

Now, there was a sameness about each day that made her want to scream. With all the people in the house, it was important to follow a timetable, but she had become a slave to it.

She dressed by seven so she could spend time with Shelby before the office staff from Howard Drilling arrived downstairs at eight-thirty. Then, as the day passed

with one business crisis after another, she would run up
and down the stairs. Making sure the nurses gave Shelby
his medicine. Checking to see if he was awake. Delivering messages. Asking advice. The oil game dripped into
her blood. The excitement, the gamble.

The evenings were the only quiet time for her. Months
ago she would have passed the time watching TV, but
now, sitting beside Shelby while he slept was her only
relaxation.

"Crystal?" Shelby whispered with a scratchy voice
that doctors said would never heal. "You still here?"

She moved to his bedside. "I'm still here, darling."

"What time is it?"

"A little before ten."

His hand covered hers. As days went in Shelby's life,
this had been a good one. He had not almost died.

"You need to get some sleep, baby."

"I was just making sure you were resting quietly. I'll
tell the nurse to wake me if you have any trouble during
the night."

"Go on to bed. I'll be all right."

She leaned down and kissed his hand. "Okay.
Night."

She was almost at the door when she heard him whisper, "In case I forget to tell you, baby doll, you're doing
a great job. I wouldn't have made it through this without
you."

He didn't see a tear roll down Crystal's face as she left
the room. It was the first time he had ever complimented
anything but her body.

She held her head high and walked next door to her
room. As she undressed, she thought how Shelby had
changed. It was almost as if he were another man behind
all the scars and bandages. And tonight, he had proven

it once again. He had been grateful, something the old Shelby had never been. He was grateful for her.

Crystal grinned. Helena said tragedy changes people. Stirs up their hearts, makes them realize what's important and what's not. Maybe Shelby had found his heart.

When she sat on her side of the bed, the message machine on her private line blinked at her. Crystal punched the button.

"You're not going to believe what happened, Crystal!" Randi's voice came through loud and clear. "Frazier's Department Store just called. They want to add live entertainment over the holidays, and they want me to be the lead singer. Just think, Crystal, every night I'll be singing, and everyone in Nashville shops at Frazier's around Christmas. I'll be sure to get other gigs from it. And the best part is they're paying me a thousand a week plus a clothing allowance to spend in the store. Imagine that."

Randi's laughter came through the line. "My last night is the eighteenth, then I'll be heading home. Thanks for letting me borrow your car. Spread the word to the other girls. I'm on my way. I can feel it."

Crystal smiled. Randi needed a bit of good luck. She was tempted to go see if Shelby was still awake and tell him. He had always liked Randi. He used to tease about her talent, or lack of it, but he had always wished her well.

A light tapping sounded before Crystal could make up her mind. The night nurse poked her head in as she did every evening after she ran a vitals check. "Mr. Howard is resting nicely. Don't worry about him tonight."

"Thanks." Crystal liked the way the nurses from Dallas were so polite, so professional. "Good night."

She leaned back thinking of all that had happened today. One day at a time Trent was cooperating with the workings of the company. He seemed to have given up fighting with her and decided to work her to death to get her out of the way. New bids were going out every day along with more work crews than Shelby had ever kept going at one time.

Ten minutes passed. Crystal had lifted the remote from her nightstand, but hadn't bothered to click on the TV. The light tapping came again, startling her this time.

"Mrs. Howard?" The nurse opened the door a few inches. "I saw your light still on and hoped you wouldn't be asleep already. I have a phone call. Would it be all right if I took it downstairs? I won't be long."

"Sure." Crystal pulled on her robe. "I'll stay with Shelby 'til you get back."

When Crystal entered Shelby's room, she was surprised to find him awake and restless.

"Where's the night nurse?" he asked.

"She went downstairs."

"Good. I was just thinking about you."

She moved to the machines. "Is everything all right?"

"Everything is fine. Come over here," he said, sounding angry and frustrated. "Closer, baby doll."

Crystal thought of the night he had tugged at her gown and made her open her top. She hesitated.

"Come here," he ordered in his low voice. "I don't bite."

She crossed to the side of his bed. "If you want me to strip, I'll do it, but I have to lock the door first. I don't want the nurse seeing me."

She closed her eyes, afraid he might say he didn't care who saw her. But he didn't say anything. Before the accident her stripping had been almost a nightly ritual. Sometimes she didn't mind, telling herself he enjoyed it, but mostly, she hated being groped, knowing the man she loved thought of her as just a body. And she hated the way he'd brag about the details of their private life to anyone who would listen.

When she looked up, he was watching her.

"I'd like…" He sounded tired. "I'd like you to lie down next to me. As close as you can get without having to touch me."

"But…"

"Just do it, Crystal."

Cautiously, she stretched out along the side of the bed as best she could. Her fingers trembled as she gripped the sheet to keep from tumbling off. There was no room for her beside him, but she tried.

"What do you want?" She forced any fear from her voice.

"I don't want to be by myself anymore. I just want to know you're next to me until I fall asleep."

Slowly, she relaxed. His breathing slowed. He made no move to touch her or demand anything.

"Thanks," he whispered just before he fell asleep.

"You're welcome," she answered just as softly.

When the nurse returned, she followed Crystal out into the hall. "You really shouldn't be…"

Crystal looked at the nurse and raised her chin slightly, ready to fight.

The nurse lowered her gaze. "Oh, never mind. If you like, Mrs. Howard, I could order a bed that's a foot wider. It wouldn't make any difference with his care, but it might make you more comfortable."

"Order it then."

The nurse smiled. "You understand it wouldn't be wise for you to fall asleep. If you rolled or swung your arm while that close to him…" She didn't have to say more,

Crystal had not lived every day around him without being aware of what might happen.

"I understand. I just want to make him feel less alone."

The nurse nodded her understanding. "Good night, again, Mrs. Howard."

"Wake me if…"

"I will. Try to get some sleep."

Saturday, December 11
12:30 p.m.
Helena's Choice

Helena unfolded from her car and headed for her first day of work since before Thanksgiving. She and J.D. decided she needed to take a few days off and rest. After all, the store could get by without her for a while. It had been great fun to sleep in and then watch movies all afternoon. They went for drives to nowhere and talked until dawn once. She finally laughed and said she had to go back to work to get some rest. No one would believe what a time they had enjoyed.

As Helena locked her car door, she noticed Anna's new white Range Rover circling, looking for a place to park. Helena stood and watched. It was always grand when the lot was full.

The Rover, after running over the curb, landed in a spot by the street. Meredith Allen and Anna Montano climbed out laughing.

Helena could not hide her smile. "What have the two of you been up to?"

"We've been picking out poles for Frankie's place.

Which would have been a challenge even for Martha Stewart." Meredith tried to straighten up but a giggle crept into her voice. "The man's not only hairy, he's color-blind. It's hard to talk paint with someone who only sees gray. At one point he was sure he wanted purple."

"It—it is not as easy as one might think choosing j-just the right lamp pole for a bar parking lot." Anna hooked her arm around Meredith's. "I—I was lucky to have help."

Meredith's eyes sparkled. "At one point, we were standing in the lot all acting like poles so Frankie could decide how far apart he wanted us."

Anna agreed. "I—I got—" she hesitated, looking for the right word "—hit on."

Helena could not think of any two people who would look less like they belonged in the local dive. Anna, in her black wool, calf-length coat and fine silk scarf. Meredith, with her jingle bell earrings and white bulky sweater that made her look like a polar bear.

"She did!" Meredith answered Helena's frown of disbelief. "If I hadn't been there to fight him off, some trucker from out of town would have found him a 'good buddy' today. Anna would probably be halfway to the state line by now."

Both women burst out laughing.

Anna pretended she was lifting a huge belt around her waist. "I reckon," she tried to sound like a local, but was hopelessly lost. "I—I could take you for a ride, little lady. I will even let you blow the horn."

The women folded over in pain from laughing so hard.

"Have you two been drinking?" Helena found that hard to believe, but their behavior warranted her asking.

Meredith looked so guilty it would be a waste of time

for her to lie. "I'm not due back at the courthouse for another half hour. I'll sober up by then."

Anna patted Meredith's arm. "We had to accept Frankie's offer. It would not have been polite to turn him down."

Helena pulled them inside and up the back stairs before half the town saw them. "Mary will have a pot of black coffee. You can drink it while I order sandwiches delivered from next door. That should sober up you barflies." She could not hide a smile as she thought of how she would tell J.D. tonight. He had learned all about Anna and Meredith from Helena. He told her once that Kevin Allen spoke of Meredith with respect, as if the little schoolteacher were the anchor in his life.

Helena followed as Meredith and Anna giggled all the way into the office, having a great time trying to imitate the voices of everyone in the bar. Helena could not believe the little schoolteacher and the fine lady were crazy enough to drink what Frankie gave them. She was tempted to stomp into his place and give him a piece of her mind. Maybe while she was there, she could pick up the two brains Anna and Meredith seemed to have left behind. They could not even tell her what they drank, only that it was green and tasted like frozen key lime pie.

The pair giggled their way through three cups of coffee and a sandwich each before they finally calmed down. Helena tried to look over her mail while she listened to them talk. Meredith promised to go out to Anna's place and see her art. Anna agreed to help Meredith paint a wall of her classroom to look like a forest.

"Well," Helena finally broke them up, "did you get Frankie to agree on lamp poles?"

"We did," Meredith said, winking. "Or rather I did, while Anna flirted with the trucker."

"B-but he was so handsome." Both women laughed at her lie.

"We'll call the order in today." Meredith smiled at Helena. "Frankie should have the poles by Christmas."

She stood and set her cup down. "I have to be getting back to work, much as I hate to."

"I—I also must go. I've been gone for far too long." Anna joined Meredith at the door. "Thank you, Helena, for the lunch."

"Anytime," Helena answered, thinking how she had known both women for months and this was the first time she had heard them laugh. Maybe green-frozen-key-lime-pie drink was not so bad. "You girls be careful."

Helena stood at the window and watched the two widows walk down the front stairs and through the store. They wound through crowded aisles packed with racks of clothing and people.

Once they left, it took Helena a few minutes to realize something was wrong. "Mary! Mary!"

Her assistant rushed to her side. "Yes?"

"The store!" Helena had to make herself slow down and breathe. Her chest felt like an elephant sat atop it. "The store is packed with too much merchandise. People can't move around freely, especially the large women who are trying to shop. This is insane."

"I know we're crowded," Mary answered, "but we had to put all the new stuff somewhere. The back is packed with spring shipments the twins ordered while they could get them at a five percent discount."

"New stuff?"

"Paula and Patricia ordered women's sizes. They thought they were ordering by ones, not by the dozens. So everything they ordered one of, we got a dozen. Two, we got two dozen. Six, we got six dozen."

"I understand the principle, Mary. You don't need to continue to frighten me to death."

Helena could not breathe. She had nothing against women's sizes, those women needed clothes, too, but the larger sizes were not the image she wanted for Helena's Choice. Her patrons were willowy like her mannequins. Many times she did not order even the twelves and fourteens in a style, because the dress would not hang right on a woman with much meat on her bones.

Helena's heart pounded when she thought of all the large sizes going out of the store in her high-quality Helena's Choice bags.

"Mary," Helena whispered, trying not to frighten her employee. "Would you be so kind as to get my pill box from my purse."

"Of course."

As Mary hurried on her mission, Helena slowly lowered herself to her chair. More than a week ago, she had stopped taking the third pill she had to swallow every day. She told herself she didn't need the digoxin for chest pain. If it got bad, she had her nitroglycerin. There was no need in using both.

Mary handed her the small box and Helena took the tiny pill, placed it beneath her tongue, then relaxed back in her chair.

"Are you all right?" Mary worried over her. "Should I call the doctor, or an ambulance?" People in Clifton Creek rarely called an ambulance; it was easier to get in the car and drive to the doctor. If someone did not have a car, they could always yell for a neighbor to drive them. An ambulance in front of a home usually meant someone died.

"No, I'll be fine in a minute. I've just been a little tired lately, can't seem to get enough sleep."

Mary did not look relieved. "Does your chest hurt? Are you short of breath? Do you have a pain in your arm?" She circled once more. "Or is it your leg? I can never remember."

Helena forced her hand to move away from her heart. "It's only the angina acting up again. You know how it gets when I overdo it. I thought I was ready to return, but maybe I should stay home a few more days. The holidays seemed to be taking a toll on me this year."

Mary handed Helena a cup of water. "Don't worry about the store. The twins will help me handle it. I couldn't believe it when we put plus sizes out for the first time, but I've been surprised. Women I've never seen in here before are shopping. And I can't tell you the number of men who've been in to buy their wives clothes who have never shopped Helena's Choice before. They don't even want us to wrap the box. They want their wives to know where the gifts came from."

"How are the sales?" Helena took a deep breath, preparing for the worst.

Mary hesitated, then smiled. "The best we've ever done. If this holds, we'll have a record year."

Helena did not respond. Swiveling her chair, she looked out the window into her store. "Wait until I tell J.D.," she whispered as she watched the flow of customers. "He is not going to believe it."

By one-thirty that afternoon, the tuna sandwich and the drinks Frankie served were at war in Meredith Allen's stomach. The third time she ran down the hallway past Sheriff Farrington's office, she saw him glance up and frown.

A few moments later, with her head an inch above the toilet, she heard the ladies' room door open. If she thought there was any possibility of vanishing by flushing herself, she would have tried. No one else was in the building. She knew who it was.

"Meredith?" he yelled. "Meredith, what's wrong?"

For a second she remained completely still, hoping he wouldn't notice her kneeling in the first stall.

"You're not supposed to be in here!" she finally said in her most authoritarian voice. "This is the women's restroom."

His hand touched her shoulder. "Are you ill?" He brushed her forehead with his fingers. "You're burning up. What's wrong?"

Meredith was positive that if wanting to die would get her there, she should at least be in purgatory by now.

Granger stepped to the sink and began soaking paper towels. "How long have you been ill? Do you think you caught something? I could take you to a doctor." He stopped talking while she vomited, then continued as if he had not noticed the sound. "Maybe it's food poisoning. The truck stop's been passing that out with the two-for-one burrito bags lately."

He handed her the first towel and Meredith wiped her mouth. She rocked back, sitting on the marble floor in a very unladylike sprawl. She did not even want to think about how she looked and knew she did not have the energy to stand.

Granger knelt down to her level. "Meredith! Is there any chance you're...?"

If she'd felt better, she would have laughed. He looked even paler than she felt. "No, Sheriff. No little deputies." She giggled at her own joke, then frowned. "I can't have children."

"Then what?"

Meredith raised her eyebrows and addressed the class idiot. "I'm drunk." She wondered if being drunk in a public restroom was a misdemeanor or a felony. She felt sure it was some kind of crime.

He stood. "You're what?" His voice echoed off the walls of the tile room, making her head pound.

"Anna Montano and I went to see Frankie about the lamp pole Randi knocked over. He was kind enough to serve us his special for lunch."

"I may have to shoot Frankie," Granger said calmly as he leaned down and pulled Meredith to her feet. "But first I need to take you home."

"No, I can work." Before she could issue her declaration, she jerked away and leaned above the toilet once more.

When she finished, he waited with a clean set of wet towels.

"I'm sorry." She flushed the toilet.

He helped her up again. "Meredith, you're not the first drunk I've seen, and you probably won't be the last. Think you can make it home?"

She nodded. Surely there was nothing left in her stomach to lose.

He put his arm around her shoulders and walked her down the hall. At his office, he picked up his keys off the desk and the pager from its nest. He flipped a switch on the phone. Then he helped Meredith out the door and to his police car. He opened the passenger door. "I make most drunks ride in back, but if you swear not to mess up my car, you can ride in front."

She looked up at him as she slid in. He showed no sign of kidding.

They were almost to her house when she remembered she had forgotten her purse.

He promised to lock the office and bring her things by later when he made his rounds. If she felt better by then, he said she could ride downtown and pick up her car; otherwise, he would have one of the deputies who came on duty at five help him get it back to her house.

"That's not necessary," she replied.

"Adam won't mind. Where are your keys?"

"They're in the car."

He glared at her. "Meredith, you shouldn't leave your keys in your car. That's just asking for a crime to happen."

"Nobody would steal my car parked at the courthouse

and if they did, they'd better be a mechanic or they'll be sorry."

"You need to get rid of that pile of junk."

"It gets me to work and back." She resented him calling her car names. The pile of junk had been hers since college.

They did not say a word to one another for the rest of the ride. He drove and she concentrated on not throwing up on his clean car.

He walked her to her door, but did not offer to come in. She was glad. Meredith had been so humiliated she didn't care if she ever saw Granger Farrington again.

Reaching for her house key in the huge pocket of her sweater, Meredith opened the door and faced him. "Thank you, Sheriff. It was nice of you." She had to tell him how she felt. "But you don't have to look after me. You don't have to check on me if you see me in a bar, or start my car, or make sure I'm warm, or anything else. I'm not your responsibility."

Meredith closed her eyes. If he said he was just doing his job, she swore she would club him with her hatchet.

"Get some sleep. You'll feel better."

He acted as if he hadn't heard a word she said. He just turned around and walked back to his car like she was number 247 on his list of official duties for the day.

Meredith wanted to scream, but her head might explode at the sound. So she went into her house, crawled onto her unmade bed and took the sheriff's advice. She fell asleep.

Dreams haunted her. Not nightmares of monsters and torture. Worse. Dreams of Kevin, burned and calling for her. But she couldn't find him. She could hear him, smell the mixture of oil and burning flesh, but she could not reach him.

In her dream she ran and ran, calling his name, fighting vines and roadblocks and chains, but never reaching him, never able to help.

Suddenly, the dream was over and Meredith found herself alone in her dark bedroom. Her huge sweater was twisted around her as tight as a straitjacket.

She stood and fought her way out of the wool, then stripped off all her wrinkled clothes and headed toward the shower. For a long while, she let the water run over her face and body and wondered if she could have made any bigger fool of herself today. Granger had only been trying to help and she had snapped at him. He was right about her car. It was a piece of junk.

She dried off and put on Kevin's old high school jersey. It almost hit her at the knee.

Wandering into the kitchen, Meredith searched for something to eat. An old apple. Half a sandwich. The bread was hard, but the chicken salad still smelled good. There was also a quart of orange juice that had aged at least one season in her refrigerator.

Nothing sounded good. She glanced at the clock. Too late for the stores, and drive-throughs were beyond her budget for this month.

Someone tapped on her door. Meredith straightened from rummaging in the crisper as Granger let himself in.

He looked surprised to see her awake. "I'm sorry— I thought you'd be asleep. I was just dropping off your purse and some soup." He set the bags down on the chair nearest the door and backed out.

"Wait!"

He hesitated.

"You brought soup?"

He smiled, realizing she wasn't still mad at him. "Soup,

crackers and cookies. I figured when you finally sobered up, you'd be starving."

"I am." She moved to within a few feet of him. "I'm sorry about the way I acted when you were only trying to help."

"Forget it."

"Would you stay for soup?"

"All right, but I cook." He lifted the bag and waited for her to lead the way to the kitchen.

Handing her the cookies, he removed his coat and unloaded groceries. He'd also brought along milk with three different kinds of soup.

"I didn't know what you liked." He shrugged, offering her the choice.

Meredith was busy fighting with the cookie package. "Any kind," she finally said as she broke the cookies open and glanced up in time to catch him watching her.

"Want one?"

He shook his head. While she ate four, he warmed tomato soup and poured them both a glass of milk.

They ate at the bar, with their knees accidentally bumping together from time to time. She told him all about the agreement made with Frankie. There was something very comforting about being with a person that you've already made a fool of yourself around. She had no more false pride to lose. Even the fact that she was only wearing an old jersey didn't worry her. After all, he'd seen her in far less.

When they finished, he did their dishes, along with several others sitting in the sink. She watched him, thinking how out of place he looked in her little kitchen in his spotless uniform. She liked the gray at his temples and the solidness of his body. An ounce of fat wouldn't dare land on Granger.

She wondered what he would say if she told him she wanted a *king's x* from all the things she had said to him. Like the kids on the playground, she wanted to cross her first two fingers and suddenly have all the rules not apply. She wanted to say she needed more than his once-in-a-while lovemaking, and part of her wanted him tonight. If she had to play his game and not touch him when he made love to her, she would. She just wanted him to lie beside her and hold her, just for tonight.

But if she begged him to stay, she would have to face tomorrow and the next day and the next. She did not want to be his midnight lover whom he came to see when he thought no one was looking.

Something she remembered a teacher saying to a college class drifted through her mind. The best example you will ever give your students, is the way you live your life. The professor was trying to tell future teachers that they cannot live one way and teach another. The "do as I say and not as I do" was never much of an example.

If Meredith continued to live an honest life, she would have to be honest with herself. She was not like those women on TV who sleep with a man whom they had known for hours, then move on to another. Meredith knew that if she gave her heart it would have to be all or nothing. That's how it had been with Kevin despite their problems. That's how it would have to be if she loved again.

She wanted a man to stand beside her, to grow old with her. If it was that or being alone, then she would have to be willing to accept solitude.

"Thanks for the supper, Sheriff."

"You're welcome." He dried his hands.

"Do you think we could be friends?"

"I'd like that." He grinned. "Would that mean I could call you if I had car trouble?"

Meredith smiled. "You bet."

"And if I needed a friend to, say, walk into Frankie's place with me, you wouldn't mind tagging along?"

She fought to keep from laughing. "I'd do that for a friend, and I'd be sure to keep my mouth closed and not try to interfere. And I'd try to keep from bossing you around if we were friends, even if you were drunk."

Granger shook his head. "That might be a hard one, since I seem to need a lot of direction." He studied her closely. "But I'd try not to leave my keys in my car, my back door unlocked, my purse in plain sight...."

"You're making a real effort." Meredith stopped him before he listed all her shortcomings. "Now, if you'll just promise to curb the drinking, I think we could be buddies."

He winked at her. "It's a deal."

She started to offer her hand, then reconsidered. "Well, good night, Sheriff." She moved to the door as she spoke.

"Do you think since we're friends, and I'm making all this effort, that you could call me Granger?"

She opened the door. "Good night, Granger."

"Good night, Meredith." He stepped past her and walked to his car without a backward glance.

She watched him pull away, wondering if they could ever be friends when she could still feel his hands stroking her breasts. The memory of their night together was so vivid even now it made her ache inside. But one night could be written off as a lapse in judgment. Any more would be an addiction that would tear her apart with its limitations.

Roughnecks worked no matter what the weather. If it got bad they might all be served a "fifty cent overcoat" —a long draw of corn whiskey.

December 17
Montano Ranch

The wind swept down from the north and large flakes of snow swirled across the flat land. Anna had tried to paint all day but it was useless. She hated winters in Texas. What little beauty the country managed to hang on to during the other seasons disappeared with the cold. Everything faded to a dull brown. Not tan, not chocolate, just brown. The mesquite trees that could almost be tall bushes when green were now only squatty, thorny, useless sticks. The tall grass that swayed in fall, shook in winter, brittle with age.

She watched the sun set, knowing she would look north as soon as darkness fell. There she could see Zack's light. Then she would feel the warmth of memories.

Carlo and several of the men drove over to Dallas to pick up a load of new mares. They would not be home until tomorrow at the earliest. If the promised storm hit early, they might not return until Sunday.

Several of the hands took time off. With the cold and the holiday season, the work on the ranch slowed. Horses were, as always, well taken care of, but their exercise time was shortened on days like this.

Her brother worried about her being alone at the ranch with only a few hands and the oil field workers still squatting near the rig. He insisted on leaving her the old Colt revolver usually kept in the barn to kill snakes.

Anna hated any weapon. Her earliest memory of a handgun had been watching her father put down a beautiful mare. The men on her family's ranch stood in a circle, but she could see between them. Her father knelt down, stroked the horse's mane while he placed the barrel of the gun where the bullet would pass straight through the mare's brain. The shot echoed in her nightmares for years. Not even her mother's explanation that her father had saved the horse a slow painful death made Anna feel any better.

Anna glanced at Carlo's gun resting on the corner of the hearth. It would be in exactly the same spot when he returned.

She had not visited Zack's place for several nights. In truth, she was a little ashamed of how forward she had been, kissing him so boldly when they said goodnight. She was a woman who knew her place, her role. In her twenty-six years she never stepped beyond that place, except when she was with Zack. The first night she climbed over the fence started an adventure. Anna had no idea how it would end.

Tonight she felt even more alone than usual. Meredith called and talked a long while, then at seven Helena phoned to check in. The older woman sounded tired, but assured Anna she was getting plenty of rest. They made plans to visit Crystal. Anna volunteered to do Crystal's shopping. Crystal wanted to put up a big tree for Shelby with presents all around the bottom. She made the effort of inviting Shelby's children and grandchildren, hoping to have a real family Christmas.

Anna feared Crystal would be disappointed, but still wanted to help her try. She planned to buy gifts anyone might enjoy just in case Crystal wanted to pass them out to the nurses and employees of Howard Drilling.

Anna looked around the great room of her cage. She had not bothered with one decoration. Carlo thought it was proper not to celebrate, with her still in mourning. Anna had bought Bella a teapot and ordered Carlo a new wallet with hand tooling on the leather. The two gifts were as yet unwrapped.

She remembered the Christmases of her childhood with everyone laughing and yelling and eating. Davis had promised her that "next Christmas" they would go back to her home. A promise he had made since their first year together. But somehow "next Christmas" never came. There were always more horses coming in, being sold or needing special care.

She tried to read. Tried to watch an old movie. Tried to eat. Nothing held her interest while she waited for sundown. She would go over to Zack's and tell him she was sorry she had been so forward the other night. She might have given him the wrong impression. She was not ready for a romance. All she needed was a hug now and then. She would survive with that.

As soon as his porch light came on, Anna ventured to the walkover. She knew the path well by now. She crossed over, then sat on the bottom step and watched Zack moving across his huge front windows. She could not help but laugh. He was trying to decorate a tree and doing a miserable job.

He did not notice her until she stepped on the porch.

He hurried to the door, mumbling and frowning. "I didn't expect you so soon."

She took a step backward. "I—I could leave."

"No." He hesitated as if afraid he might frighten her. "Don't go. I just wanted to have the tree up when you came." He glanced at the disaster behind him. "But that may be July."

"Not going well?"

"No." He held the door. "I could use some help, if you'd consider coming in."

When she did not move, he quickly added, "Or I could stop for tonight and we could sit on the swing. This isn't something that can't wait."

"I can help," she said slowly. "Then we can sit on the swing and look at what we have done."

When she passed him at the door, she was so close she felt his warmth, but she was careful that they did not touch.

His furniture was so sparse, she considered asking him if he was moving in or out. One comfortable chair in front of a bookshelf filled with mostly paperback books. One couch on a worn rug with a coffee table decorated by scattered water rings and dents. There were no pictures on the walls, but the hardwood floors were polished to a royal shine and the room looked recently painted.

Bella's doing, Anna thought.

Zack read her mind. "My wife took most of the furniture when she left. Actually, when we married, she got rid of my junk claiming it was worthless. If I'd have known the marriage wasn't going to make the year, I would have stored a little of the junk in the barn."

"I like the space. Too much furniture weighs the room down."

"That's true. I could drive a herd through here."

She moved to the mess by the window. "I like your tree."

"Thanks. I got it half price, it being so close to Christmas." He looked as if he regretted telling her about the cost of the tree. "The ornaments were in a box my mother must have put in the attic. I haven't seen them in years." He picked up one yellowed satin ball. "I'm afraid they're in pretty bad shape."

She lifted one of the balls. "Do you have any paint?"

"Sure." He raised an eyebrow. "What color do you need? It's probably in the barn. My father never threw any paint away as long as there was enough left to cover the bottom of the can. I inherited his disease."

"Yellows, as many shades as you have. And bright blue and red."

He shrugged his shoulders as if he thought she was wasting her time, but headed out the kitchen door toward the barn.

Anna looked around. The kitchen table was stacked with papers, mostly bills in disarray. However, the books on the shelves were placed in careful rows, almost like a treasured library. To her surprise, huge travel books filled the bottom shelf and each had tiny slips of paper sticking from them as if someone had marked pages in each book.

She decided to work on the coffee table. By the time she covered the old table with newspaper and spread the dilapidated ornaments out on the floor, Zack had returned with several buckets of paint and a few small worn brushes.

Without a word, she went to work doing what she loved most in the world. Painting. He straightened out the lights and got a few strings to work while he watched her. When he finally had the tree in place and the lights evenly circled around, her first few ornaments were dry enough to hang.

He sat on the floor across from her as she worked. "They're beautiful. I've never seen anything like them."

Anna smiled. "Thank you." If she had her brushes, she could paint intricate designs on each ball, but with one-inch brushes that had seen better days, she made bold strokes with circles, starbursts and wavy lines.

The tree became magic, one ornament at a time. He did not talk as she worked, but each time he stood to add a ball, he stepped back and admired the tree. When she painted the last ornament, he carried it to the tree as she stood and stretched.

"You're an artist, Anna. A real one, like I've never seen before."

"I enjoy it."

She did not move as he slid his arms around her and worked the tired muscles of her back. They had been together for hours and he had not touched her. He was not embracing her now, only making her more comfortable.

"Tired?" As he relaxed her back, he swayed slightly, almost as if they were dancing.

"Hungry," she answered honestly.

"Well, the least I can do is feed you after you saved my tree. I think I've still got some of them funny crackers and tea."

She frowned.

"Baloney sandwiches?" He laughed when she made a face. "No wait. After all that work, you need a real treat. How about a baloney bowl with cowboy beans and onions in it?"

Anna raised her eyebrows. Ten minutes later she stared at a thick slice of baloney that had bowed to the shape of a bowl when fried. It was then filled with grilled onion and canned beans. Anna was not sure she could eat it.

But Zack acted like he was serving a delicacy. "My mom used to make this for me when I was a kid." He put a slice of flat yellow bread on her plate. "Corn bread," he added when she stared up at him with an eyebrow raised. "It tastes really good crumbled on top of the beans."

She seriously doubted anything could improve the taste of a baloney bowl filled with beans.

They ate at the coffee table while sitting cross-legged on the floor. She was surprised at how good the odd food tasted.

When he finished, Zack leaned back against the couch and stretched his long legs out beside her. "You're a great artist, Anna. I'm not just saying it to be nice. You should have your work in one of those high-priced studios in Dallas. Or maybe down on Sundance Square in Fort Worth. They've got Remingtons and Russells side by side in a gallery down there. It doesn't get much better than that."

"And you, Mr. Larson, are a terrible cook."

He did not seem to mind her honesty. "I know, but at least it was edible." He glanced at her empty plate.

"I was starving."

"So am I." His voice lowered, his frankness frightening.

Without another word, he leaned across the little table and kissed her.

Anna pulled away and stood. It had come time to deal with what had happened between them the last time he had walked her to the stile. She spoke slowly, trying to make the words come out without stuttering, but knowing it was hopeless. "A-about the o-other night."

She felt the warmth of his body behind her, but he did not touch her.

"What about it?" He didn't pretend not to know what she was talking about.

"I—I am not sure I am ready." She fought for words. "I am not sure I will ever be ready."

Zack folded her into his arms. "It's all right." He felt her tremble but she did not step away. "Take your time, Anna. I'm not going anywhere. Only, do me a favor. Don't go kissing me like that unless you want me to follow you home. You'll never know how hard it was to stay on my side of the fence the other night."

Her body relaxed against his. He was not going to push her into anything. "A fair request."

"Now that's settled." His hand slid down her arm to her hand. "Let's see what the tree looks like from the porch swing."

He did not try to kiss her again or touch her in any way that was improper, but somehow their nearness had changed.

Wrapped in blankets, they sat on the swing drinking their coffee and tea but now, his every touch was somehow different. He was making love to her with each slight caress and she knew it. The moon brightened the cold night. She saw his face clearly. He looked deep in thought.

"Tell me why you read travel books." She wanted to hear him talk. He was unlike any man she had ever known. Being with her seemed his only goal. He treated each hour as a gift.

"I don't know. I've collected them since I was a kid. I love it here, but I'd like to see other places someday." He talked about all the countries he'd like to visit, all the beaches he wished he could walk on, all the roads he would wander down if he had the time.

Anna listened, not telling him that she had seen many of the things he described. The gentle sway of the swing kept time with his voice, making her almost believe the world was a wondrous place.

She had never known the pleasure of seduction. Davis kissed her twice before he proposed. Then he had seen little of her before the wedding. After they were married, he saw no need for courting.

She could not help but wonder if Zack had any idea how his slight touch affected her, now. The way he ran his hand up and down her back, playing along the imprint of her spine. How he brushed her leg as he rocked the swing. Or how his breath warmed her cheek.

Anna leaned against his shoulder and watched the lights of the Christmas tree twinkle through the window. "It is beautiful."

"That it is." He kissed her forehead. "Thanks for helping me."

"You are welcome."

"Want'a stay the night with me right here? We could leave the tree lights on all night."

"Yes," she answered honestly, "but I have to be up early tomorrow. I am going shopping with the other widows."

He did not need more explanation. She had talked of Helena, Meredith and Crystal before.

They rocked for several minutes before she added, "I may not get to come back for a while."

His muscles tightened slightly as if he were forcing himself not to say a word about when she might return. She knew she was hurting him and he was trying not to let it show.

He did not ask her to explain. No questions. No strings. He had promised.

Cupping his chin with her hand, she whispered, "It is after midnight. Walk me to the stile."

He stood and helped her up, then retrieved their coats and hats from inside. They strolled, hand in hand to the walkover, slowing as they neared.

She did not want the night to end but reality had to win out this time. And she knew even after she left him, she would still have her memories. Sometimes she thought their few hours together were the only cherished memories she had. The only time she had been allowed to just be herself were the times she had crossed the fence and stepped onto his land. He asked nothing. He might never know how much he gave in return.

Anna took the first step and faced him.

"Come back when you can," he said with his head too low for her to see his eyes. "I'll be waiting."

"How long?" she whispered. "H-how long will you wait?"

He looked up, straight into her eyes. "Forever, Anna. I'll wait forever."

She leaned against him and kissed his lips. She was not sure what she had ever done to deserve finding him, but suddenly she knew she could not let go. When she crossed the fence she was not going back to life. Life existed here, with him; the rest was the dream. Zack was her reality.

This time he was ready for her advance, he did not hesitate. His arms closed around her, pulling her to him as he returned her kiss completely. His hands moved inside her coat and beneath her blouse, hungry for the feel of her skin. His kiss was eager, awkward in haste.

Anna pulled away suddenly and tumbled over the stile,

almost falling. She ran several feet before she turned around, knowing he would be there, watching.

"Well." She laughed. "Are you coming? You said you would come home with me if I kissed you like that again. I never thought you were a liar."

He jumped over the steps as she ran toward her house. She made it to the patio before he caught her.

For a moment he just held her, breathing against her hair. Then, he gently pushed her against the wall and pressed his body along the length of hers. "I'm not a liar," he whispered.

His kiss was wild and hungry, as if it were essential to living. She answered his need, starving for the nearness of him.

He had half her clothes off by the time they stumbled into her house. Neither of them noticed a lamp tumble as he drew her toward one of the overstuffed couches.

"Wait!" Anna pushed him away, laughing and kissing him even as she tried to untangle from his arms. "I will be right back."

He took a long breath and let her go without asking her reason.

When she returned, he had turned her stereo to a country station and unbuttoned his shirt. The lean curve of his chest and stomach drew her artist's hands as if she could memorize each line and reproduce it one day in clay.

"Are you sure?" He kept his hands at his sides as she brushed her fingers across his chest. "I could leave if you want to stop. If you're not sure. Anna, I want you so bad and that isn't going to change, but I don't want to hurry you."

She spread the blanket she had gone after across the couch. "I am sure." Her voice trembled.

She sat on the blanket not knowing how they would get

back to the wildness of a few minutes before. She needed to feel alive, but knew there was far more to them than that. She needed him.

He knelt in front of her. "I'll never hurt you, I swear."

His callused hands moved over her body, pushing the silk blouse off her shoulders. "You're so beautiful. You deserve a lot more than the likes of me."

She leaned forward and kissed him, pulling him gently back with her to the quilt her grandmother had made. The only words that came to her mind were in her native tongue. She had to make him understand with her actions.

And she did.

December 18
Dawn
Montano Ranch

An icy sunrise sparkled against the windows, reflecting frozen shafts of dawn light. Zack jerked, reacting to the front door rattling a moment before Anna could pull fully awake. He moved while she was still trying to figure out where she was. A warm blanket covered her and the warmth of Zack's nude body molded against her side still warmed her. He was not in her dreams; he definitely was in her house.

He turned his head into her wild hair. "Anna! Anna you are in my arms. I thought I might be dreaming."

The memories of the night washed over her groggy brain. They had made love like two awkward fools the first time. She accidentally shoved her elbow into his eye, he pulled her hair, they bumped noses. They laughed and apologized and made up.

The second time, they got it right. And the third had been heaven. She knew it then, deep inside, all the way to her soul. They were meant for one another. They would

be together until they were both too old to remember what
they had done this night.

The door to the kitchen rattled, then opened.

Zack jumped off the couch, waking Anna fully in
his haste. He had his pants pulled on by the time Carlo
reached the great room.

"I made it back early. The horses were not…" Carlo
stopped as he looked into the great room.

For a moment Anna's brother stood there as if he had
turned to stone. Snow sparkled in his hair and two days
of stubble covered his face.

Slowly, his entire body swelled in rage.

Zack stepped in front of Anna as she frantically
searched for her blouse. "Now hold on, Carlo."

Anna watched anger building in Carlo like steam in a
boiler. Zack looked worried, but not frightened.

"We can talk about this," Zack tried again.

Carlo did not look like he planned to reason.

"I don't blame you for being upset." Zack pulled his
shirt across his shoulders. "But she's a grown woman who
knows her own mind. It's time you let go of some of that
brotherly guard."

Anna agreed but could not get her voice past the fear
blocking her breathing. She stared at Carlo.

Suddenly, Carlo came at Zack like a wild bull in full
charge.

"I will kill you!" he screamed as he landed a blow
against Zack's ribs before Zack could react.

Zack was better prepared for the second blow, but only
defended himself and did not strike out at the man who
might soon be his brother-in-law.

After a few more assaults, Zack must have known
Carlo planned to make good on his promise, so he started
hitting back.

Anna screamed, knowing she had to help, had to stop this before one of the two men were dead. Begging her brother to stop, she moved closer.

Zack glanced at her. He seemed to be saying, "It's all right. I can take care of myself. Don't worry, Anna. Don't be afraid."

But before he could say anything, Carlo landed another blow hard against Zack's jaw.

"Hold on!" Zack tried reason one last time. "There is no need…"

Anna stepped between Zack and her brother as Carlo raised his fist once more. She cried, pleading with Carlo in two languages for she knew he would not stop until Zack was dead. She begged for his life.

Carlo's fist flew into the side of her face, knocking her off the ground. She tumbled against the hearth like a broken doll.

"I will deal with you later!" he yelled. The toe of his boot slammed into her middle, sending her rolling against the brick. "I will make it so you will never leave this house again. I will see that no one ever looks at you again."

Anna watched knowing Zack was not a fighter. He told her that, except for a few times when he had been drunk, he had never hit anyone in his life.

But he fought now. He fought for his life. He fought for Anna.

He plowed blow after blow into Carlo's stout body, paying no mind that Carlo hit him back, no pain seemed to matter. They rolled across the room, toppling chairs, breaking tables and lamps. Carlo swore at him in two languages and laughed each time he drew blood.

Zack tripped over the rug and hit the floor with a thud. He tried to stand but the fight was taking its toll.

Anna watched in horror as Carlo lifted a wrought-iron floor lamp high like a weapon.

The first blow slammed into the side of Zack's head. The second into his rib cage. Each drew blood.

"No!" Anna screamed. "N-no! Put it down. You will kill him!"

Wiping the blood from his eyes, Zack tried to block the next assault, but Carlo swung the lamp once more.

Anna pulled herself up on the hearth, feeling the hits as if they were on her body and not Zack's. Blindly, she grabbed the Colt Carlo had left for her. With shaking hands she pointed it toward her brother.

Carlo laughed without fear. "Say goodbye to your lover, Anna! You will not see him again in this lifetime." He raised the lamp higher to make sure the impact would crush his bones.

Zack fought to get out of the way but he was fading in and out of consciousness.

The lamp started toward his head.

A shot rang out.

The world shifted to slow motion with the sudden explosion. Carlo looked surprised, then turned his anger toward his sister. The lamp fell from his hands tumbling against Zack's legs.

"Anna," Zack managed to whisper before he fell backward.

The wide-open Texas land had an edge to it, never quite calm. It bred risk takers like white water breeds danger. Generations descended from desperadoes, wildcatters and gamblers.

Granger wasn't sure which he hated most: ice, or people who thought they could drive on it. He'd been on the roads since before dawn and finally found a minute to check in with the office. Inez was on the morning shift, but busy on the phone. Granger figured he'd do some paperwork and let Adam handle the roads for a while. He would send Inez home to read her spy novels on her own time.

When he walked through the door, he heard Inez scream, "911 coming in!" If her voice had been a little lower, she would have made a great extra in a WWI film. The whole battlefield could have heard her yell.

Calls to the department were common, but folks never used 911 unless it was something horrible or somebody had died. Even then it was usually natural causes or an accident so the hospital handled the call, because things like murder never happened in Clifton Creek. The last emergency call that came through had been the oil rig fire several months ago.

"Montano Ranch!" Inez yelled with her hand over the bottom half of the phone. "There's been a shooting and a rape!"

Granger grabbed the extra phone. "Sheriff Farrington…" He didn't get time to say more before the caller started shouting.

Granger knew it was Carlo Vangetti by the accent. He had talked to Carlo enough months back to remember his voice well. "Calm down, Carlo. We're on our way. Yes, we'll bring an ambulance."

Inez was already on the other line giving the hospital instructions to send out Will, the only full-time medic in town. "Trouble at the Montano place again. Trouble again."

Granger hung up his phone. "Get any details you can. Call Adam and tell him to back me up. The dented fenders will have to wait."

Inez nodded, her spy novel forgotten.

Hitting the lights and siren buttons, Granger sped out of the parking lot. He knew Inez would get calls about the noise, but he didn't want to lose a second. He flew past Meredith pulling into work, her car clanking and sputtering as always.

The roads were bad, but once he hit the Farm-to-Market cutoff, it was a straight shot to the Montano place. The ambulance lights blinked in his rearview mirror, a half mile behind.

A dozen men who looked as if they worked on the ranch stood around in front of the main house as the sheriff pulled up.

Granger jumped from his car. "What happened?"

"Don't know," one of the men said. "I thought I heard a shot, but there was no answer when I knocked. Carlo would be real upset if we bothered Mrs. Montano for no reason."

Ignoring questions, Granger ran up the steps and pounded on the front door. "Carlo! You in there?"

He thought he heard a yell but the place was like a fort. Granger stormed around the side of the house and tried the door near the garage. None of the men followed. They acted as though some invisible line prevented their stepping any closer.

The side door opened. Granger turned and waved the ambulance onto the driveway, then stepped inside.

He crossed the kitchen and noticed Carlo leaning against the wall with the phone clenched in his fist. Dark blood spots from his body had marked the wall in several places.

Adrenaline must have been shooting like wildfire through his veins, for he talked as fast as he could in two languages and none of it made any sense. His normally dark skin was pale. He must have lost a great deal of blood, but a fire still smoldered in him as if he had one more battle yet to fight.

"Settle down." Granger tried to stay calm, but Carlo's panic bombarded him. Blood dripped from several spots on his face and arms. His knuckles were raw, and his left pant leg was soaked in crimson.

Granger put his arm around Carlo and tried to maneuver him to a chair, but the stout man would not cooperate.

"He must have broken in sometime last night!" Carlo yelled beyond the kitchen to the huge living room as though someone else needed to hear him besides the sheriff. "He was beating Anna when I checked on her this morning. Then the bastard shot me."

"Who?"

"Zack Larson." Carlo looked like he wanted to spit the words out. "That worthless rancher from next door. Davis never liked the man. I should have been more careful about leaving Anna alone. It is my fault."

The boys from the hospital banged in through the door with supply boxes and a stretcher. Will was the only hospital employee who drove the ambulance, and Granger wondered if he didn't sleep in the back on one of the stretchers. Will had talked the nursing program at the college into requiring each of their students to volunteer shifts to help him, so there was always a kid or two with him.

Will took one look at Carlo and nodded toward Granger as if silently saying he would take over now.

"Where is Anna?" Granger tried to get Carlo to look at him. After seeing her brother, Granger did not want to think about what shape she might be in.

Carlo did not answer. He swatted at Will and his assistant as though they were flies bothering him.

"We need to find her and get her to the hospital." Granger tried to get past Carlo. "I'll worry about Larson later."

Carlo grabbed Farrington's shirt with bloody hands. "She is fine! Wants to be left alone. Do not touch her, or I swear I will…"

"Now settle down, Carlo. No one else is going to hurt your sister. I just need to have her checked out for injuries and get her statement." Granger pulled out of Carlo's grip.

"I will give you her statement." Carlo shouted as Will and the two volunteers moved in on him.

Granger ignored him. While the medic examined Carlo's cuts and wound, the sheriff stepped into the great room. He had been here before, after Davis Montano's funeral. The place reminded him more of a hotel lobby than a home.

Now, it was a wreck. He had seen bar fights that left a room in more order. Sunlight knifed its way through the east windows, slicing the room in sections. A quilt lay crumpled on the couch, clothes were scattered across the floor, Travis Tritt's voice echoed through the rubble from speakers mounted high on every wall.

The smell of blood blended with the scent of a piñon fire that burned low.

Granger almost tripped over a body in the shadows. "Guys, we got another man hurt in here," he shouted toward Will.

"Let him bleed to death!" Carlo yelled. "He raped my sister!"

Granger knelt and touched Zack's throat. He was still alive, though judging from the wounds he wouldn't be for long if he didn't get attention.

Carlo struggled with the two young men trying to get him on a gurney. "If you put that man in the ambulance with me, I will finish killing him before I get to the hospital. I swear."

Granger saw Will jab a shot into Carlo's arm. "Just relax, friend. We're going to take care of you." Will motioned, instructing his two assistants.

Carlo jerked away with the last of his strength. "I do not want you to take care of me. I want you to hang Zack Larson. He tried to kill me. He hurt my sister."

Will and his helpers were used to handling drunks and cowboys at the rodeo. Before Carlo could react, they rolled him onto the gurney and strapped him in.

The medic signaled for the assistants to get the patient to the ambulance while he hurried to Granger's side. "Is Larson alive?"

"For now."

While he shouted orders to the young men now outside, Will cracked open his toolbox of medical supplies. He worked like a pro. "I'll get him stable and to the hospital. He's had a bad blow or two to the head. Which puts him in a great deal more danger than that Italian with a nickel's worth of lead in his leg."

"What about Carlo's threat? Can you transport them both?"

"The shot I gave Vangetti will keep him sleeping like a baby for a while." Will grinned. "We'll give him a local and take care of that leg. The only danger he's in is dying of a heart attack if he doesn't calm down."

As one assistant returned, Granger stood and looked around the room.

"Anna!" he called. "Anna!" He walked carefully, afraid he might stumble over her also. If Carlo was telling the truth, she could be hurt or even dead.

He noticed the gun on the hearth and let out a long breath. If she'd been assaulted and was armed, it could be dangerous. Most of these ranches had several guns around the place.

"Anna." Granger moved through the house. "Mrs. Montano, it's all over. You can come out now. You're safe."

He'd worked enough rapes in years past to know that the last person a victim wanted to see was a man. Anna might know him, but Granger doubted she would trust him. Maybe the uniform would help her know she was no longer in danger. The lady didn't like talking before, and after what must have happened to her, he held little hope she would give him a statement.

"Anna?"

The master bedroom was locked, but he heard her whimpering. "Anna. Are you all right?"

"G-go a-away." Her voice was so low he barely heard it.

"I'm here to help you, Anna. You don't have to be afraid anymore. Open the door." In a big city he might have been more insistent, telling her she was a witness and if she didn't cooperate she could be held in contempt of court. But in Clifton Creek that kind of thing wouldn't fly. He had to be careful.

"I—I'm all right. Go away."

"I just need to ask you a few questions."

A silence followed. He could hear her moving toward the door.

"Open the door," he said, leaning against the wood.

"N-no," she whispered from the other side.

"I can help you."

There was a long pause before the door opened a few inches. "I-is Zack still alive?"

"Yes. We're taking him and your brother to the hospital. You want to ride along with me?" Granger wanted to push the door open, but he couldn't frighten her more.

She raised her head slightly and he saw the bruises. It looked like Zack Larson had done a thorough job of beating her. "G-go away. I—I will be fine."

Granger couldn't force Anna to cooperate. She was like a frightened animal who'd been wounded.

"If we're going to file charges on the man who did this to you, we're going to need your help."

"G-go away." She closed the door. A moment later the lock snapped in place.

Granger heard Adam's voice coming from the living room. The deputy had made good time.

He hated leaving Anna, but he wasn't sure he was doing any good.

They were rolling Zack out when Granger stepped back into the main room. "You want me to wait for the woman?" Will asked. "We've got a nurse over in the next county that can do a rape exam."

"I'll bring her," Granger said. "Adam, see if you can get Helena Whitworth on the phone. Maybe Anna will go in with a friend by her side."

Adam stumbled over a lamp. He had been a deputy long enough to wear out several uniforms and outgrow a few.

"And be careful," Granger snapped. "We got a crime scene here, and I'm not at all sure what happened." Something bothered him, but he couldn't quite put his finger on it. Carlo's account didn't fit the facts.

"Breaking and entering. Rape. Attempted murder. Zack Larson won't be seeing freedom any time soon," Adam mumbled as he headed for the phone on the kitchen wall. He carried an attitude that said he had seen it all during his years as deputy and already knew who was guilty.

"Thanks." Granger frowned. "Saved us a lot of time sifting through this mess. How about we just go hang the guy like Carlo suggested?"

"That would be too good for him, hurting a fine lady like Mrs. Montano." Adam shook his head. "I remember back several years ago when Larson wasn't even out of high school. Caused all kinds of trouble. Appears he hasn't changed his stripes."

Granger memorized the room as Adam tried several numbers to find Helena Whitworth. The gun was too far away to have fallen from Zack's hand and Zack didn't look like he could have been in any condition to circle the room after he'd shot Carlo.

Will stepped back inside to grab his box of supplies.

Granger followed a hunch. "Bag his hands for me, Will?"

"Which one, Carlo or Zack?"

"Both. I'll be in as soon as I can to run a powder test."

Will waved and disappeared out the door.

"No luck," Adam yelled from the kitchen. "I talked with Mrs. Whitworth's daughter at the store. She said her momma might have taken the phone off the hook to sleep in."

"Try Meredith Allen at the courthouse." Granger frowned. "No, wait. I'll call her."

He took the phone and punched the number to the county clerk's office. When he heard Meredith's voice, he took a breath before saying, "Meredith, this is Granger. I need you to come out to the Montano Ranch. I want you to drive carefully, but get here as fast as you can."

Granger hung up the phone.

"What'd she say?" Adam asked.

"She said she's on her way."

Adam didn't look like he believed the sheriff. "Didn't she ask any questions? Like what was going on? Or why we'd want her out here in the middle of nowhere on a cold day like this?"

"She knew I wouldn't have asked if I hadn't needed her." Granger smiled to himself. "You'd better head to the hospital. As of right now, Zack Larson is in our custody. Don't let him out of your sight. I don't want anyone talking to him if he comes to. Understand? No one."

"You got it, chief." Adam headed out. "Do I smell overtime?"

"Looks that way. Call Inez on your radio and see if she can get hold of someone from campus security. Maybe

Phil can handle the calls coming into our office until we get this settled. With the college out for holidays he's not doing anything but circling empty buildings. And tell Inez to order lunch delivered on me. She's to stay on the desk until I get back."

"She'll have time to finish a whole book." Adam laughed as he casually saluted goodbye.

Granger watched him leave as he retrieved his equipment from the trunk of his patrol car. Using the kitchen table, he spread out everything he would need. By the time Meredith arrived, he had already taken a dozen pictures and collected samples of blood. He'd also bagged one of the iron lamps that had blood and hair on it as well as the small Colt.

Meredith took one look at the room and whispered, "Anna?"

"I don't think she's hurt bad, but I need to get her examined at the hospital." Granger hated telling Meredith, but he needed her help. "Her brother said Zack Larson raped her this morning."

He wasn't sure how he had expected Meredith to act. Cry probably. Maybe even fall apart. But she didn't. For the first time, he saw it. The steel inside her. The teacher who must have wiped bloody noses and cleaned up after sick children a thousand times. The one who had to be calm, no matter what the chaos.

"You can handle this, can't you?" He met her gaze.

She nodded and he realized behind the reindeer sweater and necklace of Christmas lights was a soldier who had faced the front and lived to tell about it.

"Her face is bruised." He led Meredith down the hallway. "If you suspect any other injuries, we need to deal with them first. Try not to handle her clothes any more than necessary. They're evidence. And get her to tell you what happened if you can."

Granger tapped on the door. "Anna, Meredith Allen is here to see you."

The bolt clicked open.

Meredith stared at him as she turned the knob. "I'll worry about Anna first and your evidence second." She stepped into the room before he had time to say more.

He watched as she knelt beside Anna and opened her arms. Without a word, Anna leaned toward Meredith and hugged her tightly.

For a long while he heard Anna's crying and Meredith's soft, comforting words as he went about the careful job of collecting details. There was no sign of forced entry, but Granger knew few ranchers bothered to lock their doors.

His pager sounded, blinking the hospital number.

"Adam," Granger said, when he finally got the deputy.

"Sheriff," Adam's voice sounded relieved. "I was afraid you had trouble with the snow and ice. I thought you'd be here by now."

Granger hadn't bothered to look out. When he glanced through the kitchen window, he was surprised to see huge snowflakes covering the ground. "We're still here. Mrs. Montano hasn't agreed to come in yet. How are Zack and Carlo?"

"Carlo is being prepped for surgery. The bullet's lodged just behind his knee. Doctor wants him to spend a night, maybe two. That's if everything goes all right with the removal.

"Zack's too full of painkillers to say much. He took twenty stitches across his skull and another five over an eyebrow. Somebody hit him with something besides a fist to do that kind of damage. He's also got a couple of cracked ribs."

"When can we move him to a jail cell?" Granger was more worried about someone getting to Larson than Larson running away. The roughnecks, the ranch hands, someone might decide to make him pay back once word got out that Anna had been raped.

"Doctor says he can go tomorrow morning if nothing's still bleeding." Adam hesitated. "I might be able to take him out to the county jail after the sun's up, but with this snow, it's not going to be an easy drive. And you know how they hate checking people in on Sunday."

Granger knew what Adam was thinking. But taking his chances against the storm seemed easier than trying to watch all the doors and windows in a hospital. "We'll take him up to the cell on the third floor above the office until he sees the judge Monday morning. We'll make sure he has plenty of blankets and take shifts staying with him. He'll be all right up there for one night."

"Sounds like a plan," Adam voiced one of his favorite responses.

"I'll check in with you as soon as we're on our way back to town." Granger hung up the phone as Meredith walked into the great room. She stepped over and around things, careful not to disturb anything. "How is she?"

"Bruised and cut a few places, but all right." Meredith looked tired. "She won't talk much, only to say she's not leaving this house. She's not pressing charges and says she doesn't want to see anyone, including you. She's frightened, truly and completely frightened. And it is more than just for her own life. I'm no cop, but I'd say she's protecting someone with her silence. Or maybe saving someone."

"What?" Granger was angry at himself for being

surprised. How many rape cases had he worked over the years he was in Houston? Thirty? Fifty? And how many went to trial, one? But this one would have been easy. A woman in her own house, minding her own business. A brother who saw the act. No unknown assailant, no dark alley. This time he had more evidence than he'd be able to sort through in a month. Only the lady wasn't talking. The state could press the charges against Zack, but without Anna's testimony they wouldn't have a chance of getting a conviction.

The phone startled him from his thoughts.

"Yes," he said when he took the call.

"Sheriff?" Adam's voice came across the line.

"What?"

"I almost forgot to tell you, there was no powder residue on the hands. I checked between the thumb and finger. Learned two facts—Zack didn't shoot Carlo, and Carlo didn't shoot himself."

This time Granger showed no sign of being surprised.

"Maybe the gun fell and fired accidentally?" Adam guessed. "Or maybe Zack washed his hands after he fired."

"Maybe," Granger mumbled as he hung up the phone.

"Where is Anna?" He looked at Meredith. Carlo's sister was the third piece to this puzzle. The only other one in the room who could have fired the gun.

"Showering," Meredith answered.

Granger fought to keep all emotion from his face. "She just destroyed evidence."

"She figured that," Meredith answered. "There's no need for you to hang around. I'll stay with her."

"We'll go after Zack on trespassing charges and attempted murder." Granger sounded determined. "Anna may be afraid to testify, but her brother won't be."

The new man at the rig site was called "the worm" because he got all the grub jobs. He would be called that until another new man was hired, or until he lost a finger.

"What do you mean, the ambulance is not available?" Crystal fought down panic so thick in her throat it threatened to choke her. "The ambulance is always available." With Shelby's life-threatening condition, it was the only safe way of transporting him. And she needed him transported immediately.

"Mrs. Howard?" The nurse yelled from the second-floor landing. "We need you as soon as possible."

"Look." Crystal nodded to the nurse then turned her attention back to the phone. "As soon as it's available, send it here. My husband's having trouble breathing. We need to get him into X-ray as soon as possible."

Crystal didn't bother saying goodbye. She dropped the phone and ran upstairs. "What is it? Is he worse?"

"No worse. No better," the nurse answered honestly. "He won't calm down. He keeps asking for you."

Crystal charged through the door and into the make-shift hospital room. The scene before her would have frightened her three months ago, but now it seemed normal.

Machines surrounded a man who was more mummy than person. What skin showed was raw and newborn, or scarred and withered. Patches of fine hair dotted his head. His left ear would have to be completely reconstructed. He'd lost most of the use of his left hand, and no one knew if he would ever walk again once he healed enough to try. *If* he lived long enough. If infection or hypothermia or pneumonia or a hundred other things didn't kill him first.

"I'm here," she repeated as she had for months. "You're going to be all right, Shelby. I've called an ambulance. In a few hours, your breathing will be easier."

He mumbled something between short breaths, and she leaned closer.

"Don't leave me," he whispered. "Please, don't leave me."

Crystal took his right hand. "I'm not going to leave you. I promise."

"You got every right." His voice was so rough no one else could have understood his words. "No one would blame you."

"We'll get through this, darling. I swear." She held his hand and waited. The nurses tried to make him comfortable. Finally he dozed off.

Crystal didn't let go of his hand. She thought about their five years together. The good times and the bad. In truth, the past months fell more in the good times category than in the bad, if all she weighed was their relationship. Since the accident, she'd been more of a partner. More of a wife.

Laying her forehead on the edge of Shelby's bed,

she tried to forget all the things Trent had said to her yesterday.

Shelby's son had stopped by to tell her he would not be coming for Christmas. He and his sister had agreed the children didn't need to see their grandfather in such a condition. Why have them get to know the old man now, Trent said, when Dad may not make it through the winter.

The fact that Shelby might like to see the children was not a consideration.

Trent talked on of other plans they had made as he casually walked over and closed Shelby's door when the nurse stepped out.

"Since we have a few minutes alone," he spoke as if Shelby wasn't in the room. "I've something to offer you. Call it an early Christmas present."

He pulled out a thick envelope and spread the document on Shelby's tray.

Crystal guessed Shelby was awake, but as always when Trent came to visit, he chose not to speak.

"This is all fair. Elliot Morris made sure of that, though he didn't want to prepare the document at all. Threatened not to, until I told him I'd go to Dallas and have it done. Then, he came around. I knew you'd know it was on the square if old Morris did the paperwork."

Trent straightened, proud of himself. "My sister and I are willing to offer you the value of one third of Howard Drilling. We can pay you a lump sum up front, then installments over the next thirty years. You have to agree never to contact this family again once your divorce is final or make any further claim on Howard Drilling."

"But Shelby?"

"Don't worry about him. He'll continue to have round-the-clock care." Anger fired Trent's face. "I'm almost bankrupting the company with this offer, but it will be worth it to get my father out from under your control. You may say you're talking things over with him, but it's you making all the decisions. I understand you've even taken to visiting the sites to make sure I'm following through at my end."

"I visit the sites because there are things that need checking. I'm not interested in your offer." Crystal fought to remain calm. Trent no longer frightened her.

"Think about it, Crystal." He always made her name sound cheap, on the rare occasion he used it. "My father could die any day, and you'll get nothing. Not his house, or any money or any part of the company. His will leaves everything to his children and, if you fight us, you'll bankrupt us all. This way you walk away with a fortune, and we get to keep Howard Drilling in the family where it belongs."

Trent paused, letting the last word sink in. "Even if he lives another year, you'll never have your sugar daddy back. He could never be a husband to you, not the kind a woman like you needs. It's too late for him to change his will now. There's not a court in Texas that wouldn't throw out an attempt with all the drugs he's taking. But if you play along with us, you'll be set for life. All you have to do is sign."

Crystal cried against Shelby's sheet as she remembered Trent's words. He was right about so much. Eventually, Shelby would die, maybe in a week, maybe in a year, and then she'd have nothing.

Trent reminded her that if she'd been the one hurt, Shelby wouldn't have stayed with her. She knew Trent was right. Shelby wasn't the type of man to sit beside a hospital bed.

Then why hadn't she signed the paper? Why hadn't

she taken the money and packed her bags? No one would blame her. She'd already stayed longer than most of the town thought she would. She could have taken the money and gone someplace where no one knew her. She could start a new life without hospital runs and medicine checks, and business problems.

"Mrs. Howard?" The nurse drew her attention. "The ambulance is here. He's parking in the garage so we won't have to take Mr. Howard out in the cold."

Crystal pushed aside the last of her tears. "Good. I'll get my coat. I'll be riding in the ambulance with my husband."

A wildcatter is a man in the oil business willing to risk it all. The word probably came from the term "wildcat bank" which originally referred to a bank in Michigan that went bankrupt in the 1830s. On the banknotes was a picture of a panther.

Crystal watched the traffic in the hospital hallways as Shelby waited for X-rays. She had spent so much time in the place, no one noticed her anymore. The staff was too busy to worry about her, anyway. A woman was in labor in one of the front rooms, some man was in surgery in the wing that had been set up for operating rooms, and a prisoner must be three doors down from where Shelby slept.

She helped herself to a cup of coffee at the nurses' station and offered one to the deputy on guard. Everyone in town knew old Adam. There were even some who thought he should have run for the sheriff's job a few years ago. He liked to "talk cop." No one could ever get a clue out of Sheriff Farrington, but Deputy Adam loved to impress anyone who would listen with his inside knowledge.

"What's up?" Crystal handed him the coffee.

"Nothing much." Adam grinned his thanks. "Just a shooting this morning and a rape. When all the evidence is in, it may go down as breaking and entering, assault and even attempted murder."

Crystal leaned against the hallway wall. She heard the nurses say they were going after a bullet in some guy's leg so Adam must be telling the truth and not just making up something to pass the time. "Slow morning, huh?"

Adam laughed. "You might say that. I've seen busier ones."

Crystal didn't want to get him started on some old story that he'd had years to color. If she had to waste time talking to him, she might as well find out what was happening so she could tell Shelby.

She nodded toward the operating room. "Anyone I know in there with a bullet in him?"

"Can't say," Adam answered. "Sheriff said to keep this one under wraps. My job is to guard the suspect, not the victim." He pointed with his head toward the door behind him. "Got the rapist in there."

"Come on, Deputy Adam, I know everyone in town. Don't you think the word will be out in a matter of hours? You might as well be the one to tell me."

"I'm under orders. No one gets in. No one talks to the prisoner on my watch." He twisted as if being tortured from inside. "But I can tell you, it'll have ranchers and roughnecks all upset. Might even have an effect on Howard Drilling."

Crystal tried a few more times, but Adam would not say more. Normally, she wouldn't care what the locals were doing to one another, but he had said it might affect Howard Drilling. And if it affected Howard Drilling it would affect Shelby.

She strolled down the hall to the X-ray room and sat in the plastic chair. After a few restless minutes, she walked back past the deputy and went to the restroom. When she returned, Crystal slipped into the door between Deputy Adam and the X-ray room.

The room was empty. Crystal crossed to the connecting door that opened into the hospital's whirlpool bath. On the opposite side of the room was a side door that connected to the room Adam so diligently guarded.

Crystal told herself she would just open the door slightly and have a look at the bad guy. Because of her days in bars and running with the wild crowd, she figured she probably knew most of the men who even thought about committing a crime in this town. Or, if he worked for Howard Drilling, she might recognize him. Either way, she would be better prepared when bad news came down.

But when she opened the door, she couldn't see much. A tall, lean man lay atop the sheets. He had on worn jeans and no shirt or shoes. There was a long white patch across his left ribs and another over one eye, but they could not begin to cover up all the bruises on him. The bandage wrapped around his head was stained with blood in several spots and looked like it would fall off if he moved.

Crystal stepped closer. She had a hard time believing this was the criminal. He looked like someone had tried to kill him. But he must be the bad guy. This was the room Adam was guarding.

She tried to figure out what the man would look like without the swellings, bandages and bruises. He did not appear familiar, but she definitely thought he would fit in the "fine-looking" category once he healed.

As she leaned closer to brush his brown hair off his face, he opened one eye.

Crystal jumped back, expecting a monster to break out of the bandages and lunge at her. Then, she noticed one of his wrists was handcuffed to the rail of the bed. He wasn't going anywhere.

He didn't move. "Who are you?" Hatred and anger blended with the pain in his voice.

"Crystal Howard," she answered like a fool. She shouldn't have told him her name. He might be a rapist and an attempted killer now, but he'd probably escape from Deputy Adam and come after her just because she told him her name.

"What do you want?"

"Nothing." She backed away, unable to think of a lie as to why she was in his room. "I'm sorry to have bothered you."

"Wait."

Crystal was already at the door. What was he going to do, ask her to help him escape? "I have to get back to my husband. I cannot be talking to you."

"You know Anna?"

Crystal paused. What a strange question for him to ask. "Anna who?" She wasn't going to give him another name so he could go on a crime spree when he escaped.

"Anna Montano. She said you were her friend."

"Yes." Crystal took one step back into the room. Afraid of what he might say about Anna. Afraid not to listen. "If you hurt her, I swear I'll…"

"Is she all right?" He snapped in frustration.

His words shattered her planned threat. He was in agony far deeper than any of the cuts and bruises could make. He was not thinking of himself. For some reason he was thinking of Anna.

"I don't know." Crystal tried to think of the last time she had talked to Anna. Two days? Three?

The man turned his face away from her. Crystal glanced at the chart beside his bed. The name at the top read, Larson, Zack. She moved to the exit and slipped away. She hurried back to her chair in the hallway.

Deputy Adam did not look as if he had even noticed she had been gone. He was busy trying to talk the nurse out of another cup of coffee.

Crystal stood and walked as far down the hall as she could from the deputy. Making sure one of the hospital staff wasn't watching, she pulled her cell phone from her pocket and dialed Anna.

No answer.

Next, she tried Meredith. Anna rarely left her ranch and if she did, she might be with Meredith or Helena.

No answer. Crystal began to panic. She tried to think of reasons they wouldn't answer. Maybe they were shopping?

"Mrs. Howard?"

Crystal jumped, dropping her cell phone.

"I'm sorry to have startled you." The nurse knelt to help pick up the pieces. "I just wanted you to know that the X-rays are complete and we've given Mr. Howard a breathing treatment. He's much better and shouldn't have any more trouble for a few days."

Crystal didn't say a word as she followed the nurse to Shelby. She knew cell phones were not allowed, but for some reason the nurse had not said a word.

"How are you, darling?" She tried to sound cheery, but the bandaged prisoner's question haunted her.

"Much better," Shelby mumbled. "Tired. Can we go back home now? I'd like to get some sleep."

She took his hand. "Would you mind if I stayed in town a few hours and did some Christmas shopping? Helena can pick me up. I'll have my phone with me should you need me."

"Go ahead. I feel sure I'm out of any danger until the

next time life decides to thump me. You'll probably be back long before I wake up."

Surely Helena would be home, Crystal thought. "I'll be back before it's time for your evening medication. And don't forget, I have my cell if you need me."

"Be careful," Shelby whispered, already half-asleep. "The ambulance driver said it's icy outside."

Crystal stared at him a long moment before she slipped from the room. He had actually acted like he was worried about her. Like he cared.

When a man on the rig yelled, "Duck, or no dinner," everyone needed to stay alert to live long enough to eat the next meal.

Helena combed slowly through her silver hair, then twisted it into a neat bun as smoothly as she had every day for the past twenty years.

"I'll be careful, dear, I promise, but when Crystal called, she sounded like she needed me."

J.D. did not comment. He had always hated her independent streak and loved it at the same time. But what frustrated him most, she guessed, was that she knew it.

Helena sighed, no longer pretending to have the energy she once had. "I'll be back before dark, maybe sooner. Once I settle Crystal down, I'll probably have time to stop by the store for a while. Not that they need me much anymore. Yesterday, Paula even called it 'our' store, like suddenly my store had become a group project."

She stood and smoothed her dress. "If you have the wine chilled, I'll tell you all about Crystal's problem when I get home."

He barely looked up from his book as she waved goodbye, and for a moment, he seemed no more than a shadow in his chair by the window.

Crystal was waiting for her between the front doors of the hospital. Helena did not even have time to get out of her car. Crystal jumped in.

As always, Helena did not bother with small talk. "Where to?"

"The courthouse. I want to see if Meredith's car is there. She told me she works every Saturday, but no one's answering the phone in the clerk's office or at her place."

They circled by the courthouse. No old Mustang cluttered up the small lot.

"Where to next?"

"Anna's place." Crystal chewed on the corner of her lip. "I'll fill you in on the way out."

Helena might be in her sixties, but she drove her Buick with both skill and speed. J.D. always teased her that she thought the speed limit was the minimum daily requirement for each road.

They pulled onto the Montano ranch fifteen minutes later. Neither was surprised to see Meredith's old car parked out front.

Meredith met them at the door.

Helena gave her a quick hug and asked, "What can we do?"

"I don't know." Meredith led them inside. "Anna's been pretty beat up, but she's resting now. She won't tell me anything. The sheriff told her she could put the man who did this to her in jail if she'd make a statement, but she won't say anything. It's like she thinks her silence is protecting someone."

"Crystal said they have Zack Larson in custody." Helena circled the room, looking at the damage. "He owns the place next door." She was putting the pieces together in her mind and, as always, thinking things through.

"He was here," Meredith verified. "Carlo Vangetti says Zack shot him when Carlo tried to help his sister. They took Larson and Anna's brother to the hospital in the same ambulance."

Helena stormed suddenly. "If I get my hands on that Zack Larson, I'll kill him myself. What kind of a monster would do such a thing to Anna? She's frightened of her shadow as it is and every man she's ever known has been a bully. There is no telling the damage something like this will do to her."

"Wait a minute," Crystal whispered. "Something doesn't make sense. Let's reason this out for a moment."

The other two women stared at Crystal in surprise, but she continued before they could say anything. "If Zack Larson beat up and raped Anna, why would his first question be 'Is Anna all right?' It doesn't make sense. He sounded like he was worried, really worried about her."

"Anna's only question was 'Is Zack still alive?'" Meredith added. "She didn't even ask about Carlo and he was the one shot."

The three women froze. The only sound in the great room was the wind whistling in the fireplace.

"Do you think…" Meredith started almost afraid to say the words.

"It could be," Helena added.

"We have to be sure before we tell anyone," Crystal reasoned. "No one is going to believe us."

Suddenly, all three women talked at once. Theories flowed around the room. After an hour they agreed to collect more information, let Anna sleep and meet back at Anna's tomorrow afternoon.

While Helena and Meredith tried to pick up the broken

furnishings, Crystal excused herself and walked out the front door.

"Where's she going?" Meredith watched as Crystal ruined leather heels tromping through the snow toward the burned-out rig.

"She's going to talk to the oil field workers," Helena guessed. "And from what I hear, they'll tell her anything they know. She's built a lot of respect with them over the past months. She's not just Shelby Howard's wife anymore. She's one of them."

"But it's a half mile to those trailers."

Helena smiled. "She'll make it. She also knows our cars wouldn't. Those roughnecks might say anything on the phone, but they won't lie with her facing them down. She's a wildcatter's woman, and my guess is they all know it by now."

"Can you stay here with Anna tonight?" Helena did not wait for Meredith to answer. "I'll try to track down the housekeeper Anna uses. She'll know where everything goes." Helena picked up a piece of a lamp. "Maybe she'll agree to come out and help. This might be a good time to gut the room and start over. None of this looks like Anna."

Meredith nodded. "I didn't plan on leaving Anna alone tonight, even though Carlo sent word from the hospital that there was no need for me to stay." She leaned close and touched Helena's hand. "And how about you? How are you feeling today?"

"Better than I've felt in a long time. There is work to do here. Crystal's right, something doesn't make sense, and we can't depend on one overworked sheriff and a few dimwitted deputies to figure it out. I'm a workhorse. Put me out to pasture and I'll surely die."

"Randi's coming in tonight, and she's promised to stay

with me," Meredith added. "Crystal's already told me,
I'm to keep her away from the new poles at Frankie's.
Having her with me out here should keep her far enough
away from any trouble in town. Maybe Randi can talk to
the hands on the place. Someone in the bunkhouse must
have heard the shot."

"It's a ways to the bunkhouse, but it might be worth
a try. Tell Randi to check it out," Helena agreed, feeling
like she was suddenly one part of a detective team.

"Granger told me when he got here the hands were all
standing around outside, like they were afraid to come
in."

"Randi probably knows most of the help." Helena
dusted her hands together. "Maybe they'll tell her things
they wouldn't tell us. Ask her to piece together anything
she can on Zack. Someone must know him. He's lived
here all his life."

"What about you?"

Helena shook her head. "I vaguely remember his
mother, but she died years ago. His father drank himself
to death, I think. To tell you the truth, I barely recognize
Zack Larson when I see him on the street."

Helena laughed. "J.D. says I know everyone in town,
but line them up and I'd miss a few."

"If Larson was here with Anna and they were friends,
then who shot Carlo? Who beat them all up?"

"We'll find out," Helena promised. "If Zack Larson is
guilty of hurting her, heaven help him. If he's not, then
we'll have to help him."

"**I** don't care what you and the widows came up with, Meredith, I'm not letting Zack Larson out of jail." Granger looked quite official, leaning forward in his chair. "By the way, which one of you has been making trips down to Sam Houston State to pick up a Criminal Justice degree?"

Meredith glared at the man she once considered intelligent.

"And aren't you supposed to be staying with Anna? Why are you and Randi leaving your post?" The sheriff glanced from Meredith to Randi, who did not seem to be listening to his lecture at all. He had a feeling she probably acted the same with anyone in authority since she had been in the sixth grade. He did not even want to think about what she offered in trade for all the gossip she collected from the Montano ranch hands.

"We were with her all night," Meredith answered. "Bella came by the Montano place after she brought Zack some clothes and found out what was going on. She said she'll stand guard over Anna until we get back."

Granger started again, this time with that "I'll try to be patient with you" tone in his voice. "Look at it this way. Half the men in town want to kill Zack Larson, including Anna's brother. The man is safer in here for tonight. After he sees the judge in the morning, we'll take him to the county lockup. I know his kind. He's a loner. If I did let him go, the first place he'd head would be back to that run-down ranch of his, and I'd have no way of protecting him."

Meredith knew Granger did not exaggerate the danger. Folks clustered around town, talking about how something needed to be done about Zack Larson. Most of it was talk, but what if one drunk, or friend of Davis Montano, decided to take the law into his own hands? Could Granger and a few old deputies stop him?

The sheriff glanced over at Randi, who perched on the wide windowsill to watch the snow. She obviously did not see herself as part of this discussion.

He turned back to Meredith and tried again. "I can't let a man go because the widows took a vote. That's not my job. I'm the one who catches them, the courts are the ones who let them go." He smiled at his attempt at humor.

"Yes, but you're holding an innocent man," Meredith insisted. "Doesn't that bother you?"

"Why are you so sure he's not guilty? Because Crystal heard him ask about Anna? Maybe he was worried that if he killed her he'd be going up for murder, not just assault."

Meredith did not answer, so he continued, "Or maybe I should unlock him because Anna asked about him? Did you women ever think that she might have asked because he scared the hell out of her and she was hoping he was dead?

"I've got my own misgivings, but nothing strong

enough to let the man go. He *was* in a house where he didn't belong at a time that's not usually considered visiting hours. He was undressed. Anna was beat to a pulp. Carlo was shot."

"But I stood right next to you when Adam called from the hospital to tell you there was no powder residue on Zack's hands. He didn't fire the gun that shot Carlo." Meredith walked back and forth in front of the sheriff as though she were lecturing. "And I saw you measure the space between the weapon and Zack. He couldn't have fired the gun, washed his hands, then fallen unconscious half a room away. He wasn't the one who shot Carlo, and he didn't hurt Anna."

"Then get her in here and let me talk to her. All she has to do is tell me who, besides Zack, beat her near to death, and I swear I'll put that guy in jail and let Zack out."

"She can't come. She's too afraid. But you should see the way she looks when someone says Zack's name. She's worried about him, not afraid of him."

Meredith rubbed her forehead. "I don't know, maybe she thinks if she tells the truth Zack and her might both die. It's that kind of terror I see in her eyes. She cares about the man and somehow thinks she's helping him by remaining silent."

"That's not enough." Granger shook his head.

Randi finally unfolded from the window. With her slender limbs and fringed jacket, she looked like a daddy longlegs spider on the move. "I know what would be enough," she said calmly. "I read it in your report."

Meredith and Granger both looked at her as if they had forgotten she was there.

Randi widened her stance. "You're a man of detail,

Sheriff. In your report you wrote that you turned off the stereo."

"So? I always write down things like that. You never know what's important."

"All right. This is important. What was playing?"

Granger frowned. "I don't remember, some country-and-western station."

"Zack Larson didn't rape Anna Montano." Randi smiled as if she'd made her point. When the other two did not respond, she added, "Anna loved classical. Drove us all crazy every time we were around her. It was her house, her stereo, so the music would have been her choice. Classical, not C-and-W. A man doesn't take time to change the radio to country if he's chasing her around the room to rape her."

"Maybe, maybe not." Granger frowned, obviously angry that he hadn't thought much about it. "Look, since yesterday morning I haven't had more than an hour's sleep. Why don't you ladies come back tomorrow?"

Meredith leaned into his space. "Let me talk to him, Granger." She almost knocked his keys off his desk.

"No way." Her nearness bothered him, but he didn't back down. "I've tried to talk to him a dozen times. He won't say a word. He won't even admit to knowing Anna, much less going over to her place."

"Then let me talk to him," Helena Whitworth demanded as she walked through the sheriff's office door.

Granger stood, almost bumping noses with Meredith in his haste. "Mrs. Whitworth, I was just explaining to Mrs. Allen…"

Helena handed him a paper that had been folded neatly in half. "I'm too old to argue. I brought a letter from Judge Lewis stating that since Zack Larson has no relatives that we know of, I can visit him as his next of kin."

Granger's frown was becoming a permanent part of his face. "I've never heard of such an exception."

Randi laughed. "Great, Helena. You've adopted him."

"No, I'm just visiting Zack Larson. I woke the judge up from his nap. It doesn't seem right for a man who's lived in this town all his life not to have at least one person visit him. If the rest of the city counsel considers themselves the town fathers, I can play the town mother once in a while."

Granger shook his head. "What makes you ladies so sure you're right? Did it ever occur to you that Zack may be guilty?"

"It might have." Helena tilted her head slightly. "Until his housekeeper, Bella Johnson, told me he's been drinking tea lately. English tea."

Granger threw up his hands. "That settles it. I'm letting him out. If he drinks tea, he couldn't be a bad person."

None of the women thought the sheriff was the least bit funny.

"Bella told me the same thing when she brought Zack up a set of clothes this morning." Granger tapped the letter against his hand. "But Bella spent half her life living in a bottle. Zack's family probably offered her the only job she could get and keep. She'd say anything."

Helena raised her chin as though peasants were questioning the queen. "She worked for Anna, too. Bella may have taken a drink now and then, but I believe she's honest. She wouldn't lie."

Meredith almost felt sorry for Granger. He could handle the drunks and the troublemakers, but he had no idea how to handle the widows.

She watched as he paced the office, rereading the letter from Judge Lewis. "All right, you can see him for five minutes. But you'll have to climb the stairs, the elevator isn't working."

"I'm sorry, officer. I can't." Helena lowered her thin body to the nearest chair. "I've been having dizzy spells lately. I have no plans to climb any more stairs than I have to this day."

Meredith smiled. Helena played her part so well. She wouldn't have been surprised to hear the older woman call Granger "young man."

"You'll have to bring him down here." She said the words casually, as though ordering an extra course at dinner.

Granger had met his match. Helena Whitworth had not managed a successful store and the town by giving an inch to anyone. Meredith had no doubt there would be another letter from the judge if Granger didn't start moving.

"Just wait here, Mrs. Whitworth. Adam and I'll bring him down from the third floor." The sheriff looked at Meredith and Randi. "I don't want either of you in this office when I get back."

After he left, the three women stood staring at one another in silence for a long time. They all knew the risk they took. Crystal said the hospital planned to release Carlo by the next shift change. He had already called and had his men post a guard at the gate of the Montano Ranch. Anna would not answer the phone, she was in no shape to leave, and as soon as Carlo got home and demanded Bella leave, Anna would be all alone. They would no longer be able to get to her...or save her.

If they were going to help Anna, Zack might be their only chance.

"I've never done anything like this in my life," Meredith whispered as she wiped her sweaty palms on her pants and reached for Granger's keys. She circled them around the desk as though they were a toy.

Randi shrugged. "This is just Saturday night excitement for me."

Helena straightened. "We do what we have to. I see no crime in that."

"Hope the sheriff agrees with you," Randi added.

When they heard footsteps on the stairs, they sprang like rabbits.

Randi took her place on the far side, at the bottom of the stairs. Her long leg stretched up to the fourth step as though she were a ballerina warming up.

Meredith stood on the other side near the marble column. She slipped her hand up along the back side, feeling in the darkness for what she hoped was still there.

Helena waited just inside the office, watching the men come down.

Adam held Zack Larson's arm at the elbow. Granger walked a few steps ahead. As always, he appeared aware of everything around him.

Meredith watched Granger's face, knowing the second Helena started her faint without looking in the older woman's direction. The lawman's eyes widened. He opened his mouth to shout and rushed toward his office door.

Adam and Zack were two steps from the main floor when Meredith rose to her tiptoes and threw the emergency switch.

All power went dead. The hallways blinked black.

Deputy Adam let out a long shout as he stumbled.

Meredith grabbed Zack's arm and pulled him behind the pillar. She was surprised he did not fight her. It was like he was in a coma and no longer cared one way or the other what happened.

It took her a few seconds in the darkness to shove the

key in the lock of his handcuffs. "Hurry!" she whispered. "Take my Mustang just outside the door."

He responded as if someone had yelled fire and he had no choice but to run. Long sure steps echoed off the marble floor as he headed for the closest exit. A second later, Meredith heard the door open and shut.

She raised her hand and flipped the switch back on. No one, probably not even the sheriff, knew about the emergency switch. Only janitors, and janitors' daughters who had once danced in the hallways.

"What the hell?" Adam rolled across the floor like a basketball in need of air.

"What happened?" Granger yelled from the office.

"I fell," Adam mumbled as he rubbed his knee. "Hurt my leg. I swear something ran between my feet a moment after the lights went out. Tripped me right up. This place must have rats a foot long."

Randi stood at the bottom of the stairs where she had been when the lights went out, her red Ropers looking as innocent as Ropers can look.

Meredith hurried to where Granger still held Helena. "What's wrong? Helena, are you all right?"

"I'm fine, dear. Just felt a little faint there for a moment." Helena looked pale, and very fragile. "Thank goodness the sheriff caught me or I could have had quite a fall."

Granger carefully sat Helena on the nearest chair. "How's Larson?" he yelled toward Adam. "Did he fall, too?"

There was a long silence before Adam's disgusted whine echoed off the courthouse walls. "Larson's gone."

Granger was out the office door and into the hall

before Adam's words died. "Gone! Where could he have gone?"

The sheriff didn't wait for an answer. He scanned the hallway. The only unlocked door was that of his office. There was nowhere for Zack to hide. "If he didn't come past me…" Granger stormed to the side door in time to see the tail lights of Meredith's car disappear.

"You want me to get the highway patrol on the line, Sheriff?" Adam limped toward Granger.

"No," Granger answered as he crossed back into his office and opened his gun rack. "I plan on following him. Looks like he's heading away from his ranch. Probably figures that would be the first place we'd look. Since he's in Meredith's old car, I've got a good chance of catching him before he can get to the New Mexico line."

"Can't blame him for heading away. If he goes anywhere near the Montano spread, they'll shoot him on sight."

Granger's angry stare met Meredith's. "What did you have to do with this?"

Meredith stood as straight and tall as she could. "I planned the whole thing. Turned off the lights. Tripped Adam. Left my keys in my car. I helped him escape." She crossed one hand over the other, praying he wouldn't notice how violently she was shaking as she laid his keys back on his desk.

Granger wasn't watching. He grabbed a rifle before turning back to her, a tired smile brushing the corner of his lip. "If I believed that for one minute, I'd lock you up right now."

He disappeared out the side door with Adam limping at his side.

"Men." Randi shrugged as she looped her arm over Meredith's shoulder. "You can't fool 'em no matter how hard you try."

In the oil business, once you hit oil you dropped pipe and the money started rolling in. The early fields of Texas were full of men with "pipe dreams."

Sunday, December 19
7:25 p.m.
The Breaks

Zack turned south toward what everyone in town called "The Breaks." He knew the dirt roads out there near the river better than the sheriff knew the streets. When he had been a kid, he'd spent thousands of hours riding across them on a dirt bike. If the car held up over the hard snow-packed trails, he knew he could lose Farrington.

His head throbbed as if someone was sitting in the backseat taking a swing at it with a hammer every few minutes. He gripped his side feeling a stabbing pain in his ribs every time he twisted. But, none of it mattered. With pure determination pounding through his veins he had one purpose—Anna. He had to find Anna. Nothing else, not even his life mattered.

The entrance to The Breaks was hidden on one side by an old bait shop covered over by trumpet vines, and the town cemetery on the other. During the summer, you could tell the time of day by the traffic on the old road. Fishermen at dawn, families picnicking in the afternoons, bikers looking for the back trails and weekend adventures, and lovers who arrived after dark.

When Zack dipped out of sight of the car following him, he turned off his lights and drove more by instinct than with the help of the pale quarter moon. Cottonwoods twisted beside the road, spilling inky shadows over the snow. The old Mustang blended like smoke through the turns, weaving near the river and around brown grass as tall as the roof of the car.

Twenty minutes later, Zack pulled out on the far side of The Breaks and took the back road to his ranch. The car slid off the road several times, running into the pasture, knocking down fence poles until finally he saw the lone light of his house.

Zack let himself take a deep breath for the first time. He'd made it home. Maybe it made no sense. The sheriff would find him eventually. He had sworn never to tell anyone about Anna, and he knew her brother would kill her if she tried to talk. The sheriff left her with one hell of a choice: if she testified she might free Zack, but she would condemn her brother. And Carlo would kill her before he would let that happen.

So Zack figured he would probably go to jail for a few years. But like a homing pigeon, he wanted to come back one last time. He did not blame Anna for remaining silent. Hell, he had had a lifetime of bad luck. Why would he expect it to change just because she came into his life? He just wished he could hold her one more time.

When he pulled into the yard, he saw Crystal Howard at his front door. For a moment he thought of circling his place and heading for parts unknown. The last thing he needed was more trouble.

She yelled at him before he reached the porch. "The hospital called on my cell. Carlo is on his way home. Can you get Anna back here before Carlo makes it to their place? I figure you got about ten minutes. If you can, we'll get her to safety."

"You know?" he said, fearing he had said too much by even asking about Anna at the hospital. There was no way she could have learned anything about Anna and him.

"We know little," Crystal answered, directly, "except that Anna is in danger, and it isn't from you."

There was no time to talk. He ran to the walkover and crossed the fence. The path to Anna's house was twisted and slippery, but he made it as fast as he dared. He wouldn't be much help to her if he fell and cracked open what was left of his skull. But the drugs for pain made it feel like he was moving through water. His feet would not maneuver as fast as they should.

Zack fought to clear his head. He took in deep gulps of the cold air and concentrated on one thing—Anna.

A few lights were on at her place. Zack felt his way along the patio until he found the sliding doors. The second one he tried opened.

He entered the house, afraid of what he might find. The memory of the fight still hung in the air. He could almost hear the echoes of Carlo shouting and Anna crying. The smell of the fire he and Anna built late that night still lingered, spiced now with the hint of gunpowder. The feeling that he'd die of pleasure, the fear he'd die of pain now blended in the silence of the huge room.

But no sign of the fight or the loving remained. Not even the quilt. Everything was back in order as if the hours had never happened.

"Anna?" Zack whispered her name. Maybe she wasn't even here. Crystal and the others could be worried about nothing. Anna might have gone to stay with friends.

But Zack knew she had no friends except for the widows and Bella...and him.

He flipped on the light in the kitchen. "Anna?" he called.

The sound of a round being chambered clicked in the silence.

"Take another step mister and you're a dead man," Bella's voice ordered from the darkness of the great room.

Zack moved into the light so she could see him. "You'll have to kill me to stop me," he answered. "I've come for Anna."

Bella smiled and lowered the weapon. "Evening, kid. I didn't expect to see you here tonight. Some guard I am, I must have fallen asleep on the couch." She met his stare. "I might just be falling back to sleep right now."

Zack nodded, understanding what she was saying.

Slowly, he crossed from room to room. He remembered seeing Anna being hit, falling, holding the gun. She was hurt, and probably frightened. If she knew Carlo was coming home, she might even be hiding. Time was running out for him to find her.

"Anna?" he called as he stepped into her bedroom.

In the shadows, he saw her, huddled in a corner with her grandmother's quilt wrapped around her.

"Anna." He couldn't move, afraid of what he might see if he came closer.

"G-go away." Her voice sounded hoarse as if she'd cried all she could. "I—I almost got you k-killed, Zack. G-go away before I do. Just go away and forget about me."

She shifted, and he saw her dark eyes. There was a calmness about her as though she had accepted her fate.

She was giving up any chance they might have in the hopes of keeping him alive.

"That I can't do." He fought the urge to draw closer. "The way I see it, we've got two choices. I can stay here to face Carlo and probably his men, or you can come with me. Crystal's waiting for you at my place. She promised to take you somewhere safe."

He walked toward her.

"If I leave, he will kill me," she whispered, "and then he'll kill you."

Zack knelt in front of her. "If you stay, he'll kill you, Anna. Maybe not tonight, or next month, but eventually."

"I know. He wants control of the ranch, and the only way he can get that is to control me."

Zack brushed her dark hair from her eyes. "Come with me. Somehow together we'll work it out."

When she raised her arms, he lifted her, blanket and all, ignoring the pain in his side and shoulder. She held tightly to him. He walked out of the house the way he came. Bella looked sound asleep on the couch when he passed the old woman, but he noticed a smile on her lips.

They did not say a word to one another as they crossed the darkness between their ranches. He sat her on top of the walkover, climbed it and lifted her once more in his arms. When he turned toward his house, a huge Buick pulled up next to the Mustang he had borrowed.

Or stolen. The way his luck was running, he would be charged for that, too.

Three women climbed from the car, an old woman, a cowgirl and what had to be a schoolteacher. Helena, Randi and Meredith. Anna had told him too much about each for him not to recognize them, even in the shadows. The widows had assembled.

They all turned and watched as he walked toward them with Anna in his arms.

"Be careful with her," Helena ordered.

Zack frowned. He wasn't about to drop the only wonder in his life.

"Set her down inside." Crystal held the door. "I'll get her some tea."

"Now, don't you worry, girl." Randi followed Zack into the house. "No one is going to hurt you again."

"I will not talk to the sheriff," Anna said over Zack's shoulder.

"You don't have to talk to anyone about what happened at your place if you don't want to," Randi promised.

They clustered around her, forgetting about Zack. He wanted time with Anna, but he would wait. He was not sure, but he would swear all four of them were talking at once. And Anna...Anna smiled.

Finally, Helena raised her hand and called the meeting to order. "I've got one question, Anna, and I need an answer even though we think we all know the truth."

Meredith sat on one side of Anna, patting her hand. Randi stood behind her on guard. Crystal offered her tea.

Helena looked straight at Zack. "Did this man hurt you in any way?"

Tears bubbled in Anna's eyes. "No," she answered without stuttering.

"Good. We didn't think so, but I was prepared to shoot him if we'd guessed wrong."

Zack looked at Helena, trying to figure out if she was kidding. The woman did not look like the type who would ever handle a gun. But what he didn't know about women would fill volumes.

He backed into a corner, fighting the pain in his side as he watched them pamper Anna. It felt great to have her here, safe and among friends. He had almost driven himself mad thinking about what might be happening to her. Now, he had a feeling that no matter what happened to him, these women would see Anna through this.

They were somehow connected to each other. He read once that people chose to love one another. These five women had made that choice. The bond was more than friendship. A comradeship he felt honored to be allowed to watch.

Lights blinked like static lightning across his windows, slamming him back into crisis. A line of cars and pickup trucks were coming at full speed directly toward his house.

Zack headed for the old rifle he kept mounted over the fireplace.

"Wait." Helena stopped him. "Let us deal with them. You stay with Anna."

Zack shook his head. This was his land, his fight, his problem.

Helena didn't back down. "They're not going to bother us, but they might shoot you on sight."

Randi shoved his shoulder. "Sit down, cowboy. Tonight's not your rodeo."

Without another word, Helena, Randi, Crystal and Meredith went outside to the porch. Zack lowered slowly to one knee so he could see Anna's face.

"We know he's in there! Get out of the way!" someone shouted in the frosty air. Car lights shone like footlights in front of the porch.

"Yeah, who's gonna make us, Tucker? You?" Randi

yelled back at the line of men moving toward the house. "Step one foot on this porch and I'll be visiting your wife tomorrow telling her what kind of man you are."

"There is nothing happening here, gentlemen," Helena announced. "I suggest you all move on about your business."

Zack watched Meredith shade her eyes with her hand. "Butch Colwell, what do you think you're doing here frightening us? Put that rifle down."

A young man in the front lowered his gun. "I was told Larson kidnapped Mrs. Montano. I come to help."

"Do you think if he kidnapped Mrs. Montano, I'd be out here visiting him?"

"No, ma'am."

"Well, why don't you take Kirk there with you and go on home? The two of you haven't changed since grade school, still looking for a fight you can get involved in."

"I will not go home!" Carlo yelled as he slowly climbed from the pickup, his leg in a cast. "That man stole my sister and I will take her back."

Randi stormed. "She ain't no sack of potatoes Zack drug across the property line. If she wants to be with him, there is nothing you, or anyone else can do about it."

Zack felt Anna's hand touch his bandaged forehead and he forgot about the circus outside.

"Are you all right?" She brushed his hair away from the cotton.

"I've had better days." He smiled. "This probably isn't the best time to talk, but I want you to know what happened between us, it was real...." He couldn't think of the right words with people in his front yard shouting they were going to kill him. "It was something that's never happened to me before. It was..."

He heard Crystal ordering all oil workers to leave if they still wanted to have a job come dawn.

"If I thought there was one chance in a million you'd say yes, I'd ask you to marry me." He wished he hadn't told her his thoughts. She could buy and sell him and everything he owned with pocket change.

Zack looked out the window. Carlo ordered his men to move the women over and go after Anna. But the men weren't moving. Colonel Travis should have had these four ladies at the Alamo.

"There's one chance in a million," Anna whispered as she leaned and kissed the bandage over his eye.

It took a moment for her words to sink in.

December 19
9:00 p.m.
Larson Ranch

Meredith stood at the corner of the porch and stared at Granger as he watched from the back of the crowd. His rifle was propped against his shoulder; his finger looked like it was resting on the trigger guard. He had come to bring Larson back but now, he was hesitating. She knew he could have stepped in and handled the crowd, but he was letting them do it.

Thanks to the huge windows of Zack's home, Anna's statement was being played out before everyone's eyes.

About the time Carlo called a charge to save his sister, everyone in the crowd saw Anna push Zack's shirt aside and kiss the bandage covering his broken ribs. It did not look like the kind of thing a woman did to a man who raped her, shot her brother and kidnapped her from her home.

The mob moved back, no longer wanting to follow Carlo. They could see Zack gently holding her, whispering to her as lovers do.

The crowd had no way of knowing that he was promising to stand with her no matter what the storm. He made his oath for a lifetime, not just for tonight. The men outside might not hear Zack's words, but they could see Anna's face as she smiled up at him.

Granger swung over the rail of the porch, dipping his hat to the widows as though he hadn't seen them in a while. "Nice job," he commented casually. "Next time I need crowd control, I'll be sure and call you ladies."

They all looked out over at the pickups and cars. Men were leaving quietly, as though they had been caught eavesdropping.

Carlo was the only one who did not move. "I am not leaving without my sister!" Despite the crutches, he stepped onto the first step on the porch.

Granger glanced at the widows, almost as if he was considering letting them handle the stout man. Any one of them would gladly cut Carlo to pieces. "You've done enough for one night, ladies," he said. "It's time I earned my pay." He moved to the step directly above Carlo. "I'm afraid, Mr. Vangetti, that you'll be riding back with me. At least as far as the county lockup."

"I do not think so." Carlo seemed to believe that if his voice was louder than anyone else's then he must be right. "I have done nothing, Sheriff, but protect my family."

Granger watched Carlo carefully. "You see, Mr. Vangetti, it's against the law to file a false report. Zack Larson didn't rape your sister, and he didn't shoot you."

"You cannot prove that!" Carlo shouted.

"Yes, he can," Anna whispered from the doorway. She slipped out onto the porch, staying well behind Granger. "You forget, Carlo, I was there."

"You would send your own brother to jail?" Carlo looked surprised at the possibility. Anger crept into his words. "That would not be a wise thing to do, Anna. Not for your sake, or Zack's."

Randi stomped toward the edge of the porch, her hands already balled into fists for a fight. Carlo's size and volume didn't frighten her.

Before she issued a death threat that he would have to arrest her for, Granger slid between them and took Carlo by the arm. "How about you come along as a guest of the county tonight? Let your sister have some time to think. Give you a chance to settle down."

Carlo swore as Zack walked up behind Anna and placed his hand on her shoulder. The Italian took powerful breaths like a bull about to charge.

The sheriff's grip tightened around his solid arm.

Carlo tried to jerk free, but it was hopeless. He might be a fighter, but he was smart enough to know now wasn't the time. With an angry oath, he stopped struggling with Granger. "You must take him in, also."

With the help of Adam on Carlo's left side, Granger turned Carlo toward the patrol car. "We're not in the habit of arresting a man for loving a woman." He glanced over his shoulder. "Sorry about the lock up, Larson. No hard feelings."

Before Zack could answer, Carlo demanded, "You can not leave him here with my sister."

"He's well chaperoned." Granger opened the back of his car and gave Carlo a helpful shove as he glanced back at Meredith. "'Course, I suspect they're all criminals, but I'm too outnumbered to haul them in."

Meredith opened her mouth to say goodbye to Granger. He hadn't spoken to her, but she'd felt him watching her from the time he walked up at the back of the crowd. There was something comforting about knowing he was there.

Before she could think of anything to say, he was gone. She watched his taillights disappear and realized she had probably ruined any chances of them ever even being friends. Eventually, he would figure out that she had told him the truth, she had set Zack free, and even though it was the right thing to do, she'd broken the law. They lived in different worlds. She believed in doing what was right, he believed in following the law. Once in a while the two views were not parallel.

"Thanks for the loan." Zack returned the Mustang keys. "If you'll bring it out some weekend, I could work on that engine. Maybe make it run a little smoother for my next getaway." He lowered his head. "You saved my life tonight as well as Anna's. Thanks."

Meredith did not know what to say. Before Zack could move, she wrapped her arms around him and hugged.

At first, he didn't react. Women hugging him was not something that happened to him often. Slowly, he put his arms around her and patted her on the back.

Meredith fought tears. She told herself she just needed someone to hold her for a few minutes. She needed her heart to stop pounding. She needed to know it was all over and they were all out of harm's way.

But Zack's arms gave her little comfort. He was not the one she wanted. The man she needed would never offer.

Meredith pulled away and gently embraced Anna. "You're welcome to come home with me," she volunteered. "Randi and I will try not to keep you up talking."

Anna shook her head. "I want to stay here tonight."

The women moved away from Anna and Zack with hugs but few words. They knew what they had done and why they did it. There was no need for thanks.

At Helena's car, Meredith asked, "You want me to follow you home? Or Randi can drive you and I'll follow." Helena had been a rock during the trouble, but now she looked so pale it frightened Meredith.

"No, dear. I promised J.D. I'd be home by dark and I'm

already late. He'll be worried about me. I'd best hurry." She climbed in her huge car and pulled away.

Randi moved to Meredith's side. "He's not dead to her, is he?"

Meredith shook her head. "Does it matter?"

They waved goodbye to Crystal and folded into the Mustang.

"I don't suppose I could interest you in stopping off at Frankie's on the way home?" Randi propped her foot up on the dash.

Meredith laughed. "No way."

"Then, how about the Dairy Queen? I'm starving. A life of crime always makes me hungry."

"Now, that's a deal. Let's go crazy and order banana splits."

Randi leaned back and frowned. "I'm living on the wild side now."

But she laughed all the way through her hamburger and fries. By the time they ordered their banana splits they were Butch Cassidy and the Sundance Kid, reliving their night of near death and riotous adventure.

They finally waddled out to the Mustang and drove back to the courthouse to pick up Randi's car.

"I must have left the lights on in the office," Meredith said as she pulled into the lot. "It won't take me a minute to turn them off, then I'll meet you back at the house."

"All right." Randi climbed out. "I'll stop by and pick up something for breakfast on my way. It's the least I can do."

Meredith started to argue that shopping was not necessary, but in truth she couldn't remember having anything in the house to offer for breakfast. She watched Randi drive away in her newly painted car, thanks to Crystal, then huddled into her coat and ran for the side door. Maybe ice cream on a night like this had not been such a good idea. She was freezing inside and out.

The hallway of the courthouse was dark, but her lights were all on, as well as one in the sheriff's office. Meredith's shoes tapped along the marble as she tried to remember even going in the county clerk's office earlier. She could have sworn the office was dark when she threw the emergency switch. There had not been time to go into the office. Helena, Randi and she had headed straight to Larson's ranch, knowing Crystal would be waiting.

Meredith flipped the lights off and stepped back out into the hallway.

Granger stood in his office doorway in silhouette. She couldn't see his face, but his stance was official as always.

"I'm sorry. I must have forgotten to close up the office." She moved toward him, feeling like she was reporting to the hall monitor. "That's not like me to forget something like that."

"You didn't leave them on." He stepped out, blocking her path. "I turned them on hoping you'd notice when you came back to pick up Randi's car."

Meredith stopped walking, confused by his action. She swallowed, telling herself not to be afraid. If he locked her up, he locked her up. She was not going to explain or apologize.

"I thought you'd never get here." He cut the distance between them in half. "I was worried that you'd managed to find the last icy spot of pavement between Larson's and town."

"Oh, no. We had no trouble. Randi and I stopped for a hamburger and got to talking." Meredith wanted to scream "What business is it of yours?" but she rambled instead. "We decided to forget calories and have a…"

Granger put his hands on her shoulders. For a second she thought he was going to shake her.

But he drew her to him and kissed her hard on the mouth.

When he moved an inch away, Meredith continued, "banana split."

"I know." She felt his words against her cold face. "I can taste it." He leaned down and kissed her again, this time softer, longer.

She knew there was probably something she should say. Maybe she should even pull away and run. But all she did was wrap her arms around his neck and lean against him, feeling like this was her first kiss on the porch of her parents' house when she was sixteen.

He moaned against her lips as he slipped his hands inside her coat and pulled her closer. His body warmed the length of her.

When he finally moved away, he whispered against her hair. "I've been wanting to do that all night."

"I have to go," she answered, afraid if she stayed any longer she would make a fool of herself. "Randi is waiting for me."

He took a long breath and let her go. "I heard you tell Helena that Randi is staying with you."

She closed her eyes trying to remember where she was...who she was. He no longer touched her, but she could still feel his arms, his lips, the warmth of him against her.

"Good night, Granger," she said as if the kiss had not happened. All she wanted to do was stay and kiss him again. But, Randi waited and now was not the right time.

"Good night. I'll see you tomorrow."

A stranger might have thought his farewell formal, but Meredith heard the promise in his voice.

December 19
10:00 p.m.
Pigeon Run

Helena hurried up the stairs as fast as she could. She wanted to get into her robe and relax. Most of the evening she had been fighting a nagging pain in her chest and now, finally, she could forget about everything and breathe easy.

All she needed to do was rest, she told herself. Everything would be better once she made it back to J.D.

As she entered their room, he poured her a glass of wine. She did not tell him she had been feeling dizzy earlier, or that she'd thrown up the soup she'd had for dinner. She blamed both on the excitement of the evening, nothing more. Nausea and dizziness were little inconveniences she had learned to live with over the past few months. Like the flu or a cold, they would pass eventually.

And, in truth, when she leaned back in her favorite chair and finished her first glass of wine, she did feel better. The pain eased a little and she relaxed. Home was the only medicine she needed.

Following a lifetime of routine, she got out her yellow

legal pad and wrote several notes with her plans for to-morrow. Meetings, things to check, messages to Mary. The last entry said simply, "remember to tell the girls I love them."

J.D. was right, she should make it a habit. She had spent far too many years seeing the twins' shortcomings. It was time she noticed a few of their talents.

As she calmed, she told J.D. every detail of the evening, laughing with him about how adventurous she had been and almost crying when she described the way Anna and Zack had looked at one another.

Exhaustion finally seeped into her very soul. The wine eased the discomfort in her chest. Helena decided she would not take the nitroglycerin. All she needed was a good night's sleep.

The ache grew sharper when she removed her jewelry and placed it in her jewelry box, but Helena never went to bed without making sure her clothes were properly cared for. Her cashmere coat was brushed and put in its place, ready for the next time she needed it. Her shoes were dusted inside with powder and buffed. Her dress folded neatly and placed among cleaning, ready to be taken out.

From her desk she lifted the silver dollar J.D. had given her and walked slowly to bed. The pain lessened a little when she lay down. She nestled into J.D.'s waiting arms and drifted to sleep.

An hour later, her heart forgot to beat. Her hand opened and the silver dollar rolled across the floor.

J.D. pulled her closer.

Dreams drove the drilling. Dreams of being rich. Dreams of power. Dreams of belonging.

And for some, the lucky ones, dreams of home.

December 20
After midnight
Howard House

"Shelby? Are you awake?" Crystal tiptoed into Shelby's room. She'd heard the night nurse go downstairs for her midnight dinner. Crystal was still far too keyed up to sleep.

"I'm awake," he answered. "Though I convinced the guard I was asleep, otherwise she'd never relax and leave me alone."

Crystal hesitated. "Would you rather I leave?"

"No. Come join me. We might as well party while we have the chance."

Crystal slipped into his bed, careful not to get too close. Her white satin pajamas didn't make a sound. "I miss sleeping with you, darling. Not the sex so much, just the sleeping."

She paused, thinking of how much a part of their marriage had been the sex. He had taken great pride in "how often" and "how long." Her words now must have hurt him and that had not been her intent.

But he surprised her by answering, "I know. I feel the

same. Sometimes I wake up late at night and try to pretend the hum of the machines is the sound of someone
breathing next to me."

They lay beside one another for a long while before
she said, "I feel something tonight, Shelby. A changing
in the wind. Like after tonight the world will somehow
be a different place, and we can never go back to the way
it was."

He didn't comment.

"I know you think my feelings are dumb, but don't
make fun of them. This one is too strong." Closing her
eyes, Crystal almost felt the velvet of a magician's cape
floating over her. When it lifted, her world would have
shifted.

"How about I never make fun of your feelings again?"
Shelby's voice was so low she would not have heard it if
she hadn't been inches from him. "How about I never say
anything you do is dumb? How about I call you darling
from now on and drop the baby doll?"

She twisted so she could see his face. The sight of him
still frightened people, but his looks no longer bothered
her. "I don't mind the baby doll. I kind of like it. It makes
me feel like I'm still just a kid."

"It's not good enough for you, and I'm finally realizing
it never was." He sounded cold somehow, angry. "And
what I'm saying has nothing to do with the offer Trent
made you. I've thought about that though, and I've decided you should take the third of Howard Drilling. Get
the money and get on with your life. You deserve better
than to be stuck with me."

"I'm not going to take the offer." Crystal could not
believe he suggested it. "If I have to, I'll fight both Trent
and you on the point."

"I'm not who you think I am, Crystal. I'm tired of living a lie. I'm not your husband."

"Shelby, don't get upset. Trent always upsets you when he comes. I don't know why, but he can say three words and you complain for days. And of course you're my husband, being burned doesn't change that."

"Are you listening to me?" Shelby's voice cracked. "Have you heard one word I've said?"

"No," Crystal answered in the formal voice she used to conduct business downstairs. "And I'm not going to until you start to make sense. I'm your wife. I love you more right now for trying to make me leave than I've ever loved you—so why would I even consider Trent's offer?"

She rose up on one elbow and frowned at him. "If you think for one minute that I'm leaving you, you'd better think again. So give up on trying to make me walk out the door. I'm not listening."

She wasn't sure, but she thought she heard him laugh.

"You sound just like Helena Whitworth."

Crystal smiled. "Maybe I do. Maybe the old girl and I have a lot in common. I'm finding out I'm more of a fighter than I ever thought I was. Who knows, in a few years I may be running this town and everyone, even folks I meet on the street will call me Mrs. Howard."

"But Trent promised you—"

"I don't care about the money. I never have, but I couldn't convince anyone of that before the accident, not even you. Now, if I stay, you'll know it's because I want to. The day I got called to the hospital, all I could think of was myself. I guess maybe if Trent had made the offer then, I'd have run. But that was before you needed me. Before the accident I'm not sure you really knew I was alive. Before we began to work together like a team I didn't feel like I was good at anything."

"I'll never be the man you married."

"You're already more than you were before the accident. I see it in how you take the pain without complaint. In how strong you are when I get frightened. You're my hero now more than you ever were before."

He slowly moved his hand and touched her fingers. "You know, I think I'm falling in love with you, Mrs. Howard."

Crystal smiled. "Well, it's about time."

Around old boomtowns weeds now grow over the foundations of derricks that changed lives and land forever. Once in a while someone notices a faded sign of a flying red horse or a wildcat brand carved into wood and remembers how the hunger for oil blew across Texas like a powerful wind.

December 23

As Crystal Howard predicted, there was a changing in
the wind blowing across the prairie town of Clifton Creek,
Texas. It whirled through the narrow streets and blasted
down Main, as if trying to mix directions until there was
no north or south, no east or west.

Somehow it seemed fitting that the plastic, lamp pole
reindeers Helena had always complained about were
blown down before her funeral procession moved past
the courthouse.

Though the roads were icy, the polished black funeral
limos glistened in the morning light. Everyone who did
not attend the service lined the road in their cars, bumper
to bumper, all the way out to the cemetery. As the casket
moved past, each car turned on its lights and left them
on until the last car had cleared the street.

Helena Whitworth was buried in her new wool suit
with her cashmere coat folded over her arm and her favorite scarf in her hand. Paula insisted on that, saying her
mother would never want to be caught unprepared for the
weather.

Helena's Choice bore a huge wreath on the door and

was closed until one. The twins thought of closing all day, but Mary reminded them it was the Christmas season and their mother never would have missed the entire day's sales.

The townspeople considered Helena their friend, but there were four special pallbearers who walked behind the casket. Crystal Howard in classic black, Anna Montano with her arm tucked into a sling and a hat shadowing her face, Randi Howard in a pleated prairie skirt and black Lucchese boots, and Meredith Allen in the same simple navy dress she had worn to every funeral for the last ten years.

Though most of the women cried, Crystal, Anna, Meredith and Randi did not shed a tear. Someone whispered it was because they had so much sorrow to bear, but the women knew different. They all decided Helena was exactly where she wanted to be. She was with J.D.

At the graveside, most people stayed in their cars. They all watched as Helena's daughters said their last goodbye. Paula clutched a page from a yellow legal pad in her hand. Patricia was too busy trying to corral her children to remember to place the rose Pastor Wayne had handed her on her mother's casket.

When the family moved away from the grave, Meredith expected the cars to leave, but no one did. Then she realized they were waiting for them, the widows, to finish their farewell. She chose to believe it was out of respect and not curiosity.

Randi stepped forward first. She spread her gloved hand out on the casket.

Anna was next. She placed her fingers on the box and whispered a prayer.

Crystal brushed a few snowflakes from the mahogany.

Meredith added her ungloved hand to the others atop the casket. She wanted to say something, but words would not come. Slowly, the four hands came together over Helena's coffin. They crossed as true as points of a compass from four different directions.

No one said a word. No one had to.

The wind circled snow in the air and blended with the fragrance of flowers from beside the grave. Slowly, each stepped away walking past the huge Whitworth stone where Helena had had her name carved beside J.D.'s months before.

Randi looped her arm in Crystal's. "How about I go home with you for Christmas? We'll split all those presents you piled beneath that huge tree and open them like they were all bought just for us."

Crystal grinned. "Sounds great."

Zack stepped forward and put a gentle arm around Anna. They had a flight to catch in a few hours to Italy. She wanted to spend a week with her family and then the new year seeing Rome with Zack. They planned to stay away long enough to give Carlo time to pack. They had agreed not to press charges and to give him a dozen broodmares if he would be gone when they returned.

Meredith watched them leave, knowing they would be married by the time she saw them again.

She turned toward her car. Sheriff Farrington waited halfway between her and the Mustang. As she passed him, he removed one of his gloves and took her hand, then fell into step with her as if he had done so a thousand times.

"I knew you'd be freezing," he mumbled as his warm hand covered her fingers.

Meredith smiled, realizing the whole town was probably watching. "You're holding my hand."

"Well, it was either that or follow behind you picking up frozen fingers as they fell off."

Meredith stopped walking and faced him. "You're holding my hand, Granger."

He smiled down at her. "That I am."

* * * * *

A HAPPINESS KEY NOVEL
FROM *USA TODAY* BESTSELLING AUTHOR

EMILIE RICHARDS

If you've got friends, you can do anything.

Five very different women find friendship—and
unexpected love—on the barrier island known as
Happiness Key. As each of them faces challenging,
unexpected changes in their lives, a tropical storm
is brewing…and five friends will soon discover
just how much they need one another.

sunset bridge

Available wherever books are sold.

MIRA | HARLEQUIN®
™ www.Harlequin.com

MERI238

New York Times and **USA TODAY**
bestselling author

SUSAN MALLERY

is back with a charming new trilogy!

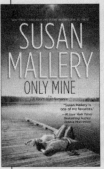
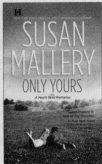
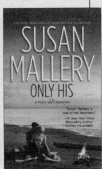

August   September   October

The town of Fool's Gold, California,
makes headlines for its lack of men.
Can three determined women
change that once and for all?

"Warm, funny and sexy…a satisfying, rewarding read."
—*Library Journal* on *Finding Perfect*

Coming soon!

HQN™

We *are* romance™

www.HQNBooks.com

PHSSMT2011